THE PRIVILEGED

Emily Hourican grew up in Brussels, and is a well-known Irish feature writer. She launched in journalism as the editor of *Himself* magazine, and then edited the *Dubliner* magazine in its early heady days of being hipster avant la lettre. For the past decade, she has been a regular with the *Sunday Independent*. Her first book, a memoir, *How To (Really) Be a Mother* (2013) is a funny, honest account of how she learned to stop faking it as a mother, and become her own version of the real thing. She lives in Dublin with her husband and three children.

www.emilyhourican.com
@EmilyH71

The Privileged
EMILY HOURICAN

HACHETTE
BOOKS
IRELAND

First published in Ireland in 2016 by HACHETTE BOOKS IRELAND

2

Cataloguing in Publication Data is available from the British Library.

ISBN 978 1 4736 2823 6

Typeset in Bembo Book Standard by Bookends Publishing Services. Printed and bound in Great Britain by CPI Group (UK) Ltd, Croydon, CR0 4YY.

Hachette Books Ireland policy is to use papers that are natural, renewable and recyclable products and made from wood grown in sustainable forests. The logging and manufacturing processes are expected to conform to the environmental regulations of the country of origin.

Hachette Books Ireland
8 Castlecourt Centre
Castleknock
Dublin 15, Ireland

A division of Hachette UK Ltd
Carmelite House, 50 Victoria Embankment, EC4Y 0DZ

www.hachettebooksireland.ie

For David

The edges of the lawn were burnt after weeks of sun and no rain. Yellowish-brown and sticking up in dry tufts, like the horsehair from an old sofa. Lunch was nearly over but they lingered, willing the bell to stay silent, to leave uninterrupted a moment that seemed minutely aware of its own glory. Around them, a steady wall of sound built up. The buzz of flies and bees joined the more distant sounds of birds and the hum of the gym fan, working overtime to cool the few dedicated hockey players who hadn't seized the obvious excuse of the day, who didn't realise that a day like that was an excuse for anything. The air between them vibrated with its own steady tone, as the girls sat in a hollow at the centre of it all, a protected place of their own.

'Every day is going to feel like this once we get out of here and into proper life,' Amanda said, rolling over and staring straight up at the sky. 'All glorious, all perfect. All ours.'

'Our only problem will be how to do them justice,' Laura agreed solemnly.

'You're so conscientious.' Amanda laughed. 'Surely sometimes we can have something without deserving it.'

'I don't think we can,' Laura said. 'I think you have to earn everything good.'

'You would,' Amanda said. 'Stella, what do you think?'

'I think sometimes you can take what comes, if you want it. Even if you can't see how it's meant for you. Even when you're half-inclined to look around and see who it's really for.'

'Well, I think it's all meant for me,' said Amanda, shutting her eyes and letting the heat soak through her to the dry grass beneath.

'You think everything's meant for you.' Stella laughed. 'You're the most entitled person ever.'

'The most entitled and the most benighted,' Amanda sighed. 'Think of everything I have to do in return for what I get.'

'What — like turn up on time?' Laura teased. 'Put up with everyone thinking you're wonderful?'

'All of that and far worse,' said Amanda. 'But not for much longer. Once we're out of here and can start doing what we want.'

Across her, Stella and Laura looked at each other. The future, when Amanda spoke of it, seemed a most delightful place, one they would walk into with her, and be perfectly sure of a welcome. Behind them the ancient chestnut tree at the edge of the lawn stirred in the wind, its branches scraping, like a dry cough.

Chapter One

New York 2015

STELLA'S MOBILE RANG AT THE SAME TIME AS THE white button on the phone in front of her began to flash. Everything was always urgent, a world of people striving, driving hard. She stared at the button, gathering her thoughts for the seven-way conference call.

'Hello.' She answered her mobile by instinct, conditioned by the 353 country code to respond. Whoever it was, and only those closest to her had that number, she'd tell them to call back. The white button was still flashing.

'Stel, it's Amanda. Something bad.'

Laura, God bless her, so sweet and hesitant about herself, got straight to the point where everyone else was concerned. Her years of training as a journalist meant that she didn't waste time on the unimportant.

'What now?' Stella tried, failed, to keep the weary note from her voice that made her sound so much older than twenty-eight. With Amanda, it was always something. Usually something big, dramatic. *Noisy.* Sometimes she felt as if she and Laura had been picking up the pieces for years. For ever. When had she and Laura last talked for any length without Amanda hijacking the focus of their conversation? As if, even now, thirteen years on, they were still in the shadow of her considerable glamour?

And if Amanda was with them, it was always all about her. A room with Amanda in it felt like a room with a vortex into which everything, eventually, would fall. Still, it must be pretty bad or Laura wouldn't ring so early. Stella checked her diamond-studded Tag Heuer, a gift from Sean – barely eight a.m.

'There's a story in one of the papers. No names. It's one of those "guess which former society beauty has been spotted" but it's obviously her. Apparently she and Huw have locked themselves into the house in Knightsbridge. Boarded up the front door and shut off all the downstairs rooms. They're living on the top floor. No one is allowed in except that rat Jake. I don't think anyone else much tries any more. Someone went to Huw's family to get help, and then leaked it to the papers. They aren't eating or sleeping or talking to anyone. The place is filthy – they're filthy too. Seems it's been going on for months. It's really bad this time.'

Amanda filthy? Amanda, with her effortlessly shiny hair, golden skin and natural elegance, with her faint aloofness, sharp wit and deep laugh. Amanda O'Hagen, social queen from the age of thirteen, locked into the wedding-cake-white four-storey Knightsbridge house, where she and Huw had lived in the five years since they'd got married, seeing no one? Stella had been to the house just once, right before the wedding. It had been an interior designer's dream, the kind of thing that got full-colour photographs in glossy magazines for the rest of the world to drool over, with its impeccable grey interior walls, original stuccoed ceilings, and fireplaces big enough to stand in. There was a Picasso sketch or two, a Bacon in the dining room, a small Turner onto which the light from the first-floor windows fell at evening, making it glow with a golden fire all its own. Amanda had told Stella how much she loved that painting, joking that she would have married Huw for it, even if he hadn't been the handsomest man on earth. What must the house look like now? Stella wondered. How filthy was filthy? And why was it anything, now, to do with her?

'So what's different?' Again, that weary note.

'They packed Dora off a few months ago, back to Mrs O'Hagen.'

'Right.' Stella, lawyer now before friend, considered the implications. 'And if Amanda is sending Dora back to her mother, that can't be good.'

'Not good at all, I'd say, when you think how long she spent keeping the two of them apart. Apparently Dora thinks she's on holiday. She's due to go home in a couple of weeks, but Mrs O'Hagen's been talking about trying to get her into St Assumpta's, so she can keep an eye on her.'

'Oh, for Christ's sake, Laura. Isn't that where this whole mess started? Mrs O'Hagen and St Assumpta's?' Stella found she was shaking, her breath coming unevenly.

'If they *must* go giving boys blow jobs, at least this way we know they're *St Augustin's* boys …' Laura drawled.

It had been their catchphrase for years, ever since Amanda had heard her mother say it to her father, while Amanda was getting ready to go to Dargle's, the rugby-club disco, where all the boys and girls from smart Southside schools went on a Friday night. Amanda had been fourteen. Now, it no longer seemed funny, even though the three of them had screamed with laughter over it for years. It had been the one thing guaranteed to break the ice between them when they met up after a separation, with increasingly little in common.

'Laura, I'd better go. I'll call you back, right?' The little white light was still flashing. Her assistant had put her head round the door twice already, looking slightly panicked the second time. Stella reached out to push the button that would bring up a huge digital split-screen showing the seven participants in the conference call. Two were down the corridor, in their own twenty-seventh-floor offices, but the rest were in Tokyo, including Sean. Beautiful Sean, with his strawberry blond hair, his white-white teeth and the one drop of west-of-Ireland blood from which he had forged a complete identity. A man in the mould of John F. Kennedy, Stella thought, now seven thousand miles away from her. Also seven thousand miles away from his two perfect children and blonde WASP wife.

The white light was still flashing. They were all waiting for Stella, who had – as always – every possible fact relating to the case neatly categorised in her mind. She had read the depositions and documents with such meticulous attention that even the Japanese clients were impressed. She had a talent for hard work and fact-retention, which meant she was being fast-tracked through one of New York's oldest, most established legal firms. Push the button, Stella, she thought. Deal with Amanda later. But she hesitated. Mrs O'Hagen and St Assumpta's. Where it had all started. Amanda, at fourteen, the most beautiful girl she'd ever seen.

She remembered their first meeting, the first time she'd gone to Dargle's. Her parents had finally relented, after a year of Stella's begging: 'Please! Everyone else is allowed go.' That wasn't strictly true. There was a fairly even split between girls like Amanda O'Hagen, who were not only allowed to go but handed wads of cash to buy themselves a new dress, get a spray tan and their hair done, and girls like Stella, whose parents felt they were still too young for nightclubs. They probably believed the media reports about underage binge drinking and blow jobs in the bushes.

'You're too young,' her parents had said, time after time. 'If you're going to Dargle's at thirteen, God knows what you'll be up to by fifteen. All-night raves and acid parties.' They had relented when she was fourteen, dropping her and Laura a couple of streets from the club.

'We'll walk from here,' Stella had offered, not wanting to be seen getting out of her mum's old silver banger. Laura was an unusual bright orange colour, her face caked in tan foundation. She was normally pale, with pink cheeks, and fine blonde hair in a short pageboy, the fringe clipped neatly to one side. She had that kind of hair – neat, biddable – which stayed in clips, not like Stella's unruly mop of dark curls. She was wearing a very short flouncy flesh-coloured skirt over bare legs, an off-the-shoulder T-shirt that said 'Pussy Posse' in sequins, and shoes so high she couldn't walk.

Stella hadn't deviated much from her usual dress code –

skinny jeans, a white tank top, a grey Chloé jacket her mother had given her when it became obvious she was never going to get into it again, and Converse. But she was woefully underdressed for the event. All around her, girls in micro-minis, with tight strappy tops and hooker heels, backcombed hair and fake lashes, were converging on the door at Dargle's. Despite the cold April evening, no one else wore a coat or even jacket. The sky was an orange glow, their breath coming in misty puffs as the girls faked nonchalance. There was a studied coolness in the way they slouched, but they betrayed their nerves in odd fidgety movements – the hand that didn't know where to go running through perfectly straightened hair, the sudden, high-pitched laugh, all of the tell-tale signs that said they were fourteen, not twenty-four.

'What if they don't let us in?' Laura muttered, clinging to Stella's arm for balance. Her teeth were chattering with nerves and Stella could feel her arm shaking slightly as it gripped harder.

'It'll be fine,' she said, looking up the line to where two burly doormen were looking through girls' bags, asking what school they were from, and leering at each other over their heads.

'Look,' Laura nudged her, 'there's Amanda O'Hagen.' In that crew of giggling, sniggering, nervy teenagers, Amanda stood out like a fully grown movie star. Her honey blonde hair framed her perfect face, with the slanting cobalt-blue eyes, and rippled down her back. Her teeny-tiny dress was white *broderie anglaise*, tight and low-cut, exposing the tops of her breasts and stopping barely short of her bum, but saved itself from looking slutty by the almost girlish prettiness of the fabric. It was the couture version of the hooker outfits surrounding them. Her high silver-coloured platform shoes were tied at the ankles. She neither fidgeted nor giggled.

With her was a gaggle of the girls who attended her at school, at the shopping centre, the park, anyplace Stella had ever seen her. They were clearly content to exist in Amanda's shadow, to be the foil and setting she required. They didn't, Stella noticed, bother her with too much of their chatter, addressing only the odd remark, to which she seemed to respond with a gracious inclination of the head and that small upward curve of the lips that could have been a smile or simply acknowledgement. The doormen behaved towards her as if she was indeed the superstar she seemed. No vulgar jokes. They treated her with, Stella thought, respect.

The evening was a mess of music she didn't like – too many chant-along choruses and guys punching the air. These weren't the girls Stella knew from school – bitchy, confrontational, some matronly, some indifferent. Suddenly, they were all the same, writhing and contorting themselves into supplicating shapes, always with one eye on the boys. When they danced, it was as if all they were missing was a pole. They slid up and down against each other, tossing their hair and licking their lips. Or bent forward at the waist with straight legs, bums stuck out, then up, chests thrust forward, hips gyrating. But everything was punctuated with the same disarming, supplicating giggles and dissembling shrugs, a rush to show irony rather than intent. Condensation ran down the blacked-out windows and walls, and a faint smell of bleach and sweat hung around them.

Girls staggered into the loos in pairs, tiny bottles of something strong and sticky hidden in their cleavages or in the lining of bags, then out again, laughing all the louder. Stella could see Laura chatting to a couple of the girls in their year, but their eyes flicked over her to the side room where cans of Coke and

7Up were on sale, and a large group of lads had converged to push each other and swagger. Stella went outside.

The stands, orange in the street lights, with their own faint hum of glories gone, were empty, except for a few huddled couples and a group of boys smoking and passing a bottle covertly around. Beyond the walls, Stella could hear the steady roar of traffic, proof that in the real world it was still just half past nine on a regular Saturday night. The playing pitch looked black, disappearing into shadow halfway across, with the opposite seating entirely obscured. Stella headed in that direction, thinking she might understand it better from an outsider's perspective, looking in, not at. She moved softly, her Converse making no sound on the wet grass. A sudden slight movement took her by surprise. To her left, in the front row of the darkest side of the stadium, an inky shadow separated slowly into three distinct ones. More boys, she thought, and was about to slip away, certain they hadn't seen her, when she heard a moan. It was a girl. She stayed motionless, waiting for her eyes to make some sense of the tableau before her.

The girl's white dress caught her attention first, then the gleam of a pale shoe, tied on at the ankle. It was Amanda, but Amanda with her head flopped forward, slumped in the stadium seat. A boy was seated on either side of her. One was smoking, head thrown back in the attitude of a docker taking respite after a long day. The other, Stella was pretty sure, had his hand up Amanda's skirt.

She started to move noiselessly backwards but another faint moan stopped her. The boy with his hand up Amanda's skirt now had the other in his trousers, while the one with the cigarette was tugging at her dress to expose more of her breasts. None of it looked right to Stella, who prided herself on Not

Walking Away – indeed, she was always recounting the virtues of getting involved. Years later, looking back, she knew that a faint silvery path, alternative to the one she thought she was treading, had branched out beside her that night, and that her feet had shifted towards it.

'Amanda!' she called. 'Amanda? Your dad's here.'

Silence.

'Amanda!' Feigning annoyance now. 'Amanda, come on! He's asking for you.' She moved forward, turning her head from left to right as if she was scanning the stands. By now the boys were getting up, gathering cigarettes and a bottle. Seeing Stella, they muttered at her and slouched off, hoods up and heads turned away so that she couldn't see who they were. Amanda remained where she was.

Stella grasped Amanda's shoulders and sat her upright. Her eyes were half-closed and her mouth slack. Was she drunk, or stoned, or what? And what was Stella going to do with her now? 'Amanda, can you hear me?'

A low response, incomprehensible.

Get Laura, she decided. But what about Amanda? Might the boys just come back if they saw her alone? She felt a wave of protectiveness for a girl who, until now, she had only ever seen in control of every situation. Amanda was smart as well as beautiful. She shone at school, on the debating team and at hockey. 'Stay there,' Stella murmured. 'I'll get help.'

Laura was outside, talking to a thin boy with droll blue eyes and a cow's lick. She came immediately when Stella interrupted them. On the way back across the pitch, she filled Laura in on what had happened. Amanda was exactly where Stella had left her, except that her eyes were now fully closed and her head lay at an angle against her shoulder.

'What's up with her? Why won't she wake up?' Laura asked.

'I don't know. She can't just be pissed. Or not that pissed. Maybe she's on something. Whatever, we have to get her out of here, and not back through the club.'

'Why us? Why not get Sally or Nadine? They're her friends.' Laura sounded petulant.

It was a fair question, which Stella couldn't really answer. But letting St Assumpta's two most notorious gossips in on the action, then watching them drag Amanda through the crowds of curious teenagers, who would all stop dancing to stare at her, felt wrong. 'Would you want Sally or Nadine looking after you if you were in that state?' She gestured towards Amanda.

'No, but they're not my friends.'

Stella knew that Laura wasn't going to fight her. 'Is there any other way out of here?'

'There's a side gate beside where I was talking to that boy, but it's locked.'

'Can you find a bouncer and get him to open it? Tell him a bit of what's happened. I bet you anything they don't want anyone seeing Amanda like this either.'

'Okay, but what then? Where do we take her?'

'Your house?'

Laura's mother, Nessa, was often out in the evenings. She had once been muse to the country's most celebrated portrait painter, a man who had believed himself to be Laura's father. He had discovered his error and Nessa's silent duplicity only when Laura was nine and her mother, in a drunken rage, had spat it at him one night during a row about money, whereupon he had walked out of Nessa's life and, by extension, Laura's. At nine, she had felt too old to forge a relationship with the man who turned out to be biologically connected to her, and too young to insist on staying close to the man she knew as her father. That left her with no father, and often no mother. Nessa had readily made her peace with the idea of leaving Laura alone for long periods. It was either that or let life float past her, taking all the dreams she had had as a young girl in the dreary midlands town of her birth. And, indeed, once Laura had grown too old to be taken to parties and dumped on beds with the coats, all she required was to be left alone with her books and her homework.

'Okay, mine. Nessa's certainly not going to be home tonight. Richard Long is in town. She was pouring half a bottle of Shalimar over herself as I was leaving.' Laura always called her mother 'Nessa'. It was one of the many signs of the sisterly level on which they operated: friendly, not hierarchical. 'God. Imagine Amanda O'Hagen in my house.' She laughed.

Once the doormen had grasped the situation, they were more than happy to open the side gate discreetly and let the three girls out onto the road. 'She'll be fine,' one of them said to Laura. 'Let her sleep. She'll be grand in the morning. Won't remember much of this.' He exchanged a furtive look with his companion.

They got a taxi, even though Laura's house wasn't far, because they couldn't drag Amanda through the leafy streets of middle-suburban Dublin. They made her pay for it. Stella searched her wallet, finding wads of cash, then took out her mobile phone. Amanda, of course, was one of the few girls in school to have one. 'Let's hope she calls her mother "Mum",' she said, with a look at Laura. 'If they're on first-name terms, I'm never going to work this out.' She scrolled down, relieved to find 'Mum' between Moneypenny's Salon and Muttley's Pet Grooming. '"Staying at Nadines, back tomorrow,"' she typed. 'Let's hope she really is as independent as she seems.'

Amanda's phone beeped. 'Mum' flashed up. 'K. Don't forget lunch w Alice @ 2'.

'Golly. Amanda's mother is fast.' Laura fell into fits of laughter. So did Stella. After the tension of the last hour, anything would have seemed funny. 'Should we text Nadine and say Amanda's gone home?'

'Nah, forget it. I bet Amanda wouldn't bother.'

Laura's house was a red-brick mid-terrace Victorian from the outside, Moorish and exotic inside. Polished floorboards strewn with rugs in deep reds and purples; huge, highly polished copper vases, ornate candelabra and low-hanging, dim lights. Nessa had made deliberate efforts to keep modern life from intruding. There was no electric kettle or toaster: water was boiled in a copper saucepan and toast made on the Aga. In the bathroom, the antique, claw-footed bath was rarely filled because the water-heating system was old and wonky.

A jumble of paintings and sketches, probably as valuable as the house, hung on the walls. Some were by the man who had believed himself to be Laura's father and who had marked her birthdays with a picture of her – Laura at three, solemn-eyed and direct; Laura at five, a new wistfulness upon her; Laura, eight now, and chubby, but still with that open, appealing gaze. Others were by contemporaries, less lauded than he, but ready to toss off a sketch as thanks for a meal or an impromptu party. Yet others were by Nessa herself, largely from the days before Laura, when she had been the celebrated portrait painter's student and before she had had the misfortune to become his muse and mistress – landscapes, still-lifes, a tiny self-portrait, with a beguiling energy and lightness of touch.

'What now?' Stella demanded. They had hauled Amanda out of the taxi, up the steps and through the door.

'Can we just put her upstairs? Enough already!'

'Fine. That bouncer said she'd sleep it off. I suppose she will. Your room?'

'Okay. You and I will have to share the other bed.' Laura's room had two tiny wooden truckle beds with surprisingly comfortable mattresses. Tucked into one of them, still wearing her white dress, hair spread across the pillow, Amanda looked about ten years old. She was by now deeply asleep, snoring faintly. Downstairs, they could hear her phone beeping manically. Probably Nadine and Sally trying to find out what exciting things she had got up to.

Stella and Laura left her, and made hot chocolate in the kitchen. In Laura's house, this meant grating cooking chocolate into two hand-made mugs, then adding maple syrup to sweeten it. Nessa, when she was with them, added a dash of rum to hers. They chatted about what they would say to Amanda in the morning, and speculated on what had happened to her. 'Even if she knows, I bet she won't tell us,' had been Laura's verdict, shortly before they went to bed. There was no sign of Nessa, though it was long after two.

Before she settled down to sleep, Stella banged her head on the pillow eight times. It was her system for waking up – eight bangs, eight o'clock. It never failed her. She wanted to be awake by the time Amanda opened her eyes. The strange feeling of protectiveness that had caught her earlier had stayed with her. She didn't want Amanda feeling disoriented and frightened at the strange surroundings.

But when she opened her eyes, light was streaming into the bedroom, and Amanda was sitting up in the small wooden bed, staring straight at her. Her cobalt eyes were undimmed by any shade of fear or awkwardness. 'Your house or Laura's?' she said, sounding faintly amused, her brief, blue gaze like flashes of sky between trees seen from a fast-moving car.

'Laura's.' After all that, it was Stella who felt awkward, wondering if they had overreacted the night before. Behaved in a foolish, uncool way. Such was Amanda's self-possession, she felt an explanation was instantly needed. 'We didn't know what else to do. You were so ... I don't know. So ...'

'Drunk?'

'Actually, I'm not sure. You were ... out cold. And there were these boys. In the stands ... We thought the best thing was just to get you out of there, without making a big fuss. Put you to bed and let you go to sleep. You seemed like you were asleep already in Dargle's.'

There was a long pause. Amanda stared at her, consideringly. 'Boys?' she finally said.

Stuck in the beam of her gaze, Stella felt she now knew how a rabbit must feel as it tried to summon the willpower to bolt. 'Yes, two of them. They were, well, they were—'

'I'm sure you did the right thing,' Amanda cut across her. Neither then nor at any other time did she ask what exactly had happened that night. Something that surprised Stella every time she thought about it. 'What about Nadine and Sally?'

'We didn't tell them anything.' Laura was awake now, sitting up beside Stella, sounding proud. 'We just bundled you into a taxi and brought you here. We made you pay for the taxi,' she added.

Amanda's top lip twitched. Even after a night of mysterious debauchery, with make-up smeared under her eyes and a rumpled dress, she looked bewitching. A little younger, a little more reachable than the Amanda they were used to, but still beautiful.

'I suppose I'd better go. Even my parents might be concerned by now.' She spoke with such precision that Stella found herself wondering if she had had elocution lessons.

'Oh, we texted your mum. From your phone. To say you were staying at Nadine's. Your mum said be back for something at two o'clock with someone called Alice.' Laura's words tumbled over each other.

'Let's just hope Nadine had the sense not to go back to mine,' said Amanda, with a laugh. 'She was supposed to stay over.'

Stella was appalled, but Amanda laughed again, a real laugh, not the fake 'get lost' sound that Stella heard her make at school. 'She'll have worked something out. Shall we have breakfast?'

℃

Nessa was in the kitchen, wearing a heavy black silk kimono with pairs of white dancing cranes hand-painted onto it. 'Poached or scrambled?' She waved at a box of eggs. 'Richard stayed the night so, for goodness' sake, don't go bursting into the bathroom. The lack of locks makes him nervous. I'm sure embassy life doesn't usually involve teenagers surprising one at one's ablutions. Not likely to be his sort of thing at all, even with teens as pretty as you.' This was addressed to Amanda, now wearing a pair of Laura's jeans and an old football shirt.

'Scrambled, please. And I'll knock first. Can I help with the eggs?'

Amanda made toast instead, at Nessa's request, spreading it with plenty of butter, eating it and the eggs when they came. Stella had expected her to pick at her food and talk about diets. Amanda even offered to wash up, and was charming to Richard when he came down, looking so buttoned-up and prim that Stella wondered what on earth Laura's scatty mother saw in him ('It's the opposites thing,' Amanda said later, knowingly).

'Come with me,' she'd suggested to Stella and Laura, when she was getting ready to leave. 'Come and meet Alice. It'll be a real treat.' Her voice held a faint hint of laughter.

Nessa had no objection, and Stella's parents wouldn't expect her back for hours, so Stella and Laura said yes. In the taxi (Amanda, they learned, always took taxis: 'Never wait for a lift, never depend on anyone for your freedom of movement,' was one of her maxims), she said to Laura, 'Your mother paints very well.'

'How did you know which ones were hers?' Laura asked. Nessa's pictures were mostly unsigned, or with a signature so scrawling as to be illegible.

'They look like her. A bit wild and unconventional on the surface, but with a disciplined core.' Both girls stared at her in amazement. How on earth did she come out with such things? Especially, Stella thought, since it was so very true of Nessa, whom she had known from childhood in all her many moods, and whose wispy dark hair, forever escaping its pins and tumbling down her back, and swirling silk skirts hid a personality that could be steely and implacable when it came to the things she considered important – art, food, love, and the development of Laura's personality.

'She doesn't really paint now,' Laura replied. 'Hasn't for years. But she was good. I wish she'd do more.'

'She's probably scared. She seems highly perfectionist.'

Again, they were astonished at her perception.

'How could you tell?' asked Laura.

'The scrambled eggs. She spent ages making them. They were the best I've had.'

By now they were far out of the city. On either side, green fields and hedges flew past. The odd glimpse of a modern mansion behind tall trees, or sunlight glinting off solar panels, indicated that they were in a land of wealth. A tiny village sprang up around them, a couple of shops selling organic duck eggs and home-made preserves, then a larger shop filled with French-style country furniture and antiques. A little tea room, furnished with the excess of the antiques shop – Louis Something chairs in palest green and a highly polished mahogany sideboard – advertised 'fresh home-made elderflower cordial' and 'home-made brownies'. Country living for rich city folk, thought Stella, whose parents lived close to the city centre because most of what they cared about – art, theatre, decent bookshops – was gathered there, and because they were damned, they said cheerfully, if they were going to drive Stella everywhere she wanted to go. 'We're not raising you to be helpless,' they told her. 'You need to be master of your fate.' They believed in self-reliance and ambition. They believed in Stella.

The taxi was turning into a pair of massive white wrought-iron gates and up a long drive, bordered by chestnut trees. Around a curve, Amanda's house appeared suddenly. Solid, three-storeys, made from caramel-coloured stone, with deep-set windows and a slate roof. Ivy crept across one side of it, enveloping four of the nine top-floor windows in its leafy embrace, softening the gentle aspect of what was certainly the loveliest house Stella had seen. To one side was a small lake, its surface broken by reeds and water lilies, a couple of moorhens paddling among them, and behind it, an expanse of manicured lawn, with more ancient chestnut trees. In the far distance a couple of horses stood out against the sky. On the other side was a red-brick walled garden. 'It's so beautiful,' she murmured.

'Even my parents can't ruin the exterior. It's protected,' Amanda said. 'It makes them furious. And the name, Belleville. They'd love to rename it White Orchards or something.' She laughed. 'Sometimes I wonder why they bought it.'

Stella assumed she was joking, or trying to defuse the embarrassment of belonging to such glory, until they entered the house, where the aggressive black-and-white floor tiles in savagely polished marble, and black-and-white-striped wallpaper, broken up with mirrors in harsh designs — one shaped like the sun with jagged rays spread out in a fan around it, another made up of interconnecting heart shapes — caused her to reconsider. Amanda's parents' taste clearly owed everything to a certain type of magazine, and nothing at all to the spirit of the house. Amanda's heels clacked across the tiles, echoing into the vast space left by high ceilings and the generous staircase spiralling into the upper reaches. Almost immediately a voice sounded from a room to their right.

'Amanda, is that you?'

Amanda's mother — it had to be her, there was a distinct resemblance — appeared in the doorway, one hand poised lightly on the frame. She was wearing a shiny black dress that ended just above the knee, her toned arms bare, her hair — a shade lighter, more Nordic blonde than Amanda's — smooth and sleek. The careful make-up and subtle Botox made her look not old, but not young either. You could never confuse them for sisters, Stella thought critically, even though it was impossible to believe this woman was anyone's mother.

'Good. You're back in time for Alice. But you'll need to change,'

– her mouth made an expression of distress at the football shirt and jeans. 'How was last night? Did you meet anyone?' They were to learn that this was Mrs O'Hagen's invariable question after Amanda had been out. 'Anyone', they were also to discover, did not usually include the people they knew.

'This is Stella and Laura. Friends from school.' Amanda avoided answering her mother's question.

'Nice to meet you.' Mrs O'Hagen's gaze flickered across the two girls and back to Amanda. She had the same carefully modulated tones as her daughter.

'I'll go and change,' Amanda said.

'Yes. Then I want to hear all about it,' her mother answered.

Stella and Laura followed Amanda upstairs, past alcoves with large vases, some replica Ancient Greek, some unashamedly modern, in leopard-print or zebra, to her bedroom on the top floor. Thick white carpet, high windows with deep window seats, a couple of pretty watercolours on the walls, and a carved wooden four-poster bed draped with gauzy white curtains and heaped with golden cushions of every size. For a time the girls were silenced by the opulence. It didn't for one second try *not* to be the golden bower of someone's little princess. There were no pictures of bands or teen idols, just one framed poster from the movie *Natural Born Killers* with Juliette Lewis from her good angle, looking thin and sexy and bad.

'How do you sleep?' Laura eventually asked, indicating the mass of cushions.

'I throw them all onto the floor every night. Ivana puts them back every single morning.'

'Every single morning?' said Laura.

'Yes.'

'God. She's like the Sisyphus of soft furnishings,' said Laura

'Nice!' Amanda said. 'That's it exactly.'

Suddenly, the three of them were laughing. For the first time on that strange morning, Stella realised they could be friends. That Amanda, under the poised and immaculate exterior, wasn't all that unlike her and Laura. That she was funny.

'Ivana's the housekeeper,' Amanda went on. 'She's from Ukraine. My mother has a thing about cushions. She thinks they're elegant. She has a thing about housekeepers too. They can't be Irish. She thinks the Irish would be judgemental. And gossipy. Ivana told me once that she sometimes dreams about cushions.'

'I suppose you have a pony too?' Stella asked, half for fun and half-enviously.

'Used to. Now I have two show-jumpers. One's a brute. I hate him. But my mother thinks I'll meet the right sort of person eventing or at hunter trials. She even bought herself a pair of jodhpurs, until she saw the other mothers in jeans and Hunter wellies. She can't quite bring herself to don the wellies, though, so the pressure's off for the moment.'

Amanda changed into a grey silk top and jeans that looked as much like the pair she had borrowed from Laura as a pedigree Saluki resembles a Jack Russell-cross. However, Stella noted that she folded Laura's jeans and football shirt carefully and put them into a Brown Thomas bag. She slipped on a pair of Tod's loafers. 'We'd better go down. Like I said, you'll love Alice.'

○3

Alice was a fright. Probably Mrs O'Hagen's age, but determined to act Amanda's. She ate nothing, just drank a good deal of icy white wine.

Mrs O'Hagen missed nothing. Even when she appeared to be engaged in conversation with Alice — an endless list of who did/wore/saw/bought what — she was monitoring everything Amanda did, said and ate. 'Have more fennel, it's good for the blood, but I think that's enough crab cakes,' she interjected at one point, and almost imperceptibly shook her head when Amanda reached for dessert — tiny blood-orange and chocolate mousses in shot glasses. Stella could see herself and Laura losing points because of the eagerness with which they put away the delicious food, but otherwise Mrs O'Hagen largely ignored them in a way that made them feel she had put them to one side and might come back to them later.

When the food was finished, she turned fully to Amanda. 'So, Amanda, tell us about last night. Did you meet anyone?' Her tone was wintry. Clearly, Amanda's earlier efforts to avoid the conversation hadn't been successful. Stella wondered if they ever were.

'No, there wasn't anyone there. An empty room.' Amanda's voice was monotonous, weary, rather than sarcastic.

'There must have been *some*one. Or why on earth go? What about that nice St Augustin's boy — Gerard Hurley? The one whose father is a member of New Forest with your father.'

'I don't know. I didn't see him.'

'Well,' Mrs O'Hagen said, with a horrid little laugh, 'I don't know why you bother going, or why we pay for new clothes for you to go, if you're not going to meet anyone nice.'

'Oh, but remember the *thrill* of your first nights out as a teenager,' Alice interjected on a shriek. 'I still get goosebumps thinking about it. The expectation, the excitement. The sheer wonder of it.'

Mrs O'Hagen was boot-faced.

'Mum's first nights out as a teenager were probably round the back of Stillorgan shopping centre with a bottle of cheap vodka,' Amanda said coldly.

There was a long, awkward silence. Stella expected an explosion, but Mrs O'Hagen simply looked at Amanda, who looked back. Blue eyes to blue eyes. A battle of ice.

Mrs O'Hagen turned to Alice. 'I meant to ask what you thought about the new restaurant that opened in Dún Laoghaire – Joly's?' Her voice betrayed no emotion, only the years of work that must have gone into creating it.

❧

In time, Stella was to learn that Mrs O'Hagen never entered battle unless she was sure to win, and only then if the victory was worth having. Whatever her many failings – as a mother, a wife, a woman – she had strengths. She was clear-sighted, focused, ruthless when she felt the need. She was also, Stella discovered, largely indifferent to taunts about her past. She had grown up on a dull housing estate, part of a sprawling hinterland of such estates that fanned outwards from the hub of the city. Without centres, without attraction or distinctive features, their roads and undistinguished houses ran into one another, back gardens marching in formation, pressed down by the thick air of apathy that hung over them, and skies that seemed lower than in other parts of the city, even on a sunny day. Some had washing lines that whipped viciously in the wind, or broken toys bleached of colour lying in sad heaps. In others, thick-set dogs of fighting breeds barked, deep and depressed, at the end of short leashes. Nature, which might have softened and subdued, seemed to disapprove, and sent only weeds and clumsy heaps of mud.

The children of the estates made their own rules, their own

society, adapting to the physical environment. They congregated close to whatever spark seemed to connect them with the broader current of life – a chipper, a Chinese takeaway, a newsagent's – they would hang in the doorways and within the circle of light on dark evenings, chattering, stirred not by aspiration so much as the simple and insistent desire to get out. The older ones were charged with minding little ones by mothers whose notion of childcare was to get rid of them in the mornings and not see them again until after night fell. No one moulded or shaped them, no one steered them towards an ambitious or even coherent future.

Some of them sniffed glue or drank cheap vodka. The girls might allow a hasty fumble in the scrapland, sometimes more, enough to get them pregnant and caught, like flies, in the sluggish amber of their physical environment.

Mrs O'Hagen – Marie Heneghan as she was then – had had it harder than many. The early death of her father, followed by the unacknowledged slide into depression of her mother, set her apart. The few events of the estate – a new car, a new television, a holiday – were never theirs, and the practical sympathy of neighbours dwindled until the daily dispirited scraping of money and resources was something they did alone.

An early consciousness that she was an object of pity had stuck hard. Even after Marie had married young – the boy from two doors down, who turned out to have a genius for property deals – and left the old life so far behind that she seemed genuinely to remember very little about those days, she had still a hatred of sympathy. Admiration she craved and envy she was easy with, but sympathy chilled her.

Much later, Stella asked her about her family. 'Like anyone else's,' Mrs O'Hagen responded, looking surprised. 'Like families were then.' She seemed to have stepped out of that life as cleanly as someone stepping onto a bus, but she had brought with her a strong belief in the possibility of the upward thrust, and a dislike of anything she deemed ordinary. Better to be wicked, outrageous, even vulgar.

In their new world, Mr and Mrs O'Hagen's background was perfectly respectable. Many men, with teams of lawyers and advisers at their beck and call, had grown up in rags and on their wits. They made their own present, unconnected with their past, based on what they saw in magazines and on TV, things they wanted and could afford.

They were different from the adults Stella had grown up with, the lawyers and university professors of her parents' circle. They spoke less, but moved with greater purpose. They had a simplicity of vision and a frank admiration of excess that she found intriguing, even though she secretly despised it, just as she had been brought up to. Later, when Amanda's life gathered up so much of hers, she knew her parents worried. 'It's not your world,' they would remind her, after hearing the second-hand story of some spontaneous late-night trip by private jet to Ibiza. 'You won't live a life like that.'

'I know,' she would respond, laughing. 'And I wouldn't want to. I'm only visiting.' She couldn't see that, even as an outsider, she was at risk from the subtle distortion of view.

But she was quick to work out the angular division between men and women in that group and see where power lay. The possibility of being replaced lent a brittle edge to much of what those women did, to the acquiescence of their domestic lives and the shrill competition of their social ones. There, too, Mrs O'Hagen was unusual: she lacked the shifting, reactive insecurity that propelled most of them. Her ambitions went well beyond holding on to what she had.

Chapter Two

Dublin

AFTER SHE AND STELLA HAD HUNG UP, LAURA reflected on how American Stella was getting. All that 'right?' stuff, and the way she said it, impatiently, as if you'd be a moron not to agree with her. And she had seemed so deliberately, carefully, underwhelmed by Laura's news of Amanda. Laura guessed it was the five years of New York life and handling multi-million-dollar litigations, having to play it cool always, look as if you were a couple of steps ahead. The residue was a kind of hard-boiled veneer that she seemed unable to drop.

Since Amanda's wedding five years before and Stella's move, Laura and Stella had seen each other far less, and Amanda almost not at all. The closeness of their childhood and teenage years had worn away so that it no longer felt easy. They now sometimes regarded the other with a sidelong glance, as if wondering who this person was. When Amanda was with them, she stared straight ahead, seeming dazed, as if she, too, was struggling to remember their bond and was looking for the thing that would throw them back into instinctive sympathy with each other.

The last time Laura and Stella had met was when Stella had come home for her parents' wedding anniversary, a weekend visit. Two days of Stella drumming her fingers, criticising, barking at waiters and grilling Laura about her plans.

'How's work?' she had demanded.

Work, Laura had had to admit, was pretty terrible. But Stella wouldn't listen when she tried, haltingly, to explain why.

'You need to confront this,' she had said. 'Take this directly to your editor and get some resolution. You need to close this down. This is bullshit, Laura.'

Laura knew it was, but she wished Stella would stop telling her what to do, snapping advice, like a pike snapping at flies on the gently moving surface of a pond.

Laura could see her now, as plain as if she was up on one of those conference screens she spent her life in front of. Impeccably cut grey suit, the skirt reaching to exactly one inch below the knee, crisp white shirt, dark hair cut into a sleek bob, all hint of childish curls straightened. Funny, she thought now, it was actually Amanda who had created that look for her, had grabbed a brush and hairdryer one day in her bedroom and said, 'May I?' gesturing at Stella's unruly mop. She had expertly wielded brush and dryer until the curls fell into a shining helmet, accentuating the dark eyes beneath the now-straight fringe. Black heels, probably

Gucci, and long, tanned runner's legs. Laura could even picture the way she would duck her head slightly to one side now, tucking the sharp scimitar of hair behind one ear as she tapped irritably at her keyboard. Where had the other Stella gone? The sweet Stella with chewed nails, Converse and skinny jeans, hair in a high, messy ponytail. The Stella who had had a mania for experimentation, who tackled her parents on perceived injustices, confronting what she saw as their prejudices and narrow-mindedness, while they laughed, indulgent, delighted to have such a bright daughter. Laura, at her side, had always felt tongue-tied and dim-witted, unable to marshal her thoughts into the dazzling black-and-white that Stella achieved so effortlessly. Where Stella was abrupt and decisive, she was beset by endlessly multiplying points of view, the need to feel she had been fair to everyone.

Laura knew she spoke too slowly, too haltingly. She also knew she was funny, but very few people stuck around long enough to find that out. They grew impatient with her drawn-out delivery and went looking for people who could throw down punchlines and one-liners with speed and verve. Laura, with her delicate pink-and-white complexion – 'perfect peaches and cream', Nessa had always said – that was still too often suffused with a mottled red. As a child she had blushed at everything. These days, she was better, but that fiery glow still rushed over her far too often. Only when she wrote could Laura find her voice, distil all she felt into coherent argument and follow a single line of truth through the maze. She knew she was capable of more than anyone allowed her to be, but she couldn't work out which she wanted most: to sneak up and surprise them one day or find a way to thrust her personality before them now?

The hesitancy of her delivery was why she wrote for a living. Not that it was much of a living. Or that she particularly loved the stuff she wrote, at least not recently. Six months ago, she had been content – she was a news reporter on the country's biggest-selling paper, the only job she had ever wanted, covering politics, current affairs, scandals, murders, corruption, and the odd agricultural fair – 'all human life', as her editor used to say with conviction. Then she was asked to 'pop into' her editor's office. Petrie was icy and unpredictable, a glacier with the heart of a volcano. She had a habit of staring in silence which made her most aggressive superiors quail, and her subordinates babble idiotically. Laura's hands shook slightly as she tapped on the frosted glass door.

'Laura,' Petrie cooed, 'sit down. This will only take a minute. I'm sure you have more important things to be doing...'

She let the sentence hang, until Laura muttered, 'Uh, yes, of course,' then continued.

'*This* came this morning' – holding up a sheet of white paper, covered in blue biro writing – 'from a Ned O'Sullivan. One of yours?'

'Yes,' Laura stuttered, staring at the impeccable six-inch heel of Petrie's black patent leather shoes. She can't ever have worn them outside, Laura thought, wondering if actually, as was rumoured, Petrie lived somewhere in the office. Certainly no one had ever arrived before or left after her that Laura knew of. 'He's one of the sources I spoke to for the piece on moneylenders last week.' She produced the information in a rush, knowing that if she drew it out any longer, her voice would fail entirely.

'Except that he says he never spoke to you, and that he has been clearly identified in the piece, even though you didn't use his name, and that he thinks he has been defamed.' Petrie didn't rush. Her words were smooth and slow. 'Isn't that right, Ed?'

Only then did Laura really notice that the news editor, Ed Grout, a dapper little man with bright eyes in ancient, wrinkled sockets, was sitting to Petrie's right. He cleared his throat. Both sat looking expectantly at Laura.

'But he's lying,' Laura gasped. 'Of course he spoke to me. And I don't see how anyone could identify him unless he identified himself.'

'Did you record the conversation?' That was Grout.

'No.' Laura hung her head. 'It was on the phone. My recording thingy wasn't working. I took notes.'

Long silence.

'Well. I'm sure what you say must be true,' Petrie's emphasis on the word *must* served only to highlight her incredulity, 'although I do think it would be more careful to record these conversations. For your *own* sake. I'll let Legal deal with this.' She indicated the scrappy letter. 'Oh, and don't worry, Laura.' Petrie smiled kindly at her. 'It doesn't matter *at all*.'

By which Laura knew that it mattered very much.

It might have died down within a couple of weeks – as everything did, in the world of daily deadlines – except that a property developer who owed almost a billion and had moved to South Africa, having openly declared that he had no intention of repaying a penny, and whom Laura had been courting for months, suddenly gave a huge interview to Richard Callan, her exact contemporary and rival. This was the 'bullshit' that Stella had referred to.

'How can it not be weighed in the balance?' Laura asked the guy who had the cubicle next to hers, an older, more experienced journalist. 'All the good things I've done, against the one minor slip.'

'There is no balance,' he responded. 'There is no track record. Only today. Imagine a fresh fall of snow covering every one of your footsteps every night. Or a giant eraser rubbing it all out.' He had laughed.

'So I'm literally only as good as my last story?' Laura asked.

'Exactly. The story before that is finished, gone. Who cares that you once persuaded a senior politician to admit to adultery on tape, or got a confession out of a killer, or whatever? What have you got for us *today*? *Now*?'

'Nice world we live in,' she responded.

And indeed, since those incidents, Laura had been conscious of a certain *froideur*, and what looked like deliberate attempts to sideline her, usher her in the direction of more junior stories or – almost worse – human interest. She'd been asked to cover the city's literary festival, talk to a chef about his new restaurant. What next? The Bouncing Baby competition?

These thoughts made her squirm because she felt certain that the sidelining was common knowledge within the large, open-plan office she shared with thirty-odd other journalists. Some, she reckoned, were sympathetic – the ones who had themselves tripped and fallen in their time – but others, particularly Richard Callan and Ed Grout, who preferred Richard to her for his abilities as wing-man on a night out, were, she guessed, delighted.

The open-plan office with its flickering fluorescent lights had filled up around her, journalists and sub-editors of varying degrees of seniority, each with their crate-sized patch, some adorned with photos and personal scraps, others deliberately blank. Laura stared fixedly at her computer, knowing she had to get outside, trying to calculate the best way to do it without attracting attention. She could feel Richard staring at her from the other side of the room, and she was starting to breathe a little more quickly, even to sweat. Her heart was beating fast and she could feel the prickle of panic starting under her arms and spreading along her back. She had to get out of there, but how? The door was so far away, with so many tables and so many watchers between her and it. Stay calm. Deep breath. *Think.* Keeping her head down, she slid the phone receiver off its cradle, holding it low behind her cubicle wall. Determinedly not looking at it, she discreetly keyed in her mobile number, then allowed it to ring, long and loud, before reaching down, with her other hand, grabbing her BlackBerry and almost shouting, 'Hello, Laura Butler.' Then she waited a moment, said, 'Jack, howr'ya?,' loudly again, before, ostentatiously, starting to mutter into the phone. Carefully replacing the landline receiver, she stood up, saying, 'Just give me a second,' into the mobile, and made straight for the door, filled with purpose, an intrepid reporter on the scent of a story. And she knew she wasn't imagining that everyone else in that grey open-plan office was covertly watching her. Except Richard, who was staring openly.

She got downstairs and outside and leaned against the wall, nearly choking on the cigarette she'd lit. Her heart was still thumping, and she began to understand why people who had panic attacks thought they were suffering heart failure.

This was not the time to be making a poor showing. The paper was in trouble – all papers were in trouble – and the latest round of cuts had been savage, with more to come, if office gossip was anything to go by. And an office full of professional snoops and spies could usually be counted on for accuracy. The rumours were vague enough and accurate enough to spook them all, and ensure a fractured response. Instead of banding together, tackling the coming trouble as one, there were splinter groups and factions, suspicion and paranoia.

She needed a proper story, a scoop. Something no one else could possibly land. If she was ever going to set her own agenda and be seen to do so, she needed something to mark her departure.

Unfortunately Amanda was it.

CB

Amanda. Most dazzling beauty of her generation. The golden girl who had made the dream marriage, transporting herself effortlessly into the rarefied world of the very rich, the very famous and the very sought-after. Who had lit up the social scene of the city for a few years, then disappeared from view into something altogether too fabulous for any of them to follow. Now living the life of a recluse, in squalor, too locked into a depraved cycle of decline even to answer the phone. Too lost even to see her child.

The path back to those heady days shimmered in front of Laura. The years between contracted so suddenly that the nearness of all those yesterdays jolted her.

CB

'I thought I'd wait for you. I've seen you getting off the bus before, so I knew that was how you travelled.' Amanda swooped gracefully out of a dark green car, Ivana at the wheel, just as Laura reached the school gates, taking her arm affectionately. 'Shall we wait for Stella?'

'Her dad drops her on his way to the law library. She should be here any minute.' Laura found herself a bit tongue-tied. This Amanda – school Amanda – was totally different from the girl who had woken up in her bed on Saturday morning and worn her scruffy jeans, hair tied back in a loose ponytail. Laura didn't understand why the invisible barriers that separated them hadn't re-formed now that they were at school. She had never expected to be acknowledged again, once the walls of everyday closed about them all.

'Her dad's a lawyer? That explains it.' Amanda laughed.

'Explains what?'

'Stella's intellectual poise. Her way of asking questions. Always about the small, technical details. Like a cross-examination. Not always a friendly one either.' She laughed again.

Laura knew exactly what she meant. It was a way of *going on* that Stella had. Coming back again and again to a point that you thought was unimportant, attacking it from different angles. But she wondered if it was a bit disloyal to admit she knew what Amanda was talking about, so she dug around in her bag instead, wondering what Amanda had brought for lunch. Or did she eat the canteen food? It seemed unlikely.

It was a chilly morning. The school looked even greyer than usual. Certainly the country's rich-list didn't send their daughters to St Assumpta's for its architectural beauty. All the way in on the bus, Laura had wondered what might happen. Would Amanda just pretend the weekend – that strange night in Dargle's, breakfast with Nessa, lunch at Amanda's mansion, the trip to see her show-jumpers in the gentle glow of the afternoon sun – had never happened? They had walked through the gardens together, she and Stella idly playing a game they had begun as small children. 'Black or White', they called it.

They played because it was funny, and because they believed that you could tell a lot about a person from their answers.

'Guest or host?' Stella had asked Amanda.

'What?'

'Which are you better at being, a guest or a host?'

'Um. Guest, I think.'

'Okay, friend or girlfriend?'

'Friend, definitely.'

'Right. Laura, your turn.'

'Soloist or orchestra?' Laura asked.

Pause. 'Orchestra?' said Amanda.

'Liar,' said Stella, with a laugh. 'Soloist, clearly.'

'My turn,' said Amanda.

'Go on.'

'Tennis or hockey?'

'Hockey,' said Stella quickly.

'Critic or chef?'

'Critic, I think,' said Laura.

'Diarist or memoirist?'

'Good one! That's very clever.' Laura and Stella cheered, swapping looks with each other, looks that said, 'Maybe this is real …'

It had been just her and Stella for such a long time, two fish out of water in St Assumpta's, two little outsiders. Her, because of her single mother, her small, arty house, the lack of sun holidays in Marbella and Quinta do Lago, skiing in Verbier, Christmases in Bali. Stella could have fitted in if she'd wanted to. Her parents could easily afford the trips, the shiny black Mercs, the designer clothes, if they had wanted them. Instead, they drove a beaten-up Volvo, went to places like Bilbao to visit the Guggenheim, Amsterdam for the Rembrandts. If they went to New York, they never went near Saks or Bergdorf Goodman. Stella's father said they sent her to St Assumpta's only because of the world-class education — it had produced a couple of female CEOs and a well-above-average smattering of the best lawyers — and definitely not for the kind of company she would be keeping. In fact, laughing, he had forbidden her to make friends. Except Laura, of course, whom they knew from the local junior school. She had been Stella's best friend from the day, nearly a week into the first term, when she had found Laura almost unable to breathe with terror as Nessa said a jaunty farewell at the classroom door, indifferent to the fact that every other girl had a desk to go to, a place to hang her coat, the name of someone who might be a friend, where Laura had nothing, knew no one. Stella had silently taken Laura's hand and led her to a seat beside her. 'You can borrow my colours if you don't have any,' she had said kindly.

Later they had been the only two girls in that class to go on to St Assumpta's, although Nessa had never told Laura who paid her fees. 'Don't need to know,' she trilled, each time Laura asked, smartly ending the conversation.

Laura always suspected Stella might have liked to make more friends, but the other girls, once they discovered that her dad didn't play golf with theirs and her mother didn't go to the same charity lunches, had decided for her, leaving her coolly alone.

Just then Stella appeared, and Amanda had taken their arms and walked them through the yard, talking in a low voice about the curriculum or something equally innocuous. Laura saw Nadine and Sally start towards her, then stop in astonishment, because Amanda waved slightly at them, but didn't pause.

ॐ

By break time, it was done. The entire school knew of Laura and Stella's unbelievable reversal of fortune. They might have been curious, some envious, a couple downright furious, but that was it. And Stella and Laura had been right all along. There was an inner circle, and now they were part of it. Hidden paths opened smoothly before them. Even in the inner circle, though, Amanda was still the sun around which all else revolved. No plans were hatched without consulting her, and dates were readily changed if they didn't suit her. Purchases were made only after she had been consulted.

'Navy or grey?' Some weeks had gone by. Lunch over, Nadine produced two identical dresses, fitted wool with short, flouncy skirts, from a smart carrier bag. They had been sent on approval from Missy Mo, a boutique that specialised in keeping the mothers close and getting the daughters young.

'Grey. Navy is for nuns and you don't have a nun's complexion.' Amanda had barely looked up. Nadine instantly restored the navy to the smart shopper with 'Missy Mo' scribbled across it in powder-blue. Amanda nodded at her, a dismissal.

'Is it always that easy?' Stella asked, with a laugh.

'No. Sometimes I have to pick their summer holidays. Even their boyfriends,' Amanda said. 'And once I had to choose which parent one of the girls should live with during a divorce.'

'God, how awful. How did you choose?' Laura was horrified.

'I tossed a coin.' Gurgle of laughter. Laura believed – hoped – she was joking.

Amanda didn't seem to do anything special to deserve the flood of attention. It was the essence of her that demanded it.

She appeared unaware of her effect, and yet, Laura noted, she wasn't slow to wield her power when she felt it necessary. She required an awful lot of attention, and company, during her after-school appointments. Trips to the vet or dog-grooming parlour with Muttley, a toy Pekinese, with bulging eyes and rolling gait, whom Amanda loved without affectation; visits to the various professionals who added the subtle practice of their art to Amanda's natural beauty – nail people, hair people, skin refinishers – all of whom took delivery of Amanda as if she were the Venus de Milo and they responsible for the burnishing of a masterpiece. For all that she affected to despise her parents and their lifestyle, Amanda never said no to the money, and spent it much as her mother did – in boutiques, department stores, salons, on taxis and fast-food joints.

'Why would anyone spend a hundred quid on a cushion?' Stella said one day as they wandered through a department store after school, idly picking up and admiring things they had no wish to buy. 'I just don't get it.'

'I do,' said Amanda. 'It's because they can. And other people can't.'

'So it's the last bit that's the attraction?' Stella sounded disapproving.

'I guess.' Amanda shrugged.

'Why don't you do something really good with all your influence?' Stella asked as they crowded together into a small patch of sunshine slanting across the schoolyard.

'Like what? You're not going to suggest I go for student president? I think that's more your thing.'

'No, not that. But what about Celestine?'

'What about Celestine?' Amanda sounded baffled. Celestine was a girl in their year who, if Stella and Laura had been invisible until Amanda lighted upon them, was all too visible. Slow of speech and movement, she was the butt of jokes and cruel shorthand for anything that occurred that seemed particularly stupid. 'That's so *Celestine*,' the popular girls would say, perhaps with a glance to where she sat alone. Always alone. Laura knew that Stella had long been bothered by the cruelty of barbs that cost the perpetrator little thought but hurt when they reached their target. She had talked about it several times to Laura, suggesting ways that maybe they could help Celestine, even though they knew there was nothing they could do.

'Maybe you could make everyone less mean to her,' Stella said.

'But why?' asked Amanda. 'I don't know her. Or like her.'

'But it seems awful that people should be so cruel to her. It's not fair. Her life must be a misery. I tried being nice to her a few times, but it never made any difference. But if *you* did ...'

Amanda was reluctant. 'I don't know what you think I could do,' she said. 'And I certainly don't want to hang out with her.'

'You wouldn't have to,' Stella said. 'I've thought it all through.'

'Of course you have.'

'All you have to do is show everyone that they ought to leave her alone. Invite her to sit with us a few times, in assembly or at lunch, and you know very well that the other girls will get the message. Once you're not mean to her, it won't be cool for anyone else to be mean to her.'

'But I never was mean to her,' Amanda pointed out. 'I was never anything to her.'

'And now you're going to be nice to her. Please?'

'You really mind that much?'

'I do. I really do.'

'Okay, fine, I'll do it.' And she did. The next morning in assembly, she called Celestine over, loudly, publicly, and made space for her on the bench. Later, at lunch, something similar, so that there could be no doubt. Celestine didn't say much, took almost no part in the conversation, but she sat meekly within the protection of Amanda's popularity. Enough soaked into her to give her the colour she needed.

'Thanks,' said Stella, some days later, giving Amanda's arm a gentle squeeze. 'You see how well it worked?'

'I did it for you,' Amanda said, 'not for Celestine. Who, by the way, isn't even grateful.' Indeed, Celestine had seemed faintly suspicious, even relieved to slip back to solitude, although she was now, Laura noted, left fully alone rather than goaded and mocked.

'I can see she's not. But I am,' Stella said.

'I don't see why you should be grateful,' Laura whispered to Stella later. 'It was your idea, not Amanda's.'

'Yes, but she did it, and I'm glad.'

The three of them talked constantly, but not of the things Laura had expected. They didn't talk about boys or clothes or music very much. In fact, Amanda seemed to prefer dwelling on the future rather than the present. They talked of what would be – Stella with her usual highly specific, determined ambitions: 'Law. Human-rights law. I want to make a difference, change things, fight the bad guys on behalf of the good guys – people caught up in wars and revolutions, women who lose their jobs for getting pregnant, people wrongly accused.'

Laura, vaguely, but with passion: 'It has to be something I can do in my own time, without people hurrying me up or looking over my shoulder. Something creative, but not painting. I'd never try that. Can you imagine?' They all shuddered.

Amanda was vaguer again, but filled with twice the enthusiasm: 'We can be whatever we want, don't you see? We can get away from all this, and make our own lives.' By 'all this', Laura took her to mean her home life, as much as the dull trappings of school and life as a sixteen-year-old in the suburb of a small capital city on the fringes of the wider world.

They usually did what Amanda wanted, Laura remembered, but often what she wanted was simply to hang around at their houses: Dargle's on a Friday night, then a sleepover at Laura's – she had an affection for the little box bed, claimed she slept better there than in her own four-poster – and breakfast with Nessa the next morning. For a time, the similarities between them blinded Laura to the differences. All three were only children, with the kind of fraught parental relationships that often spring from the sheer visibility of basking alone in the sun of attention without siblings to distract and camouflage. They could relate to the intensity of intimacy each one experienced as a burden, could laugh at the loneliness of being just one when their parents' hopes and fears were so many.

Nessa adored Amanda for her looks and for what she described as 'her strange, still quality'. 'Amanda,' she said to Laura, 'doesn't twitch and fidget the way other girls do. She has chosen to be beautiful.' Laura had thought the stillness was just part of Amanda's general poise, but apparently it was more than that. Something holy.

'What do you mean? She just *is* beautiful.'

'Yes, but she's also clever, and funny, when the mood takes her. She's kind and affectionate to the few who get past her guard. But what's the one thing we all see and remember about her? Her beauty. Amanda *plays* beautiful, just as much as she *is* beautiful.'

Laura pondered her mother's words. She supposed she could see what she meant: Amanda did rather allow one to admire. And she didn't ever screw up her face and make freaky expressions the way every other girl Laura knew did. She didn't self-deprecate or goof. In fact, she took herself seriously.

Amanda came often to the little house. She loved curling up on the battered chesterfield and reading Nessa's odd books, everything from an eighteenth-century hen breeder's manual to satirical novels. One in particular she read again and again, *Cold Comfort Farm*, about Flora Poste, a girl full of energy and practical resolve, who ordered the lives of those around her with a sure touch.

'I need her to sort my life out,' she said to Nessa, when she had finished the book for the first time. 'She'd be able to manage my mother, and tell me what I'm supposed to be doing. And Flora, what a nice name. If I have a little girl, I'm going to call her Flora. It's old-fashioned but strong.'

Nessa talked to Amanda about art, showing her images from the huge glossy books she spent so much of their money on. She even sketched her one day, to Laura's amazement. The sketch was still there on the living-room wall of the little house Nessa had left to Laura, where Laura still lived. In it, Amanda was half-turned away, her face in three-quarters, long neck curved into an appealing C-shape, heavy hair coiled loosely at the nape, eyes half-closed so that the long lashes swept down towards her cheekbones.

The fire had been lit, even though it was only late September, because there had been a sudden turn in the weather. The girls had finished their homework and were shelling chestnuts for a chocolate and chestnut pudding Nessa was making. Except that Nessa had lost interest in the pudding, picked up a pencil and torn a sheet out of one of Laura's sketch pads. 'Don't move,' she said to Amanda. 'Stay exactly like that.' Her pencil moved quickly, lightly. Looking over her mother's shoulder, Laura could see that it was a perfect likeness, capturing exactly Amanda's quality of being elsewhere, even while she looked at and spoke to you.

While sketching, Nessa talked to Amanda about the role of a model, the power she had to shape the vision of a great artist, to inspire someone's best work through her own interpretation of the world. 'Great art,' she said, pushing a strand of her hair out of the way, 'is often a collaboration. The result of a meticulous adherence to personal truth, refracted through the lens of another's experience. This is true of fashion and filmmaking as much as painting.' Laura had only the dimmest notion of what her mother might mean, but Amanda nodded slowly as if she not only understood but was considering the information carefully.

It wasn't the first time Nessa had talked to Amanda in a way she never talked to Laura, as if Amanda was somehow her own age and understood the ways of the world. Sometimes she talked to her about men, quite as if Amanda had the same considerable experience.

'You give them only what you want, but in a way that makes them think they have *extracted* it.'

Laura had a vision of some of the boys they knew coming after them with a crowbar, levering … what? The only thing she really knew boys wanted was sex, and surely it couldn't be that. She understood, somehow, that that wasn't what Nessa had meant, that she was talking about something more subtle, psychological, but at that point she gave up, baffled. Amanda, however, had laughed and agreed with Nessa.

There was an instinctive understanding the two had, a

way of being together that was so unlike the tight, twisted relationship Amanda had with her own mother, where every move the other made just wrestled them tighter together. Laura could see why Amanda responded so eagerly to Nessa's funny abstractions.

In contrast, where Nessa was expansive with Amanda, talking to her at length about anything and everything, she could be uncommunicative with Laura, refusing to tell her more than the bare facts of her life. Laura had once asked how on earth she had come to be conceived so soon after the break-up of what had been the great, defining relationship of Nessa's life. The answer was startlingly brief.

'I did it quite deliberately. I was celebrating my freedom.' And, for a long time, that was all Laura knew about the complicated situation involving the celebrated portrait painter, the unassuming man who turned out to be her real father, and Nessa. And of all the bewildered longing that Laura felt when she thought about families – real families, with a father and a mother and set times when people came home and saw each other, asking boring questions about school and work and really meaning them – Nessa didn't want to hear. 'That's not our life,' was all she said, when Laura tried to explain the regret she felt for something she'd never had, adding darkly, 'There are worse things than our way,' by which Laura presumed she meant safe, predictable nuclear families. That Laura might not agree seemed of little interest to Nessa.

The effect of Amanda on Laura's relationship with Nessa was a curious one. Amanda joined the dots for Laura and Nessa, providing a third in what was a too-sharp relationship. But she also opened the door of possibility for Laura, showing her clearly what she had always suspected she lacked: the status brought by money and nastiness. Nessa was never nasty to salespeople, waiters, people in queues, and she had no money. And so she was patronised, treated with familiarity and sometimes contempt. Nessa seemed not to notice, but Laura did, and she burnt with hot indignation for her. For both of them. The deference that greeted Mrs O'Hagen and Amanda was very evident to Laura. Amanda's life forced Laura to question the things Nessa had always taught her daughter to prize – intellect, integrity, good taste, organic food – and conclude that perhaps Nessa was wrong. Amanda's house had none of those things, as far as she could see, yet it hummed and pulsed with an ambitious energy. Things happened there that didn't happen in the little house where Nessa drifted in and out of attitudes.

Mrs O'Hagen had frequently talked to Amanda about modelling, suggesting she get some photos taken and go along to an agency, or meet such-and-such a person who could introduce her to fashion photographers. Amanda had ignored all this, saying modelling was for idiots, and citing as an example a girl in their year with very long legs and a small head who had appeared in a couple of photocalls for betting companies.

'Standing by Stephen's Green in a bikini in November, her legs blue under the fake tan. I mean, please!'

But after a conversation with Nessa about muses, in which Nessa had dangled examples such as Fellini and Giulietta Masina, Lucian Freud and Caroline Blackwood – Amanda seemed to think differently about modelling.

Stella's parents were not as easily won over by Amanda. They knew enough about her parents to be prejudiced but acknowledged that Amanda had what they called 'wit', which they valued highly. They enjoyed the funny stories Amanda told about the parties and lunches she went to, things her mothers' friends said, the importance they attached to getting their hands on a particular designer dress, even though they knew half the women in the room would have a variation of the same thing.

Amanda was a good mimic and had an understanding of what her audience wanted to hear. She never mocked her parents too overtly, Laura noted, because she sensed that Stella's parents wouldn't like that, would think it not really on. When she spoke about her parents, the anecdotes were carefully crafted. She never began sentences with 'my mother says', as did every other girl they knew, even though her mother's attempts at control over her life were to continue unabated for many years.

Everywhere they went, Amanda's phone would ring or ping, her mother wanting to know where she was, what she was doing, what she had decided to wear to the Grovers' lunch on Saturday. Had she entered Gingerbread and Little Miss into the jumping section of the next agricultural show? Amanda never said, 'Hello' or 'Hi', just 'Yes?' with a flat note in her voice. But she nearly always took the calls, patiently answering her mother's questions but volunteering nothing.

'No, I didn't … No, no. Not yet … Yes, okay … Okay, yes. See you later.'

She was like a child trying to slide out of a room without being noticed, Laura thought. It was the very quality of stillness that Nessa had noted in her, and it seemed to have its origin in a desire to remain unseen. At the heart of Amanda, Laura sometimes thought, there was a locked room, a place she didn't show anyone, or even go into much herself.

She had a passivity that you didn't notice at first because, wherever she was, a swirl of activity went on around her. She was so sought after, always being phoned, texted, collected. She could pick and choose between invitations, and was almost better at saying no to things than she was at saying yes, all of which made it look as though she was in perpetual motion, running from a game of tennis to a lunch, home to change then out to a party, followed by early breakfast and a horse show, or an interview for a magazine. And yet there was something else too, quite different from the surface glitter: a point where all the activity died away to a deep, still pool – where only the surface was ever touched by ripples.

'I've got the best invite ever.' There was a bubble of mirth in Amanda's voice, so irresistible that Laura refrained from saying that she had retired to this quiet corner of the library to get some work done. Laura usually stayed at school until well past five o'clock, even when she didn't have hockey practice. That way, by the time she got her two buses home, she was mostly done with homework and ready to join Nessa in the kitchen, to chat and chop while they prepared dinner.

'Well? Go on.' Laura closed the biology book she had been reading.

Amanda had come straight from tennis. She was wearing immaculate whites, her long brown legs disappearing into snowy ankle socks and trainers, hair in a swishy ponytail. 'It's a twenty-first.' She paused expectantly. Sure enough, Laura weighed in with 'I thought you didn't bother much with those any more.'

Now seventeen, Amanda had grown out of Dargle's and hanging out at friends' houses when their parents were away, sneaking the odd glass of Southern Comfort. These days, she went to proper grown-up parties, where there were fridges full of champagne and expensive white wine, usually some guy ready to whip up complicated cocktails, real DJs and grown men who vied furiously to drop her home. The calibre of party grew better and better as the circle widened of people who wanted to know her.

Part of it was through modelling. After that chat with Nessa, Amanda had signed up with an agency, and almost immediately was offered more work than she could have accepted without quitting school. She turned down most of it. Here, Mrs O'Hagen had proved herself adroit. 'We'll market you very carefully,' she had said to Amanda one Saturday, when Laura and Stella had stayed over. 'Leave them wanting far, far more than they can have. And you'll only do editorial. No photocalls. No advertising, unless it's a really *top-tier* campaign. We'll make you a face, a personality. If you can't do a job, we'll say it's because you're at Cheltenham, or in New York for a film première. We'll build you slowly, slowly. It's not as if you need the money.' She laughed, a chilly tinkle.

It was around that time that Mrs O'Hagen had shown an unexpected interest in Laura. Amanda had let slip – deliberately, Laura suspected – the complicated relationship with the celebrated portrait painter. Except that she hadn't revealed how complicated it actually was, had just said the man was Laura's father. The next time Laura had gone over there, Mrs O'Hagen had cornered her and begun to coo about how they *all* admired his art.

'How exciting for you to have such a close connection with such a brilliant man. Do you see much of him? Has he ever painted you?' She had more questions, though she didn't wait long enough for Laura to answer any – 'Do you paint yourself? How much do you take after him?' – until she got to the killer blow: 'Why don't you invite him to lunch here one day? I can think of so many people who would love to meet him. And perhaps he might even get a few commissions. I know how an artist's life is.' She had stared expectantly at Laura.

Laura hadn't known how to explain the way things were. 'He's not, I mean, he was … but …' In the end, she had just stammered, 'He doesn't like parties. And he never eats lunch.'

Mrs O'Hagen had been offended, had given Laura a cross look and said, 'Well, we'll see,' then click-clacked her way across the aggressive black-and-white tiles and out to her waiting car.

'Fool,' Amanda had said cheerfully later. 'You should have strung her along, made her believe you could actually bring him to lunch. She would have been much nicer to you.'

'But why did you tell her about him?'

'I was trying to give you a decent back-story,' Amanda had explained, with a laughing, sideways glance. 'You know, make you more interesting. And show her that it's silly to dismiss people the way she does because they can turn out to have a lot more going for them than she sees.' From that, Laura learned two things. First, that Mrs O'Hagen had 'dismissed' her, and that Amanda did, in her own indirect way, try to stand up to her mother.

After that one incident, Laura never again got the feeling that Mrs O'Hagen had a pivotal place for her in the careful scheme of her life, but an odd sympathy grew up between them. She realised she enjoyed being visible to that strong-minded woman, and she wanted other people to see her too. Mrs O'Hagen might have lacked charm but she had magnetism, force of character and energy, all things that Laura, with her wavering nature, was susceptible to in others. When you were in the full glare of Mrs O'Hagen's attention, you wanted to stay there.

It put her subtly at odds with Amanda and Stella. 'If you gave more, she'd ask less,' Laura ventured one day to Amanda, after Mrs O'Hagen's usual post-night-out grilling.

'She always wants more, no matter how much you give,' Amanda said. 'There's no such thing as enough for her. She's like a particularly aggressive nineteenth-century nation, constantly pushing at the borders, trying to expand and colonise.'

'Well, I think, actually, she's not that bad,' Laura dared.

'Then you don't know her,' Amanda said flatly.

'Laura, she's a nightmare,' agreed Stella. And that had been that. Mrs O'Hagen was officially, for all of them, a 'nightmare'. Except that Laura saw for the first time that it was possible for them to differ about something important. Amanda had her beauty, the golden setting of her background. Stella had the force of her direct personality and a sense of humour that was a challenge. Laura had nothing obvious. And she began to know how much she yearned for something, some recognisable name or look or style, something that would stand behind her and project her worth to the world.

And here was Amanda now, ready to divulge the details of her latest invitation.

'Normally, I don't bother with twenty-firsts. But this is for James Marsfield, son of Lord Brinsley. Drumcranig the house, is amazing. Everybody goes there. Politicians, poets, film people. James is at Trinity, but he has friends from all over the world. I got invited by the photographer who shot me for the *Sunday Herald* magazine last week. He said he knew James would love to meet me. I asked if I could bring a couple of friends, and he said yes, as long as they were girls and pretty.' Laura could see that Amanda, normally so cool, was really excited. Clearly, this party was a big deal in ways that she didn't understand.

'When is it?' she asked.

'Saturday. Say you're free! Then we can work on Stel and her parents.' So Laura said she was free. Nessa never much minded where she went, trusting Laura to be sensible and not get herself into impossible situations. In fact, when Laura told her where they were going, she laughed.

'I used to go to parties there,' she said. 'Very good parties they were too. I remember one where the then British ambassador disappeared with Rosalind Hayes, whom everyone knew was sleeping with a really ferocious IRA terrorist. She was gorgeous, but mad. The daughter of an English earl, but very anti-establishment. It nearly turned into a major scandal, our very own Profumo affair. The ambassador got a stern talking-to, and the earl was dispatched by the British government to bring Rosie home. Pity. She was a lot of fun.' Amanda was there when this story was being told, her eyes like saucers. Laura could see that she was hooked on the possibilities Drumcranig offered.

To their surprise, Stella's parents were quite excited too. 'That's a fairly louche scene,' Stella's dad had said, laughing, 'but I can see why you'd want to go. It'll be interesting. You'll need your wits about you. And you can't stay all night, which is what the rest of them will be doing. You have to be home by twelve thirty, even if it feels like the party's only starting then.'

Stella promised, although they had already decided they would all stay over at Amanda's – she lived much closer to Drumcranig than they did, so it made geographic sense. But also, as Amanda pointed out, her mother would combust if she couldn't get a full account of the party immediately they got back. Mrs O'Hagen was more excited than Laura had ever seen her.

'It's about time,' she had said coolly, when Amanda told her, but the glitter in her eyes belied her attempt at laid-back. She and Amanda then had a huge row about what she was to wear. Mrs O'Hagen wanted to dispatch her for various beauty appointments – tanning, eyebrows, nails and so on – but Amanda refused. It was the first time Laura had seen her openly defy her mother.

'That's not the way I want to look,' she had said. 'Tans are tacky. And those people will know that. Turning up bright orange with perfect nails, a blow-dry and a tight little dress will immediately tell them I'm not worth bothering about.'

'Not bright orange,' her mother had said. 'A subtle glow. And since when did having decent nails and hair make anyone look anything except well groomed? What's wrong with that?' She had looked baffled, and appealed to Stella and Laura for back-up: 'What do you girls think?'

'That it doesn't really matter all that much, one way or the other, although of course it's fun to pretend it does,' Stella had said, true to her convictions, but surprised at her own daring. Mrs O'Hagen looked hard at her, then turned to Laura.

'I'm sure you're right,' Laura said in a rush, trying to please everyone, 'but surely the best thing is that Amanda feels comfortable ...' She trailed off. The idea of Amanda feeling uncomfortable in any social setting was so clearly ridiculous that no one even answered her. She felt stupid – she could feel that Mrs O'Hagen had acted on the silent, fragile sympathy that seemed to exist between the two of them, and that Laura had let her down because she was not yet brave enough to go against Stella and Amanda.

Mrs O'Hagen was even more confused when Amanda had popped in to show herself off before they left on the Saturday night. She was wearing a black silk and cashmere dress, perfectly plain although beautifully cut, which hugged her curves seductively and ended just below the knee. Her hair was loose, brushed into gentle waves, and she wore very little make-up, just a slick of fire-engine red lipstick.

'But that dress is ancient,' her mother said.

'I've only worn it once.'

'It's last season.'

'So much the better. Trust me.' Amanda softened slightly. 'I know what I'm doing. Really. I want to do this my way.'

Mrs O'Hagen had given Stella and Laura a despairing glance, although Laura noted that she seemed to perk up when she ran her eye over them, mentally comparing them with her daughter. Both were more obviously dressed-up than Amanda – Stella in a short floral dress that just avoided being too pretty because she was wearing it with opaque tights and chunky heels, and Laura in cream lace, one of Nessa's from years before, that they had shortened. Lately, Stella had taken to wearing a lot of black eyeliner, and her eyes were appropriately finished with an upwards flick that gave her a slightly haughty look. But even so, despite their efforts – and they had both found themselves very excited as the day drew nearer – Amanda eclipsed them. They knew it, Amanda knew it, and Mrs O'Hagen knew it. Laura saw her smile tightly to herself when she had finished the once-over.

Chapter Three

Dublin

SEEN FROM A DISTANCE OF YEARS, THAT PARTY had been a milestone. But Laura wondered if a small part of her had known it even at the time. It was as if, that night, they had found a tiny door at the back of all the other dull and careful parties they had ever been to, and crept through it to a glittering, exotic wonderland.

&

Ivana drove them, nipping around country lanes in the little black Merc the family allowed her to use when on errands for Amanda. One window was down so she could smoke, TLC's 'Waterfalls' was blaring from the stereo and they were all singing along.

It was late September, but the day had been so glorious that it was still bright out, with a cold mist rising off the ground now, gradually melting into the warmer air so that everything low down had a gentle smoky blur. There was a faint smell of autumn – a tart, clear, appley smell – which made Laura think of the nights when it would become really cold, dark by five o'clock, their frosty breath on the playing fields as they trained under orange floodlights. 'It's nearly autumn,' Stella said, as if reading her mind. 'I hate autumn, when summer ends and there's nothing but winter to look forward to.'

'I'm glad summer's over,' Laura said. 'What I hate are the dog days, when you're clinging on, still hoping for a bit of warmth because winter seems so extreme. By now I'm ready for it.'

'It's all going to get better from now,' Amanda agreed, her face glowing with excitement.

They had been climbing gently, steadily, and now they rounded a bend in the road and saw Drumcranig beneath them, glittering white in the evening light. From that distance, the house was like a bright jewel, tucked under the side of the mountain, with an inky lake spread out at its feet and a mass of trees in their early autumn glory ranged around it.

'It looks like it's on fire,' Stella said.

And, indeed, the blur of orange, red and yellow leaves were just like flames, leaping around the pure white of the house, but whether to protect or consume it, Laura couldn't tell. 'You'd expect some kind of a huge sea creature to rise up out of that lake and attack anyone who went near it,' she said.

'"Weaving spiders come not here."' Amanda laughed. 'We'll be okay. We're here for the right reasons. The creature will know it.' The air seemed to change as they descended into the valley, thickening with a thousand specks of dust and whirling mites until it gathered itself into a living stream and rushed along beside them, keeping pace with the car, ready to push them through the giant rusty gates, should there be any impediment. There wasn't, even though the gates looked as if they hadn't been opened in years, and Nature had almost clawed back to herself the road on the other side, jolting them over potholes and tufts of grass, until they came to the house. It was smaller than Laura had expected, and, close up, the vision of serenity and seclusion it had given off at a distance was marred by a frenzy of activity. Dogs, people and cars were milling around purposefully.

The girls got out and stood, slightly bewildered.

'I am come back at two o'clock. I am meet you here,' Ivana said, and Laura saw Stella look momentarily anxious at the deception she would be forced to practise on her parents.

Then Amanda grabbed her arm. 'Come on, let's do it.'

The front doors were wide open, leading into an enormous hall painted crimson, with faded floor tiles in a curly green-and-yellow pattern. It was big enough to have its own fireplace, over which hung a huge painting of a man in black robes with two hounds at his feet and a complicated compass in one hand. A big battered velvet sofa stood to one side of the fireplace, in which logs were burning, and the floor shone with such a gentle sheen, the glow of ages, that Laura couldn't help thinking of the savage black-and-white in Amanda's house, and what might have lain there previously. An elderly lady wearing layers of brown was sitting on the sofa, changing out of a pair of mud-encrusted wellies and into a battered pair of black court shoes, while a small dog yapped at her.

'Quiet, Dibs!' The woman who came towards them had short blonde hair, pale blue eyes and a surprisingly deep voice. Where Mrs O'Hagen was ageless because her face was so smooth and unmarked, despite a heavy, grown-up look to it, this woman had exactly the same effect, but the other way round. She looked so young, almost child-like, yet there were maps of tiny wrinkles around her eyes and mouth. She smiled, bringing all the delicate lines and wrinkles into relief, and Laura noticed that she looked all the more appealing for them: battered, but sexy. As if she had lived, laughed, loved, and didn't care who knew it. They later learned that she was James's mother, and a large part of the legend that surrounded Drumcranig. 'Janine, how lovely to see you,' she said to the elderly lady, proffering an arm to help her up. Then: 'You must be friends of James's. I'm Iseult. Everyone's in the back. There's a marquee,' she said to Janine. 'Can you believe it?' The way she said 'marquee', it might have been an elephant. Or a dog trained to wear clothes and do little tricks.

They went out to the marquee, only to find that most people were avoiding it, seeming to prefer sitting outside, on the chairs and benches arranged for them, or on low walls and even on the grass. There were people of all ages, which Laura, Stella and Amanda weren't used to. For them, 'grown-ups' were still beings to be treated respectfully and avoided. There were a couple of kids, with the same straight dirty-blond hair, running madly around, ignored by those whose duty it should have been to tell them to 'Be careful!' Old men in creaking three-piece suits with watery eyes and clipped accents, talking about architecture or fishing; ancient ladies dusted with chalky face powder and wearing badly applied lipstick, drinking martinis and smoking. In between, though, there were some of the most dazzling people Laura had ever seen, men and women in the prime of their lives, filled with a confidence so complete it suffused everything they did and said. Holding out glasses to passing waiters for refills, without taking their eyes from the person they were talking to, wandering from group to group, joining, without a moment's hesitation, conversations that seemed fascinatingly clever, teasing each other and laughing.

The men were all in black tie, so romantic-looking that Laura thought they could have come from a different era. Some pre-war time, when innocence itself was young. The women were beautiful, but Amanda had been right: these were not the impeccably groomed, modishly turned-out society ladies of Mrs O'Hagen's circle. They wore clothes either so plain that they were unnoticeable or so eccentric as to be slightly mad. Laura could see none of the preposterous handbags that had come to dominate Mrs O'Hagen's type of party, which every woman seemed to carry, like armour, bags with names that dripped with chains, padlocks and quilted bits.

The girls stood at a loss for a few moments, wondering how they might ever breach such a seamless flow, but then Amanda said, 'I'm going to get a drink.' She moved into the marquee, which had tiny lights set into the canopy like twinkling stars, where they had seen a bar, rather than accost any of the waiters. 'I'll have a gin and tonic,' she said to the barman, who nodded, and looked at Laura and Stella.

'Um, Diet Coke,' Stella said.

Laura said she'd have a beer: a drink might make her feel less awkward. 'Now what?' she said to Amanda, back outside. 'Do we work the room? Well, the garden ...'

'No!' Amanda said, so sharply that Stella jumped, spilling a bit of her Diet Coke. 'We just wait. We don't do anything.'

That was odd, Laura thought. She'd seen Amanda in action

at parties. She never waited, or stood at the side. She walked around until she found someone she liked the look of, then smiled at them. Invariably they smiled back, and came over to her. And that was usually that. Even at her parents' parties Laura had seen her put on a good showing. She and Stella had once or twice been paid to 'help' at those events – although the caterers Mrs O'Hagen hired were always so efficient that there was literally nothing to do – and Laura had admired the way Amanda could make a quick tour of a room, pausing here and there to chat, casting a smile one way, a little wave of her hand another, then exit, leaving her mother satisfied that she had been sufficiently 'seen'. But now she just stood, talking quietly to them about things like architecture and history. It was confusing, Laura thought, and frankly a bit dull, when everything else was so exciting.

They didn't wait for long. Within moments, a man wearing a black dinner jacket, with a white T-shirt saying 'Rock This Place', came over. He had scruffy shoulder-length hair and several days of stubble, but his eyes were bright and his shoes highly polished.

'Amanda.' He kissed her on both cheeks. 'Good, you came. I promised James I'd bring him the most glorious birthday present. If you hadn't shown up, I would have had to go searching through auction houses for something as exquisite.' He laughed heartily.

What a moron, thought Laura. He'd laid it on with a trowel.

'Isn't this something, huh?' he was saying, sweeping an arm out towards the house in front of them. 'Finest house in Ireland. Best parties in Ireland too.' He laughed again, head thrown back, making much of just how at ease he felt with it all. Amanda, Laura noted, was smiling back at him.

'This is Stella.' Amanda pushed Stella forward. 'And this is Laura.'

'Laura. Stella. Welcome. Good you could make it. I see you paid attention to my instructions,' he said to Amanda, with a wink. 'Girls, pretty ones, are always welcome.'

'This is Will,' Amanda continued. 'He's a photographer. He shot me for the *Sunday Herald* a couple of weeks ago.'

'Actually, I think she seared herself on the camera lens without any help from me,' Will said gallantly – moronically, in Laura's opinion. 'I showed some of the shots to James. He was very impressed. Come and meet him.' He took Amanda's arm, steering her across the middle of the lawn. Laura swapped a quick look with Stella. *Go? Stay here?* As one, they set off after them, trotting a little to catch up.

By now it was nearly dark, the sky a deep royal blue, and the first stars could be seen above the band of light created by the bonfires, Roman candles and fairy lights strung from tree to tree. Food had appeared, huge pots of something that steamed and smelt stew-y, on trestle tables just inside the marquee. The garden had filled, and the general hum of conversation was much louder. They caught snatches of chat as they worked their way through and around the groups.

'She couldn't have stayed with him, you know. He was frightful.'

'They tried to renew my contract at the same rate. Well, I told them where they could go with that ...' This from a bullish man smoking a fat cigar.

'... the kind of thing he writes about. His work is much darker now.' That was a woman with pale auburn hair piled on top of her head, a peacock blue velvet fringed shawl draped across her shoulders.

'Never gave him a second thought,' responded the heavy-set man with her. 'That brooding Spanish manner of his. Too weighty. Too deliberate.'

'That's what they *gave* him the Nobel Prize *for*,' said a dark-haired girl, in a slim black sleeveless dress, who couldn't have been much older than Laura. She had spoken with some scorn, as if she expected her opinion to be taken seriously. And it was. The heavy man and auburn-haired woman nodded thoughtfully.

A man whose face had been familiar to Laura and Stella for almost their entire lives, dominating television screens, stood with another group. His wasn't the only face they recognised. There were a couple of actresses, a few musicians, and at least two of the more exciting type of politician, the ones who had real power and didn't lead their lives in constant fear of being pictured doing something inappropriate.

Drink was flowing, music was starting up somewhere that Laura couldn't see and the mood of the party was moving into a higher gear. Amanda and Will had come to a halt at a group standing on the edge of the party, beside an empty swimming pool. The bottom, reached by a flight of stone steps, was neatly swept but looked as if it had been a long time since any water, beyond rain, had touched it. There was a thin scraping of lichen down the sides, and dust deep in the corners. Laura noticed all this because she was avoiding looking directly at the knot of people gathered in front of her. She was paralysed with shyness because, of all the beautiful people at the party, this lot were easily the most dazzling. Probably only a few years older than her, they could, she thought, have come from a different planet. Four boys and four girls, all wearing black except one girl who wore a cream lace dress quite like hers but exquisite. Glancing at her own dress, Laura thought how shabby it was. She wished she'd worn something more anonymous. Stella was looking coolly at the group, clearly trying to work them out, but Laura wanted to bolt back to the safety of the bar where the guests might have been just as fabulous but were at least old, and likely to ignore her. Being ignored seemed preferable to being sized up by this lot. They stood close together, at ease with one another, impenetrable. Will was doing introductions: 'This is Amanda' – special emphasis on the way he said 'this' – 'and this is Stella, and Laura.' Less emphasis on them.

A cool nod from the blonde girl in cream. A steady stare from one of the girls in black, a pixie-ish creature with cropped hair and huge eyes. Another of the girls held out a hand. 'Oh, hello.'

The fourth girl, who was small and curvy, with slightly crossed front teeth and thick, wavy brown hair, did the same kind of staring thing as her companion, but ended on a little smirk. The boys all gazed at Amanda.

'I'm James. How kind of you to come to my party.' He was tall and gangly, in his well-cut but slightly battered dinner jacket, with a mop of dirty-blond hair falling onto his forehead. He looked eager and enthusiastic, brown eyes shining as he included each of them in turn in his smile. He shook hands with Amanda, then Stella and Laura. The other three boys followed suit.

'Do you live around here?' one asked, of no one in particular, so Amanda answered.

'Not far. Just outside Glencallam village.'

'Oh. *Glencallam.*' The girl with the pixie crop put so much withering emphasis on the name that Laura winced. 'I didn't know anyone actually lived there. I thought it was all just, you know, curiosity shops and little tea rooms. For tourists.'

'Mostly,' Amanda said, carefully bland, 'but there are a couple of houses too.'

'Of course there are, Dell,' James said quickly. 'You know there are. The Finches used to live around there.'

'Hey, my parents bought our house from some people called Finch. Must be the same ones.' Amanda beamed at everybody, but immediately it was obvious that this wasn't quite the calling card she'd thought. No one smiled back. Indeed Laura saw that James looked positively pained and Dell openly hostile.

'I think we all remember *that* transaction,' she said.

'Come and get something to eat,' James said firmly, drawing the three of them closer to him and steering them towards the marquee. 'There'll be dancing later,' he told them, as they walked off. 'And really good music.' He smiled down at them all, not just at Amanda, Laura noticed. James, clearly, was nice. His friends not so much, she decided.

It was exactly the kind of party Laura was worst at, where people snapped clever, funny lines back and forth at each other, like the rat-a-tat-tat of a machine gun. Stella was much better at that sort of thing, quick-witted and with a type of cheeky sparkle that left people charmed and challenged, but even she couldn't muster much of her usual dash. She was quieter than normal, and Laura wondered if she, too, felt overawed. The idea cheered her.

Amanda, however, seemed to find her feet almost immediately, allowing herself to be presented from group to group by Will and James, who seemed, between them, determined not to let her alone for a moment. Laura watched her shimmer and glow, taking on the reflection of all around her.

'She's so good at this,' Laura said to Stella enviously, as Amanda laughed and chatted. All the same, she definitely got a little second-hand buzz, and suspected Stella did too, from seeing everyone fall before the double-whammy of Amanda's charm and beauty. The party was Amanda's. Despite the odd whisper – '… the Finches' old place. Yes. That one …' which were more resentments of an old order about to be toppled – it was a night of triumph for Amanda. They watched her modify and shift her register oh-so-slightly, subtly muting her manners to blend with those around her as she shaped a clear vision of her own future.

Laura gave up almost immediately, and knew that, despite her efforts at nonchalance, Stella was grateful when she suggested in a whisper, 'Let's sit out.' They found a low wall, put their jackets under them to stop the wet of the moss seeping through their light dresses, and settled down to watch. They had some of the stew, which was delicious – rabbit – and later some pavlova, which bore no resemblance to the perfect discs Mrs O'Hagen's caterers served but was gloriously squishy and chewy. They even drank a glass of champagne that an old man in musty black gave them, in funny-shaped glasses that were apparently called coupes. That was for the toasts, which went on for ages, and seemed to be uproariously funny, judging by the way everyone around them was bellowing. James made a lovely speech, about how grateful he was to his parents, how tonight he finally saw the point of a house that was always cold and falling down, and how he wouldn't let the tradition of great parties lapse. That got a resounding chorus of 'Hear hear!'

A helicopter buzzed overhead. 'That'll be Malcolm,' people said, looking skywards. Malcolm was the manager of a rock band, huge in America and the UK, but who chose to live in

Ireland because 'the climate's so great'. ('The tax climate,' Stella's dad told them afterwards.) Soon after he arrived – they saw him glad-handing his way through the crowd, clapping people on the back and kissing women on both cheeks – the music started up properly. First came some wild, punky traditional music, which astounded Laura with its strange intensity, played by musicians who looked old but behaved young. After that, a different band, with a female singer, played hits like Chuck Berry's 'Johnny B. Goode' and Prince's 'Raspberry Beret'. Laura and Stella danced a bit – she noticed that nearly everyone did: even the ancient were guiding each other in and out with careful concentration.

Fireworks exploded with comic panache above their heads. 'My father is childish about fireworks. He loves them,' James said. He and Amanda sat and watched them beside Laura and Stella. And, indeed, Laura caught sight of Charles, Lord Brinsley, across the lawn, his face lit up in the green glow of a shower of stars, beaming and rubbing his hands. He was tall and rangy, like James, with a similar mop of hair, except his was snowy white. Amanda now had her arm tucked cosily through James's.

By two o'clock, Laura was dropping, longing to go home. The party was still in full swing around them and Stella was clearly full of energy, occasionally dancing sedately with one of the old men and laughing at the things they told her, but Laura wasn't a bit sorry to be leaving. Just then, Amanda came through the crowd towards the low wall where she had retreated. Her hair was tousled and her eyes shone more vividly blue than ever.

'I'm going to stay. You go back with Ivana. Tell her I'll make my own way later. Someone will drop me.'

No doubt someone would, Laura thought, then said, 'But how can we stay at yours if you're not there?'

'Don't be silly. You know where everything is. The beds are made. Just go to sleep and I'll see you in the morning.'

'But what about your mother?' Stella wanted to know.

'My mother will be delighted. Trust me,' Amanda said, with a mischievous grin.

Just then the man called Malcolm pushed through the throng. 'Amanda, there you are.' He caught her bare arm in his hand. He was old, at least sixty. He was wearing a big chunky gold ring with a square emerald in it, Laura noticed, and his fingers were like sausages. 'Don't worry about her,' he boomed at the two girls. 'I'll make sure she gets home all right. I know her father.' Amanda smiled at them, kissed them both on the cheek, and waved over her shoulder.

'Let's see what Ivana says,' Stella suggested, when she saw that Laura was inclined to fuss. 'It's more her problem than ours.' They made their way back, through the vast hall with its open fireplace and the sad man in black above it. Someone, impossible to say who, was sleeping on the velvet sofa, tucked into a pile of coats.

Ivana, as it turned out, didn't say anything much. She sat, drumming her fingers on the steering wheel for a few moments after they'd told her, then sighed. 'Is not my problem. I'm not nanny. We go.'

Laura fell asleep on the way and had to be shaken awake by Stella when they got to the house. They could see a light on in an upstairs window, one they thought belonged to Mrs O'Hagen – Amanda's parents had separate rooms. They had been shown into Mrs O'Hagen's room once by Amanda, who wanted them to see the 'awful' paintings there. 'They're done to order,' she had scoffed. 'You tell the guy what colours your room is, and he creates the canvases. It's not so much art as artifice.'

They crept into the house like mice, letting Ivana go first, then tiptoed up to Amanda's room where, as promised, a second double bed was made up, with snowy sheets and a thick gold satin quilt. They snuck into it, Laura feeling like an interloper, praying that Mrs O'Hagen wouldn't come hot-footing in to find out if Amanda had 'met someone'.

Chapter Four

New York

THE WHITE BUTTON STILL FLASHED, AND STELLA
signed to her PA to delay the call for ten minutes. She needed
to remind herself why she was there, what she was expected
to say. She knew her value to the Japanese clients, what they
wanted and what she was meant to deliver. But she couldn't
snap her mind back into focus to perform for them.

It was still early enough that the day hadn't entirely gathered
itself. Around her, the office was only half-full. In as much as
Davies Darn and Slate operated socially, it was in the hours
before eight thirty a.m., and very late at night, in bars close
by, where everything that happened would be tacitly disowned
the next day. There were no in-jokes, no shared banter or office

humour. All withered in the face of relentless competition and pressure of work. Sometimes Stella wondered, Why am I here? She had to remind herself, again, that she had chosen to be there. Had wanted to be.

Her New York was the place she had dreamed it to be, but with subtle, dislocating differences. Long, hectic working weeks, days busier and lonelier than she ever admitted, evenings in her apartment, eating take-out, with the chance that Sean would call. Weekends, when she knew he wouldn't, were for walks through Manhattan and Brooklyn, imagining the places he could have shown her, stopping at bookshops, flea markets and galleries, Central Park through the changing seasons, but too often alone, or with people she couldn't reach. She had friends, mostly Irish, who were strictly for weekends, when work allowed them to meet in one of the downtown Irish bars where they could compete on the outrageous expectations of their employers, how much or little they missed home, how much they earned and who had been promoted. They were a disparate gang, who would have had little in common in Dublin but were everything to each other so far away. Not everything, she corrected herself, only some things. The surface, unimportant things. A matter of physical hours spent together rather than instinctive intimacies.

There were even a couple of girls from St Assumpta's, though none from her year, who would ask after Amanda, with a persistence that defied Stella's ability to keep saying, 'Fine.'

It was funny, she now thought, that St Assumpta's had improved for her and Laura on every level once Amanda had entered their lives. Even the teachers had seemed to take them more seriously. Could that really have been true? Probably not, she decided. It would have been appalling. She had thrived under the attention – real or imagined – but Laura had been uncomfortable with it.

'I wish people would stop trying to be friends with me,' she had muttered to Stella one day. 'Nadine asked me if I wanted to go and watch a DVD at her house. Can you imagine?'

Stella laughed. 'We used to long to have more friends in this place. Don't complain!'

'You might have,' Laura said. 'I didn't. I don't want any more friends, and certainly not from here. I don't know what to say to any of them. It's embarrassing.'

'You don't have that with Amanda, do you?' They were still marvelling at the friendship, that it withstood everything St Assumpta's could throw at it: the continuing incredulity of some of the girls, the sullen jealousy of others.

'No. She's not what I thought she would be.'

'I know what you mean. She's nicer, and funnier, and more like us, but she's also harder to read.'

'I thought she'd be bitchy,' Laura confessed, 'but she isn't. Not at all. And I don't know what she is instead of bitchy, if you see what I mean. Like, she's not super-nice either. She only did that thing for Celestine because you made her. And she's not obsessed with doing well at school, or at tennis, or hockey, even though she's good at it all.'

'It's the thing my parents are always talking about,' Stella said. 'Drive. What drives her?'

'Social ambition?' Laura was only dimly aware of what it meant, but they had heard Nessa say it about Mrs O'Hagen, as if it was something amusing but not admirable.

'Not that either.'

'Let's ask her!'

So they did, but Amanda had looked vague, and said, 'Nothing yet. But something. I'll know it when I see it.'

And after all, Stella thought now, 'escape' was a hard concept for a teenager, and in Amanda's case meant more the absence of things she knew she didn't like – her mother's oppressive attention, the weight of expectation that followed her – than anything concrete.

She was passive, biddable. The habit of obedience was trained into her, but she also, Stella realised, had a habit of silent mutiny. She didn't refuse, but when pressed by any of them to do something she didn't want to, she retreated to somewhere remote, unreachable.

As she grew older, she got better at sensing when something she didn't like was about to be asked of her and did a sudden disappearing act, usually dragging Stella and Laura with her. 'Time to go,' she would say, as some besotted guy pressed his attentions too hard at a party or nightclub. 'Faster than that,' she might urge, as they fumbled for bags and coats. Once a pushy American, many years their senior and with the butch confidence of his age, had followed her around, describing the kind of date she would have if she agreed to go out with him: 'I would not have you waiting in the restaurant to order. What I would do is, I would ring ahead and order for both of us. That way the food is sitting on the table by the time we get there. No waiting.'

'But how would you know what I might like?' Amanda had asked, trying to keep a straight face. 'Often I don't know myself. And if I do, I usually change my mind.'

'Nothing is a problem for a beautiful woman,' he had said gallantly.

'I might change my mind twice,' she said, then dissolved into peals of laughter as he, straight-faced, insisted that even that would be okay. But the laughter waned when he continued to pursue her.

'All possible haste,' she hissed at Stella, her own jacket already over one arm. 'He's about to take out a marriage licence. Get Laura, quick. I'll meet you downstairs.'

Stella had found Laura deep in conversation with a guy she quite liked. 'Why can't she go on her own? Why do we always have to come too?' she had asked crossly. But once settled in a cosy bar, with Amanda ordering drinks and re-enacting the scene, she had laughed and said, 'It's such a waste you being funny when no one ever notices because of the way you look.'

To which Amanda had responded, 'You two do, and that's enough.'

It had been a kind of fun, free of consideration and care, that Stella hadn't known much of recently. Her New York nights out were scored and carefully defined. When she went to parties now, she had objectives – people she wanted to meet, connections she needed to make – and she rarely lost sight of them long enough to pursue anything more that might have been on offer.

Because of Sean, because of being with him and yet not with him, she was cut off from the romantic possibilities around her. Because of James, she was indifferent to the sadness of that fact. Somewhere she understood that she was beginning to shut down possibilities she had once thought of, slamming doors one by one. A husband, children, the kind of noisy family life she had never known and always longed for. She was putting those things beyond reach in order to keep hold of what little she had.

She was envied by her colleagues, who saw her smooth progress towards a larger office. They would never know how much any of it cost her. How much she had given up to get it: the things she'd once thought she would do, the person she'd once thought she would become.

If she didn't take that call, she realised, she would find that even this had moved beyond her. Amanda would have to wait. She pushed the white button.

Chapter Five

Dublin

'ANYONE GOT ANY IDEAS ON THE AMANDA O'Hagen thing? This is big, a real story. We need to get in there.'

Petrie looked around the boardroom table. The regular Tuesday morning editorial meetings were something the entire office dreaded: unless you had a truly original idea, or access so extraordinary as to be practically illegal, you were going to end up looking a fool. And even when you were armed with a brilliant idea, nothing was plain sailing. How many times had Laura seen a colleague deliver their pitch, only for Petrie to fall silent, staring at them, grey eyes blank, only to say, 'No. That's not going to work. It's too obvious. We need something *wittier*, more *us*, if it's to be a real *Sunday Herald* piece.' It had happened to Laura several times. If you continued to defend your idea, Petrie would just turn away, leaving you mouthing like a fish in mid-sentence, and speak over you, in her crystal tones, about something entirely different. Sometimes, later in the meeting, she might hold up a hand for silence, and say, 'Wait a minute. I've got an idea ...' only to produce *your* idea, sometimes with a minor tweak, more often verbatim. When she did, the entire table of hard-bitten journalists would go off into rapturous applause.

'Excellent!'

'Great idea!'

'Perfect!'

Recently, it had seemed that all Laura's ideas — good, bad and indifferent — were getting the silent treatment. There was some kudos within the office to having your idea 'Petrified', as they called it, meaning appropriated. A well-received pitch earned you a whole point in the office stakes; having your idea Petrified got you a half-point. They all kept score meticulously, so the whole office knew who was hot and who was not at any given time. For a long time, Laura had hovered at just over halfway, sometimes entering the dizzy heights of the top third, then dropping back slightly but always keeping the halfway line below her. Now she was in the bottom third, with Lindsey, a large, adenoidal girl, who did picture research and never managed to get anything to anyone on time, and Matt, one-time star reporter, now a chaotic drunk who clung on by grace of an ancient friendship with the paper's owner.

Because of her slide into ignominy, the editorial meetings were hell for Laura. She didn't know how much more of the humiliation she could take. So when Petrie started talking about Amanda, she found herself twitching.

'It would take someone really close to her to get anywhere,' Petrie was saying now. 'I think Laura knows her a bit.' Laura nodded. 'But, then, I suppose many of us know her a bit. We've met her over the years, we've interviewed her. But that's not going to be enough to get through. No,' she finished, 'this calls for a real insider.'

'I know her that well.' Laura was almost horrified to hear her own voice. All eyes swivelled towards her. Petrie's widened, and remained fixed, unblinking, daring her to go on. 'We've been friends for years, since we were fifteen. We're close. Well, we always were … although I don't know how close anyone is to her just now.' Her words were coming out in halting, jerky dollops. She felt like a cat with a dead mouse, dropping it at Petrie's patent leather feet.

Petrie stared a bit longer. 'Really, Laura? You never said.' She sounded disbelieving.

'I couldn't. I always promised not to.' This was true, but it was Stella she had promised, not Amanda. Amanda would never have asked such a thing.

'But how is that going to help us? What exactly can you do?'

'I'm going over to London. To see her. Well, to try and see her.' Until the words came out, Laura had had no such plan. She and Stella hadn't decided anything. But even though a large part of Laura was filled with dismay at what she had just done, a deeper part of her knew that of course they were going. They might not have decided anything yet, but they were going. Just as they always had.

ɔ൪

The aftermath of James Marsfield's party had shown them a new Amanda, filled with ambition to do well in her school exams, happier than ever before. She had glowed so brightly in those days that Laura, when she looked back, could hardly see herself or Stella in memory's prism. As if the light that shone from Amanda simply obliterated them.

She had come home in the early hours of the morning, as the sun was casting long shadows across the smoothly manicured lawns around the O'Hagens' house. Laura woke up as Amanda crept into the bedroom, wearing a black dinner jacket over her dress, and a pair of muddy green wellies.

'How did you get back?'

'James dropped me. Malcolm wanted to – you know, the band manager – but he had to go to a meeting. Straight from the party. Oh, Laura, it was brilliant. We danced all night, then as dawn arrived we went swimming in the lake, skinny-dipping. Then we went back up to the house for a huge breakfast in the hall. Someone had put out long tables and chairs, and there were great big dishes of sausages, fried eggs, kippers, toast, and pots of tea. James made me sit beside the fire, which was still going, because I was so cold after the swim. The fireplace is so big, you could fit a table and chairs into it.' She burbled with laughter. Her blue eyes were starry. She took off the wellies and the dinner jacket, and fell into bed. It was the first time Laura had ever seen her lie down without performing her meticulous cleanse-tone-moisturise routine.

'After breakfast we went for a walk around the estate. That's when James got me the wellies. I think they're his mother's. Some of the dogs came with us. There's a whole pack of them. And when we got back, his mother – Iseult – was awake, looking amazing, even though she'd gone to bed at four, and she made me sit with her and have a cup of tea, apart from all the other guests, and talked to me about school and what

I might do next. Then she said James must drive me home immediately because my parents mustn't be worried, and that he could take her car.'

She was babbling, words escaping in a swift, joyous stream. Laura wanted to ask about the other people they'd met, especially Dell, the pixie girl, but before she got a chance, the door opened and in came Mrs O'Hagen, in a remarkable quilted silver satin robe, her hair smooth and perfect, held by a few bulldog clips, and her morning make-up fully in place – light, natural-looking, but not actually natural.

'I thought I heard sneaking feet.' She sounded neutral, much less annoyed than Laura would have expected, given that it was after eight o'clock and her teenage daughter had just come home. 'So what happened? Stella and Laura came in last night. I could tell by the footsteps. You obviously didn't.'

By now Stella was awake too. Amanda's ebullience had evaporated slightly, and she huddled down in the bed as if she were cold, but she still managed to give her mother a good account of the evening. As she talked, Mrs O'Hagen nodded. When Amanda got to the bit about meeting Malcolm, she interjected, 'Excellent! Your father knows him. I've tried to get him to come to the house many times, so he could meet you, but he's never accepted. Did he take your number?'

'God, no. It doesn't happen like that with these people.' Already Amanda sounded like an expert. 'He knows perfectly well how to get hold of me if he wants to.'

Ordinarily, Mrs O'Hagen might have pulled her up on the rudeness, but this time she let it pass. Amanda continued her tale, although she was sounding tired and flat now. Mrs O'Hagen grimaced slightly at the skinny-dipping, almost more so when Amanda insisted, 'They aren't like that, prudish and embarrassed. It was all incredibly natural. They took off their clothes and swam. No one giggled or was silly about it.'

Laura was amazed that Amanda told her mother everything, unvarnished. Normally, after a night out, Amanda squirmed her way through the post-mortem, revealing as little as possible, omitting anything her mother might be too interested in. Any chance encounters with people Mrs O'Hagen might be expected to know of or want to know were always left out, as if Amanda couldn't bear the worrying at it that would follow. Now, though, perhaps secure in the impression she had made, or just too happy to run a double life, she let it all out.

Tea with Iseult Marsfield got Mrs O'Hagen's full attention. 'What does she look like? I've seen photos, of course. I think Snowdon photographed her years ago. Sort of *gamine*, but with an *old* look about her too, like she'd seen things.'

'No make-up, quite a lot of wrinkles, but gorgeous eyes. And she asks amazing questions. And makes these *pronouncements*.'

'Amazing how? What kind of pronouncements?'

Amanda thought for a moment. 'Like, she said, "The world will always fall for you, but the better educated you are, the more interesting the world that falls will be."'

Mrs O'Hagen looked annoyed. She had often expressed the opinion that it didn't matter if Amanda went to university or not because she was so clearly destined for bigger things. But she swallowed the irritation. 'What else?'

'She said a twenty-first should be the night when your life made sense forwards, not backwards.'

'What does that mean?' Mrs O'Hagen looked perplexed.

'I can't explain it, but I know. And that's the kind of twenty-first I'm going to have.'

'Yes, we must start to talk about it. But not just yet. What else did she say?'

'Oh, just this and that. I don't really remember. I'd been up all night.' To Laura, it looked as if Amanda remembered very well, but had decided not to say any more.

'I'll send Ivana up with a cup of tea. Then you should sleep for a few hours. We have the Molloys for lunch' – Mrs O'Hagen always had somebody for lunch – 'at twelve thirty, but I suppose it would be all right if you were a little late.'

'Never mind the tea. I'm just going to crash.'

'Not "crash", "go to sleep".' Mrs O'Hagen was careful about these things. She left the room.

Amanda made a face, then settled herself into the pillows, having thrown any remaining cushions onto the floor. 'Will you guys wait till I get up? Please don't go home yet.' As usual, the transformation from sophisticated teen to vulnerable child caught them off guard.

'I'm going back to sleep too,' Stella said. 'This is way too early for me.'

Only Laura got up, unable to ignore the appeal of another glorious early autumn day. She wandered down to the kitchen where Ivana made her bacon and toast. Mr O'Hagen was nowhere to be seen – probably playing golf – and Mrs O'Hagen, who never ate before she exercised, had gone to the gym. Laura took her toast and went out into a sharp, sunny morning. The strong light made her tired eyes water, but a little breeze nipped at her neck and fingers and stopped her going back to bed. She went to the stables where Amanda's two show-jumpers and the handsome, placid hack Mrs O'Hagen had bought, in case riding turned out to be her kind of thing, stared out of their boxes at her. She rubbed their noses, feeling sorry for them.

Riding hadn't turned out to be Mrs O'Hagen's thing, and the horses were ignored, denied the chance to do what they were good at. No one should be denied that, Laura thought, feeling a weathered kind of melancholy steal over her.

She walked round to the old walled garden where, protected from the wind, she found a sunny spot and sat down, back to the knobbly red-brick wall. In front of her a thick clump of lavender was still flowering in the late-season sun. The delicate trailing creeper that swept down the wall in drifts had begun to die back, exposing the roughened mossy bricks, the cement between them honeycombed by age and rain. The odd woodlouse wandered out of its crack, or walked the grooves of cement as if they were city streets. Wood pigeons cooed and she could even hear the rat-a-tat-tat of a woodpecker on a tree somewhere behind her.

Surrounded by the peace of the beautiful grounds, she found herself wondering, not for the first time, just what was so wrong with the family who lived there. No one who belonged to such a lovely place should be so unhappy. And yet the fault-line of discontent that ran through the three was deep and obvious. Mr and Mrs O'Hagen seemed united in their appreciation of money and the things it brought them, but otherwise kept a wary distance from each other. They must have been in love once, Laura supposed, because they had married, but she couldn't see any residue of affection in the few exchanges she witnessed. Between Amanda and her mother there was so much hurt and disappointment – on both sides, she suspected – that every day seemed to add a bitter nugget to the store.

The active aggressor was always Mrs O'Hagen, but the self-contained Amanda couldn't have been an easy daughter. Mrs O'Hagen had once told Laura a story about Amanda as a small child, three or so, with a very high temperature. She had screamed repeatedly with the pain in her head, and each time Mrs O'Hagen had tried to comfort or help her, Amanda had roared, 'No! Go away!' until eventually she'd stopped trying and left the room. Whereupon Amanda had stopped crying and, watched by Mrs O'Hagen through a crack in the door, picked up an old ragged cloth doll, kissed it very gently and put it under the covers of her bed. She had climbed in beside it, cheeks still wet with tears, and gone quietly to sleep.

Mrs O'Hagen told the story as an illustration of how independent Amanda had been, even as a child. To Laura, that wasn't the way it sounded at all: Mrs O'Hagen's version had missed out the heartbreak. But it showed just how far back that fault-line ran.

The real cipher within the family, though, was Mr O'Hagen, of whom Laura had no sense at all, except that his hands were soft and his fingers delicate, with very clean nails, because she had rarely dared look past his hands to his face the few times he had spoken to her. He inhabited the house lightly, usually spotted only on his way out or in. Once in, he had mysterious recesses to which he retired: his study, his bedroom, a dressing room – inner sanctums from which Mr O'Hagen rarely emerged into communal family life. Amanda and Mrs O'Hagen were clearly used to living around him. They didn't leave any obvious or awkward gaps where his absence might be noticeable. They filled their lives smoothly and seamlessly, and made room if he showed any indication of taking part. Only once had Laura ever known either of them to suggest that he join them. That was for a day at the races, and Amanda had said, 'Isn't Dad coming?' just as they were about to leave the house.

'If he is, he can meet us there,' Mrs O'Hagen had retorted, sweeping out the door.

At the various lunches and parties Mrs O'Hagen gave, her husband surrounded himself with a knot of similar types. Even then, he seemed to be more absent than present. There was always a sort of cold gust where he was, as if he left a gap in the wall of humanity through which the winds outside the world whistled.

The sun had travelled away from Laura, to a further corner of the garden, and without it she was chilly. Judging it to be after eleven, she went back to the house, hoping that Ivana might make her more toast, or that she would find the courage to make her own if the kitchen was deserted. Ostensibly, she and Stella were supposed to treat the house like their own homes, helping themselves to food when they felt like it. In practice, they rarely dared to do so, although Stella was better at it than Laura.

'We saw you from the window. You looked as if you were growing into that old wall,' Stella said, as Laura entered the kitchen. She and Amanda were eating waffles with syrup. Laura grabbed a waffle, still hot, and smeared it with butter.

'Now tell me about the party from your point of view,' Amanda demanded. 'You must have noticed different things from me. Did you have fun?'

'Yes,' said Laura, deciding that was the truth, 'but it was a bit embarrassing, not knowing anyone. We sat there for ages and no one spoke to us, except some of the old men being polite. Stella danced with a few of them, but I didn't know the steps so I didn't.'

'Well, what were the old men like?' Amanda asked teasingly.

Laura realised that Amanda actually wanted to know. She

was so in love with all of it, even the old men were important. 'They weren't like usual old men. They were more fun. One of them asked Stella if she was a Montgomery, because she looked so like one. And when Stella said no, he laughed and said, "Not officially maybe. Lot of unofficial Montgomerys," but not in a nasty way.'

'That's right.' Stella took up the story. 'And then he asked me to dance and he was incredibly energetic, even though he seemed so old that his skin was paper.'

'It's the genes,' Amanda said. 'Aristos always have good genes.'

'More like years of living off the fat of the land while the poor got rickets and curved spines,' Stella retorted smartly. 'Don't go running away with the romance of it, Amanda. They aren't our kind of people. In fact, I bet we never see any of them again.'

She sounded perfectly pleased with the possibility, Laura thought, wondering how Amanda would take being dropped, if it happened.

'Actually, James is coming over later. I said I'd show him the gardens.' Amanda tried, and failed, to keep the note of triumph from her voice. There was a slight pause.

'Why do people always want to see gardens?' Stella murmured.

'You didn't tell your mother that,' Laura said, not because it was any of her business but because the deception interested her.

'I thought I'd keep it in reserve in case she gets cross that I won't go to her lunch party. And I really don't want her planning a big reception for him. If I give her any warning, she'll have people dressed as servants in mob caps in a double line-up outside the front door for his arrival. It'll be like *Mansfield Park.*' She laughed, still clearly high on lack of sleep and the triumph of the night before.

Stella seemed irritated, grimacing and staring at the scrubbed-pine table, and Laura wondered if the appeal for Amanda was actually James himself, or something else.

ଔ

By the time James left, late that afternoon, Laura was pretty sure that, for all his charm, it wasn't him. James Marsfield was a nice guy, funny, polite, good-natured, with laughing eyes and a gangling, careless air that was very attractive. He made a big effort with them, asking Stella and Laura if they had enjoyed the party, and seeming to care about the answer. He apologised for not having seen more of them, explaining, 'The host always has the worst time,' although he added, 'Well, almost always ...' with a laughing look at Amanda, and said that they must come back, soon, when there weren't so many other people.

'I'd love to show you the library,' he said beguilingly to Stella. 'I think you'll be interested. Some amazing first editions there.' He admired the gardens and said they were much improved since the Finches had had the place. 'Really, it had run wild. They couldn't keep it up.' And he was politely quiet about the interior of the house, although Laura suspected he must have been itching to make unfavourable comparisons with the old days.

When Amanda introduced him to Mrs O'Hagen, as she eventually had to, he continued to behave impeccably. They were in the small sitting room off the hall, where Mrs O'Hagen liked to have coffee after large lunches, or lunch when there were fewer people. The walls were papered in powder blue with a high satin sheen, and everything else was white – white carpet, two squashy white sofas, spindly white chairs upholstered in white velvet around a circular white table, and a few carefully chosen ornaments – a crystal panther prowling down a black marble plinth, an immense vase painted with pink peonies and filled with white flowers. It was the room Laura most feared in the whole house, because she was certain that, one day, she would tread mud or dog poo across the white carpet, or spill something blood-red and indelible on the sofa.

James, too, seemed to find the room unnerving. Laura caught him looking covertly around it with the faintest of smiles. Perhaps it was the panther, glittering and sparkling in the corner, jewelled eyes fixed on a spot below the table. But he rallied fast, answered all Mrs O'Hagen's questions – what was he studying (world religions and theology), where had he been to school (in England, boarding), where had he spent the summer (Italy), when was the last time he had been to the house (so long ago he couldn't quite recall, he diplomatically responded) – and refused all her offers of tea, coffee, cake or 'a drink, because I know what you undergraduates are like'. Still he said no, that he must be going, there was an awful lot to be done to restore the house after the party, and his parents were expecting him to dinner.

He left, in his little red sports car – 'so old I doubt it'll carry me home' – with a flurry of gravel and a promise to be in touch. Laura had no doubt that he would be. That he was taken with Amanda couldn't have been clearer. If she had been in any doubt, one look at Mrs O'Hagen's satisfied face would have told her as much. But despite all his efforts, and the undoubted appeal of his open, honest personality, she didn't think there was enough excitement in James to fascinate Amanda. She might love what he offered her – the world he inhabited, to be placed at her disposal – but Laura was willing to bet that that was all.

On the other hand, she wondered about Stella. There had been something – a hint of a blush, a failure to meet his eyes, in the normally oh-so-direct Stella – that had made her pause, with a faint premonition. Then she dismissed it. Surely they were above competing over boys, like Sally and Nadine would. Surely their friendship was more than that.

But she felt even more apprehensive later, when Amanda said dreamily, just before she and Stella were to go home, 'You know, he's the eldest. He'll get the title,' to which Stella instantly snapped, 'Then no wonder his mother was quizzing you.'

'She wasn't quizzing. She was interested,' Amanda said stiffly.

Oh, no, Laura thought, wondering just how much to read into Stella's snappiness, and the unexpectedly enthusiastic way she had responded to James's talk of first editions.

Chapter Six

New York

STELLA GOT THROUGH THE CONFERENCE CALL
with Japan, then another, and then an internal meeting. She
pushed lunch back in favour of a run around Central Park, as
she often did. Lunch didn't mean a whole lot to her, but running
was essential. It was how she processed things. As she pounded
around the reservoir, an ugly, sludgy grey that day, her feet and
breath seemed to drum out a pattern: *Aaaah-maaan-da, Aaaah-
maaan-da, Aaaah-maaan-da.*

She showered in one of the firm's bathrooms and left her
running gear in the locker room, from where it would be
retrieved, laundered and returned overnight. Dressed once
again in the tailored grey suit and a clean white shirt from the

selection that hung, still in their dry-cleaning bags, in her office, she ran a straightener through her jaw-length black hair and returned to her desk, where the efficient assistant had already laid out the paperwork for the afternoon's case.

But even with everything in place, her green tea in the bone china cup and an energy superfood bar beside it – her usual stop-gap if she skipped lunch – Stella was unable to enter the almost-meditative state of mental clarity in which she usually worked. The sense of peace and purpose wouldn't come. Too many images from a past she had tried so hard to subdue whirled around her head. Filled with resentment at the unwelcome intrusion, she began an email to Laura, punching savagely at the keyboard, proposing that they do nothing:

> *Amanda is going to have to handle this on her own. There's nothing we can do any more. We've done it all, for too many years, and I don't want to go back to that. I want out.*

She stopped there, because the email risked getting too personal. If she had learned anything with the venerable law firm of Davies Darn and Slate, it was to keep your emotions out of it. Do business with your head, leave the emotional stuff for family, and never write it down. 'Getting involved' was a very serious breach of protocol and Stella had schooled herself – encouraged by her now-natural inclination to put emotions at arm's length – to stay aloof. So she saved the email. She would sleep on it.

ଷ

That evening Stella was still so agitated, she had to stop herself going for another run. She forced herself to eat the poached razor clams and steamed pork with garlic and soy vinaigrette she had picked up on the way home. She didn't feel like eating, could have spent the night in the basement gym of her apartment block instead, putting her body through a session so punishing she would be guaranteed to sleep after it, at least for a few hours.

The pictures that threatened to overwhelm her were so vivid they cut easily through the years and her own desire not to see them. Amanda dancing at dawn after the Trinity Ball, surrounded by a delirious group of undergraduates all chanting her name; Amanda looking up from her lunch at Bijou's restaurant to say, 'Stella, how lovely,' and moving her chair to make room; Amanda lying across the double bed in that guy's house, so comatose that Stella couldn't lift her and had had to ask James to help; the look on James's face when he'd entered the bedroom and taken in the dishevelled state of Amanda's clothes and the guilty smell hanging in the air.

Thick and fast the images came, until Stella found she was pacing and breathing far too rapidly. Her buzzer went, shocking in the silence and thick web of memories that had built up.

'Yes?'

'It's Sean.'

'Sean!' she gasped, with relief and delight. She hadn't been expecting him until the next day at the earliest. And there had been every chance Tokyo would drag on for another week. 'How did you swing it?'

He came in, pushing his thick strawberry-blond hair back from his forehead. 'There were more depositions to be taken. Would have been at least three days. I'll have to go back, but I thought I'd come and see you first.'

He put his arms around her, and she could smell his thick,

sweaty, masculine odour. Even after thirteen hours in business class, he smelt like he'd been breaking in wild horses all day. 'Tory isn't expecting me until tomorrow. We have the whole night.'

Stella hated that he mentioned his wife so casually to her. As if the arrangement was a consensual one, whereby all three of them knew and were tolerant of a situation that Stella found appalling, bearable only because Sean excited her like no other man she had ever been with. The way his big, hard body hinted at a life more vital than that of a senior partner in a wealthy law firm, the way he smelt of sex and wide-open spaces, and a faint tang of salt, like the breakers off Cape Cod. The way he took her just as he wanted to, any way, anywhere, because he knew she loved it.

Squirming a little inside, she began to remember their phone sex sessions of the last few weeks. He still had his arms tight around her, and she could feel his breath starting to quicken. Recalling some of the things she had begged him to do to her over the phone, Stella's breath quickened too. He could do this to her, every time. Whatever it was about him that was so raw and wild, it cut right through her natural prudishness.

Later they got into Stella's big double bed, with the grey linen sheets and grey satin duvet.

'Baby, we are really good together,' he said, settling an arm around her shoulders and pulling her down towards him.

Stella smiled, though she was longing to go and bathe. As soon as he was asleep, she slipped out from his arm. Her East Village apartment was small, but it had the best bathroom she'd seen, with a window onto the street and a large bath. Never mind that she'd already had a shower, she ran a bath, soaking in Jo Malone Red Roses bubbles. After all, she was a New Yorker now. It was something she paid for daily, in the growing distance from her parents, who were surprised by her dedication to a career they thought beneath her intellectually, and a rejection of the values they had brought her up to. She paid, too, in the gap that had opened between her and Laura, and between both of them and Amanda, a gap that had more in it than simply distance. As for what Stella got in return, that was hard to reckon, but living in New York, away from Dublin and the mess she seemed to have made of her life there, was part of it.

Sinking back into the bath, she felt like a marathon runner who had smashed her personal best – bone weary but content. Sex with Sean always left her feeling like that, even if, deep down, she worried that being able to fuck someone the way they did sometimes must mean you hated them, at least a little bit.

The physical attraction between them had been immediate. She knew it, and he had said it. He was a senior partner at Davies Darn and Slate, more than ten years older, so their paths had hardly crossed in the first years of her appointment. Back then, all she really knew about him was his reputation – that he was so well connected, his weekends were spent with a *Who's Who* of New York's political and media elite. That anyone important who wasn't related to him entered the family fold anyway, via Tory, his impossibly groomed blonde wife, daughter of one of the city's oldest families, and an impressive operator in her own right. That their Cape Cod mansion, to which he commuted by helicopter every weekend, was regularly filled with the great, the good and those who wished to be known as those two things.

Stella's reputation for putting in long hours without fatigue interfering either with her grasp of detail or her looks meant that within a few years she was on many of the firm's biggest, most complicated cases – the ones that had juniors and associates eating take-out at their desks for weeks on end and going home by cab in the small hours. Because Stella had no family, she thrived on the workload and anti-social hours. Eventually she found herself on a case with Sean. And from the start his rough-edged good looks and self-confidence had gone straight to her heart. One night, late, he had offered to drop her home. In the back of the black Lincoln, his usual driver at the wheel, she had sat as far away from him as possible, achingly conscious of what the smell of him did to her. Conscious, too, that he might be aware of it. Outside, the night slipped by in flashes of light distorted by the raindrops. The streets were busy, but any sound was blocked from the interior of the sedan, upholstered in tan leather and smelling, thanks to Sean, of Gucci cologne.

Stella was tongue-tied, even though he made an effort to chat easily, asking her when she had last been home and had she ever visited the Mayo village where his family had come from.

'No,' she had said, 'but I know that part of the country. It's beautiful. Such a barren landscape, but still so full of promise. Have you been?'

'Not yet, but my wife has plans for a big family anniversary there. Only she's waiting for someone to build a hotel good enough to accommodate us all.' Stella was bothered at the casual, even teasing, way he dropped his wife into the conversation. Maybe she hadn't read the signs right. Then he went all sentimental.

'My grandmother lived in the middle of the bog, and walked five miles to school every day in bare feet. That's real grit. She met my grandfather when she came over here, even though he was from the next village back in Mayo. Those two people, together, founded a family. From that little patch of turf, they joined their blood to the great river of souls that is America. From their hard work, they created prosperity for future generations.' His eyes were moist with what actually looked like tears. He was a man practising an election speech – victory, Stella decided, not campaign.

From what Stella had heard, it was really the second generation, Sean's father, who had put the family on the map. And often in unsavoury ways, if the rumours were true. Not that it mattered. Sean Senior had achieved what he'd set out to do. The Callaghans were everywhere that mattered now. Lower profile than the Kennedys, but fewer scandals. Still, she couldn't take such a dollop of schmaltz without protest.

'I'm from Ireland, Sean,' she said. 'Everyone's grandmother walked barefoot across the bog to school.' Except perhaps her own, she thought guiltily. Long lines of solicitors, doctors and schoolteachers stretched away into genealogical history on either side, sternly admonishing her for the lie she had just told. But Sean threw back his head and burst out laughing.

'Okay, okay,' he said. 'I'll cut the crap for you. But you know what? You're a pistol!'

She presumed that was a good thing.

At her apartment, he had reached across her to open the door, telling the driver, 'I'll get it. Wait where you are.' His hand had brushed the underside of her wrist as she fumbled with her bag, and the shock that ran through her was like an earth tremor. Their eyes met, and that was it. The promise was made in that second. It was several more months before anything happened, but those months had had a luxurious quality, a deliberate waiting that could only enhance the inevitable fall. And the fall, when it came, was everything she had dreamed of in her most feverish longings. A trip to Atlanta with Sean and another colleague from the European office. The European colleague, a Dutchman, succumbed to jetlag after a long day of conference calls and negotiations. Sean had suggested dinner, and taken Stella somewhere delicious, discreet and horribly expensive, where they hadn't even bothered to pretend that nothing was happening. By dessert – the most exquisite crème brulée Stella would ever taste, they were openly entwining their fingers. He had run a finger down her cheek, saying, 'I don't much go for uncertainty. Not at my age.' Stella had said nothing. 'I'm offering to seduce you. But only if you want it.'

She had stroked the fine blond hairs on his wrist and said, 'I want it. You. I want you.' She hadn't laid down any conditions, which had probably been foolish. Perhaps that was why he felt he could talk so openly about his wife. Not that she wanted him to pretend he didn't have a wife, just occasionally to show that he was conscious of the vile position Stella was in. But she hadn't asked for anything because she didn't want anything, except him. Didn't want what he could buy her, do for her career, or socially – none of it. And that was the only way she could justify taking another woman's husband. Because all she wanted was him, and because she wanted him so badly, it was a constant ache. It started up moments after they had come, and lasted until he was inside her again.

That night in Atlanta, he had taken her back to his hotel room – an executive suite; she had a standard double – and fucked her in exactly the way she had fantasised about for so long. Straight inside the room he had pushed her against the wall, and kissed her hard until she had started to tremble. Then he had picked her up, carried her to the large, luxurious bed, and laid her down, roughly removing every item of clothing, starting with her shirt, ending, in short order, with her wildly expensive cream and black lace knickers, leaving only the matching push-up bra that Stella had bought with exactly this moment in mind. The confidence and purpose he showed in the boardroom – the confidence of three generations of immigrant dreams joyfully met by the promises of America – didn't desert him now. If anything, he was even more wilful and aggressive, though carefully controlled. He would have come quickly, Stella was certain, except that she stopped him. This was a challenge, a gauntlet he was throwing down. Here, in this deliberately anodyne, extraordinarily luxurious hotel bedroom, he was testing her, and Stella was never one to duck a confrontation.

'Wait!' she ordered, then rose up and forced him onto his back. 'Me first, I think.'

'Well, they've certainly taught the Irish a thing or two about intercourse in the last few years,' he said, when they had got their breath back, laughing at her, his navy blue eyes twinkling. Then he had twitched aside the heavy cream linen sheets. 'Try taking it all off,' he said, stroking her tiny square of pubic hair. 'You'll love the way it feels. My wife had it done. She says she can come just by crossing her legs.'

The vulgarity and the indifference made Stella catch her breath, but excited her too. After a few hours – it was still inky black outside – Sean woke her, told her to get dressed and sent her back to her own room.

'It wouldn't look good for either of us if you're seen coming out of here, right?' he said, kissing her lightly, almost politely, on the cheek. Still drunk on the best sex she'd ever had, and confident that she had passed the test he had set for her, Stella wouldn't have minded if he'd thanked her, even paid her.

She sank lower into the bubbles. Until Sean, sex had been dispensable, from the days of fumbles with boys who never met her eyes, neither during the fumbling nor when they next met. The accepted way to go about it had been to pretend it hadn't happened. That was how it had been for Stella as a teenager – a few kissing sessions outside Dargle's or at friends' houses when their parents were away, which always seemed to turn nasty when she wouldn't let the groping go any further than her top half. The boy in question would say she was frigid and stalk off. These were boys who talked and acted like gangsters, but were destined for careers in law, accountancy, banking and politics. It was a pose they would replace in a heartbeat with conventional middle-class prudery when the right time came.

Stella knew, even then, that the insults were a way of saving face, but that didn't mean they weren't hurtful. Once she had retaliated. He had been a particularly cocky St Augustin's boy, Angus Somebody. His dad was a financier, very successful, so everyone took Angus at his own estimation of himself. She always suspected he had turned his attention to her because she had a reputation for being hard to get. And when the evening ran its inevitable course – he had tried to put his hand into her pants and she had stopped him – he had flung the frigid line at her. 'Maybe if you were better at it, I'd be tempted to go further,' she had flung back. 'But you're not. You're as crap as all the rest of them.'

He had spread vicious lies about her so fast that, by Monday morning, half the school believed that she'd put out for him and wasn't much of a lay.

When she got a little older, during the years when she, Amanda and Laura had gone to nightclubs and parties, the pre- and post-sex manners improved. At least the guys had bought her drinks and devoted themselves to amusing her for the evening. And afterwards they often rang and asked her out again, or at least could manage a civilised conversation if they met by accident. But the sex itself still hadn't been the stuff of dreams. Functional, sometimes pleasant, but always inhibited. It wasn't just a question of lights on or lights off – although it was nearly always lights off – it was in how they touched each other. With reservation. Silent and diffident.

James had been different. There hadn't been any of the raunchy confrontation or bare-knuckle fucking she had with Sean, but there had been such gentleness, such tenderness, and such a connection of minds that even now Stella could hardly bear to think about it.

It had happened just once. After the first Amanda disaster. And, of course, she thought bitterly, it would have to be Amanda who brought us together, took her foot off the pedal just long enough to give Stella and James a moment, then slammed it back on.

That night had been, at first, a carbon copy of so many others. A gang of them had met for cocktails at eight. Already Amanda seemed, if not exactly high, then certainly giddy. Her eyes were huge, more black than blue, and her gaze was unfocused. She was wearing a tight black dress made of such soft leather it looked like velour. 'Rick Owens,' she said, when somebody asked.

'Jesus,' one of the girls near Stella whispered. 'My mother has a bag of his. It's tiny, and it cost a *fortune*.'

With it, Amanda had put on knee-high biker boots and a thick gold chain wound many times around her wrist. Her hair had a deep sheen, like gold that has been much worn, and swung loose around her face and down her back. James, who had picked her up, was nowhere to be seen. He must be trying to park the car, after dropping Amanda to the door, Stella thought. Amanda was always dropped to the door.

They were a year out of school by then, and Amanda was a year into the bright future everyone had promised her. She had so many offers of modelling work that she was justified in turning down most of them, without even the excuse that she was trying to create a buzz around herself. She took only the jobs she wanted, the ones that paid well in money and better in prestige. She worked with photographers who were mostly in love with her, and stylists who adored her 'look', so that with every new shoot she appeared more and more beautiful. She travelled to London, New York, Milan and, increasingly, Beijing, and had offers from agencies to move permanently to each of these places. She had even starred in one short film – she played a drowned girl who refused to leave the land of the living, just stood and dripped around her childhood home – which had done the rounds of festivals and from which, even though she had no lines in it, her agent had set her up with a whole load more castings. She had appeared in a couple of big campaigns and was earning plenty of money, although, as far as Stella could see, she still spent her father's, usually in fistfuls. Even her relationship with her mother seemed to improve, because at last they were of one mind, and in the execution of their great plan, there was purpose enough to hide the gulf between them. She had keys, cards, codes and passwords for every club in the city, from the swankiest to the speakeasies and fleapits. She was loved everywhere, for her looks, her profile, and her ability to party hard.

The three girls were then in Trinity – Laura was doing English, Stella law and Amanda, to their surprise, history of art. She didn't just want to model, or think only about fashion, she explained to them. 'I want to know the people who matter, and to them, fashion will always be rather dumb. The things they care about are art and architecture, old houses and pictures, and even the ones who haven't been to university know an awful lot. I can't talk to them about shooting a campaign for Mango, because they won't care less, so I'll learn about the things they do care about.'

Although she was the most desired girl in college, Amanda was loyal to the world that had first excited her. Which was why their little group still included not just James but each of the gang of eight who had been at his twenty-first. The girls had mellowed towards Amanda, but she was still on sufferance, Stella thought. Each time she believed they were all forging a genuine friendship, she would intercept a look, or a bitchy aside, usually about Amanda, although she and Laura got the same treatment. Just the previous weekend she had heard Sinead, a willowy blonde who looked beautiful until Amanda stood next to her, say to Dell in an undertone, while Amanda was moaning about the amount of work she had to do, 'Don't know why she doesn't get "Daddy" to endow a new wing or something. That way they could just hand her a degree.'

'Mm. Dishonorary doctorate.' Dell had sniggered. 'Dirty money and squalid past. But they could put a statue of his little princess in the new wing, so all could come and adore.'

Dell was still the most dangerous of the group. At the twenty-first she had been the one to challenge Amanda, but even though James was no longer the bone of contention – he and Amanda had never really gone out together, while he and Dell had long since ended their on-off thing – she was still a source of trouble. If Amanda dug a little too deeply into drugs, she was still only dabbling, or so Stella had believed, while Dell had chosen a more complete immersion. Their interest in narcotics brought the two girls close, but as conspirators rather than friends. Whether Dell lacked judgement, or just restraint, most of the real harm that threatened Amanda came to her through the people Dell introduced her to.

Amanda never seemed to know or care how compromised she was by some of those associations. Whether they were going down together, or Dell was facilitating a fall, Stella didn't know, but sometimes she thought she could see the crash unfolding before them. She had mentioned it to Laura just once – feeling disloyal and gossipy – because Laura was intuitive and sensitive, but her friend said, 'Don't be silly. They're only having fun. Just because we don't go for it as much as Amanda does doesn't mean it's a problem.' Then, weeks later, Laura had asked her, out of the blue, 'Do you think we do the drugs just to be a bit bad?'

Stella had considered. 'Yes. And because it's necessary. A part of being in college, growing up, having fun in the way we do. We sort of have to do them.'

'That's what I thought,' Laura had replied. 'But Amanda's different, isn't she? She has something else going on.' It was an observation that left Stella feeling chilly and nervy, although neither of them mentioned it again.

That night, Dell was being nasty, and Amanda, in her Rick

Owens dress, genuinely indifferent, possibly because she was stoned. She was trying to tell a story about something that had happened in Trinity Main Square, and Dell kept interrupting.

'Amanda, we know it's your first year, and college is still very exciting for you, but please – spare us!' she drawled. 'We've had three years of this stuff. Things that happened in Main Square are just not particularly funny any more.'

A guy called Tim, who disliked Amanda because she had nicknamed him 'Byron de Sade' for his tiresome obsession with opium addicts and romantic poets who died young, was beside Dell. He was handsome, with charcoal grey eyes and lashes so black everyone immediately assumed he was wearing mascara. He had a chalky pallor, high forehead, and thick, shiny black hair. Invariably dressed in leather greatcoats and tight black trousers, he swaggered through college like one of his romantic heroes. At first, he had been flattered by Amanda's nickname for him, until he had realised she was teasing. Ever since, he had lost no opportunity to snipe at her, though he wasn't sufficiently brave to challenge her openly. He sniggered now, saying, 'Yes, the novelty does wear off sometime in year two ...'

'This is actually funny,' Amanda said, with a slight slur. 'I promise. If you'll just listen.' Actually, it *was* a funny story: two fat American tourists marvelling at the architectural wonders – 'Gee, isn't it *old*, honey?' – and asking their guide 'is this place pre-World War Two?' only to be answered by the pompous young man shooing them around 'Madam, this place is pre-America'.

James arrived just as Amanda delivered the punchline, and found everyone laughing. He was delighted to see such harmony between his friends and the girl he adored. At times like that, he looked as if she were the very light and warmth of his life.

She never spoke to Laura about James, except in relation to his hopes of Amanda. But once she had found herself explaining: 'Watching someone whose whole focus is someone else is the surest way to see them clearly. Do you know what I mean?'

Laura had thought for a bit, then said, 'Yes, I do. There's no distraction of light in your eyes. They aren't dazzling you, so you can see how they really are.'

'Exactly.' What Stella hadn't said was that this was how she *knew* that James was lovely. That he was open, kind, sweet and funny, even as she saw him turn all these things onto Amanda in an effort to reach her. Because while he did it, Stella could take her time separating him from the romance all around him – the house, the mother, the little red sports car – and see that, beyond it all, he was good.

After the cocktail bar, they had collected a couple more undergraduates. Kids willing to experiment and investigate, who had clocked that Amanda, with her desire to make every night magical and overblown, was someone to latch on to. And Amanda, never reluctant to be admired, was happy to let them tag along.

While Dell and Amanda bickered, the night flickered around them as they moved to a quayside dive bar that mixed local hard men and auld fellas with the city's bright young things. Amanda was a great favourite of the barman, Paddy, who was a surly old git with most people but called her 'Princess' with genuine affection.

The music was good and they all danced, though not as hard as they drank. Even so, Amanda was way ahead in consumption, knocking back drink after drink, then disappearing to the one grimy loo, often with Dell or a guy called Christian, who was in first year with them. By then Amanda's eyes were bloodshot and she was starting to stumble. Her dress was smeared with something sticky, and she was messier than Stella had ever seen her. But it was a messy night, with everyone on a mission to get drunker, higher than usual so Amanda didn't stand out. Until she blundered out of the loo with blood running from her nose and her eyes rolling back in her head.

She made it into the bar, staggering and grabbing at bystanders, who shrugged her off. Then she fell, clutching at a scarf tossed lightly over someone's shoulder. A flimsy round table broke her fall, cradled her long enough for James to hurl himself through a crowd who were cheerfully unaware of any unfolding drama. He got to her as she hit the floor. Stella was right behind him. She had been watching James watching Amanda. Once he had his arm around her, he turned her, supporting the inert head in the crook of his elbow. A thin trickle of blood made its way down from her left nostril. It was the colour of summer geraniums, surprisingly pretty against her pale skin. Her eyes were white slits under drooped lids and she was shuddering. If there hadn't been an ambulance two doors down, summoned to deal with a homeless man whose profusely bleeding head had alarmed a kindly stranger, Amanda might not have survived the night. When the ambulance arrived, the homeless man had stopped bleeding and was opposed to being taken anywhere. 'Youse are cunts and can feck off,' he roared.

It was at this point that Stella had found them. While the others were frantically jabbing at numbers with shaking hands, she ran outside, not knowing what she was hoping to find, just that she couldn't be anywhere near Amanda while the thread of her life was unravelling. Flecks of white had formed at the corners of Amanda's mouth and her skin had assumed a bluish tinge. The blue lights of the ambulance had registered immediately, and a surge of relief made Stella dizzy. She lurched over to where the paramedics were closing the back of the van, while, beside them, the homeless man shouted abuse at them.

'Quick!' Stella grabbed a paramedic's arm. 'Come quick. She's dying.'

The man whose arm she wasn't holding muttered something about ringing it in, but the other guy, having seen Stella's face, was reaching to reopen the back door of the ambulance.

'Ring it in while we go,' he said to his companion. Then, 'What happened?' to Stella.

'I don't know. Her nose is bleeding and she's not responding. I think it only happened a few minutes ago.' Stella was steadier now, because things were happening.

The men cleared a path through the bar, which had emptied, and had to shoulder James out of the way to get to Amanda. He was holding her head on his lap as he sat on the wet, filthy floor. Her hair was spread out across his knees and smelt of vomit. Blood was still trickling from her nostril.

'What did she take?' the man snapped. No one answered. 'Quick!' he barked. 'What?'

'Cocaine, I think,' said Stella. She seemed the only one capable of speech.

The men strapped Amanda to a gurney and wheeled her, fast, out of the dazed and silent bar. The ones who didn't want to be mixed up in the drama had scarpered, the rest stood and stared, held fast by shock. Paddy the barman hustled the rest of them outside, but the men wouldn't let any of Amanda's friends into the ambulance.

'How old is she?' the surly one asked.

'Nineteen,' Stella answered.

'Ring her parents. Tell them where she is. St James's.' They drove off, sirens blaring, blue lights flashing icily.

Stella looked at James, who was grey under the orange streetlights. Laura's hands were shaking so badly she couldn't hit the buttons on her phone. 'What do we say to Mrs O'Hagen?' she stammered. Her teeth were chattering.

'Don't say anything,' James said. 'Tell her there's been an accident and let the hospital explain. They'll do a succinct job of it,' he said. 'Did you see the way they looked at us, and at Amanda? They hate people who do this stuff to themselves.'

'But she'll ask me questions. I'll have to say something.' Laura could barely get her words out.

'I'll do it.' Stella grabbed the phone. She felt perfectly calm now that Amanda's life and death were no longer her responsibility. If anything, she felt angry. Trust Amanda. They all did this stuff – a few pills, a few lines – but they kept it together, didn't get so messy that other people were dragged into something ugly. Well, Amanda had gotten very messy now. Not for the first time. There had been nights before this. No ambulances or hospitals, but nasty things. A guy she had had sex with, then later accused of taking advantage of her. Not officially, not to the police, she just told everyone that she'd passed out because he'd fed her speed and absinthe and she'd come round to find him inside her.

Stella had seen them leaving the nightclub. The guy was doing a master's in politics, and they had both looked happy and snuggled up together, Amanda wrapped around him, beaming. Amanda had got over the incident, but the guy in question had vanished. One of his friends later told Stella that he was crippled with depression, had deferred his year and gone home to his parents.

Now Stella made the call, explaining as little as she could to Mrs O'Hagen while still giving her the salient facts. To her credit, Mrs O'Hagen asked almost nothing, beyond the basics: 'Which hospital? Where are you?' Once she ascertained that Stella was nowhere near Amanda, and couldn't give any report as to her condition, she thanked her crisply and hung up.

'Should we go to the hospital?' Laura asked.

'No.' Stella was adamant. 'There's no point, and you need to get home. I'll ring Mrs O'Hagen again in a while. She said I could. We'll find out that way. Amanda will be fine. You know she will.'

'Okay, but come home with me. I can't sit there on my own not knowing anything.'

James came too, back to Laura's cosy little house, and indeed the warm light cast by the open fire on copper pots and coloured glass was soothing after the trauma of the night. They drank mint tea, heavily sugared, by the fire. Nessa had gone out and wasn't expected back, which meant James could stay. After a couple of hours, Stella rang Mrs O'Hagen for an update.

'The doctors say she'll be fine. They've given her Valium to calm the convulsions and will just watch her now. If the night passes without incident, she'll be discharged tomorrow. If that happens, I want to talk to you and Laura in the morning.' No recrimination, barely any emotion in her voice.

'Okay, Mrs O'Hagen. Good night. Thanks,' Stella responded meekly, relieved to have been right in her insistence that Amanda would be fine. After all, she had been saying only what Laura needed to hear, not what she truly believed.

Once the welcome news was transmitted, Laura went to bed. Stella and James continued to sit by the fire, watching it die, and piecing together the night from their two perspectives. It was the most frank conversation Stella had had with him, and through talking they learned that Amanda was much deeper into disrupting her life than either had realised. Incidents they had seen only from one side, rumours heard but never corroborated until now, combined to produce a rather frightening picture.

The night wore on and the fire went out. They drew together for warmth and comfort. They were so close by the time dawn came that when Stella placed her hand at the side of James's face, cupping the curve of his cheek and jaw in her cold fingers, he had to bend his head only slightly to kiss her.

She moved closer into him, her body melting into his, and they made love on the squashy red velvet sofa, under a woven Moroccan blanket that was scratchy and smelt faintly of earth. His touch was so gentle that Stella found herself lost in a kind of reverie. She lay beneath him, moulding her body to his, her limbs diverted any way he chose by the slightest touch of his hands.

Afterwards she buried her face in his shoulder. 'Why?' she muttered, not daring to look up. 'Why do you stay around, take all the pain? You'll get nothing, you know. There are so many other guys.'

There, she'd admitted it. There were a lot of guys, but somehow she, Laura and Amanda had always managed to pretend there weren't. And he knew immediately what she was talking about.

'Because. Because one day there won't be. There will just be me.'

'Do you really believe that?'

'I do. She's never fallen for a single one of them. And none of them loves her as much as I do. Or they love the wrong things in her.'

'"But one man loved the pilgrim soul in you, And loved the sorrows of your changing face".' Stella quoted the lines with bitterness. 'Yeats knew how you felt,' she added bleakly. 'Lucky you.'

'Exactly.' James's face had softened, and he seemed unaware of the bitter undertone in Stella's voice. It was as if she wasn't there, hadn't just had sex with him, sex that had been so loving that it felt real. He didn't need to let her down gently, she thought. She barely existed for him.

'Tell me,' she said conversationally, sitting straight up now, 'do you think I slept with you because I'm Amanda's friend? To make up to you for her bad behaviour and to comfort myself because I'm so worried about her?'

He looked appalled. Clearly, the possibility that this might not be so had only just occurred to him.

'You really are a fool.' She got out from under the rug as she said it, pulling her top over her head so that she was at least half-dressed, had half a barrier between herself and him. 'A fool for Amanda and a fool about me.'

Fully dressed, she went into the kitchen, ignoring him when he put his head around the door two minutes later, saying, 'Stella,' with quiet hesitancy. When she didn't answer, he let himself out through the front door and into the breaking light of day.

Then Stella remembered something Nessa had once said to Amanda about love: 'It begins in pity and ends in misery.' Finally, Stella could see what she had meant.

All these years later, in her deep bath, in her tiny East Village apartment, with another woman's husband asleep in her bed, she still felt the pain of that night.

Chapter Seven

New York

SEAN LEFT AT SIX A.M. THE AIR WAS STILL charcoal grey as he dressed and kissed Stella goodbye. He would, she knew, go to his gym, where he would spend an hour hitting the heavy bag and sparring with his coach, dancing around the boxing ring and taking the knocks that came his way. It was one of the tenets of his faith that he carefully counted off, like rosary beads, the insistence that one part of him was the same raw country lad his family had produced in Ireland, who needed to engage with the marrow of life, who could never be happy far from the sea. Who could take whatever life dished out and wrestle it into something good.

After the workout, he would shower, then his driver would

collect him and take him to the office. There, he would ring Tory to make plans for the evening and the weekend. Together they would decide which prize-winning novelist to invite with the first deputy mayor, a woman whose buxom figure and habit of ringing Sean for intimate chats had already cost Stella some pangs of jealousy. He and Tory would discuss the make-up of the Cape Cod party in minute detail, down to the cocktails served (dry martinis usually: Tory considered anything else tacky), and whether these should be served in the large room overlooking the ocean, or the room with the de Kooning. Sean would devote himself to these conversations with as much concentration as he brought to bear on important merger documents, drawing a thick veil around himself and Tory as he did so. He didn't need to show Stella her place in his life: it was immediately obvious and had been from their first night together. The silent rage she felt at how little he offered, how much less she asked for, fuelled her long runs and late work sessions, the lonely weekends when she trawled Manhattan's flea markets and galleries for lack of anything better to do, and the lies she told her parents about how great everything was.

She rolled over, too irritated to sleep any longer. Somehow the latest mess of her life felt like Amanda's fault too. In the shower before hitting the basement gym, she speculated that only in America would anyone shower before and after a workout. Land of opportunity and limitless hot water.

ℭ

She was in the office by eight, first of the day's coffees in hand, hoping she'd made it before Sean. For some reason it was important to her that, professionally, she kept ahead of him.

As if, that way, she could kid them both that her job was the most important thing to her, her affair with him somehow secondary. Her assistant was already there, with a list of the client meetings, conference calls and lunch appointments to come. Her dry cleaning was hanging in the coat cupboard, pristine in its plastic sheath. It looked to be a day like any other, except that the question of what to do about Amanda was still buzzing in her brain. She needed to ring Laura and settle the matter. What could they do? Nothing, she decided. The inevitability of Amanda had been written into the first overdose, like letters in a stick of rock. There could be no more pretending.

As she tried to close her mind to the mute appeal of Amanda – filthy, maybe desperate, in London – she thrust the hard-bitten side of her personality to the fore. The one that daily ignored the claims of people, with real lives, hopes and dreams, in favour of giant corporations. But the image of Amanda at her most desperate wouldn't leave her. That day in hospital, with Dora – or, rather, waiting for Dora to be returned. Even then Amanda hadn't asked for help or understanding. She hadn't said anything because, Stella knew, she believed she didn't need to. Always they had rushed instinctively to help her, until they'd felt they couldn't help any more, until Amanda had disappeared into a world so fabulous that Stella had allowed herself to believe that it was full of friends and confidants, 'A new Greek chorus,' as she had joked to Laura one day, unwilling to admit how hurt she felt, and laughing when Laura responded, 'Wait till they find out just how much epic drama they're letting themselves in for.' Where were all the exciting new friends now? Why weren't they with Amanda, helping her? Why had Laura's phone call so easily stirred up the old feeling of protectiveness that Amanda's vulnerability had always inspired in her?

Her foot kept twitching, a symptom of her irritation. She stilled it, but with an effort. She was angry, unwilling to allow the old life to surface in the new. Hadn't she crossed the Atlantic to get away from all this? Amanda and her dramas, Laura and her endless desire to placate, her own youthful self, so full of naivety and hurt. Why must they all follow, beseeching her to look back? I will not be Lot's wife, she decided. I will not look back.

So why could she not order her life as she wanted, like a smooth, well-made bed with hospital corners? Why did the old wrinkles keep showing through? She knew that it was fear of helplessness that held her back, as much as her determination to stay aloof. What if she went and could do nothing? Yes, she was tired of Amanda, her demands and needs, but the more she allowed herself to remember, the more difficult it became to ignore the appeal that Amanda hadn't made and never would.

Stella remembered the morning after the overdose, how close she had come to breaking the thread between them, and how tangled it had suddenly seemed, so that no break could have been clean. If someone needs you enough, they have a claim on you, she thought wearily, switching on her computer. It really was as simple as that.

ᛗ

The day after the overdose, when Amanda had been discharged, Stella and Laura, still terrified that their own parents were going to get dragged into the story, had cut lectures and gone to the O'Hagen house. The swelling notes of a blackbird surrounded them as they waited at the front door. Inside, Amanda was wearing a pair of striped flannel pyjamas, curled up on the sofa of the second-floor sitting room that she increasingly used as her own since her parents – her mother – had declined to let her get a flat in town. She was wrapped in a plaid rug and looked awful. She was gnawing at a thumbnail, which she did only when extremely stressed, and didn't look up as Stella and Laura entered. There was an awkward silence, then Laura rushed over to her.

'Are you all right? God, Amanda, that was scary!'

Stella stayed where she was. She had barely slept. After James had left, she had been so cold that she couldn't get warm and had ended up having a boiling bath in Nessa's free-standing copper tub, then getting into bed just as Laura was stirring, and falling into a deep sleep for a few hours. She had woken, feeling so flat and sad and old that she didn't know how she could face the day. Pretending to Laura that she was hung-over, she had managed a few bites of toast and a cup of tea, but the food had brought no spark of energy. She had just felt soggy and hopeless. Now, standing in front of Amanda, she decided that if Amanda tried to brush it all off, she would leave and not look back. Instead, Amanda burst into painful, ragged sobs.

She didn't say anything, just cried. Eventually, as Laura rubbed Amanda's hunched shoulder, Stella walked over and put her arms around her. She held on to her as Amanda continued to heave, her thin shoulders rising and falling, her breath coming in harsh gasps.

'Stop! Amanda, stop! It's okay. It's going to be fine.' Stella barely knew what she was saying, just that she had to find some way of stemming the flow of pain that ran so freely from whatever part of her Amanda normally kept closed off. 'It's all going to be all right,' she said. 'We'll get through this.' She meant it. Somehow, together, they would all get through it. Even the bits about James that the other two didn't know.

Finally, the heaving stopped, the sobs dwindled to gasps, then hiccups. Amanda raised her face, blotchy and red-eyed, her hair a tangled mess. 'I wouldn't blame you if you hated me. The staff in the hospital certainly did.' She gave a shaky laugh. 'The nurse who tended me last night was so rough, I think she would have used sandpaper on my skin if she'd had any. They hustled me out of there this morning as fast as they decently could. The nurse said they needed the bed for people who were "really ill, like".'

Stella smiled reluctantly.

'But seriously,' Amanda continued, 'I'm sorry. You saved my life, and I'm sorry I made that necessary.'

'It was Stella who saved you,' Laura said in a rush, proud of the decisive role Stella had played. 'We were all standing, staring, freaking out. She ran out and found help.'

'I got lucky,' Stella said.

'No, *I* did,' Amanda said quietly. 'They told me I could have died. Funny I don't feel worse today . . .'

'How do you feel?' Laura asked.

'Empty, headachy, mostly just flat and sad.'

Just like me, thought Stella in surprise. Maybe that's all heartbreak really was: your body reacting to being poisoned. The poison of love. The idea cheered her up a bit. 'What did your mother say?' she asked.

'Nothing yet. But she will.' Amanda rolled her eyes. 'Whatever about saving my life, thanks for coming today to take some of the heat.'

'She has a right to be angry,' Laura said.

Mrs O'Hagen wasn't angry, or not that she showed. She came

click-clacking into the room a few moments later, looking, as
always, as if she had just stepped out of Hair and Make-up.
She was wearing a cream velour tracksuit with the word 'Baby'
picked out in Swarovski crystals. The combination – heels,
tracksuit, flawless make-up, coiffed blonde hair – made her
look like a Mafia wife, beautiful, but wrong. She was in full
damage-limitation mode.

'Now that we know Amanda is fine' – she arched an eyebrow
in Amanda's direction – 'how do we handle it? We can't expect
that it won't leak out. I'm sure it was all over the city within
twenty minutes, so there's no point denying it. But I won't
have people making more of it than needs be.'

The girls stared at her, Stella and Laura in appalled wonder.
When they said nothing, Mrs O'Hagen sighed. 'The question
is: do we say nothing, or do we try to use this ourselves? And,
if so, how?' She looked at Laura and Stella, eyebrows raised
again.

There was a blank silence.

'Amanda could have died.' Laura sounded accusing.

'Don't imagine I'm not aware of that.' Mrs O'Hagen turned
her icy blue eyes on Laura. 'I am not for one second suggesting
this is acceptable,' she continued. 'I didn't think I needed to
spell out my feelings about such undisciplined behaviour.'

Undisciplined, thought Stella. If only . . .

'However,' Mrs O'Hagen said, 'neither do I see the point
of going on about all that. The main thing now is not to let it
become worse than it is. I'm presuming it will never happen
again.' She stared at Amanda.

'No, Mummy,' Amanda said dully.

'Well, then, the important thing is how we handle the
gossip, and how damaging it could be for Amanda's career.

I think, if we're careful, it doesn't have to be. It's lucky we already had you positioned as a party girl. It would have been much worse if your image had been girl-next-door. As it is, we can afford to say nothing and allow the rumours to work their own way out.'

'Are you going to tell our parents?' Laura blurted out.

'No. Why?' Mrs O'Hagen seemed surprised. Stella realised that the possibility had never occurred to her because she was incapable of seeing that this was a situation that involved other people. To her, it was entirely about Amanda. Even though she was kind to Stella and Laura, welcomed them to the house, included them in her plans, even chatted to them as if they were equals when it suited her, they were just wraiths, shadow-play. The idea of informing their parents of the kind of scene they might be mixed up in hadn't registered with her. Stella supposed she should be grateful not to be facing more trouble.

'We need to talk more about this.' Mr O'Hagen had entered the room silently and now stood in the doorway looking rough and menacing, despite his beautifully cut suit. He must have contributed *something* to Amanda's genetic make-up, but Stella could never figure out what.

'There's no point going on about it,' Mrs O'Hagen insisted. 'We play it down and carry on.'

'No. Amanda needs to stay at home more. We don't know where she goes, or who her friends are, apart from these two.' He gestured dismissively towards the girls. 'We don't know what she gets up to, and last night made it clear that we can't trust her. For Jesus' sake, Marie, this wasn't a public relations disaster – it was an overdose!'

Stella's sentiments exactly, but she was surprised to hear Mr O'Hagen second them; surprised, too, to hear him talk so much. His accent held the undertones of his suburban childhood, which made him seem more human.

'Don't overreact, Mick. This was a one-off. I'm not saying it isn't serious, but it could just as easily have been Laura or Stella as Amanda. It was simply foolishness that got out of hand.' She didn't ask Laura or Stella for their corroboration, didn't even look at them. 'And *of course* we know who Amanda's friends are and where she goes. Why, she was out with James last night, and you like James.'

'James.' Mr O'Hagen snorted. 'As if *he* can handle Amanda.'

'Amanda doesn't need to be "handled", Mick. Stop talking about her as if she's some kind of problem.'

'And taking so much cocaine that she goes into seizure isn't a problem?' His face was red now.

'Stop going on about it!' Mrs O'Hagen nearly screamed. 'We are not going to let this stupid incident ruin everything. It is never going to happen again. We have already established that. Amanda has a future, a real chance, and I will not let you destroy that. She needs to be out to be seen. Without that, she will not succeed, I'm telling you.'

'And I'm telling you that I want to know a lot more about what she gets up to.' They were shouting at each other, indifferent to the three girls, unaware that Amanda had started to cry again.

'Let's leave them to it,' Amanda finally muttered to Stella and Laura, and they escaped down to the kitchen, where Ivana made them big mugs of hot chocolate and pancakes with stewed apple. They ate in silence until she left the room, off on one of her many errands.

'At least your mother isn't too furious,' Laura said, trying to make the best of what she thought was Mrs O'Hagen's shocking attitude.

'Oh, she's furious,' said Amanda, 'but she won't let it stop her. She thinks she's a shark and she'll die if she isn't always moving forward. Always forward, always getting on. *Making progress*. No one is ever allowed to slow down or be unhappy or despondent,' she finished bitterly.

'What does she think will happen?' Laura asked.

'That the world will end and everything will come crashing down? I don't know,' Amanda said. 'But she's pathological about it. If I cried as a kid, because I fell down or something, she wouldn't even look at my knee or whatever was sore. She'd just say, "You're all right. Up you get now."'

'Well, it's very positive.' Laura tried to see the good side.

'It's not, it's horrible! It's probably the result of clawing her way out of that dreadful slum she was brought up in.'

'Hardly a slum,' Stella protested. 'Dreary suburb is all.'

'Well, whatever it was, getting out of it seems to have left her with an empathy bypass. She's always *achieving*, *doing*, *bettering*, even in her sleep, I'd say, so I have to, too. I can't just be what I am.'

There was a long pause. Stella thought about what it must be like never to be allowed to have an off moment or a bad day, to be always goaded forward, in denial of pain or sadness. Amanda's right, she decided. It's horrible. 'I wasn't sure if it was speed or coke,' she said conversationally. She had decided the best way to tackle Amanda was to pretend it was no big deal, that it could indeed have been her or Laura sprawled on the filthy floor, splashed with vomit and a trickle of blood from one nostril. Even though they all knew that she and Laura had never gone that far and never would.

'Coke.'

'Who got it for you?'

'A guy Dell knows. He's a motorcycle courier. Very handy. He'll turn up wherever you are within twenty minutes or so. You pay more, but that's part of the service.'

Presumably it was bravado that had Amanda so deadpan, Stella thought. 'That's why you left the bar so soon after we arrived?'

'Yes, I met him outside.'

'And then you spent way too much time in the loo, snorting it.'

'I suppose I did.'

'You know, I'm not sure Dell is such a good friend to you,' Laura joined in, adopting the same conversational tone.

'Oh, she's all right,' said Amanda, without much interest. 'She can be a total bitch, but that's just her.'

'She's not like that with everyone, though. It's mainly with you,' Laura said.

Mrs O'Hagen walked into the kitchen, her face set. 'Amanda, don't forget you have a shoot on Tuesday. I'd better book you in for a facial tomorrow.' From this, they all knew that she, not her husband, had won.

'All right, Mummy.' Then, to the girls, 'James rang to say he'd come round later. Shall we rent some movies?'

'Only if you agree to change out of those pyjamas,' Stella said. She had realised, after a shocked second, that of course she would have to face James sooner or later, and decided that sooner was probably better.

'*Pulp Fiction*, anyone?' Laura joked, but only when Mrs O'Hagen had left the kitchen.

Together they all worked hard to smooth paper over the cracks, put the curtain back in place and carry on as usual.

'If there are things to talk about, that you want to say, you can always do that,' Stella said, trying to make eye contact with Amanda.

Amanda kept her head bent over her pancakes. 'I know,' she said quietly, still not looking up.

It was what they always had done, Stella knew: they had pretended nothing had happened, that nothing was wrong.

ভ

When James had arrived later that day, looking tired and, she thought, faintly sheepish, she had rushed headlong to nothing, forcing normality out of the encounter, driven by fear of what either of them would say if she didn't. Afraid that she would blurt out, 'I love you,' or spell it out with every inch of herself to anyone who knew to look, and that he would have nothing to say, just a silence that said everything, or attempt an explanation: I can't. I don't.

When she had heard the wheels of his little red car on the gravel, she was first up from the kitchen table, first outside to the driveway, where she walked straight up to him and gave him a friendly kiss on the cheek. 'Hi.'

'Hi.' He looked wary.

'Did you get any sleep? I'm wrecked.' Cheerful, practical. 'But Amanda seems fine.' The same instinct that forced her to steer him away from herself guided her to mention Amanda. I'm like one of those birds that nests on the ground, she thought, beating its wings furiously to distract predators from the vulnerable young. A distracting flurry of noise and activity that put her at risk of harm, in order to avoid a greater risk. The thought made her feel desperate.

'That's good.' He looked as if he wanted to say something else, but fear drove her on.

'Come in, she's in the kitchen. But stay away from Mrs O'H if you can. She may not be on the warpath exactly, but it's not a peace-path either.' He followed quietly, as if confused by the show of strength she was putting on. One half of her wanted to stop, stand still, let the words fall out of her mouth, no matter that they could never be unsaid, and let his own words be as they were but, again, fear stopped her. She believed that the worst could be avoided if you ignored it.

It was the same fear that allowed Amanda to dictate her own terms while they danced along behind her, still too caught up in her gorgeousness and growing celebrity to see how thin the whole thing had become. Amanda had laughed and romped her way through the first year at university, taking in her stride the gossip that spilled out around the overdose, just as she later sat her end-of-year exams.

And then, when it seemed they were safe, the door that had been pushed open a mere crack on the night of the overdose was wrenched wide at Amanda's twenty-first, when Huw first entered her life. Even now, Stella found herself marvelling at the lavishness of the party. Amanda's twenty-first was the hottest ticket in town. Everyone who had the slightest acquaintance with her hoped to scrape an invitation, and indeed Amanda showered them liberally.

Thinking back now to the delight with which the three of them had helped with the preparations, how those days glowed with such warmth, she felt the full force of the distance travelled since, and saw that there was nothing inherently sad about nostalgia. Looking back at the giddy innocence they had brought to that night, she saw that the moment itself was pristine, and only her knowledge of how ugly the whole thing had since become made it otherwise. She felt sad again, for the girls they had been, and the women they were now.

ᔆ

'The marquee holds a hundred and fifty. Wait until they see how many actually turn up,' Amanda told Stella and Laura gleefully. They were in their second year at university, and between them, they felt, they knew everybody.

'How many have you invited?' asked Laura.

'I've no idea. I've been to so many parties in the last few weeks because everyone wants to host something for my coming-of-age, and I've asked pretty much everyone at all of them. Which means Will Manley has been invited about six times, but that ghastly news editor from the *Evening Tribune* has been invited too. Only once, though.'

'God, you'll have to start putting some serious misinformation out there, and hope half of them get lost, or get the wrong day,' said Laura, laughing. They were on the terrace outside the kitchen, and a light breeze was blowing, ruffling the pages of notes in front of them – playlists for the DJ, food requests, entertainment ideas. 'Let's have a guy making balloon animals! I used to love those when I was younger.'

'And a chocolate fountain! I saw one at a party once. So Willy Wonka.' Amanda's bare feet, with perfectly manicured tangerine-orange toenails, were up on Stella's chair, her long bare legs emerging from a pair of tiny denim cut-offs, and an ancient white T-shirt under her sloppy cardigan. Stella was in black leggings and an oversized granddad shirt, while Laura, who was trying out a new, more grown-up look, was wearing one of Nessa's wrap dresses, orange and white, with huge 1970s' shades, her hair in a wonky chignon. In the distance, the bells of the village church were sending out the final Saturday-night appeal.

'But how many *formal* invitations?' Stella wanted to know.

'Oh, *formal*! And I mean very formal – the card is so stiff it looks like rigor mortis has set in, and my mother has concocted a kind of heraldic sign for the family. I knew I should have got suspicious when she made me research O'Hagen in the library genealogy section. You should have seen how she sniffed when I said there wasn't anything!' Amanda smiled her bewitching smile. The one that proved, beyond a doubt, that she was the loveliest creature in the world.

'God, I know,' Stella said. 'We've seen them, remember. My parents are proudly displaying theirs on the mantelpiece this instant. Go on, though, how many?'

'I bet they're not. I bet they laughed at them,' Amanda said, without rancour. 'Two hundred cards sent out in total, with a hundred and forty-three acceptances and fifty-seven distraught regrets.'

'So who's definitely coming?'

'Well. My parents have shoehorned in a few of their cronies – people like Malcolm, of course, and Alice, the Dwyers and the Blackburns – but mainly it's our lot from college, as well as nearly all the photographers I've worked with in the last couple of years. The fashion editor and the editor of *Belle* are coming and bringing guests. Two casting directors – the one who put me up for the role in *Shambles*, and the one who didn't and was annoyed about it.' Part of Amanda's genius was her ability to shine in any light, to be the muse everyone wanted, whether they worked in high fashion or electronics.

'Lots of models,' she went on, 'even the nasty, starving ones, have said yes, and every stylist I've ever met.' Amanda wasn't liked by other models, because she was too successful, according to her; because she sneered at the kind of low-grade photocalls they had to do to survive, according to them. She had once given an interview in which she had talked about how she'd rather drive a taxi than be photographed in a bikini and an outsized Santa hat. Since then, she had been largely ostracised at catwalk shows. Still, that kind of animosity rarely counted when a really good invitation was in the offing.

'James is coming, of course, and his parents, and a cousin of his from England, Huw Something, who's very grand apparently, but James says he's fun too. Dell is bringing her new boyfriend, who is a complete jerk, the type only Dell can choose, and I'm letting her because I hope he does something awful and shames her.'

'Hey, she doesn't always choose badly. She used to go out with James, remember?' Stella wished she hadn't said anything but the words came out faster than she could catch them.

'Not really. He always said it was just friends, although she wanted more.'

'That's not fair. They were going out until shortly after he met you. Then you ruined him for everybody else, even though you don't want him.' Stella tried to smile after saying this, not that Amanda would notice.

'Who says I don't?'

'Don't what?'

'Want James.'

'Amanda, what do you mean? You can't be serious?' Laura looked worried.

'But I am. Things have been different between us recently. I've felt really close to him since the night in the hospital.' She rarely mentioned it. 'I'm thinking my party could be the perfect time to make it something more.'

So James would get what he wanted, after all. His patience, tolerance and unswerving devotion entitled him to it. He may as well be happy, Stella forced herself to believe. No point both of them walking wounded through the world.

'He loves me, really loves me, and there's something wonderful about that,' Amanda was going on. 'Besides, I want to settle. Have something good and solid in my life. I'm built on too many shifting sands. Like Venice.' She laughed awkwardly. 'I love his parents, and his house. Far more than my own.' She didn't specify which she loved more than her own, house or parents. She didn't have to. 'I'm always meaning to be happy. It's about time I started to be.'

'Wow. Always the unexpected with you, Amanda,' Laura said.

'It's different for you two,' Amanda said, picking at a thread that had unravelled from the cushion she was sitting on. 'You're happy. All you need to do is to carry on, with your lives getting better and better.'

There was a long pause. Then: 'How little any of us really knows about the others,' Stella said lightly.

'What do you mean?' Amanda looked upset. 'Aren't you happy? How could you not be?'

'How could you not be?' Laura said. 'You're beautiful, clever, rich, everyone adores you, your parents give you everything you want. So why aren't you happy?'

'She means that things can look really great on the outside, Amanda, and feel very different inside,' Stella explained. 'She's not actually shouting at you for not being happy.'

'But does that mean you aren't happy?' Amanda wasn't to be deflected.

'Who says happy is what life intends us to be? It seems to

me that everything is set up for quite the opposite result,' said Stella.

'I don't believe that,' Amanda said. 'We can be happy, all of us. And I mean to be.'

Stella could see Mrs O'Hagen passing an upstairs window. She was on the phone. From the kitchen, the sound of the radio meant that Ivana was preparing lunch. She turned to Amanda. 'And you think James can give you that?'

'I think he can give me the security of being loved, and I can do the rest by myself.'

'Hardly fair on him,' Laura muttered.

'What do you mean?'

'James is a great guy. He deserves to be loved, not just to be the protective cover you throw over yourself.'

'I can make him happy too. I know I can,' Amanda insisted. She seemed to accept their right to ask the hard questions.

'I think he'll take whatever you can give him,' Stella said, 'and try to be content with it.'

Laura was gazing at her in a way that said she was looking for something more, but Stella stared back unflinchingly.

Laura smiled. 'Well, that's settled, then. James's lucky night.'

&

It wasn't, though. Not at all. He was one of the first to arrive, with his parents, his mother looking like a grown-up Joan of Arc, in a peacock blue sheath dress, and the cousin from England, who was small, compact, with shiny brown hair worn below his ears, slanting green eyes and very red lips. Without being remarkable-looking – he was far less handsome than James – he had, in his neat frame, a distilled energy that was compelling. He looked sly and exciting.

'Amanda, this is Huw. He's staying with us for a few days,' said Iseult.

'The cousin from England, with a Welsh name.' Amanda held out her hand and smiled. 'I wrote the invitation myself.' In her gold silk dress, cut to follow the lines of her body, emphasising and framing the perfection that Nature sometimes lends to twenty-one, her hair a pile of curls heaped on top of her head and snaking down her back, she was bewitching.

'Not a cousin exactly.' Huw took her hand in his and smiled back. 'James and I were at prep school together. So were our fathers. And my grandfather was Welsh.'

'Always lovely to meet a friend of James's family,' Amanda said, with non-committal politeness and a secret, laughing look at him that rang tiny alarm bells in Stella.

'Just ask for anything you want at the bar. The guys are whizzes at all kinds of cocktails,' Amanda went on, then gave a rundown of the evening's entertainment. 'There's drinks first, then dinner. Speeches, probably, then a band at eleven, and a DJ until we agree to let him go.'

'Something that we'll decide much closer to the time.' Huw had smiled at her, but coolly. The heat of her beauty and celebrity caused most people to froth over when talking to her but not Huw.

'Of course,' she'd responded.

In the marquee, decorated to look like a Bedouin tent, tiny fibre optic lights were set into the dark velvet of the roof, arranged to represent the night sky as it would appear over a Middle Eastern desert. Vast urns of flowers, all Amanda's sweet-smelling favourites – stocks, sweet-peas, peonies, roses – were set around soft rugs and cushions meant for reclining or sitting on. At one end, there were a few low tables and chairs for those unwilling or unable to recline.

'I'll leave you here,' Amanda said to them. 'I'd better go and say hello to a few more people. But I'll see you later.' She smiled at them all and set off to welcome guests and graciously accept gifts worthy of the Three Wise Men. Each beautifully wrapped box prompted 'Oh, how kind, thank you.' As she received and thanked, Stella saw that her face lit up with such a glow that all those who, predictably, said they had never seen her looking so beautiful were right.

Stella watched as Amanda flitted from group to group, chatting, laughing, putting up her face to be kissed by elderly admirers, accepting compliments and congratulations with wit and grace.

For her and Laura it was a night to pick up the gauntlet thrown down by James's twenty-first four years earlier. Then, they had known no one, had been gauche, content to stare from the safety of the fringes. Even Amanda had been uncertain, struggling not to seem out of her depth, in her understated black dress. Tonight, she looked like a Renaissance princess, her elegance just tipping the balance of her beauty so that it seemed something unbearably precious. Her mother, in floor-length red, with gold gathering up the Grecian folds of her dress at the shoulders, looked like Hera, wife of Zeus. Magnificent and terrible.

And tonight, Stella thought with satisfaction, she and Laura, too, knew everyone. There were friends, well-wishers, compliments for them also, even presents from people who couldn't think of Amanda without automatically remembering them. A girl from Stella's law class had made three hand-embroidered smocks – 'For baking, or gardening, or just lounging around.' A friend of Mr O'Hagen's, with whom they had lunched several times, solemnly presented each of them with a handsome voucher for dinner in the city's best restaurant. 'Treat yourselves,' he boomed, gripping each of their hands in turn with both his.

It was nothing like the loot Amanda was amassing, but they were happy. And they looked good – she knew it. Maybe not amazing like Amanda, but pretty, even sexy.

Nessa was there with her latest romance, an Italian artist she had met at a retreat, who stared at the opulence around him with undisguised approval. '*Molto bene*,' he kept saying, rubbing his sensitive hands together.

'Very nice. You look like Janet Leigh,' Nessa said to Laura, and to Stella, who was wearing a floaty white dress over a shocking pink tulle skirt, and black patent stilettos, 'You've managed to keep your punk aesthetic but still look formal. Clever.'

Stella's parents were also there, at home among the bohemian, erudite crowd Amanda had collected, which even included one of her professors from Trinity. 'He's an expert in Irish art, and knows most of these people anyway,' Amanda had said, when Stella asked her why on earth he had been invited and was it so he'd give her good marks? She had an instinct and a talent beyond her years for the right mix, knowing that juxtaposition and context were the key to transforming people into the best version of themselves. 'Amanda could be a truly great hostess,' Nessa had once said. 'She understands how to create social fireworks.'

Stella was enjoying herself. The timing was perfect – a week after they'd finished their exams – and the weather was beautiful, a mellow summer evening with enough warmth to carry the promise into every corner of the house and gardens, and the food was as matchless as Mrs O'Hagen's expensive caterers and her own insistence on excellence could make it: tender lamb tagine with apricot and honey, to follow through the Moroccan theme, little spiced poussins in flat dishes, deep bowls of salad. The groups laughed, chatted, dispersed and re-formed, while the general hum of hilarity rose steadily higher.

They ate sitting in groups inside the marquee and out, at tables set on the lawn. Mr O'Hagen made a speech in which he mentioned Stella and Laura, saying he couldn't talk about Amanda, or even think about her, without immediately thinking of them too. 'Her two best friends' – 'Aaah,' went the crowd – 'partners in crime' – 'Ha-ha' – 'and guardian angels.' It was a good speech, even if it did seem like someone else's rather than his own, painting a picture of a relaxed, convivial past in which the three girls tumbled through a generous house as they became young women. But the end of his speech was all for Amanda.

'To my daughter, Amanda, who is as beautiful as she is brilliant and kind. A brightly shining star in the ascendant.'

'To Amanda!' chorused two hundred voices. 'To Amanda!'

'And to you too.' James, standing beside Stella and Laura, raised his glass to them. He reached out to put his arm around Laura and draw her in for a hug, then did the same to Stella. It was the fact that his basic decency and good manners had never suffered as a result of their night together that forced Stella to admit how little he felt. He could not, she reckoned, have been so faultless in his behaviour if his heart knew anything like the turmoil of hers, and she was astonished at how intense a reaction his almost bland kindness provoked in her. She wondered, not for the first time, if he had any idea of the storm he had stirred up.

She allowed him to hug her again now, and resisted the urge to lay her head in the crook of his neck where his clean white collar cleared his skin. Instead, she looked up, over his shoulder, and met Huw's pale green eyes. He raised both eyebrows at her in a faintly mocking smile that made Stella feel he knew all about, and was amused by, her predicament.

The band played, and people danced sedately, Amanda with Mr O'Hagen – they danced well together – then with Stella's father, while Stella danced with the Italian artist, who was much too good for her halting shuffle, and insisted on spinning her around, pushing her in and out, even trying to bend her over backwards, making her feel more and more clumsy, until Nessa came along and said, 'That's enough,' allowing her to escape with relief. Gradually, the older generation slipped away and the remaining gang drew closer in. The DJ was on now, the catering staff had left, and only two barmen remained, both fairly drunk. All the cushions had been heaped into one corner, where a gang were lolling, smoking joints, watching the dancers. Occasionally someone would reach out and grab one of the dancers, hauling them into the soft pile, amid shrieks of laughter.

'I love Irish parties,' said Huw. 'No matter how loaded everyone gets, the pressure on the bar never lets up. In England, when we get high, we stop drinking.' He leaned against the bar, a whiskey in his hand. He had, Stella noticed, made himself very much at home throughout the evening. Either he knew far more people, of every age, than he had a right to, considering the party was hosted by someone he'd never met in a country he wasn't from, or his easy self-confidence was universally winning.

'Oh, we only take drugs to be able to drink more,' Amanda

assured him, laughing. 'Our primary aim is booze. God, look at Dell! What *is* she doing?'

Dell was on the dance floor, bare-footed, waving her arms above her head and swaying in time to the music, which wasn't easy, seeing as the DJ was playing the kind of hard house that doesn't go with swaying and floating. She twirled and dipped at the waist, arms trailing.

'She's an acorn growing into an oak tree,' said Huw snidely.

'A wood nymph, tossed hither and thither by the breeze,' Amanda added.

'Tosser is right,' Huw said.

'Let's break a glass and scatter it across the dance floor. That will soon stop her.' For Amanda, who could be wicked but was never cruel, it was a surprising remark.

'She's all right,' said Stella. 'I guess she's just a bit wasted. She's not doing any harm.'

'Violence to my aesthetic feelings is harm,' Huw assured her, while Amanda laughed delightedly at him.

'Who are you, Oscar Wilde?' asked Stella, then, pointedly, 'Where's James?'

'Not sure.' Amanda looked around vaguely. 'I think he's in the garden. A group of them are playing that game where you pick up a bottle top from the ground using only your teeth.'

'Ah, the great Teeth Only Bottle Top Game – another of your wonderful Irish customs.'

Stella looked hard at Huw, to see if he was taking the piss, but Amanda seemed to have no such notion, just laughed again and said, 'Let's watch them.' Her eyes were enormous, while the faint forward set of her jaw told Stella clearly that she had been doing drugs, although not how much or what. That was the funny thing about Amanda. It showed so clearly on her immediately. Other people could be as high as kites and you'd never know. With Amanda, the jaw was always a dead giveaway, even when her speech remained distinct and her movements steady.

Huw took her arm and they walked off together. Stella began to have a strong feeling that whatever Amanda had thought she had decided about James was all up for grabs again. Sure enough, as the party wore on, she was everywhere, flitting from group to group, on the dance floor, winning the limbo-dancing competition with a fluid, graceful move that none could equal, clamouring for shots of tequila at the bar, with Huw always beside her, his hand on her arm, or his arm around her shoulders. And Amanda, who normally couldn't stand any kind of public claim on her attention, didn't shrug off the hand or arm, didn't wriggle away from him with a laugh and join another group to escape, as she usually would have done. Instead, she smiled up at him, took his hand when she staggered, which she increasingly did as the night wore to its close.

By the time dawn began to rise over the mountains in the east, revealing their lumpy shapes and flooding colour into a black-and-white world, Amanda and Huw had disappeared.

'Say goodbye to Amanda for me,' the various stragglers said to Stella and Laura, getting into their taxis, huddled into coats, faces grey and eyes smudged with black.

'We will,' the girls chorused. 'She must have crashed. I'm sure she'll ring you tomorrow.'

'Today!' The stragglers laughed. 'It's today already.'

'Of course, so it is!' They laughed back, shutting taxi doors and waving.

James came along and said he was going to drive home, that

he hadn't had a drink in hours, he was fine, and had they seen Huw, who was supposed to be coming back with him?

'Gosh, no,' said Laura. 'Maybe he just got tired and crashed out somewhere.'

'That's probably it,' James agreed, but stiffly, not quite meeting their eyes.

Stella said in a rush, 'Do you want me to go and look for him? I'm sure I can wake him up and get him out to you. He's probably on a sofa somewhere.'

There was a pause while James seemed to consider the possibilities. Then he said, 'No, let him sleep. I'll call back for him later. If you do see him, tell him to wait here for me and I'll come back in the afternoon. Tell Amanda I'll see her later.'

He got into his little red car, shivering slightly, and wound down the window as he lit a cigarette.

It was a morning without much promise. Grey and chill, a flat denial of the excitement of the night before. All around, men were packing up, taking down the fantasy land they had created, rolling and bundling and stuffing boxes in the clear morning air. Behind them, the grass was trampled and scattered with stray glasses, plates, and odd heaps of clothing – a shawl, a pair of shoes, several dinner jackets.

'It's like the circus is leaving town,' Laura said.

Stella, who privately felt that the circus might just have arrived, added valiantly, 'Great party, though!'

'Yes, great party.' James's voice sounded hollow. He revved the engine, which had its own friendly, growly sound. 'See you later. Get some sleep.' He drove off, window still down, a plume of smoke issuing from it, like a broken signal.

The girls went to their usual beds in Amanda's room. Amanda was nowhere to be seen.

They didn't talk, just went to sleep. Didn't mention it when they woke, hours later, the afternoon sun bathing the room in dim golden light, just talked about the party, the speeches, the DJ, anything except James, Huw and Amanda.

They found her downstairs, at the terrace table where they had planned the party. She was alone with a cup of coffee, wearing a silvery silk kimono. Nessa had given it to her the night before: 'Vital to have something elegant to get through the mornings after,' she had said. All traces of the party seemed to have vanished like a dream, a fairy feast you can only ever recall through dim images and flashes of bright memory.

'What happened to you? You're never early to leave a party,' Stella tried to joke, but Amanda didn't respond.

'I went with Huw,' she said finally.

'Where with Huw? James was looking for him. Where is he now?' Laura's voice was sharp, disapproving.

'He's gone. James came to get him about an hour ago. We climbed up to the attic to see the sunrise, and we stayed up there.' So that was where they had been.

'But why, Amanda? Why? You said you were going to be with James,' Laura said.

She shrugged. 'It's beyond me,' she said. 'I can't help myself.'

'Rubbish,' said Laura. 'That's ridiculous. There has to be a reason, and it'd better be a good one, after what you've done to James.'

There was another pause while Amanda stared at her coffee cup. Her hand was trembling slightly, and she looked pale, despite the golden glow of the day. 'Huw's the first man I've met who has the power to break my heart,' she said eventually, looking straight at both of them now.

'What's that supposed to mean?' Laura asked, still snappy. 'And how is it a good thing?'

But Stella got it. Suddenly she understood what Amanda meant. 'What was it Auden said in his poem, about being the more loving one?' Amanda and Laura stared at her. 'That's you, Amanda. The more loving one.'

That's me,' Amanda agreed, with a flash of excitement. 'Poor James.'

ᗉ

The more loving one had certainly been her, Stella thought now, staring out over the Manhattan skyline, seeing the old city, with its soft brown stone, reflected endlessly in the new, the shiny glass icebergs on every side of her. As if Manhattan wasn't big enough, it had this trick of projecting itself ever forward, one reflection at a time, until brought to a sharp stop by the shoreline, from which the buildings reared back in comic alarm, a hurtling mass of lemmings brought to a sudden halt.

There had been no lack of love on Amanda's side. As for Huw, she had never been sure what drew him to Amanda. Her looks, her money, her fame, but something else too. Perhaps the space within her personality for him, the room left by whatever it was she couldn't be. Was that love? The shape of the emptiness inside you that matched the shape of another? Anyway, love was never going to be enough for Amanda and Huw. Or maybe there had been too much of it for either of them.

Stella picked up the phone, ignoring the memo asking her to arrange a face-to-face with Sean via his PA. That was clearly work. Their private meetings would never be scheduled in such a way. She wondered what it could be, speculated briefly – a new case, presumably, perhaps the one that would make her senior associate – but carried on dialling Laura's number.

Chapter Eight

Dublin

'IT'S ME. OKAY, WE'LL GO. I GUESS WE HAVE TO.'
Stella had sounded almost hesitant – Stella, who never sounded
hesitant. 'Of course we have to go.'

Laura was relieved, even though she had never doubted the
outcome. Stella had always been impatient, and these days could
be downright snappy, with an over-the-top New York kind
of rudeness that Laura found almost stagey, but she was still
the bravest person Laura had ever known, with a personality as
true as an arrow. Only with James had she ever been less than
honest, Laura thought. She had never told him the simple truth
of her heart, and pretended not to know what Laura meant
when she'd tried to open the way for Stella to confide in her.

That, too, had been brave, she thought now. Too brave, really. Laura had long suspected that the effort of bottling up her thwarted love, choking it down, was what had hardened Stella into the tough, shiny creature she had become, dripping labels and sarcasm.

But that she would refuse Amanda, when Amanda needed her, was impossible. And Laura's hunch was that, this time, Amanda did need them. Her various slips and stumbles over the years, periods when she would disappear from view, eventually resurfacing a little thinner, a little less substantial, had never before made the papers. Always she had pulled herself back from the brink, back to Dora, to Huw, to the parties and openings they attended, to talk of a photoshoot or campaign or film, even if these seldom materialised now, but this time, Laura thought, it was different.

'Okay, but not for long. I can only get away for a couple of days,' Stella was saying.

'That's fine. Day after tomorrow? That gives us the weekend, and maybe Monday.'

'It's all the time I can spare. And presumably the paper doesn't want you disappearing off for any longer either.'

'Well, my time is more flexible.' Laura was evasive. She couldn't tell Stella that the paper was delighted, had urged her to go sooner, stay longer, even offered to pay for her ticket, which she had declined, out of guilty principle, and would be waiting anxiously for her copy.

'God knows what good it will do,' Stella sighed, 'but I'll see you there. Meet you at that little B&B where we stayed last time. What was it called?'

'The Knightsbridge Mews?'

'That's it. I'll have my PA make a reservation.'

'Let's share a twin.' Laura didn't know how she was going to pay for everything, except that the paper would reward her handsomely, had already mentioned the possibility of syndication and said they would allow Laura to collect the entire fee if it happened, which was generous. The story was sure to attract attention, just as the wedding had, years before.

'Any word on Dora?' Stella asked.

'I haven't rung Mrs O'Hagen yet. I didn't know what to say to her. But now I know we're definitely going, I'll ring her today and find out what she knows.'

'Okay. Gotta go.' Stella hung up.

Laura dropped the receiver and leaned back in her swivel chair. The only way she could do what she seemed to be doing – 'betrayal' hovered in her mind – was step by step, without looking further forward than the next necessary task. She believed that she could pick her way through this mess to the right path, but she knew she could do it only by instinct as each branch and fork presented itself. It was obvious that her two objectives – to help Amanda and her own position at work – were not compatible, but neither were they mutually impossible, and she trusted that the way to achieve both would present itself. She knew she didn't want to run away this time. She had always had trouble figuring out what she wanted, but had begun to know what she didn't want. She didn't want a life like Nessa's, where obscurity was relieved only by the men she hooked up with, where talent and ambition got lost. And she didn't want to continue scuttling along the corridors and across the open-plan arena of the newspaper, only ever one step from the exit. In the last few days, she had tasted the possibility of more and better, and she liked it. More power, more authority, more substance.

Only the day before Petrie had popped her head out of her office as Laura was walking past and asked her in.

'Let's get your opinion on this,' she had said, showing Laura a mock-up of the front page. 'What do you think? Is it the right balance?' And Laura had sensed an opportunity. Petrie recently had seemed newly hesitant. Where once she had chosen the weekly 'mix' – the stories to include – purely on the basis of what she knew and felt to be right, now she was trying to assess it from the reader's point of view. Would such a story appeal to *younger* readers? Would Generation Y or Z, or whichever they were on now, have any interest in this or that?

Laura knew what was driving the hesitancy, and knew, too, that her age, her proximity to younger readers, could work for her. The readership numbers were terrible – all numbers were terrible for all papers: these were uncertain times, and therefore offered great opportunities, if she could only grasp them.

She had paused thoughtfully, almost theatrically, heart hammering, and affected a cool scrutiny of the page. 'Too similar,' she said at last. 'The second leader piece needs to be stronger, more definite. Why don't you move the water protests story from the second page?'

The silence told her that Petrie was not just listening but calculating, running scenarios through her mind with the lightning speed for which she was famous, considering and discarding various options. And then she nodded. 'Good idea.'

Laura had tried to remain calm, measured, determined not to betray how excited she felt at this sudden mark of favour and what it might lead to. Because she knew, too, that it could dissipate as ruthlessly as smoke once she had filed her Amanda story, faster and more completely if she didn't. Enjoy it now, she decided, adopting one of Nessa's most sacred beliefs.

'There is only now,' Nessa would say. 'Yesterday is gone, tomorrow doesn't exist. Even this evening doesn't exist' – she would pinch Laura's arm as she said it – 'so stop torturing your hair and live *this* moment. Life's gift to you, that you seem so determined to squander every time.' Laura had stopped listening to her after a while, too hemmed in by worry. And anyway, 'Look where living in the moment got Nessa,' she would mutter to Stella and Amanda. 'She's hardly Martha Stewart.'

'She doesn't want to be,' Amanda had responded. 'She's made her life work for her. She's happy.'

Now Laura supposed Amanda was right. Nessa had been happy, had lived intensely, even during the periods when all they'd had to eat were lentils and cooking apples. Even when she'd got sick, the way she'd had of being where she wanted to be hadn't entirely left her. Not until near the end anyway.

The onslaught of the disease had started at almost the same moment as Amanda had called time on her life, and Laura had always wondered what Nessa might have done had she had any idea of Amanda's destruction, if she had been more herself. She would have done something, Laura was sure, that none of the rest of them could do.

ᘓ

Huw Edsberg had seen no need to pretend to be what he wasn't, had never bothered hiding how fascinated he was by every type of squalor, as long it was human and degrading. His impeccable manners and charm, the floppy fringe and ability to turn laughter into a razor-sharp weapon, layered over a secret wantonness, seemed at first, to their untutored eyes, to be a pose, a deliberate tussling with debauchery. Except that with

Huw it was no pose but the real thing. He had wanted Amanda, from the minute he had set eyes on her at her party-lit house, and he had taken her, without apology or assurances. And she had gone willingly. Laura couldn't hate him as much as Stella did, although out of loyalty she tried. His veneer of mocking superiority was off-putting, but he wasn't stupid, could even be surprisingly appealing when he lost himself in fanciful speculation about the motives of some friend or media figure. Laura would never have admitted it to Stella, but sometimes she thought him . . . not kind, exactly, but considerate, when he was out of the line of Stella's scornful gaze.

'Huw's coming to live in Dublin. My mother will have to agree to let me move into my own place now,' Amanda had said to them, with satisfaction, just a couple of months after her twenty-first. In that time, she had visited him in London, where he had a job in an art gallery, four or five times, usually coming home white and exhausted.

'What do you do over there?' they had asked her, over a crowded, noisy lunch in the Brown Thomas restaurant, where Amanda was constantly interrupted by women who wanted 'just to say hi'.

'Go to parties, dinner, meet people. I've met a few who'll be really useful to my career. There's a woman who knows Mario Testino well, and thinks he might like to shoot me. Sometimes we stay in, just chatting, drinking, playing Scrabble. You should see his family's London house! It's unbelievable, one of those white four-storey houses in Knightsbridge that look a bit like tiered wedding cakes. And it's full of amazing things, paintings especially.'

'You don't do much eating, do you?' said Stella, looking at Amanda's skinny arms.

'No one does much eating except you two,' Amanda had replied affectionately, giving Stella a little shove and gesturing at her plate of pasta in a creamy chicken sauce.

'So why is Huw moving over? Surely he has a job in London,' Laura asked.

'He wants to be with me. And his job is really only a stopgap. He has other plans. But until I finish college and am ready to move, he says he doesn't mind living here. He can work on his thesis proposal. That way we'll both have stuff to do in the library. I think we should find somewhere near where you live, Laura, so we're close to college but not so much in town that we can't get home quickly for weekends.'

She had it all worked out, Laura could see, had made plans joyously, and painted herself a vision of a future that was full of light. Herself and Huw opposite each other in the library, each involved in their great work, going home to make dinner together, a few pints in the local, where they would be welcomed with affection, weekends in the country, a happier relationship with her parents . . .

'I thought your mother was dead set against you moving out.'

'She was. But that was before Huw.'

'Do they like Huw?'

'Of course they do! His father's family go back to William the Conqueror. He grew up in a house that makes ours look like a gate lodge, even if half of it is shut off and crumbling. He went to Eton and then Oxford. Trust me, they love Huw. Even if he was a dunce with a squint, they'd love him. Well, my mother would.' She laughed, because it seemed the perfect solution. 'I never thought she and I would see eye to eye on something like this. It's like he was created precisely for me. And me for him.'

None of them mentioned James. There was no point. Since the night of the party, he had withdrawn from their lives. He had never made a scene or confronted Amanda, although they'd heard he had said some sharp things to Huw. He had simply vacated the field and thrown himself into the postgraduate degree he was working on. Apparently he was considering transferring to a college in London where there were better research facilities. Laura presumed the decision was a recent one, taken in the light of losing Amanda, and had tried to sound Stella out on her feelings about it, but Stella had said only, 'I can't say I blame him. He'll find much better material there.'

So Huw had moved to Dublin, arriving with a small case of clothes and a proprietary attitude. Amanda was his, and he was determined to prove it. At the time, she was taking whatever modelling jobs her mother approved of, as long as they fitted in with her college hours, and sometimes if they didn't, when the job was high-profile enough.

'A week in Milan for MaxMara? I think so. You'll just have to fit your assignments around it.' Or 'Miss a couple of tutorials so you can shoot with Johnny Barrow? Well, he asked for you specifically, and he always makes you look wonderful. So, yes, I think so.' Mrs O'Hagen was in her element.

Amanda was content to be guided by her mother. It saved her from thinking too much. In fact, as far as Laura could see, her commitment to her career consisted entirely of turning up. She would be on time and polite. Beyond that, she seemed to have little need to pour herself into it.

'When the films start coming through, I'll have to work hard. But for now, the results are just the same whether I sit and think about shoes, or throw myself into it. So why not just sit and think about shoes?' She had shrugged, laughing a little.

It wasn't showing off: Laura could see she was being perfectly sincere. And she didn't seem filled with any urgency over the film career she sometimes mentioned as part of her future. So, Mrs O'Hagen was in sole charge of Amanda's direction. Until Huw arrived.

They moved into a pretty apartment on the second and third floors of a Georgian house on Lower Leeson Street. The windows were huge, and the original plasterwork still curled across the ceilings. There was a large drawing room and kitchen on the second floor, with a generous bedroom, bathroom and study upstairs. Highly polished wooden floors and some of Mrs O'Hagen's second-best furniture and rugs meant that the place was cosy and welcoming, with a lofty serenity born of antiquity. It became instantly a magnet for their ever-widening circle of friends.

Huw, who seemed to know people everywhere, had brought his own gang, some of whom would have been James's friends too, but many were odder, grander, often older. There was an American industrialist's son, gaunt, with flapping hands and yellow skin, who laughed wildly, then retreated into silences that lasted for hours. The son and daughter of an impoverished lord, who were very interested in exactly how Amanda's father had made his money and always wanted to know what everyone did and where they lived. There were a smattering of new-rich Irish – kids like Amanda, whose parents had seen economic change and seized the opportunities of upheaval. They drove nippy little cars and carried handbags that proclaimed their origin and price tag like a heraldic cry. Or a leper's bell, as Laura had one day said, watching a girl in head-to-toe Burberry wielding her enormous leather, padlocked satchel like a weapon.

The apartment was always full of people, drinking cocktails before nights out, sipping mugs of tea afterwards and chatting. Always chatting on phones or at each other. There was a nearly permanent spare bed pulled out of the sofa in the study, and always a body, sometimes two, under a heap of goose-down quilts.

Amanda seemed to thrive on it, or perhaps it was the constant presence of Huw. Even now that he was living with her, he seemed not to like her to be out of his sight. If she went to college, he came too, waiting in the library until she had finished her tutorials and lectures, sitting opposite her while she studied, his own heap of books in front of him – something to do with early Crusader art. 'God knows what he thinks he'll find on it in Trinity,' Stella had muttered to Laura.

'Let's go,' he would whisper.

'I can't. I need to finish this essay,' Amanda would whisper back.

'It can wait. I can't,' Huw would respond, with a wink. And Amanda would giggle, fold over her books and papers, and follow him.

Often they would disappear upstairs to bed in the middle of a party at their flat, or in the afternoon while people made cups of tea and chatted in the kitchen. Once Laura had gone upstairs to say goodbye to Amanda and walked into their bedroom before realising she shouldn't have. Amanda was against the wall, dress pulled up to her waist, one leg supported by Huw, while he thrust into her hard. It wasn't the act itself, or the embarrassment, so much as the look of ecstasy on Amanda's face that stunned Laura, then still too innocent to understand what love might be.

She withdrew before they spotted her, pulling the door

quietly behind her. Halfway down the stairs she realised what was bothering her more than the scene she had witnessed. It was the squalor of the bedroom. Clothes lay on the floor with shoes scattered between them, stepping stones from one heap to the next. There was a sour smell – dirty clothes, stale sex, sweat, overlaid with Amanda's musky perfume.

'When's the last time you saw Amanda without Huw?' Stella's question, a few days later, caught Laura by surprise, so that she had to think.

'Don't know. A few weeks? You?'

'Maybe once since he moved over, so it must be six months ago.'

'Right. And?'

'I think he does it on purpose.'

'Does what on purpose?'

'Keeps her away from us. Monitors all her meetings with us.'

'It's true that he's always there, but I thought that was just because they're so in love.'

'In love is one thing. Lots of people are in love. But never out of each other's company? That's something else. That's obsession.'

'*Egoisme à deux*,' said Laura thoughtfully.

'What?'

'Like a French film. Mutually exclusive solipsism.'

'She's always going on about how this is a great love, the world's *greatest* great love. But you can't have love without freedom, and he doesn't allow her to be free.'

It was the kind of thing Nessa would say, or Amanda herself, but in the abstract. It sounded strange, too heartfelt, coming from Stella.

'Let's invite her to dinner, just her. At yours, this weekend? He can't come if he's not invited, and then we'll get to see what's going on with her,' said Laura.

'Good plan.'

Amanda accepted, but turned up complaining of being exhausted. She was certainly in low spirits. Wan, with dark shadows under her eyes and a new habit of picking at her nails.

Stella's family kitchen was clean and minimalist, with chrome fittings and sharp black tiles of unpolished marble. There were so many hard, shiny surfaces that the three girls sitting round the table were reflected back at one another from myriad angles, like different versions of the truth. Stella and Laura were in jeans and T-shirts. Amanda wore jeans, too, but spray-tight navy, with a see-through snakeskin print shirt and absurdly high heels. She was thin enough, elegant enough, to stop the outfit looking hopelessly trampy, but only just.

'So what have you been up to? It feels like we never see you,' Stella said.

'You see me.' Amanda sounded defensive. 'We were all at Trap only last weekend.'

'We were. It was great. But we don't seem to get time to catch up much.' Laura, of course, was more placating.

'Life is very busy,' Amanda conceded.

'More than ever since Huw moved over,' Stella said, fishing.

'That's true. As well as college and work, there are so many things to go to with him. He's incredibly social,' Amanda said proudly. 'And he knows everyone. People want to know him.'

She was right about that. Huw was greeted with delight everywhere he went. The half of the city who weren't already somehow related to him jostled to get close. Hostesses scrabbled to invite him to parties and dinners, then crowed with joy if he showed up. The same hostesses could often be found, as dawn broke, wringing their hands and wondering how to get rid of him.

'But how is it living with him?' Stella was fishing again. 'Doesn't it ever get claustrophobic?' Laura could see she was still thinking about freedom and the price of love.

'Oh, it's wonderful!' Amanda lit up a little. 'Seeing him, being with him, every day, is just amazing. We're almost never apart. And when we are, I miss him immediately. I don't know how to live without him any more. Loving Huw makes the world shrink. It's all simple now. Everything difficult is gone. I know what I have to do. I have to make him happy, and then I can be happy with him. I don't know how I ever lived without him. We were made for each other.'

It was a variation of the same 'great cosmic love story' they had been hearing since Huw had come on the scene. Except that, looking at Amanda now, picking through her spaghetti carbonara and taking hefty slugs of vodka and tonic, anyone would have been forgiven for thinking that she was in the throes of a depression, rather than a glorious love song.

At ten precisely the doorbell rang. Laura had just suggested face packs and a film. It was Huw, looking pleased with himself. 'I've come for my prize,' he said, with one of his studiedly charming smiles.

'Huw offered to collect me. We have to go somewhere. I was just about to tell you,' Amanda said guiltily, pushing back her chair and going to kiss Huw. He kissed her back, one arm around her waist, the other hand tangled in her long hair.

'Where are you going?' Laura asked, trying to sound easy.

'A party given by someone Huw knows.'

'Another cousin? Or a new friend this time?' Stella asked sweetly.

'A friend. The Mould Boys Club.' Huw grinned.

'Mould Boys?' Amanda asked.

'Yes, the rot of the public-school system. Dropouts and never-will-bes.' Undoubtedly Huw's greatest charm – clearly his only charm, in Stella's eyes – was that he could turn the same lazy, teasing note with which he baited those around him on himself.

'We'll come too, if that's okay?' Stella said.

Laura looked at her in surprise. They had planned to stay in, were hardly dressed for a party and, anyway, Stella hated sudden social engagements. But Stella was looking fixedly at Huw.

'Of course,' he said politely, at last. 'I'm sure you'll be very welcome.'

'Great. We'll get changed. Give us five minutes and we'll be ready. Laura, I have exactly the dress for you.'

'Okay.' Laura was still bewildered.

'Amanda, come up and get ready with us. It'll be like the old days – Dargle's and parties in free gaffs.'

'Minus the layers of fake tan,' Amanda laughed, getting up.

But Huw caught her arm. 'You're already dressed. Stay here with me and tell me what you've been up to. I haven't seen you in hours,' he said, smiling.

With an awkward laugh, Amanda sat down again, rolling her eyes at the girls. 'Call me if you have any fashion crises.'

Stella and Laura bounded up the stairs and into Stella's bedroom, as clean and minimalist as the kitchen. Stella slid open the mirrored door of her wall-to-wall fitted wardrobe, and began riffling through the neat hangers.

'What are you doing? You don't want to go out,' Laura hissed at her.

'No, I don't, but *fuck* him. He just turns up here and bags her, like she's his property. You heard him. His "prize". That's exactly what he thinks of her – like he owns her. He hates her spending any time with us, in case we help her remember who she used to be before he took over.' Her words came out like cards being dealt across a table: slap, slap, slap.

'She's the same person.'

'No, she's not! She's half of herself, and the other half is made up of obsession, vacuous rubbish about love, and drugs. She's half-wasted already. Can't you tell?'

'I thought she just seemed a bit tired and off.'

'A bit tired, off and wasted. Check out her pupils – they're pinpricked.'

'Well, what are we going to do?' Laura tried to take the edge off Stella's fury, because she didn't fully understand it, and because she could see that Stella was working herself up into the kind of rage that, with her, required a showdown.

'I don't know, but he's not going to get away with it.'

'Okay, but remember that she likes it,' Laura warned. 'Whatever he's up to, she's happy with it. So don't fight with him. It's not worth it. And if you make too big a fuss, she won't have anywhere to bolt to if things do go badly with him.'

The party was in one of the big red-brick houses around Herbert Park, owned by a couple the girls vaguely recognised from the same social pages that so often carried Amanda's photo. He was English – something to do with finance, with the same slightly drawling tones as Huw – while she fronted a gallery that sold incomprehensible art. With a sheet of shiny black hair and cross cat-like features, she was like a slightly ruffled panther.

'Huw, how lovely.' She wrapped her arms around him. Her voice was clipped, as if her words were anxious to finish and stop drawing attention to themselves. 'And Amanda.' She was just as effusive in her greeting. Rather less so when she caught sight of Laura and Stella behind them. 'Do come in. Tom's in there somewhere.' She gestured to a huge room with a glittering chandelier and pale grey carpets. 'I'll take your coats.'

The guests were uniformly handsome, some recognisable from TV or stage ('More panto than Broadway,' hissed Stella), but struck the girls as dull. 'Too glossy, no grit. It's not going to be a party that takes off,' was Stella's verdict.

'Maybe they don't want it to,' Laura said.

There were a couple of models Amanda knew, and Tom's financier friends, whom Huw seemed keen on. Stella and Laura retired to the kitchen, which had a marble island and a cream Aga that looked as though no one had ever used it. They ate pretzels and olives, and chatted with a couple of scruffy but decent guys, who turned out to be friends of their hostess's brother. 'Glen told us there would be models,' one said wistfully.

'He didn't warn us the models wouldn't speak to us,' the other added sadly.

Inside, the music had been turned up – bad techno, they decided – and people seemed to be dancing. 'More like pole dancing,' Stella quipped, watching a girl who pulled numbers out of a plastic ball after the news on a Saturday night, now wearing a silver dress and sliding herself up and down a tall, awkward-looking guy. Amanda came into the kitchen, staggering slightly, and said, 'Having fun?' to Stella and Laura.

She was slurring and the hand that held her vodka glass wasn't quite steady. She stumbled out again.

'Beautiful girl. Shame about the fella,' said one of the scruffy guys, whose name could have been Dermot.

'Isn't he the pits?' Stella agreed warmly.

'Stella …' Laura said warningly.

'Rotten,' agreed the one who might have been Dermot. 'Arrogant, ignorant toff. He's a lord or something, yeah?'

'Not quite,' Stella said. 'But generations of upper-class inbreeding and an ever-increasing sense of entitlement anyway.'

Just then there was a crash, audible over the music, followed by a shriek. Laura went to have a look. 'Stel,' she stuck her head back into the kitchen, 'come with me. Amanda's broken something.'

The something was a large crystal owl – Laura could still see its round amber eyes, staring up from a heap of shattered sparkle – and a bottle, both knocked from the mantelpiece and smashed on the hearth below. A puddle of red wine was sinking into the pale grey carpet. Shards of glass and crystal were scattered in small glittering heaps and their hostess was on her hands and knees, with a bunch of paper napkins, shrieking for tea towels, while various guests suggested remedies.

'Salt,' said one.

'Not salt, white wine,' said another.

'Just water, lots of water,' a third proposed.

Amanda just stood there, an unfocused look on her face, swaying. Huw was still on the other side of the room with the beefy financiers.

'You could help,' their hostess snapped at Amanda.

Amanda looked surprised. 'What would you like me to do?'

'Get a cloth. Do fucking something.'

Amanda was clearly infuriating her. Someone sniggered. Amanda stayed where she was, but Laura ran back to the kitchen, promising to bring a bucket of water and lots of cloths. But when she saw Stella walking over to Huw, she abandoned the clean-up effort and followed her. 'I think Amanda should go home now,' Stella said quietly.

Huw barely glanced in her direction but shrugged her hand off his arm as if it burnt. 'She's fine,' he said curtly.

'She's not. She needs to go. We'll take her. We're going now anyway, aren't we, Laura?'

Laura nodded.

'No. She stays. She's fine,' Huw said.

'Huw, don't be an arsehole. Look at her.'

They all turned towards Amanda, who was holding on to the mantelpiece, looking down at their hostess, mopping at the stain, now a dirty brown, like old blood. She was still swaying, and one of her knees was twitching spasmodically. To Laura, she looked forlorn, unmoored.

'See? Absolutely fine,' said Huw. 'She won't go with you anyway. Try if you want.' He turned back to the group, brushed off Tom's suggestion that perhaps Amanda would be happier going somewhere quieter, old chap, and homed in on the chubby, pasty-faced man around whom the group had arranged themselves. 'You were saying?'

Stella, clearly dismissed, looked, Laura thought, as if she was considering kicking him in the back of the knee, but instead she walked over to Amanda. 'Do you want to go?' she asked her.

Amanda blinked at her. 'Is it time? Is Huw going?'

'Not yet, but you could come back with me and Laura. Come back to mine and stay the night.'

'It's okay. I'll wait for Huw.'

'Come back.' Laura held her hand out to Amanda. Then, when Amanda mutely shook her head, she gave up and joined their hostess in the clean-up.

Stella tried again, for several minutes, but got nowhere, so went to find Laura, who had disappeared. She found her rinsing the bucket in the sink while their hostess thanked her warmly. The party had fallen back into its lines around them. People were dancing, chatting, drinking, flirting. 'I want to go,' Stella told Laura.

'God, so do I,' Laura muttered. 'Our hostess is scary when she's being nice. But what about Amanda?'

'Amanda will be fine. Even pissed like that, she's never short of someone to talk to.'

Sure enough, the guy who could have been Dermot and his friend were chatting to her, and Amanda was laughing, although still with a faintly dazed look on her face.

'Forget it, let's go. I've had enough,' Stella said.

〇ℬ

Later they heard from Dell, who was naturally delighted with her scoop, that Huw had left shortly after them, with the finance guys, for another party. He'd promised to come back for Amanda, whom he refused to take with him on the basis that she 'wasn't up to it'. So Amanda had stayed, and Huw didn't come back. Eventually she was put to bed in the spare room, because it was either that, apparently, or accompany her in a taxi to her flat because she was unable to speak coherently or stand. Huw reappeared the next day after lunch, which for him was still part of the night out, by which time Amanda had wet the spare bed.

'Rubbish. Who told you that?' Laura asked.

'Huw.'

'Huw?' Laura was appalled.

'Yes, Huw. He thought it was too funny. So did I. Imagine Amanda.'

Imagine indeed. At first unthinkable, the idea quickly became just another possibility, one that came with a little shrug that meant 'Why not?'

Modelling work dried up for Amanda as her impatience and unpredictability grew – 'She can't hold an expression any more,' one of her model friends told them with mock concern. 'She's just blank. Not good blank either.' Clearly, thinking about shoes wasn't working. But then Amanda's film career began to take off. Huw hadn't lied when he said he 'knew people'; the fact that they made dingy arthouse films on low budgets about strip joints and drug addicts and teenage runaways didn't matter to Amanda or Mrs O'Hagen, because the writers and directors were on the fringes of a more expansive world. People 'with a future', as Mrs O'Hagen put it, who knew people with a present. The fact that Amanda was increasingly cast within a very narrow stratum – the self-destructive neurotic, the beautiful-but-damned, innocence corrupted – didn't seem to bother them. The films were short and ostentatiously lacking in any point that Stella or Laura could make out. There would be long shots of Amanda's thin arms wrapped around her thin knees, her golden hair tumbled over her face, eyes haunted, then maybe a close-up of a scattered pouch of tobacco, the twisted strands apparently providing enough metaphor to sustain the shot.

She didn't get paid for these films, but she had no immediate need of money, and the hours weren't hard – on one shoot practically the entire cast plus the director moved into the flat she and Huw shared and seemed to film only interiors, hastily assembled scenes that depended on who was awake and how fit they were for speaking parts. Messy as they were, some of the films went to festivals, where they were described as 'hard-hitting' and 'a sombre reflection of youthful nihilism'.

Amanda began to acquire a niche following in France, where she was described as being possessed of '*un magnétisme provocant*'. That was after one short film that seemed to consist entirely of her in a pair of flesh-coloured knickers, ugly bruises evident on her thighs. There were rumours that Gus Van Sant had seen her in something and wanted to screen-test her, the suggestion of a small part in a big ensemble film about Paris fashion week. Her mood changed: she was 'done', she said, with Dublin. Couldn't wait to get out, get away, although she didn't know where, and get started, although she didn't explain on what.

The flat where Amanda and Huw lived changed too. Neither Stella nor Laura much liked going there. The gang who cluttered it were a more dismal bunch now. The chat was less, the cups of tea, drunk silently, contained more sugar, no one opened the windows, cooked anything beyond toast, or cleaned up much.

ᘓ

'Just the two I was looking for.' Amanda was in full charm mode. 'Can I bend you to my will?' Despite the black rings under her eyes, she was irresistible. 'Come back with me quickly while I get money.'

Amanda had come late into college – increasingly she didn't show up at all. When her phone beeped, she announced that she had to leave immediately. 'I have a hair appointment. I'd forgotten about it.'

Mrs O'Hagen still made regular appointments with the support cast of beauticians, hair stylists and manicurists who attended to the details of Amanda's appearance. 'I've missed so many lately, I'd better go.' Clearly, she had. The surface gleamed rather less than of old: there was the shadow of a spot on her chin, and her nails were a mess. The habit of picking at them had intensified, so that the cuticles were now ragged and chewed, and there was an inch of dark roots in the golden hair. The usually smooth aura of perfection was fuzzy and ragged at the edges, as if static had built up around it.

'Okay.' Laura was in a glow of virtue having attended all her early-morning lectures that week. Without so much of Amanda in their lives, she and Stella had found that they had quite naturally moderated their going out. Stella, she knew, was bothered by the idea that, without Amanda and the sandstorm constantly playing about her, they were both a bit ordinary. Laura didn't mind that. Sensible, she said to herself firmly, focused. And when Stella voiced her nagging suspicion that theirs was a borrowed glory, she said, 'No. It's just that we know where to draw the line, and that there's a time for being a bit focused on something other than the next night out.'

Stella had laughed wryly and said, 'I suspect it's exactly that which makes us a bit ordinary.'

'I'll come too,' Stella said now. 'We can walk you to the salon, pick up lunch and eat it by the canal when you're done.'

It was one of those warm early-spring days that come in ones and twos, and guarantee nothing. Laura had long learned to grab them.

They walked slowly to the flat, chatting about work, friends, their parents. 'Nessa isn't well,' Laura confided. 'She's having tests. We don't know anything yet, but she's certain it's cancer. She says she can feel a knot of malevolence inside her. But she also says she can disperse the knot with light from her mind, and starve it by eating only the things it shrinks from, like vegetables and Aztec seeds.' She paused, trying to keep the irritation out of her voice. 'I'm going to wait and see what the doctors say before joining in any of that. It might be nothing.'

'Laura!' Stella was horrified. 'Why didn't you say anything?'

'There wasn't much to say. There still isn't. We don't know anything. It's because we're here together, just the three of us, and haven't been in ages, that I thought I'd tell you.'

Amanda gasped. There were tears in her eyes. 'Oh, no, Laura. I'm so sorry.'

'It's probably nothing. A cyst, or just a lump – nothing serious.'

'This is my fault,' Amanda said.

'How could it be your fault?'

'It just is.'

'Amanda, you're nuts. This is nothing to do with you.' Stella was clearly furious, seeing only Amanda's need to be centre stage, the focus of every drama.

Laura, who better understood the kind of psyche behind such histrionics, said, 'If it is, then Nessa's nuts too. She didn't have to accept the malevolence.'

'What are you *talking* about?' Stella was suddenly raging at both of them. 'Cancer is a *disease*, in which cells divide and grow wildly. You get it because you're unlucky, or because you have a history of it in your family, or because you smoke and drink too much and eat crap. You don't get it because somebody else did something they shouldn't. Nessa isn't sick because of what you've been up to, Amanda, whatever that is. Anyway, it's probably nothing,' she added, seeing Laura's stricken face.

'She'll be fine. Nessa is as tough as an old boot under all the floating scarves and whimsical fragility.'

'But under the toughness, she's actually very fragile,' said Laura.

They reached Amanda's flat. From less than halfway up the stairs, they could smell cigarettes and something sweaty, mixed with the rankness of stale milk. Inside, the place was in semi-darkness but with enough dingy light to let them see that it was really filthy. All the times Amanda had groaned recently and said, 'The flat is a tip,' she had been understating the reality. The high ceilings, which once seemed to echo benignly above, now looked as though they had reared back in alarm from the squalor. There were lumpy heaps, whether of clothes or people the girls weren't sure, dotted around the room. There were definitely two bodies on the sofa, asleep or just unmoving. Along the windowsill the plants were in various stages of extremis, which was unfair, thought Laura, because the windows gave plenty of light. She went for a jug of water, refusing to allow the sinkful of greasy plates to put her off. It was certainly a source of the nasty smell that hung in the air, but not the only source.

Amanda was looking impatiently around.

'Where's Huw?' Laura asked.

'Probably still asleep.' Amanda was bent over one of the silent bodies, tugging something from underneath it.

'So what do this lot do,' Stella asked, 'when they're not asleep on your sofa?'

'Make films. Smoke heroin.'

'Right.' Stella smiled, expecting an answering grin from Amanda. Nothing came. 'You're not serious?'

'Yes.' Amanda shrugged. 'They're friends of Huw's from

London. It's much bigger over there with artists and creatives. It's no big deal. Apparently the heroin helps them think. But it makes them rotten house guests. They get up at weird hours and are always disappearing off at strange times to find all-night shops and to score. They eat too much chocolate, and leave heaps of it lying around, which is very tempting. Actually,' she walked over to the girls, who had moved closer together in astonishment at the revelations, 'I wish they'd leave. They've been here for ages now. They're starting to get on Huw's nerves. He says it's like being back at school, having them around all the time, except without early-morning chapel.' She went back to looking for whatever it was that was buried under the bodies.

'Does Huw do it?' This was Stella.

'A bit. Mostly when these guys are over. Or when he's bored. He says it helps him get over the fact that life has so many humdrum moments. Like Sunday lunch with my parents,' she said, half-laughing.

'He goes to lunch with your parents stoned?'

'Stel, we've all been to lunch with my parents stoned. It's the best way.'

'Not on heroin. A few joints maybe …'

'There's no real difference,' said Amanda. 'Except that Huw says heroin helps him understand paintings better, turns his mind on to the layers of symbolism that all great painters have in their work. He says there are far, far more than most critics realise, and he can spot them when he's high.'

Stella had admitted that, when it came to art, Huw was indeed as bright as James had said. He could talk about painters and paintings in a way none of them could. As if they were alive, spoke to him, confided in him. He could draw parallels and make connections that were spellbindingly brilliant, even if, in his eyes, it was unusual for him to find anyone worth the effort of conversation. Iseult, James's mother, could get him talking, keep him interested with her own interjections and insights, untutored but psychologically clever. A tall older man called Charles, who wrote painstaking biographies of minor, madcap historical figures and was a constant house guest at great estates around the country, had also provoked brilliant discourse in Huw through intelligent questioning. So if getting stoned on heroin helped the flow of ideas, maybe they were ignorant and bourgeois to dismiss it. Or maybe not, Laura decided.

'And you? What about you?' she asked.

'Oh, I've tried it,' Amanda said. 'I'm not really sure it's for me. Frankly, it's the chocolate they keep buying that I have trouble staying away from. All those Dairy Milks ... Anyway, I don't have any creative insights when I'm that stoned. It doesn't make me think, like it does Huw. It just makes me forget.'

Chapter Nine

New York

IT DOESN'T MAKE ME THINK ... IT JUST MAKES me forget.

Why, Stella wondered now, had that remark of Amanda's not rung more alarm bells? Why had she and Laura just let it go? She guessed now that she had been so relieved that Amanda had shown little enthusiasm for the drug that she hadn't looked further. But what about Laura? She was supposed to be the one with intuition, Stella thought. Surely she should have heard a warning.

After all, they knew Amanda had demons. There were the nightmares she woke from, sweating, a violent need to obliterate the residue of thoughts, a knot in the smooth grain of her mind that produced the kind of recklessness that had led to the first overdose. They all drank, often too much, and took drugs, because sometimes it was easier to be drunk or high than to be uncertain, hopeful, horny. Being simply 'drunk' or 'wasted' took the nuances out of whatever you did and drew attention away from it. When you didn't know how, or couldn't be bothered, to give a good account of yourself, 'drunk' could be relied on to take over, an acceptable understudy. They all did it, used it, at times. But Amanda was always different, greedier, more determined to go recklessly from fun into oblivion. And when she did, when she blanked out and had to be filled in the next day on the things that had happened, instead of being embarrassed or scared or repentant, she threw it off with a laugh, or affected a grim satisfaction: 'A hangover and a few lost hours seems a small price to pay for not having to listen to most people. They're so boring' was one line Stella remembered her delivering, when she had surfaced after a particularly messy night. And Stella had laughed, because it was funny, and easier than working out what else to do.

Now she grabbed a pristine notepad and pen from her desk. Time for the meeting with Sean, at which she must listen, nod, offer brief opinions and cool analyses, forget that she had ever seen him naked, ground against him in violent need for far more than he could give.

She checked her face in the mirror. Her hair was perfect, her eyes, despite the lack of sleep, shone. She was impeccable. Why did she always look the same, she wondered, despite the internal ravages of her lifestyle or emotional life? It was a strength, no doubt, but a curse too. No one would ever love her for her vulnerability.

'Sit down, Stella.' Sean waved at a black leather seat opposite him, across the heavy, polished dark-wood boardroom table. Outside, the windows of the skyscraper opposite were tinted blue. To one side of him Maxine, his steely assistant, would say nothing but hear and recall everything, and to the other Barrington Fraser, another senior partner with whom Stella had so far had little contact. Pudgy, with beautifully manicured hands and a watch slim enough to be a woman's around his thick wrist, his well-cut suit hinted at shapeless horrors beneath. She was surprised not to see more people. Sean generally summoned a full house. He liked to feel the energy of the firm harnessed to his will, a team of associates quivering on their marks, awaiting his signal.

'This is complicated.' He twitched at a thread hanging from his cuff, not because there was a thread, but out of habit. 'It can't ever go further than the people in this room. No one else in the firm has buy-in. You understand?' Sean was in full Master of the Universe mode.

Stella nodded, keeping enough eye contact to seem engaged, professional. While she had to work hard to keep the intimacy of their private moments from spilling into the office, she had the impression that once he was through the plate-glass doors every morning, he didn't associate her with the wanton, demanding lover of his later hours. Maybe her own bisection of self was so good that she made it too easy for him.

'This is a quiet case. Wrongful dismissal. Could get messy.'

Stella was silent. This was far outside her experience. From the start she had worked on major litigations and mergers, having shown herself to have a mind of abacus-like clarity when it came to document review, able to fish out the one pertinent piece of information from a mass of irrelevancies. 'We're handling it for Carter Armstrong.'

'But he's —'

'Yes, Carter Armstrong of Morgan Brown.'

'Our rivals?'

'Exactly. They can't deal with it in-house. They need distance, and have no expertise in this field.'

'I'm not sure I do either. I haven't done employment law since university.' She forced herself to say university, even though 'school' was what wanted to slip out. She tried to curb the steady inward drip of Americanisms because she knew Sean liked her for her Irishness, her difference. Sure enough, his blue eyes crinkled slightly.

'We're doing it as a favour to Carter. He may be working with the wrong guys, but he's a friend.' Of course he was, thought Stella. Same preppy, privileged upbringing, same army of Latino house staff, same impossible-to-get-into pre-kindergarten that pretty much guaranteed entry into an Ivy League university fifteen years later. She had never met Carter, never even seen him, but the name was enough. And Sean's description of him as 'a friend'. He reserved that for the guys from his college fraternity, and the thugs down at the boxing gym. 'You can handle it,' Sean promised. 'An associate with a grudge, trying to make trouble. They want it to go away, but not if that means paying out. They say she's crazy and has no case, just couldn't take the pace of life in the fast lane.'

So it's a she, thought Stella. Okay. One of the many sucked into the funnel system that big law operated, vacuuming up the best and brightest graduates every single year, working them to shades, then spitting them out gradually in ones, twos and threes, until only those with the capacity to endure, to grind forward, despite exhaustion and the mounting anxiety that affected every aspect of their lives, whether it was decisions about grocery shopping or relationships, were left. From that battle-scarred pool, a few more fought their way out and into the upper echelons, to the rarefied land of senior partners, where the thick carpets and sound-proofed doors disguised the hollow rattle of reality. She understood that hollowness. And she still wanted it. What she didn't know was why. Barrington Fraser still hadn't said a word.

'Okay, but why me?' she asked. 'Why not ask Naomi?' Naomi had joined Davies Darn and Slate at the same time as Stella, had shown the same intelligence and ambition, plus a similar kind of physical magnetism. But Naomi had had two babies in three years and, instead of coming back to work at the usual pace, had permanently sidelined herself by asking to leave at five o'clock every day and taking days off when one of the babies was sick. These days, she managed the interns and handled small, relatively unimportant pieces of litigation from an office half the size of Stella's on the floor below.

'I'd like you to do it.' Sean paused, waiting for Stella to drop her eyes. When she did, he continued smoothly, 'It shouldn't take much time. This is Mickey Mouse, I'm telling you. This shouldn't knock the Sato litigation off course. Which reminds me, I have to go back to Tokyo at the end of the week. I might need you to come with me.'

Just forty-eight hours earlier Stella would have met his gaze calmly and said, 'Certainly.' Inside, she would have been dancing with glee, knowing that they would be able to travel on the same flight – she wasn't a partner, so they were allowed to fly together: the firm would never jeopardise itself by putting too much expertise into the same potential danger. She would have been anticipating evenings spent openly in restaurants, legitimate colleagues in an anonymous city. Nights in the vast eroticism of a bland but luxurious hotel suite, proving again and again that there was no such thing as enough for either of them. She would have been planning a shopping trip just for lingerie, already debating between the demure sexiness of peach and lace, or the all-out raunch of ink-black satin, knowing that, lithe, young and supple as she was, she could wear either to effect. Blast Amanda, she thought yet again.

'I have personal business back home. I may need to be away until Monday.'

There was a heavy silence, full of conjecture and studied disapproval. Associates in Davies Darn and Slate didn't have private lives. Not that they brought to the office, anyway. Not if they wanted to get on.

Her years of dedication stood to Stella. The fact that she had never taken a sick day or come in late, had rarely left while there was daylight outside, had never faltered with a crucial piece of information. She could see Maxine playing all this through her mind. She nodded almost imperceptibly. Sean nodded coolly, Barrington Fraser heavily.

'I wouldn't if it wasn't important,' she said, secretly furious with herself for not remaining silent and toughing it out.

Sean nodded again. 'Okay. We'll catch up when I'm back.'

Did that mean she wouldn't see him before he left? she wondered wildly. Or was this just for show, for public consumption?

'I'll have the Morgan Brown files delivered to your office.'

She was dismissed. She left, well aware that her strange defection, short-term as it was, would be the subject of discussion as soon as the door closed. Barrington Fraser was following her with his paunchy grey eyes, two slugs out for a slow but purposeful walk.

☙

The files were delivered, just two boxes. Emails, employee evaluations, notes of meetings, internal memos. Stella felt giddy at the lightness of the paper load. She was going to enjoy this. She didn't like people who mistook what they were getting into, then made it someone else's problem. She would do a brilliant, subtle job of dismantling this case, and Sean would be impressed.

Stella's cleverness at document review wasn't just that she had a nimble mind and an accurate memory. It was her ability to string a story out of the most unpromising material, to see where bits of a jigsaw fitted together, and the way in which minute pieces of blue, put together, would form sky or sea or something coherent. She could read, remember, and create a story out of long, dreary streams of factual material. Nothing, she had discovered, was entirely impersonal, and it was this that allowed her to recall the vital missing component when others couldn't. Buried beneath the business decisions, the unfortunate mistakes and *force majeure* of the international markets, there was always something human. A hint of exhaustion, an error of judgement, the ghostly shadow of a disrupted night with a small baby, an emotional trace that could be felt more than seen, which made her fingers twitch almost before her mind had registered it, and pulled the swamp of information into focus.

As she began to put together the story told by the files on Sarah Travers, the woman who was claiming wrongful dismissal, and her life with Morgan Brown, Stella found herself searching for the kernel that would explain the woman to her. Once she had done that, Travers could be processed and neutralised, but not until.

To Stella's relief, Sean texted 'Dinner Sheng Wang 9' before she had finished for the evening, so she didn't have to contemplate another night alone.

Sheng Wang's was noisy and small, with cheap tables and plastic chairs. The food was good but not outstanding. They were never likely to meet anyone from Sean's world there, slumming it for the sake of 'the best Chinese in the city', or anyone from the firm. They sat close together, and even before Stella had finished her Chow Zhou chicken with steamed broccoli, her arm was pressed hard against Sean's and his hand was on her thigh, inching between her crossed legs.

'What's the personal business?' he asked.

Usually, they talked about work. They didn't have much else. No common ground to explore together, no shared interests to be nurtured into something intimate, no social life to gossip over. Plus Stella suspected that he approved of work-talk, because it made him feel he was still on billable time. But she had known he would move outside that this time. She had wondered how much to tell him. He knew almost nothing about her beyond the moments in which they were together, except that she was an only child, her father was a lawyer, and she had been the smartest in her class at the subjects that were important to her. This, she felt sure, matched his image of her – straightforward, ambitious, alpha-in-the-making. He knew nothing of the lost nights, the unarticulated yearnings, the dreams of doing good in the world that she had ditched. She had told him about her early interest in human rights, but as if it were a childish fancy, rather than something lost to her because she hadn't the energy to pursue it and had instead chosen to bury herself in the best-paid job she could find. Youthful radicalism, she knew, he would understand, even approve of. It was okay to have been a 'goddam Commie' as a kid, just as long as you faced up to the real stuff when it came along.

'It's a friend who's in trouble.'

'She must be a close friend.'

'I guess she is. It's hard to say. I haven't seen her in a while, but there's a lot of history there.'

Would he ask for details? Would she tell him? They didn't have intimate conversations. They had fenced off the place where they met, and neither ever stepped outside that arena. But could they?

'She's a friend from school. Amanda O'Hagen.' She wondered if the name would mean anything to him. It didn't. Tory, his wife, might have stirred a little, cast her mind down the track of memory to retrieve whatever quivered slightly in response, but Sean just nodded. 'There were three of us who used to hang out,' Stella said, 'always together, but things went wrong. For all of us, I suppose. But mostly for Amanda.'

'She lost her job? Money?' He picked at his teeth with a hollow plastic toothpick, reached across her to pick up the remains of the chicken dish she hadn't eaten, and skewered a piece.

'No. Much more than that.' How to put into words the growing sense she had that whatever curse had been laid on Amanda applied to herself and maybe to Laura too. Sean looked at her, with enough of a smile to show those dazzling white teeth, eyes crinkling at the corners. 'Tell me. Do you believe in loyalty?' she asked him.

'Sure.' He stopped eating.

'Even if being loyal stops you being other things? Stops you seeing things you should see? What I mean is, can loyalty sometimes be the easy way out? The thing you can use to avoid making difficult decisions?' She wondered why she was asking him. Because he was there, she supposed. Because she had to ask someone.

'There's a thing called blind loyalty,' Sean said. 'That's where it gets dumb.'

'So there is a limit to it? Or should be?'

'Of course. Anything that gets in your way that much isn't worth sticking with. You gotta know when being loyal makes you stupid.'

'But are you sure? What if that's not right? What if you're meant to choose a path and stick with it, whatever happens?'

He waved a dismissive hand. 'No. When it's not in your interests any more, you drop it.'

'Okay. Well, what about sticking by someone when they're in trouble? If the trouble is their own fault, you've bailed them out a thousand times before and that one time you can't face doing it again? And you think they'll be fine, so you just walk away, and they aren't fine?' Her words were coming in a rush and she knew she wasn't being at all clear. Sure enough, he looked momentarily confused, then bored.

'Let's go.' He leaned forward, interest lost. 'I want to fuck you right now.'

They went, Stella dropping the thread of her story abruptly. Inside her apartment, Sean picked her up and made straight for the bedroom. He threw her onto the bed, pushed her skirt up to her waist, exposing her lilac silk knickers, then dropped his own trousers, already straining at the crotch, and entered her, thrusting hard. 'We'll do it better in a minute,' he said, when he caught his breath. 'I just love that you still make me feel I need you so bad I can't wait.'

Stella wondered then why she had tried to draw him further

into her life, when he so clearly could not be drawn. She wasn't dishonest enough to pretend that there was much more to her own feelings for him than the way he smelt, the way he held her, hard. The way he made her feel that any disgrace was worth the risk. But maybe there could be, she had thought. Maybe if he knew her, knew her life, there might be real depth to the passion between them.

'Do you want a drink?' she asked afterwards.

'I'll have a whiskey. Can't stay, though. Tory will be expecting me.' He put on the few clothes he had taken off and Stella threw on an old silk shirt of his, left behind one night after some fancy dinner when he had buzzed her, swaying and dishevelled, very late, because he 'wanted some hot Irish ass'.

She poured him a whiskey, two ice cubes, and a glass of white wine for herself, and they sat beside each other on the sofa. On her own, she didn't much bother with booze during the week. Exercise was a far more reliable buzz. But Sean liked her to have something: 'I'm not gonna sit here and drink on my own like some dumb alco fuck,' was how he put it.

They discussed the Morgan Brown case. 'I don't get it yet,' said Stella. 'There's nothing in any of the documents to explain why she would go off on one like that. No build-up. And I don't see why they wouldn't just pay her a reasonable sum and let her go satisfied. I just don't get it.'

'You don't need to get it. Just get rid of it. Make it go away. Send her back to fucking Bridgeport, or wherever she came from, and you can go back to the real work.'

'I wish I was coming to Tokyo with you.' Stella changed the subject, because she wanted to see if it was possible to draw him towards intimacy, to offer him a view of her interior life and see if he would take to it.

He put down his glass – a heavy crystal tumbler that Stella had bought for his whiskey on one of her weekend flea market visits. 'I gotta go. It's late. Never mind about Tokyo. We'll have other trips. Come here.' He reached a hand across, grabbed hers and pulled her towards him, wrapping her in the hard circle of his arms. 'We're good, right, you and me?' he said, his cheek crushed against the side of her head.

'We're good,' she mumbled. They were good. Sean, more than anyone, made her live in the precise moment of their meeting. Forced her to, so that she neither looked ahead nor referenced the past, because there was never time. She could hear his heart beating steadily, then his breath quickening as his hand moved beneath the white silk of her shirt, reaching her breast, rubbing against it, hard, with the flat of his palm. His other hand reached behind to cup her ass, while Stella bent to kiss him, unzipped his trousers again, and climbed on top of him, moving smoothly.

'Does no one ever notice you going home looking such a mess?' she asked later, laughing, as he yet again rearranged his clothes.

'No one bothers to look at me the way you do,' he replied, with a grin.

Stella knew it wasn't true, that he was observed carefully by dozens of people, for dozens of different reasons, but she liked that he had said it.

After he left, she returned to the papers she had brought home with her, looking again for the clue that would reveal the heartbeat of the Sarah Travers case. She read dozens of emails from and to her – neat, professional, curt even. The emails were largely requests for things she needed – particular files, travel details – or confirmation of things she knew that others wanted spelled out. She seemed efficient, clipped. Until one, sent at 3.11 p.m. on a Friday afternoon to Carter Armstrong, in which she added, at the end of a paragraph detailing progress on a case, the line 'It won't happen again.'

What wouldn't happen again? Had she broken down in tears of exhaustion during a meeting? She wouldn't be the first. Thrown a coffee cup at another associate, in a frustrated rage? Again, not unheard-of behaviour. Arrived late to the office? Worn flat shoes or a dowdy jacket? Forgotten a vital detail or file? It could have been any one of a hundred things that transgressed the unwritten but adamantine code of behaviour for ambitious associates, but it was, at last, the chink Stella had been looking for. The place where the thread snagged and could be unravelled. All she had to do was pull gently.

Chapter Ten

Dublin

LAURA TIPPED HER SCRAMBLED EGGS ONTO THE
toast, and grabbed the first plate that came to hand – an ugly
white one that Nessa would never have permitted in the house.
Some friend had brought it round as part of the sympathetic
meals-on-wheels service they had operated in the months after
Nessa's death, so Laura wouldn't have to cook, and she had
never got round to returning it. She didn't bother dusting the
eggs with a tiny pinch of cayenne pepper, or chopped chives,
as Nessa would have, simply plonked the plate on her knees on
the sofa in front of the TV. She was conscious of how inelegant
the whole thing was. Soon she would need to start packing for
the next day's trip to London. What kind of clothes to bring?

What on earth would they find there? Would they even be able to get into the house? Via Mrs O'Hagen, she had spoken to the police inspector at the local station in London, who said they had sufficient grounds to consider a forced entry. So, yes, she supposed they would get in.

She wasn't watching television, didn't much, but she couldn't bear the solitude of the kitchen, which had been the scene of so many intimacies between her and Nessa. The kitchen was where they talked, preparing meals – Nessa carefully chopping ginger or garlic, pounding turmeric or coriander seeds with the pestle in the black slate mortar Laura had given her for Christmas one year, bought on holiday in Morocco and brought back bundled in her clothes. With the table between them, the buffer of food and each dish's deadline, they could talk with ease about school, love, Laura's plans, Nessa's many money problems – 'I'm not going to let them get me down,' Nessa would say resolutely. 'There is always money. Somebody always has it. It's just a question of finding who, then figuring out what they will part with it for.' It was an attitude that Laura deplored because it meant they never had quite enough, and never knew where their next funds might come from, but she had to admit that her mother was right. There had always been money somehow, available from somewhere. 'The pursuit of money is perfectly respectable,' Nessa would say, 'as long as that is what really inspires you. But talking about it, scheming over it, lamenting the lack of it – never!'

Nessa might have given up painting and drawing herself, but she had a remarkable eye, could spot the one good piece in a room full of bric-à-brac and trinkets, and had a genuine love of haggling – could tussle amiably over a couple of quid until the owner not only agreed to her offer but thanked her profusely for the experience – that meant she made a living as an occasional art dealer, which was curtailed far more by her own lackadaisical attitude to it than by any external resistance. Laura sometimes wished she would just knuckle down and get rich by turning over simple pieces – landscapes, watercolours of fruit – with huge mark-ups to people too rich or stupid to care that they could have got them cheaper. But, no, Nessa bought only what she loved, and sometimes couldn't bring herself to part with it, even when she found a buyer. Like the sketch of the two haggard men by a wintry roadside that she had unearthed at a flea market in Paris one weekend. 'Flemish, eighteenth century,' she had said happily. 'Look how ragged and hungry they look, but still so crafty around the eyes.'

Laura, looking now at the sketch, hanging on the wall opposite her, recalled sadly the intensity with which Nessa did everything. The vital way in which she had gone about her life, almost to the end. Yet what had she left behind? A grieving daughter, a handful of bits and pieces, some decent. Nothing much. Not even a very strong impression on the minds of those who had known her, but maybe that was their fault, not hers.

If Laura knew anything, it was that she didn't want to die in the way Nessa had. She thought again, angrily now, of all Nessa's clever aphorisms, her little sayings and scraps of wisdom, the maxims of Truth, Art and Beauty by which she had lived her life, and how badly they had let her down in the end. Dying poor and overlooked, a public patient in a busy, overcrowded hospital where only a certain basic decency, it seemed to Laura, had prevented her from being ignored by the medical staff. Their decency meant she was fed, her few and reasonable requests attended to, but no one, Laura knew instinctively, busied themselves much about her survival. In that final analysis, on the third floor of a hospital where need would always outweigh what it was possible to get or be given, everything that Nessa held dear had been shown to her daughter as useless because she had died.

'If she was right about any of that stuff, she would still be here,' Laura had said to Stella, in the days after Nessa's death, when Stella had flown in from New York, arriving rigid with stress because she was in the middle of a big litigation and couldn't really spare the time, but knowing that Laura needed her. 'About the life of the mind and living on your own terms and all that. But she was wrong, so she's dead.'

'That's not the way it goes,' Stella had tried saying. 'It's not a competition, with life as the prize for the victor, and death for the losers. Plenty of horrible people live and good ones die. God, or Something, might sort us out after we die, but no one comes along and does it while we're still alive. Life isn't a reward for having the right beliefs.' But Laura had refused to be comforted.

'If Nessa was right, she'd be here,' she insisted stubbornly. 'Can you imagine Mrs O'Hagen dying like that?' Stella had to admit that she couldn't. 'She would have fought every step of the way, got the best doctors and consultants and surgeons from across the world to defy the cancer, no matter how far advanced, and she would have lived. Nessa just let it happen. She resigned herself and tried to be gracious because that was what she believed in. She thanked the doctors and nurses for doing the slightest thing for her, even though they did as little as possible.' Laura's voice broke. The tears she tried so hard to hold back – she had discovered that the more she cried, the more she wanted to cry – threatened to choke her.

'But Mrs O'Hagen has the money to get the best people and force them to help her. It's not the same thing.'

'Yes, and why does she have money? Because she made that happen too. She didn't trust to *Providence* and *Art* and *Truth*.' Laura put such withering emphasis on the words that Stella gave up. Laura knew, she presumed, that time would mellow her bitterness, allow her to realise that the tragedy of Nessa's death didn't mean anything, that it just was. But she never did, persisting in the belief that, in the battle between Nessa's Way and Mrs O'Hagen's Way, Mrs O'Hagen had won, simply by virtue of being still alive. To the victor the spoils, she thought, allowing the bitterness to wither some of the pain she felt because it was easier to be angry than heartbroken.

Amanda hadn't appeared. She had rung several times, speech slurred and meandering, with increasingly frantic stories about the problems she was beset by. She had babbled about lost keys and Huw being unable to take her to the airport, until Laura had finally snapped, 'Don't come. You've barely seen Nessa since she got sick anyway,' and Amanda, hurt, had sworn that of course she would be there. Except she hadn't been. Laura had thought she would never forgive her, never speak to her again.

'She can't help it,' Stella had said quietly. 'You know she would be here if she possibly could. If she isn't, it's because she can't. I think Nessa would have understood.' And Laura knew that Nessa would have understood, had in fact understood, so she forced herself not to let Amanda's failure become a breach between them. But despite her resolve, it had added another bitter nugget to the heap, and widened further the distance between the three girls.

At the funeral, Nessa had been laid out in a wicker coffin that Laura privately thought shabby and ugly, but which Nessa's friends insisted she would have liked: 'No waste, you see. She hated waste. The idea of paying a fortune for something solid made of oak that is only going to rot in the ground!' Then they saw Laura's face as she heard 'rot in the ground' and stopped.

'Nessa was thrifty,' they had said, once Laura's face had settled. 'Frugal. She didn't like needless expense,' they had concluded happily. Across the room, Laura could see Stella, trapped by an old man in a baggy mac, being lectured about something.

'They're wrong, of course,' a sharp voice had said at Laura's elbow. 'Nessa wasn't thrifty, she was shockingly profligate sometimes.'

It was the celebrated portrait painter who had been Laura's father for the first nine years of her life, and whom she had hardly seen after Nessa had revealed the truth. 'And as for hating waste, she practically made a virtue of it.'

Laura thought he was right. Nessa had had a magnificence of mind that didn't allow her to calculate profit margins. 'She never threw away food,' she said, with what she felt was a startling lack of brilliance.

'No, maybe not,' he conceded, 'but she threw away opportunities, talent, goodwill, recklessly. Except where you were concerned. She didn't squander anything that you needed.'

Laura had felt the lump rising in her throat again. 'Isn't it funny how little any of us knows anyone?' She gestured towards the group of women close to them. 'Those are her closest friends, and when they talk about her, I don't recognise the person they're describing, except in brief flashes when they recall a phrase of hers or something she liked, like a dish or a colour.'

'Brief flashes of knowing is all any of us gets,' said the portrait painter. 'It's enough. Will you come and sit for me?' he asked.

Laura had said she would. 'Although it will be terrifying to see the passage of time so clearly marked. The last picture you did of me was years and years ago. I'll be like Dorian Gray.'

The painter had ignored the joke. 'This was always a face that had a lot in it,' he said, gently cupping her chin with his hand.

Since then she had sat for him a couple of times, at his studio on the top floor of a Georgian house, looking down into the locked garden at the centre. He played music he thought she should know about – Latin American jazz, African drum music, opera – and made her delicious things to eat in his tiny kitchen: buckwheat blinis with caviar one day, Welsh rarebit, sausages with black truffle. They talked about anything that entered their heads: painting, fashion, books, food, the best place to buy flowers, Laura's grief.

'Grief is like a heap of stones,' he had said to her once. 'The heap never gets any less, nor does it soften, but the stones acquire a shine, with time and use, and then they thin slightly as you wear them away.' It seemed as good a description as any that Laura had heard. So far, her pile seemed unchanged, though. Just as dull, just as lumpy.

The room where she sat now looked the same as when Nessa had left it, but fainter. The glow was less intense. No matter how much attention Laura paid to shining the shiny things, brushing the brushable ones, polishing and cleaning, the mistress was no longer there, and the house and its belongings didn't bother putting on the same kind of show for Laura. Nessa's personal things were still dotted about, but subdued now, and Laura sometimes felt as if she were simply perching among them, her imprint so faint that it was almost unnoticeable. The only things she had got rid of had been gifts to Stella, Amanda and a couple of Nessa's closest friends. She had asked them to choose something by which to remember her mother. Stella had taken a watercolour Nessa had done of the Smithfield market, shaggy black-and-white horses with bowed heads – 'The very essence of the dumb beast,' Nessa had said of one, which stood in an attitude of patient dejection, slumped over huge, feathery hocks – and their mean-eyed masters, boys with faces that were lean and lacking either food or affection. Amanda had asked for the sketch of her that Nessa had done, but Laura had refused to part with it: 'I know it's of you, but it's the only thing she finished in years, and I want to keep it.' Instead, she had offered Amanda a pair of tortoiseshell combs picked out with tiny jewels with which Nessa had held up the heavy weight of her hair. Amanda had finally made it over from London, weeks after the funeral, full of apologies and explanations that didn't ring true, and the things she had done to mark Nessa's passing in her own way.

'I went for a walk alone in Hyde Park and thought about everything she taught me and how much I learned from her.'

'More likely took a bumper load of drugs and spent it passed out in a dark room,' Laura had said later, on the phone to Stella, her own pain encouraging her to jeer, even though she knew that Amanda was trying to make up for not coming to the funeral, for failing in friendship.

For the tortoiseshell combs Amanda had been grateful, saying, 'I won't wear them, but I want something that was physically close to her, that still might have a little bit of her left in it.'

Laura didn't believe anything could be left after a person had gone. She still couldn't get over the fact that Nessa's smell – essential oil of rose and jasmine, a hint of Shalimar perfume, garlic – which lingered on everything Nessa wore, had vanished from the entire house, without trace, almost as soon as she'd died. Laura remembered hunting through the house in the days after the funeral, trying to find something where the smell was still lingering. Finally, she had caught a faint whiff of her mother on an old pair of pyjamas. The next day even that was gone.

The loneliness in the months since Nessa's death had been far more intense than Laura let on to anyone. There didn't seem to be very much in her life except work, which was why it had become so important. If she'd had just one person she could talk to . . . But now that Nessa, with her profundities, absurdities and intense articles of faith, was gone, who was that person? Stella was too far away, had become too remote, and although Amanda had a gift for subtle mockery that put everything into perspective, she had set it aside.

'Promise me you will really live,' Nessa had said to her, one day near the end, her breath faint and wheezy. 'I worry that you don't put enough of yourself into the world. You're still holding back, still waiting.' She was accusatory, this being the worst of sins in her eyes. 'There will be no signal, Laura. No bell will ring to tell you that life has begun. Only to tell you that it's ending.' Her eyes had filled with tears and Laura had seen clearly how very much she minded. And how much she knew. Earlier, the doctor had asked her, 'You do know what is happening, don't you?' but not unkindly.

'Yes,' Nessa had answered.

'How do you feel about it?'

Nessa had shrugged her thin shoulders. 'Sure what can you do?' she had said, with resignation that was only skin deep. Beneath it, Laura could feel her disappointment, astonishment, that she should be called out of class so early.

One of their last conversations had been about Amanda. Laura had tried to describe the way in which she felt that what happened to Amanda affected her and Stella also. 'We're not just ourselves, we're each other too,' was as close as she had been able to come to it.

'Then be careful,' Nessa had said, raising herself on one thin arm. 'Remember that it wasn't just the Sleeping Beauty who fell asleep for a hundred years. It was the whole castle. Even the flies on the windows.'

CB

Amanda never did graduate. She dropped out a few months before her finals, to the devastation of her professor, who strongly believed that the originality of her mind would eventually outweigh the steady slump in her work and commitment. But Amanda had, at last, reached something like critical mass in France, following a première at which she had worn a vintage Saint Laurent dress, black crêpe, with the entire back panel cut out and replaced by gorgeous lace work, so that her back was both revealed and concealed. It was classy and sexy, and incredibly French. After that, she was launched. And she was finally cast in a feature film by Antoine Huddart, avant-garde director of challenging nihilistic movies about the destructive inevitabilities of modern life. Amanda was to play the role of allegorical temptress, seducing the young hero from his bourgeois life into the squats and shooting galleries of suburban Paris.

'It's not much of a role,' she confided to Stella and Laura, with disarming candour. 'I mean, I don't have any back story or motivation that I can work out. I think I'm just supposed to drift around looking irresistible and bad. But at least it's a full-length film, and it will go to Cannes and places, and I'm getting paid, and something is bound to come of it. Huw thinks I should do it, and he says a couple of months' filming in Paris will be good for both of us. There are galleries he wants to visit, and I think he's a bit sick of Dublin.'

Not half as sick as we are of him, the roll of Stella's eyes suggested, but she only said, 'Why do you have to leave so quickly? Couldn't you do your finals first?'

'Shooting starts almost immediately, and my scenes are all being done early. Anyway, Huw thinks I should go and acclimatise and get used to being there.'

'And your mother?'

'Oh, you know Mummy. She wasn't particularly keen on my doing a degree in the first place. That was strictly till-something-better-comes-along for her. But we're going to have a huge party for your graduation, and to celebrate my first big film. We'll book Trap and invite everyone, and get our own DJ, and the next day my parents want us all to have lunch at the house, to mark the beginning and the end of everything.'

It had certainly done that, Laura thought now, except that it had worked the wrong way round. Amanda had meant the end of the life of studying and exams and being children still, and the beginning of something more exciting, more grown-up, the freedom she had always longed for. In fact, that night had marked the end of the instinctively honest bond between them, and the start of their three lives running parallel but no longer linked. They were kept apart by the things they couldn't speak of.

Later, when it was just the two of them and Stella said yet again that she didn't see why Amanda couldn't wait a couple of weeks, do her exams and then go, and that if Antoine Huddart wanted her that badly, he could surely delay shooting, Laura said, 'But she's hardly likely to pass anything now. She's done no work for months. And I'm not so sure the film would wait for her. I mean, I got the feeling that Amanda was eager to say yes very quickly because she didn't know if the offer would hold good.'

'Right,' said Stella. 'She's running out of options?'

'For the moment, anyway. Think about it: she's burned a lot of bridges over here recently. Her studies have been a joke for ages. Much as Professor Greene wants to pass her, I don't think he could. She needs new pastures, new interests. You know that panicky feeling we all have of what on earth to do next? I think Amanda has it worst.'

Stella nodded. 'I know what you mean,' she said, and Laura could see that she did. The shelter of school and college were nearly over. The easy bit – of putting one foot in front of the other and following the path laid out for them – was at an end. Soon they would all have to find their own momentum. Even Stella, who knew exactly what she was going to do – a legal internship at Amnesty International while she continued further law exams at night – and who rarely felt uncertainty, was secretly terrified by the formlessness of what lay in front of her. Laura had a good idea of her own path – work experience on the local Southside paper and constant submission to every magazine in town, followed, if life were fair, by paid work on a decent paper – but was far less sure of her ability to pull it off. Anxiety clawed at them both, surfacing each time they forgot to subdue it. Amanda's life, though surely far more fabulous, was also far less clear-cut, and Laura knew that, despite her best efforts at the old insouciance, she too was apprehensive.

Then, as if the apprehension acted on her like a brake or a warning signal, Amanda did one of her sudden about-turns, swapping excess for virtue and moderation. She slowed down the drinking and partying, began lunching in the few wholefood places that had appeared in the city, rather than the canteen with its plates of chips and sausages. She looked fresh, bouncy, animated from within by a secret laugh.

'I'm living like a Frenchwoman,' she said, when they commented on her new ways. 'I'm in training for when we move to Paris. I'm eating small amounts of exquisite things, and paying careful attention to my nails and the tying of a scarf. I can see why they do all this stuff. It takes up so much *time*. You're never bored as a Frenchwoman because there's always an anti-cellulite cream to be rubbed in or facial exercises to be done. It's a real hobby. I think that's the secret for them – it's not just window-dressing: it's a habit that needs to be fed.'

Early read-throughs for the film were going well, and Amanda said she felt she could make something of the role. 'It's still not much of a part, but the director is amazing, and we click, and he says he'll have more work for me afterwards. If I have to be a *muse*' – she made a funny, deprecating face – 'then maybe I can be his. He's got enough talent not to let us both down.' She was excited, energised.

'Maybe one day you could be the master, not the muse,' said Stella. 'Make stuff, not just be in it.'

'Maybe.' Amanda looked unconvinced. No one else had ever suggested to her that there was another side to the camera for her.

Before she moved to Paris properly, there was the great party to organise. Amanda threw herself into this with zeal. 'How about Come As You Were as a theme?' she asked Stella and Laura. They were sitting on a bench outside the college library, faces turned towards the feeble sunshine. Around them, bells pealed the hour and students scurried. 'That way people can really wear whatever they like. Dell can squeeze herself into a school uniform and give the boys a cheap thrill. Laura, you could probably wear a romper suit and get away with it. Stel, you can leave your hair so that it goes into the crazy curls you used to have.'

'What about you?' Stella asked.

'I'll wear the Dries Van Noten dress from the first shoot I did for *Glamour* magazine. If it still fits me.'

'Of course it'll fit you. You're skinnier now than you've ever been,' said Laura, looking at the place where Amanda's delicate collar bones protruded from the grey cashmere sweater she wore over tight black jeans. 'I mean, if it doesn't fit you, no one in the entire world will ever be able to wear that dress.' That much was probably true. The dress was a glorious deep purple – 'Like the bad queen's nightgown,' was how Laura had described it when Amanda had brought it round to show them – long, with an asymmetrical hem that trailed along the ground and gathered at the back so that it almost made a fishtail effect, a straight bodice and one thick shoulder strap.

'Hair?' Laura liked the way Amanda always followed through on her dress ideas, always had a theme, even if it was a vague one.

'Up. Lots of little curls, the way they did it for the Ophelia shoot, but softer. Now we need to decide on music and decorations. Do we have food, or not?'

'Not,' said Stella. 'If we have food, people will eat. We don't want them to eat. We want them to dance.'

'True,' Amanda said. 'I think the music should be quite free. Anything, basically, as long as it's good. Now, what about drugs?'

It was a serious question. For big nights, they generally decided in advance what they would take. Acid or mushrooms were for the type of evening that had a visual component, like the cinema, pills for where dancing was the only priority.

'A few lines of coke? We don't want to be too messy, and everyone will want to talk to us, so we'd better be reasonably together,' said Laura.

'Suits me,' said Amanda. 'And remember we've got that big lunch with all our parents the next day, so we don't want to be too wrecked. And then we're off, two days after, to Paris! Huw has found us an apartment in the Marais. I haven't seen it yet, but he says I'll love it. Oh, girls, I finally feel as if this is it, that grown-up life is really starting.' Laura was reminded of Amanda's joy when Huw first moved to Dublin, the way in which she was projecting her fantasy onto a clean canvas. What had happened to that picture – studious days in the library, charming dinner parties, a balance of study and play for them both? Instead she had a filthy flat with a permanent round of temporary inhabitants, no degree, bitten cuticles and the same emptiness inside. But Amanda was gushing on, 'Imagine being in a different city from Mummy' – Laura could see how that would be good – 'and with Huw. Heaven! We won't really know anyone at first, so I suppose we'll have to spend most of our time on our own.' She was weaving a cloth of shimmering gold out of the pictures in her head.

Laura felt she herself could have described them with pinpoint accuracy: small restaurants with red-and-white-checked tablecloths, candlelight, *pastis* in late-night bars with an assortment of musicians and painters, afternoons at the Louvre or drinking coffee and watching Paris go by, Huw content and relaxed, needing nothing but her. The images were every bit as fantastical as a tourist brochure's. More, because Huw was in them, and brought his own jagged edge to everything. Somewhere inside she felt a knot of irritation with Amanda. Must she always do this? Make them all jump through the hoops of her self-delusion?

'What about us?' Stella asked in mock sorrow.

'I'll always have you. That's the point of us,' said Amanda, tucking their arms through hers. 'I won't be gone for long, you'll visit, and then I'll be back, and if I'm not, you'll just have to visit more. Maybe we should all make a plan to go to New York,' she continued, in sudden excitement. 'We could, you know. It's the one place where all our worlds collide perfectly. Stel, you could get a job with one of those huge law firms and earn a fortune. Laura, you could work for *The New Yorker*, or the *Wall Street Journal*, and I could model and make films. I could persuade my dad to buy an apartment there, and we could live together.'

'I don't think Huw would like that,' Stella said.

'He'd love it.' It was one of Amanda's deliberate blind spots, that Huw, Stella and Laura were great friends.

'Anyway,' Stella said, 'I don't want to work for one of those law firms. They're the corporate equivalent of a giant Play-Doh machine – they just scoop everyone up, green, red, blue, pink, churn them into a generic version, a kind of muddy brown, then spew them out again. And the only thing that makes it worthwhile is the obscene amount of money that you never get to spend because you're working so hard. You end up being one of those morons who has a "concierge service", someone to collect your dry-cleaning and stock your fridge with your favourite expensive bottled water because you're too *busy* and your time is too *valuable*.' Her sarcastic inflections were getting wilder. 'I'd rather stock my own fridge, thanks. And I want to do *meaningful* work, not endlessly chase the metal filings that fall when giant companies grind up against each other.'

'And I'm quite unlikely to get a job on the *Wall Street Journal*,' Laura said. 'One day, maybe,' she added, seeing Amanda's stricken face. 'If we all work hard, and get to where we want to be, maybe we can converge on New York later, and take the city by storm.'

'Okay, back to the party.' Amanda sounded a bit deflated. She was chewing a thumbnail, always a bad sign. Laura could see that, despite trying to be a Frenchwoman, she had inflicted terrible damage on the skin around the nail, bitten it until it bled, as far down as the knuckle, leaving behind painful-looking ragged scabs. But she cheered up quickly, proposing various cocktails and wondering should they have going-home bags. 'We could put eye masks and herbal hangover cures in them.'

'An all-day breakfast roll would be even better,' Stella said.

'You know James is coming?'

'What?' The word jerked sharply out of Stella's mouth.

'When did that happen?' Laura asked, with an eye on Stella.

'Well, he *might* be. He's definitely coming to the lunch but he might make the party as well.'

'But why?'

'He wants to see us graduate, of course. Well, you graduate, and me flunk out.' The happy way Amanda said it, they could see she didn't really consider she was flunking. 'I texted to tell him about the lunch, and he said he'd like to make it, so I told him about the party too.'

'Are you in touch much?' Stella blurted out.

Laura was surprised. Usually, she maintained a rigid self-control, never asking about James and rarely dropping his name into conversation. This time, though, she clearly couldn't resist asking, even though she looked as if she dreaded the answer. Laura had never tried to find out if there was any contact between Amanda and James, had always presumed that there wasn't, that the break James had made had been a clean one. So she waited for the answer too, for Stella's sake. 'Not much, every once in a while.' Amanda was gathering her things, seeming barely to pay attention to what Stella was saying. 'I must go, I said I'd meet Huw.'

After she'd left, there was silence between the two girls. Was it staggering indifference or a total lack of awareness that caused Amanda to be so callous? Laura wondered. Stella was very good at masking her emotions, but surely the way she felt about James should have been apparent to anyone who cared enough to see.

'It'll be fun to see James again,' Laura said cautiously, not sure how much sympathy or acknowledgement Stella would welcome.

'Yes. I suppose.' Stella sounded defeated, so that Laura, in a rush, decided to venture further.

'Does not seeing him hurt less than seeing him would?' she asked quietly.

'I'm not sure.' Stella didn't bother with denials. 'The idea of seeing him scares me. I've got used to not, and to not expecting to. And I don't think about him all the time. I try really hard not to. But somehow he's just always there in the background of my mind. It's like the beat of my mind is his name, said over and over again so that I'm hardly aware of it, except when everything goes quiet and I can hear it.'

As a description of love, it made far more sense to Laura than Amanda's extravagant ramblings. It had the hint of sadness that she always associated with love, the knowledge that no matter how intensely people felt for each other, they were still separate, with separate destinies that might take them away from where they wanted to be.

'Why do you think Amanda has asked him to come back? Is it just what she said? To be friendly?' Laura asked.

'I don't know. She knows exactly how he feels about her, so surely she must know that it isn't very friendly to keep reeling him in when she feels like it. I wish she'd just let him go,' Stella said savagely.

'Maybe she's getting sick of Huw, and wants James back as insurance,' Laura suggested.

'I doubt it. You know what she's like with Huw still. The shining light of conviction radiates off her, like sun on snow. I think she doesn't bother much about what James thinks. She's too used to not considering him. Or anyone,' she spat.

'Well, I don't see why he comes,' Laura said stoutly. 'He's an idiot if he keeps letting her do this. And if he can't see that there are better things for him.' She looked sideways at Stella, still unsure how much frank discussion she was prepared to take.

'He can't help it,' Stella said sadly. 'He's in love. What else can he do except what she asks him?'

'Then he should stop being in love.'

'So should I,' said Stella. There wasn't much Laura could say to that, so she said nothing. They fell silent again. Then, 'Bugger Amanda O'Hagen,' Stella said viciously.

Chapter Eleven

New York

THE NEXT DAY, STELLA'S LAST IN THE OFFICE before London, she arrived, green tea in hand, to find a meeting with Sean and Barrington Fraser electronically added to her calendar for three o'clock. Presumably, this being a city and an industry in which everything operated at top speed, like her mother's old Moulinex blender permanently on the highest setting, they would expect a substantial progress report. That gave her the morning to follow the tiny thread she had snagged the night before. It also gave her an excuse to tell her PA to hold all calls – the PA knew very well that Sean was not included in 'all' – which gave Stella a wonderfully luxurious feeling, as though she was playing truant. She kicked off her shoes and ran a quick search for 'Amanda O'Hagen Huw Edsberg London' on Google. There were still only the vaguest reports of 'growing concern around limited signs of activity' in the London house. Concerned 'friends' were quoted as saying that they hadn't seen Amanda in several weeks, and that she had seemed 'agitated' before that.

'How do we know they're even there?' she had asked Laura the night before.

'They are. Or, at least, one of them is. There are signs. Lights go on and off, that Jake guy gets in and out through the back way apparently. Sometimes a window is opened. Police have been keeping an eye on the place. They say they have enough reason to believe there are drugs on the premises, which entitles them to effect an entry. Mrs O'Hagen has been able to persuade them to wait until she gets there before they go in.'

With that, Stella had to be content. She settled down to her boxes of documents.

Three hours later, after two more green teas and a protein bar that made her tongue feel like sandpaper, she was bewildered. There was nothing there. Or nothing that made any sense. There was no build-up, just a sudden deterioration in relations. There were emails requesting Sarah Travers's presence at 'employee evaluations' to 'discuss her recent performance', but nothing that Stella could see that had led to them. There didn't seem to be any properly documented evidence of a fall from grace, except internal memos and emails, mainly between Carter Armstrong and his partners, about their 'growing concern' over Sarah Travers's behaviour. Nowhere was there a clear moment or event that had led to such overt hostility. Unless the case went to trial, she would have no opportunity to depose the plaintiff, which meant no opportunity to ask questions and get answers.

'There's nothing there,' she said to Sean and Barrington Fraser in the boardroom. She had changed her shirt, putting on a perfectly ironed pale pink silk one in place of the lilac she had worn that morning, which contrasted delicately with her charcoal suit over bare brown legs and high black heels. The holiday feeling of the morning was entirely gone. She felt nervous, aware of how much work she had to do before leaving that night, and that her assessment of the case so far wasn't likely to be popular.

'What do you mean, nothing?' Sean barked.

She had been right. 'There's no sign of any misconduct on her part. There is a clear and proper trail of internal memos, employee evaluations, notes of meetings and so on, but all are after the fact, and make no direct reference to the grounds for complaint. There is apparently an attitude problem, but no information as to where it originated.' Stella was deliberately being as brusque as possible. 'Sarah Travers denies it at every turn, and there is nothing concrete to suggest that she is wrong. Her work is not in question – she brought in a big client in the middle of all this – and no one suggests it is, although there are plenty of concerns voiced over whether or not it will *become* an issue in the light of her attitude problem. Which she denies it has. Morgan Brown have done their due diligence around the dismissal, but they are entirely missing a vital part of the picture. All there is, is *this*.' She produced the email in which Travers had written, 'It won't happen again.'

'That's it?' Sean sounded incredulous.

'Yes. There isn't anything else, and the timing is right. After that email, the firm start to get behind monitoring her.'

Sean remained silent. Thought heavily for a bit, watched by Barrington Fraser.

'She's unstable,' he said finally.

'Really?'

'How should I know? But it's a good place to start. Stella, we didn't ask you to go all Sherlock Holmes on this for us, just to make it go away. Morgan Brown and Carter Armstrong don't want this to go to trial.'

'Then they should pay her off. Properly.'

'Bad precedent. They don't wanna do that. So you make it go away. You find what you need to make the stuff stick, and you write an opinion that will shrink the nuts off Sarah Travers's two-bit attorney. Can you do that?' He looked at her with chilly speculation, the grey eyes calculating.

'I'll do my best,' she said stiffly. She wondered if Barrington Fraser was going to sit in on all their office interactions from now on, his paunchy eyes following her every move. How could she find something that wasn't there? Maybe she *had* overlooked something, a key piece of documentation that explained how Sarah Travers had called a client a moron, or refused to take a call because it was four o'clock on a Saturday morning, or turned up drunk to an early meeting. Had she somehow 'gotten involved'? It wasn't all that hard to prove oneself unworthy of the trust implied by the substantial salaries paid to associates: one slight step out of the strictly delineated lines could do it. So why wasn't there anything to suggest that Sarah Travers had done so?

Stella's weekend case was packed and stowed behind the door of her office. Associates at Davies Darn and Slate did not make a parade of their social lives by flaunting suitcases or travel plans. In it were her jogging gear – she had a feeling that the only way she was going to get through the weekend was with a lot of running – two pairs of J Brand jeans, a couple of shirts and a blazer. She would travel in her work clothes and make do with the jewellery she had on that day: diamond studs, and the watch Sean had given her. She had had her hair blow-dried that morning, and it would have to last. Lunch was out of the question – she buzzed her PA and requested take-out from the Japanese place down the block. Then she settled down to the documents again, from the beginning, trying as she read to figure out who Sarah Travers was. And what, she wondered, would her own life look like if suddenly spilled out of a sealed document pouch? Who would Stella Dwyer be if viewed in just two dimensions, with faint hostility, by someone she had never met?

And what about to someone who did know her? Had known her before? Would the passage of time seem to have delivered an unexpected result, or was this where she was always headed? Stella realised that the last time she was conscious of feeling like just one person, rather than two, separated from herself by what she had done, was the day of the graduation party.

From a distance of five years, she could clearly see what had been only dimly obvious at the time – how the simple code of their teenage years had grown at odds with the complex, grown-up situations they found themselves in. You never told on a friend, they knew that, but they also knew they should tell someone a bit of what they suspected about Amanda. You never let a guy come between friends, but neither were friends supposed to take the guy you wanted, once they knew you wanted him. Had Amanda known? She had never said.

Stella recalled the rage she had felt when Amanda had dropped in so casually that she had invited James to the graduation party, and how quickly it had dissipated. The anger in that moment had been real but unsustained. It had flared up violently, then dwindled away, so that they had carried on as they always did, teasing, joking, affectionate, and Stella had done her best to separate in her mind the Amanda she loved, the friend she cared for, and the Amanda she was so furious with, who behaved with such arrogant disregard. She remembered the expression on Sean's face as he described the limits to his loyalty, the point where he reckoned it became 'stupid'. In his mind, clearly, nothing justified that. Maybe he was right, she thought. Maybe blind loyalty was a kind of pathology.

She still marvelled at the knotty thread of emotions she had been able to carry with relative ease: loving Amanda, hating her, determined to protect her from all the things she could see frightened her, then wanting to see her exposed, ruined, destroyed. And yet everything had seemed to belong easily in its own moment, rather than spilling out and contaminating another, so that she had been capable of wanting the best for Amanda while also wanting her to understand, for once, that the things she did, she did to all of them, not just to herself. Mostly, protectiveness won. But not always, she thought now, remembering the night of the party.

ভ

That afternoon, they had agreed to meet in college, then go and change at Laura's, because Nessa (then just 'not well' rather than the 'sick' she would soon become) wanted to see them before they went out. 'She's not ill exactly,' Laura had explained. 'At least, they still don't know what's wrong, and maybe it's nothing, but she's pretty tired. They're still doing tests.'

When Amanda arrived to meet them, they could see she wasn't happy. Her face was mutinous, and she had a mauve hat on. 'Look, they've ruined it!' She pulled off the hat, exposing ludicrously curly hair. 'It's like a 1980s' perm. We might have picked Come As You Were as the theme, but this is *not* how I was. It's awful.'

It was impossible not to agree, thought Laura. The curls were tight, hard, springy. Poodle-like. 'What are you going to do?'

'I can fix it.' Amanda ran a hand impatiently through the curls. They resisted furiously, then sprang back into bristly shape immediately. 'I need my straighteners and a steamy bathroom. Come with me to the flat. I'll grab some stuff and then we'll head to yours.'

The day was dull with a faint mist. The skyline had retracted and the buildings along the Grand Canal huddled into themselves as though suspicious. On the water a mournful swan drifted past. 'Poor thing,' said Laura. 'You never see them alone, unless they've been separated from their mate. They don't like it.'

The steps leading up to the flat were dirty, with drink stains that the night's rain hadn't washed away, and cigarette butts tossed casually on the ground.

'Your landlord mustn't be pleased,' said Stella.

'Oh, he hates us,' said Amanda cheerfully. 'I think the best thing that ever happened to him was us giving notice and moving to Paris. He's a friend of Daddy's, so he's never said too much, but I can see it in his eyes. I thought we shouldn't even bother looking for Daddy's deposit back, but Huw is insisting we get it.'

Stella twitched with irritation at this further proof of Huw's voracious sense of entitlement, but she said nothing. They went up the stairs, not speaking, and entered the flat, where Stella and Laura again marvelled at the strange smell, and the fact that Amanda lived there like that. I wonder will they turn the Paris apartment into the same sort of dive, Stella thought, staring at the mottled carpet. Then she felt Amanda, beside her, stiffen, and heard a sharp gasp from Laura. Looking up, along the truncated hall corridor and into the sitting room, she saw a perfectly framed tableau, backlit by the soft light coming in through the large front windows, bordered by the door frame.

Huw was sitting on the sofa, legs splayed apart, hands behind his thrown-back head, eyes shut. Beside him was a sheet of tinfoil and a lighter. A lit cigarette was smoking in the ashtray balanced on a heavy hardback book. Crouched between his knees, a girl with short black hair, lips pursed around his erect penis, was moving her head rhythmically up and down. They stood, said nothing, barely breathed, watching, until, with a loud gasp and a sudden upward thrust of his hips, Huw came. Only then did Amanda react.

'Dell!' Her voice came out as a wild shriek. It was indeed Dell, they could see now, sitting back on her heels, an expression of dismay on her face that would have been comical were it not so ghastly.

'Amanda!' Huw was struggling with his fly, trying to stand and get fully dressed at the same time. He wasn't managing very well, seemed to be fumbling wildly, his eyes unfocused, not helped by Dell, who clearly didn't know where to look or what to do. She was in his way and he bumped into her as he stood up, knocking over the book and the ashtray.

Amanda turned on her heel, Stella and Laura flanking her, and was through the door, down the stairs and outside before Huw caught up with them.

'Amanda, wait. Talk to me.' She didn't say a word, just looked at him for what seemed an age, then shrugged off the hand he had placed on her arm, and carried on down the steps.

'Amanda?' It was a question, almost a plea, a note none of them had heard from him before. Stella and Laura hurried after Amanda and they walked in silence for a while, trying to catch hold of where they now were. Their feet directed them towards Laura's house as the sun broke through the fine mist. By the time they reached her door, there was a soft light slanting over the black slate roofs around them, picking out stone chimney pots and aerials in sharp relief. Still, Amanda hadn't said anything. Stella's one attempt at breaking the silence had been not so much ignored as subsumed into the intense soundless pool around them. After that, she gave up. Anyway, she was ashamed at how fast her mind had spun off to James, and what he would make of this, appalled to find herself thinking that he would now get what he wanted. That all he had to do was be sympathetic and not too I-told-you-so, and Amanda would inevitably be his. For all that she had – oh-so-nobly – told herself that his suffering hurt her almost more than her own, the thought of him happy with Amanda was unbearable. After all, she decided, astonished at the new harshness within her, she'd rather he was miserable than that he and Amanda should be happy together.

She suddenly recalled the last time she had seen him. He had rung her unexpectedly one day, to say he was leaving for England shortly and could he see her before he went? There was something he wanted to talk about. They had met in a café near Trinity, on a day so wet that the city seemed to have closed in around the steamy window where they sat, raindrops slithering sadly down the glass panes. Stella had done her mental preparation well, so that when James, after telling her she looked nice and asking after the various parts of their lives that intersected, had said, 'How is Amanda?', she wasn't taken by surprise, had been expecting it.

'She's fine.' Stella didn't know what else to say then. Besotted? Happier than she had ever been? Neither seemed an appropriate answer, not to James, who didn't try to disguise his feelings.

'Will you keep an eye on her? Sorry, I know you will. It's just—' He broke off. 'It's just that Huw, well, he can be slightly odd.' He paused again, and Stella could see that even now he was struggling to voice criticism of someone who ostensibly was a friend. It wasn't James's way. 'He was always wild at school. He hung out with a very druggy crowd, boys who were smoking weed at fourteen and turning up at the Fourth of June celebrations high on cocaine and skunk. He survived, because he was bright and the beaks didn't really want to see what he was up to. Some of that crowd were removed from school, and Huw calmed down for a while, but university seems to have set him off again. And the old crowd were waiting for him in London when he got there, all of them years more advanced by then. Huw has a taste for that sort of thing, and he seems to have the constitution, but not everyone around him is as lucky. There was a boy at school with us, then at Oxford with Huw. He hasn't ended up so well … I saw his father at a party and he told me his son is in South America, trying to get clean by doing one of those shamanistic peyote trips. Which sounds like swallowing a spider to catch a spider, if you ask me, but I suppose he felt he had to do something. The point is, Huw certainly hasn't been helping him to get clean.'

And you're probably understating it, thought Stella, because it's the type of thing you would do. 'Why on earth did you bring him to Amanda's party?'

'Oh, I'm kicking myself for that, trust me. I brought him because he was there. He had come to stay. I know now that he needed to get out of London for a while, although at the time he just told me he wanted a change of scene. What else was I to do with him? I had no idea Amanda would take one look at him and ...' He didn't finish. He didn't need to. For the first time, there was a steel girder of bitterness in his voice.

'So what do you want me to do?'

'I don't know really. Just ... keep an eye on her. Huw might be different when he's here. Maybe he's looking for a way out as well, and Amanda is his peyote trip. It might be okay. But if it's not, let me know and I'll help if I can.'

'By killing Huw? Because I don't think she can be warned off.' Stella was only half-joking. Killing Huw seemed a very attractive proposition.

'No, probably not.' James fell silent.

Stella promised she would let him know, if there was anything to know, and finished her coffee. 'I'd better go.' She felt awkward, aware of how badly she wanted to lean into the crook of his arm, feel that it was just the two of them, together, in a wet and empty world.

'Stella ...' A faint red glow appeared along his cheekbones, and she knew he was going to say something about 'them' when there was no them. About what could and could never be. Whatever it was, she couldn't bear to hear it.

'Gotta go. Library calls.' She grabbed her bag from under the table, which was suddenly too full of his elbows and arms, too close to his broad shoulders and strong neck, fighting the urge to throw her arms around him and cry for the whole lot of them.

In the house, Amanda made straight for the sitting room, where Nessa was curled up on a battered plum velvet sofa, with a fringed shawl draped around her, her head resting on a cushion. She was reading a hardback copy of *Middlemarch*.

Stella wondered whether or not to go in with Amanda, but she shut the door almost in their faces, and she saw that Laura made no move to open it. They stood outside, awkwardly, and heard no sound from inside the room.

'Let's get something to eat,' said Stella, and they moved towards the kitchen, where Laura began making prawn and pea risotto.

'Bloody hell,' Stella began, almost pleased Amanda was gone so they could talk about what they had seen. 'What the fuck was that?'

'The end of everything, by the look of it.' Laura sounded more upset than Stella had expected.

'That's a good thing, though, no?' she asked, bewildered.

'I guess so. But not like that.'

'Better like that than not at all.'

'I don't agree. This will shatter her. It's so ugly, so cheap. She won't be able to deal with it. I just hope Nessa can say something to her that will help. It was her entire world, present and future, that she lost there.'

Later Stella found out that Nessa had said something very similar to Amanda: 'Infidelity is one thing. For some men it's just a fact of life and can be forgiven. This, the ugliness, the crudity, can't. And shouldn't be. Be glad you found out now, while the angels are still on your side.'

'But why would Dell do such a thing?' Stella asked.

'That's easy – revenge. Must have seemed the perfect blow to strike for James, all those years ago. Funny, she must have cared more about James than she ever let on.'

Makes two of us, Stella thought sadly, seeing Dell in a slightly different light. That they had both been hurt by Amanda, out of love for James, made her feel a kinship with Dell that she could never have imagined. 'What I don't understand,' Laura continued, 'is Huw. Why would he do it?'

'That's easy. He's a jerk.'

'Maybe, but he loves Amanda. Wants her, anyway. I don't see where cheating on her fits in with his plan.'

'God, it's not going to be much of a party, is it?'

They heard Amanda in the hall outside the kitchen, and hurriedly busied themselves chopping, heads down so that she wouldn't see that they had been discussing her. As if they could have been discussing anything else, thought Stella. Amanda's face was still set, hard, with no trace of tears.

'Let me help,' she said, taking a knife from a drawer and joining Laura at the chopping board. 'But I'm not doing onions.' Her bottom lip wobbled, but she held firm, and they quietly cooked and ate their way through the next hour, feeding Nessa her dinner on a tray, using the mismatched but delicate china she preferred, and chatting with her about only the most innocuous things. Until dinner was cleared and washed up, Laura and Stella weren't even sure the party was still on, until Amanda said, 'We'd better get dressed. It's nearly time to go. It is in your honour, you know. You have to be there to greet your public as they arrive.'

'Are you sure?' Laura began.

'Of course I'm sure. Come on. I still need to sort out these curls. We'd better get started.'

Chapter Twelve

Dublin

THE APPROACH TO TRAP HAD BEEN LAID OUT with red carpet and large planters containing stiff box hedge on either side. A banner with 'Congratulations Stella and Laura' hung above the door. 'You should have put your name in,' Stella said, nudging Amanda.

'Time enough. This is your night,' Amanda answered. The bouncers smiled and hugged them all. Down the stairs they could hear the steady throb of the music.

Stella linked Amanda's arm. 'You sure you're up to this?' Amanda nodded, grabbed their hands and squeezed hard.

Through the padded double doors, the room was aglow with fairy lights and candles, and the wistful strains of Rod Stewart's

'Forever Young' rose to greet them. It was a song they all loved for its unashamed sentimentality and that hopeful 1980s' drum beat, and for the way it seemed to grasp the poignancy of the present when seen through the prism of the possible future, the swift passage of everything and the preciousness of their now.

'That's how I want to be loved,' Amanda had said, years before, during one of their many late-night conversations about life, their future, love and the universe, with the song playing in the background. 'By someone strong enough to want only the best for me, who sees me as perfect and to be protected.' She took a deep drag of the joint they were sharing in her bedroom, windows wide open to a clear, starry night, the heady smell of dew-wet grass rising to them. As she leaned farther out to blow away the smoke, catching at the tea-rose silk dressing gown that slipped from one golden shoulder, her hair tumbling about, it didn't seem possible that any other fate should await her.

It was only afterwards that Stella remembered that the song was a father's benediction for his child, and not a lover's declaration.

Now, they stood silent in the doorway, immobilised, as the music swung past them. People began to surge towards the door, clapping and calling congratulations to them. Still they stood. Suddenly Amanda uttered a sob. Laura turned to see tears rolling steadily down her cheeks, taking mascara and eyeshadow with them in grimy trails. She ran for the Ladies. After a moment of shock, Stella and Laura ran after her. Inside, she was sobbing violently, shaking, the sounds coming out of her mouth more like choking than crying. They went to her, one on either side, patting her shoulders, hugging her, saying, 'Don't, Amanda, don't. It'll be okay …'

The Ladies was done up like a kind of boudoir – chairs with curly legs and a divan upholstered in shiny peach. Powder puffs and tasselled perfume atomisers dotted various surfaces.

'It's my heart,' she said finally, when able to produce any words along with the tearing sobs. 'It's broken.' The way she said it, Stella thought, was as if she had never heard the expression. As if she was simply describing an actual physical fact rather than uttering a cliché.

She cried, and then she stopped. Concerned and curious friends put their heads around the door at intervals, but were waved away by Stella and Laura. Gradually, Amanda reached the hiccuping stage which meant that sleep would follow. Except that sleep wasn't the narcotic Amanda desired. 'Get me a drink,' she said. 'Get me two drinks, strong ones, and then I'd better get out there.'

'Would you rather just go home?' Laura asked.

'No. He's spoilt enough things. Tonight I'm going to celebrate.'

'But your heart isn't in it.'

'My heart will never be in anything again. I'd better start getting used to it.' She sat up on the counter, between two sinks, and began fumbling in her bag for make-up. Laura left for the bar, Stella having suggested Manhattans because they were the strongest thing she could think of. 'I didn't think other girls would be a problem,' Amanda said quietly. 'I knew there would be problems, but I didn't think it would be that.'

'No, I guess not,' Stella said soothingly.

'I mean, why would he cheat on me? With Dell? I'm not vain, but …' She trailed off.

'You're a hundred times more beautiful, so it's not that. It's something else.' She resisted the urge to tear Huw down for

Amanda, drag his many failings into the open for her to see. Be smart, she told herself. Play a Socratic game. So instead she asked, 'Some inadequacy of his own?'

'I suppose so. Though he doesn't seem to show the inadequacy anywhere else.'

This was true, Stella thought. Huw was possessed of endless self-confidence in every situation. Whatever his troubles were, they ran very deep down, like an underground river that forced its way to the surface through the boulders of his personality.

Amanda repaired her face as best she could – a pretty good job, Stella thought, considering – and Laura came back with a tray of drinks. They grabbed a glass each, clinked them solemnly together, and Amanda tossed hers back in one go. She reached for a second and downed half of that.

'Okay. Let's go,' she said, squaring her shoulders, then applying a final slick of vermilion lipstick. The crying had made her eyes huge, and the dark shadows imperfectly concealed below them gave her a slightly louche air, but she looked good.

Out at the bar, Stella and Laura tried to stay close to Amanda, but waves of people wanting to chat, compare notes on exams, summer holiday plans, the next stage of everyone's career, drove them apart. Whether the news had travelled, or the stricken look on Amanda's face at the mention of his name put them off, the girls didn't know, but very few people mentioned Huw. Maybe they were just glad not to see him, thought Stella, as Sinead chatted about the restoration atelier in Florence where she was to spend the summer.

'I'm glad to be getting away, to be honest,' Sinead confided. 'Things have got a bit weird, don't you think, in the last while? Everyone seems so ... jangled, so at each other's throats. Dell has gone really odd, and Amanda … I don't know what's been up with her at all. Even my mother has noticed. She asked me if everything was all right the other day, and said that I didn't seem to be spending as much time with my friends as usual.' She took a slug of her gin and tonic. 'And I'm really not. Because my friends, except you and Laura,' she gave Stella's arm a squeeze, 'have all gone a bit psycho. I hope the summer sorts things out. It's all such a pity.'

Stella could see that Sinead really did mind. Was she particularly perceptive, or was it blatantly obvious that they were all falling apart? She could see Amanda at the other side of the bar, knee deep in admirers as usual, and doing a fairly good impersonation of insouciance. Amanda caught Stella's eye and winked at her, and Stella felt a sudden wave of admiration for the perfection of her poise, the effort she put into self-control. She's quite old-fashioned and Victorian in her way, she thought, not all modern and touchy-feely.

Telling Sinead that she was sure they were all just stressed about results and feeling the pressure, that things would go back to normal soon, Stella left her and made her way to Amanda, reaching her at the same time as Will, the photographer who had invited Amanda to James's twenty-first, and Laura, who appeared from the other side of the room. Will had put on weight, and was wearing black jeans so tight they squashed his arse to nothing and made him walk like a penguin, with quick, constricted steps. Around his waist was a thick studded belt, drawn in under a podgy stomach. He smelt of Calvin Klein unisex perfume.

'Don't forget who discovered you, darling, as you disappear off to queen it in France,' he said to Amanda, reaching out to put his arm around her waist, pulling her close to him. 'And remember what happened to Marie Antoinette.' He swayed with laughter at his own joke.

'I won't forget,' said Amanda, coolly, 'but, really, this isn't my night. It's about these two, my gorgeous friends.'

'The Holy Trinity,' said Will, immediately expansive, prepared to include them all within the circle of his arms and charm.

'Holy Travesty, more like,' Stella said.

'Or Troll-y Trinity,' added Laura. They all laughed, leaving Will discomfited, Stella could see. He bowed stiffly at them, more like a penguin than ever, and waddled off.

'Oh dear, we weren't very nice,' said Laura, laughing. 'And I suppose he's right – he did sort of discover you.'

'He did not,' said Amanda, crossly. 'He just got there first.'

The guy they still mockingly called Byron de Sade joined them then, full of his own plans for the summer, his pallid face shining greasily in the dim light. 'I'm going to circus school in Bordeaux,' he boasted. God, thought Stella, can't anyone do anything normal, like wait tables? 'I'm going to learn how to swallow swords. I'll teach you when I get back.'

'Oh, good,' said Amanda. 'Then we'll all have a better chance of swallowing those ridiculous stories you tell about yourself.'

Byron looked furious, and Stella realised that Amanda was more than a little drunk.

And then James arrived, late, having missed all the drama, but the joy of seeing him was perhaps all the more for that. 'You're like the cavalry,' Laura said. 'I feel everything's going to be better now that you're here.'

Stella's emotions were more mixed, but she knew what Laura meant. There was a kindness in James that made you feel everything really would be okay. Although not for herself, she thought, or not in the way she wanted. He laughed, said, 'I doubt it,' but was obviously happy to see them. He reached forward, tried to hug all three of them at once, which nearly made Stella fall over. They bore him off, having dispatched de Sade to the bar for more drinks, and, in a dark corner, filled James in on everything that had happened. First Nessa's illness, or what they knew of it, then Amanda and her plans for France, and finally, told by Stella at Amanda's insistence, the incident with Huw that afternoon.

'Dell is such a stupid bitch,' Amanda hissed, when the telling was done. She clearly hadn't stuck to the agreed plan as far as drugs were concerned. Stella felt giddy, a little bit high after a couple of lines, but Amanda was swaying, eyelids starting to droop.

James refused to join them in trashing Dell. 'This is Huw's doing, I'd say. If we knew a bit more, we'd see that Dell is getting a rubbish deal too.'

'She's a bitch. I don't care what excuses anyone gives, that girl has been nothing but shit in my life from the start.'

That's probably true, thought Stella, though God knows what kind of a force Amanda had been in Dell's life.

'Let's go and dance,' she suggested to Amanda, to distract her, and because the DJ was playing Happy Mondays' 'Step On'.

'Okay.' Amanda drained her drink, another cocktail, and they hit the dance floor, followed fairly promptly by three or four guys all keen to twirl Amanda round. Later, Stella saw her wrapped around Christian – or, more accurately, hanging off him. She clearly couldn't stand unaided and her eyes were starting to roll. She looked wanton, and incredibly sexy.

'Should we take her away?' she said to Laura, who appeared at her side.

'No, leave her. I mean, what else was she ever going to do tonight? You heard her. It's the end of everything, in her mind.'

'Well, the beginning, if you ask me, but I guess yes, let her process it in her own way.'

From then, things got messy for all of them. The cocktail habit had caught on, and half the room seemed to be swilling Margaritas and Manhattans. Which meant that everyone was wildly drunk. Stella had long lost count of how many she had had, but knew it was enough to make sure that lunch at the O'Hagens' would be a more-than-usual trial. Still, Huw hadn't appeared, and that was something. Neither had Dell. She had feared he would turn up and force a showdown, or that Dell would saunter in, trying to pretend that nothing had happened. She wondered if they were somewhere together. Perhaps they were a couple already.

'Not likely,' said Laura, when Stella mooted the possibility. 'That's not what it was about. They're too alike, those two. Both watchful and tough. They both need someone more gentle and biddable. Like Amanda. Like James.'

'Biddable indeed,' said Stella, watching Amanda wrapped around Christian. 'God, she's pissed.'

'What should we do?' asked Laura in concern.

'Have another drink,' said Stella.

They didn't exactly play catch-up, because Amanda had so clearly outstripped them, but they drank heavily, throwing back the cocktails and shots that friends bought them. Hands seemed to be everywhere, reaching for them, encouraging them, applauding, clapping them on the back, handing them drinks, cigarettes, joints. Sometimes a hand beckoned and they went into a cubicle and did another line of coke. After one of those, Stella, leaving the loo, stumbled into James and would have fallen, but he grabbed her arm, pulled her towards him and steadied her.

'Whoa there,' he said. 'Are you okay?'

'Never better,' said Stella, leaning back against the doorframe and smiling up at him. The coke she had just snorted mapped out a route for her, a daring new route, and she decided to take it. She leaned in to him, her shoulder angled towards the curve of his neck. 'And you?' she asked. 'Having fun?' She was looking up at him with deliberate provocation. He gazed back at her, surprise and something else in his face. She held his eyes, long enough for the noise and babble around them to recede to nothing. Until there were only the two of them in the entire world. Until he knew it too.

And he kissed her. Of course he did. The coke told her that he would, that he couldn't not. She kissed him back, more passionately, slipping her tongue into his mouth, and wrapping her arms around his neck. She pulled him towards her, at the same time thrusting her body into his. And she knew he felt the charge exactly as she did. She knew the precise moment lust made his legs weak so that he, too, had to lean back, pulling her with him until he found equilibrium against the wall, his arms tight around her waist, one hand moving up towards her hair, her neck. And then, just as she was ready to gasp that maybe they should go somewhere else, he stopped. Pulled back and tried to smile at her, a queer look in his eyes. 'Sorry,' he said, his breath ragged and uneven. 'I shouldn't have.'

He let her go, sidestepped so that they were no longer close enough to strike sparks from each other. And instead of taking his hand, saying yes, you should, and laying her head

on his chest, Stella smiled the knowing, teasing smile the coke
gave her and said, 'Darling, it's a party. Don't be so serious,'
and went back into the room full of dancing, laughing well-
wishers, with no further scrap of joy in the night, but still
playing the part the coke had given her. When she saw Amanda
beckon James onto the dance floor some time later, then twine
her body around his, wrapping her arms around his neck, in
the precise spot where Stella's had been, and kissing him on the
mouth, she did nothing, said nothing, just turned away with a
shrug, another laugh and, later, another drink.

The party rolled on, louder, shriller, than she could really
bear, so that when Laura found her, suggested they get Amanda
and go, she agreed readily.

'Where is Amanda?' she asked. Since seeing her with James,
she had carefully turned away from any group or corner that
might have Amanda in it.

'Check the loos,' Laura said. 'She might be crying again.'

'Okay.' On the way they ran into James. At least they hadn't
left together, Stella thought, trying to smile coolly at him.

'Have you seen Amanda?' Laura asked.

'Not recently,' he responded, with an evasive look at Stella.

'We're checking the loos. Come on.'

'You go. I'll wait here,' said James.

'Oh, just come. Nobody cares if you pop your head around
the door,' said Stella, suddenly impatient of his impeccable
manners.

There indeed Amanda was, slouched on the divan. Her
make-up had run, her eyes were wandering, her hair was
wild and unkempt. Her dress had ridden up, and beside her,
kissing her neck, his hand down her top, was Christian. De
Sade was leaning against a washbasin, rolling a joint and

leering at them. It was, thought Stella suddenly, transported back to a cold, foggy night, very like the scene on the very night they had met Amanda at Dargle's. Had they really come so far, just to be back there?

'Christian,' Stella snapped, 'stop it.'

'Piss off, Stella,' he said amiably. 'This is none of your business. Is it, Amanda?' He turned Amanda's face up towards his and shook her head from side to side. 'See? She doesn't want me to stop.'

'Christian, she's completely out of it. You're being a disgusting perv. We're taking her home.'

'Oh, fuck off, Stella. Stop being such a do-gooder. Amanda's a big girl.' Byron de Sade sounded much less amiable than Christian. Stella could see he was thoroughly enjoying Amanda's humiliation. She and Laura took one each of Amanda's arms, and tried to heave her up.

'Ah, come on,' said Christian. 'My one chance, my one big night with Amanda O'Hagen. Don't ruin it!' He grabbed Amanda's hand, pulling her back down. Caught between the three of them, she flopped like a rag doll. Glancing at James, Stella saw a flash of pain on his face, but it was nothing like the bare, beaten look he had had at Amanda's twenty-first, when Huw had first entered the scene.

'God, what has she taken? She's completely out of it,' Laura said, trying to get Amanda's weight disposed in a way she could manage.

'Christian, any idea?' Stella asked.

Christian looked sly, then tapped his nose. 'I don't know, Toto, but it sure ain't Kansas,' he said.

'Oh, piss off! If you're not going to be helpful, then just get lost.' Laura was uncharacteristically vehement. 'Amanda, come on,' she said.

Amanda slurred, 'Don't worry 'bout me. I'll see you later.' She tugged her other arm out of Laura's grasp and slumped beside Christian. Stella was about to begin the awkward process of hauling her up again, when a vision of Amanda kissing James rose before her. Instead, she said, 'Okay, fine. Stay. If you want?'

'I want,' Amanda mumbled.

'You see? She wants!' Christian crowed.

'Okay, but be at Laura's before twelve, because that's when my parents are picking us up.'

'I'll leave a key for you,' Laura said anxiously, with a startled look at Stella. 'In case you come back before we're awake. You can just sneak in and sneak into bed. Sure you won't come now?'

'She's sure,' said Christian. 'Aren't you, pet?' He took Amanda's face in his hands again, but this time made her nod.

Stella felt sick, but all she said was 'Okay, if you're sure. We'll see you later. Have fun.'

James made a noise of disagreement, half-grunt, half-sigh, but Stella ignored him. Let him deal with it for once, she decided. If he felt he had the right to step in, he should do so. He didn't. Instead he followed them out and upstairs.

'Are you sure we should leave her?' Laura asked, at the top. 'I mean, Christian and Byron aren't exactly responsible.'

'She'll be fine,' Stella said. 'You heard her, she wants to stay. She's much more able to face those lunch parties on no sleep than we are. Come on, I've really had enough of this place.' Her desperation to leave was so strong that she swept the rest of what she felt beneath it.

And despite Laura's worry, she prevailed, and said goodbye to James, who was looking uneasy but irresolute. She and Laura got into a taxi and went home, almost in silence.

ରଃ

Safe in Laura's bathroom, Stella vomited, her body finally rejecting everything she had taken, and what she might have done.

She lay in bed, shivering, then passed into a deep, dreamless sleep that felt like a rehearsal for death.

In the morning Amanda arrived early. She looked tired, pale, but seemed determinedly bright.

'Did you stay much longer?' Stella asked, following her into the bathroom, which still smelt faintly of sick. 'Don't tell me you've been up all night?'

'No. I got some sleep at Christian's. Eventually,' Amanda said.

Stella gave her a sharp look. She was washing her face, scrubbing at last night's make-up with a muslin cloth and something that foamed and smelt of honey. There was a pause. 'Right. I presume he didn't give you breakfast. Shall I make coffee and toast before we go?'

'Coffee. No toast,' said Amanda, now smoothing something peachy and glowing into her skin so that she looked flawless.

'So was it a good night?' Stella needed reassurance that everything had been okay. That leaving hadn't been the act of betrayal she secretly feared, just the normal thing to do when one friend wanted to stay out and the other was tired and wanted to go home.

'It was fine.' Amanda was doing her eyes now, obliterating all traces of exhaustion with careful layers of colour.

Stella's relief was so intense she felt dizzy. 'Okay, I'll make the coffee. We're going to need it! I wonder how much cutlery your mother has laid out today.'

Amanda gave a wan smile. 'I suppose Huw never turned up?' she asked suddenly, half out of the bathroom.

'No.'

Chapter Thirteen

Dublin

DAWN WAS BREAKING. LAURA LAY IN BED listening to the sound of the house waking up, creaking gently, the mysterious daytime taps and gentle knockings that replaced the equally mysterious night sounds. She needed to get up, pack for her lunchtime flight, but was trying to centre herself for the challenge ahead. Petrie had rung her late the night before – no apology, of course – and talked through, yet again, what they needed, what she assumed Laura was offering.

'Obviously we need an exclusive,' she barked. 'We can't have Amanda talking to any other paper. In a while we'll discuss with her what magazine and TV she can do, but for now, just us. Got that?'

Laura, heart sinking, had said she had.

'Does she have an agent?' Petrie continued.

'God, I don't know. I doubt it. I mean, she never did that I know of ...'

'Right. The angle is the obvious one: the descent into hell, but write it for plenty of contrast, the golden past contrasted with the squalor of the present. What about the mother?' she said, suddenly changing tack.

'She's meeting me there,' said Laura, realising for the first time what that actually meant. That she would have to confront Mrs O'Hagen too.

'Good, a few quotes from her will help, but nothing libellous. Steer clear of any suggestion of fault. Don't say he made her do it. And, Laura?'

'Yes?'

'Amanda can see her quotes, but not copy. Got that? I know she's your friend, but don't make any rash promises because you won't be allowed to keep them.'

'Okay.' Laura had hung up, feeling sick. For all that she wanted her shot, wanted to step out of the uncertain, halting person she had always been, she didn't want to lose Stella and Amanda. She wanted their friendship and love, and she wanted new respect at work. Maybe both weren't possible.

Laura had never been any good at working things out – plans of action, campaigns, military-sounding stuff, which Stella was so adroit at. Laura made lists, painstakingly drawing up pros and cons, totting them up and forcing a solution from the outcome, then often changed her mind at the last minute and did the opposite, out of a stubborn reluctance to do as she was told, even by herself.

'Just do what you want to do,' Amanda had said to her once.

'It's the only true way to decide anything. Never mind other people and what *they* want. You can't guess for them, only for yourself.'

'But I don't ever really know what I want,' Laura had replied. 'Or, at least, I do, but then I change and want something else just as much.'

'Well, do what Stella and I tell you.' Amanda had laughed. 'We'll decide for you.'

And for a long time, she now thought, they had. Or not so much decided as proposed, and she had simply followed. But recently she had felt the stirrings of the old stubbornness, a strong wish not to do what anyone told her, to pick her own path and plod steadily down it, knowing now what she wanted at the end of it. Recognition. Position. Money, dammit, she decided. They owed her. Or Amanda did. All the years of picking up pieces, and now it was time to get something in return. She would ask Amanda outright, as a favour, to let her write the story. Or as payment for favours already done. Once Amanda said yes, Stella would have no choice. Laura felt certain that one good story, one big scoop, could put her in the position she needed to work at the subtle chinks she had begun to feel rather than see in Petrie's façade, to winkle at them until they grew large enough to squeeze herself through.

Funny, she thought then, how Mrs O'Hagen's endless lectures on the advantages of worldly position should have slid across Amanda, making no dent in her determination to be swallowed by love, and soaked so deep into Laura.

She remembered the chilly but efficient kindness Amanda's mother had shown during Nessa's illness, and the way she hadn't come to the funeral. She wondered again who the *real* Mrs O'Hagen was: the one who had sent things to Nessa, punnets of perfect raspberries, pheasant, or the one who hadn't come to honour her passing, or the one who had hosted the graduation lunch, where she had revealed so much of herself?

ঙ

The sun had been bright and hard that day, making the trees and fields seem brittle, austere. They would get no sympathy from Nature, Laura had realised, as they drove out of the city. Her bones felt sore, her stomach churned, her head ached and she was blotchy and pale underneath the hastily applied make-up. Her dress was wrong, too wintry for the day, and Mrs O'Hagen would know it.

Stella's father was driving, her mother chatting brightly about some piece in the morning paper. Beside Laura, Stella sat bolt upright, probably trying not to vomit again, with Nessa squashed in beside her and, on the far side, Amanda, leaning against the window, eyes shut.

Laura shut her own eyes. The shapes and colours flashing past the window made her feel sick. She thought about the night before, trying to put her finger on the bit of it that bothered her. There had been so much drinking, so many drugs, that there were blurs where she needed images to be sharp.

Amanda had set the pace, but they had followed more closely than they usually did. Partly, she thought, it had been solidarity. A recognition of her need to blot out the sordid events of the afternoon, and their own role. 'A guard of dishonour' was how she phrased it to herself. She remembered the way the party had worked on two levels that couldn't seem to connect. How on the surface it was a good party, one of the best. Loud, raucous, with just too many people and enough hilarity to keep them all afloat. But on the other level it had been muffled and she had been watchful throughout, worried, with an edgy kind of alarm that didn't have any specific focus but kept triggering itself over small things. The look on Stella's face when she'd come back into the room, James close behind her and a hundred silent things in the gap between them. The abandonment of Amanda's dancing and the joylessness of her overt flirting. Mostly, the scene in the loos before they'd left.

In that kind of state, Amanda always protested that she wanted to stay. They didn't listen to her. That was the deal. They scooped her up from whatever sofa or chair she was on, or steered her off the dance floor, ignoring all her protests that she was still having fun, and bundled her into a taxi, trying to disguise how out of it she was from the driver, who might refuse to take them if he knew. The next morning they would regale her with stories of the close shaves they had saved her from – 'You were talking to that guy with the long fingernails from college, then one you once said was so boring he made you want to cry, except last night you seemed to find him *fascinating*' – and Amanda would laugh, hide her head under the duvet and swear it couldn't be true, that they were making it up.

So why had they left her the night before? There had been something odd in the room, a tension, as she and Stella had struggled to get Amanda up and out, which had had nothing to do with the state Amanda was in. She tried piecing together the exact sequence of events, knowing only one thing for certain: that Stella was always the one who insisted they drag Amanda home with them – 'We're not leaving her as prey to maggots,' she would say firmly – but that last night it had been Stella who had given up, walked away. It had been an overwrought day, that was true, and Stella was more out of it than usual, and there was no doubt that playing bodyguard to Amanda could be very trying. But, still, something niggled about it.

She felt slightly guilty, she decided. That was it. Even though it was no big deal – Amanda had probably been about half an hour behind them. After all, Trap didn't stay open all night. But if we'd insisted she come with us, she'd have got another hour or so of sleep, Stella thought. There was something particularly miserable about the exhausted way Amanda was slumped in her seat.

She continued to muse over the night before, different moments resolving themselves into something clear out of the mass of noise and colour. The photographer waddling stiffly away, like a penguin, when they teased him made her want to laugh again, but the confusion on James's face, when he'd looked from Stella to Amanda, worried her. Any wavering on his part, any hint of interest, would be far worse for Stella than the flat impossibility of now, she thought. Then the greedy look on Byron de Sade's face came back to her. She wanted never to see him again. I must remember to tell Stella and Amanda, she thought. We need to ditch him now, before he tags along with us into adult life. She nudged Stella. 'Let's never see Byron de Sade again.'

Stella seemed alarmed. 'Why?' she asked.

'Because he's horrible,' Laura said.

'Did he do something?' Stella said, wary.

'Not in particular,' said Laura. 'He's just a horrible person, and we need to get rid of him now before he thinks he's a friend for life.'

'Good plan,' Stella said. Then, 'How do you think she is?' She flicked her eyes to Amanda's slumped form.

'Not great,' Laura answered. 'She looks terrible. But, then, so do I. You don't look great either.'

'No, I guess not,' Stella said. 'She said she got some sleep at Christian's, though.'

'Better than nothing After all, she's got to tell her mother about Huw. Tell her something, anyway, about why he's not there.'

'Jesus, a Mrs O'Hagen lunch party is exactly what none of us needs today.'

ᙝ

In the years since they had first met Amanda, Mr O'Hagen's wealth, always impressive, had apparently substantially increased. Even the rumblings of disaster seemed not to have touched him, because he had been smart and swift, moving ahead of the shock waves of financial collapse. He was regularly cited, along with four or five other men whose names they had all grown up with, as an example of what could be done by hard graft. 'He's the guy Croesus goes to when he's short of a few bob,' Christian had said, reading the Sunday paper, which contained a list of the country's richest, one morning over brunch. 'They say he has the Midas touch. He clearly put his hands all over Amanda.' He had laughed hard at his own crude joke.

There was no sign of any substantial change to the house, though. There was a basement gym now, and a helipad behind the stables, but from the front, all was as it had been on their first visit, on just such an early-summer day, Laura now recalled.

Through the wrought-iron gates and into what had always seemed to her to be a kind of dream sequence. The ancient beauty of the house, gently buoyed up by the patchwork of fields and gardens around it, proffering itself to view, like a hand holding out a pretty stone, but all the while, Laura was conscious of the sharp interior of the house, pulsing at the heart of the picture, like something wrong.

'Aha, the hall of mirrors,' Stella's father said happily, rubbing his hands in satisfaction as they were shown in by Ivana, who hugged the girls warmly. He greatly enjoyed Mrs O'Hagen's entirely uncompromising taste. Amanda, woken at the last minute, went silently upstairs to change. She didn't suggest that Laura or Stella come with her, so they followed their parents into the main drawing room, with its thick cream carpet overlaid by woven rugs in subtle, expensive Oriental colours. A large, Regency-style couch upholstered in plum-and-white-striped satin and scattered with cushions dominated the room, surrounded by spindly chairs and occasional tables, all covered with photos, mainly of Amanda, always staged and posed, never candid shots. In every one, she was staring straight at the lens. The overall effect was faintly aggressive.

Mrs O'Hagen was wearing ice-blue, fitted around her still very impressive bosom, with panels at the side that cleverly distracted from the thickening waistline. Her hair was carefully coiled and held in place by a silver clasp, her make-up light but perfect, and her eyes the same ice-blue as the dress.

'Nessa, John, Sandra. Girls. How nice,' she said, coming towards them, hands outstretched to clasp theirs. Her touch was firm and cold. (Much later, when Laura tried to hold Nessa's dead hands as she lay in her coffin, tried to fit her warm fingers around and under the unyielding, marbled flesh, she thought of Mrs O'Hagen's chilly clasp.) Mr O'Hagen nodded to them, smiling briefly, then turned back to the man beside him. Various people were dotted around the room, intimates of the O'Hagens, including Alice, whom they had met their first day in the house, and Malcolm, whom Mrs O'Hagen had once hoped would help Amanda's career. He must be there to underline the fact that Amanda has made it, thought Laura. Sinead was there, too, pretty in pale green, like the first delicate sign of spring. She smiled at her.

'Where's Amanda?' Mrs O'Hagen still had hold of one of Laura's hands.

'She's upstairs, changing,' she said. The curiously light blue eyes looked into hers consideringly. Mrs O'Hagen always considered. Everything was weighed in the balance with her, even seemingly trivial matters.

'And Huw?'

Laura didn't know what to say. Had Amanda told her mother anything at all? Better play it safe, she decided. 'I'm not sure. Amanda knows ...' she muttered.

Stella, who had been uncharacteristically quiet all morning, had moved off to get a drink from a tray held by a waiter – Bellinis and Bloody Marys, by the look of it, with glasses of cold white wine. Laura wondered if a drink would make her feel better, or much worse. Deciding she couldn't actually feel much worse, she grabbed a Bellini, downed it quickly and reached for another.

Stella winked at her. 'We're going to need it,' she murmured, gesturing at Alice, who had started a story of what she had said to the salesperson in Brown Thomas, what the salesperson had said back, and the crushing retort she, Alice, had produced.

James arrived with his parents. Laura, standing beside Stella, felt her jump when she saw him, then turn away. Iseult, his mother, was exquisite in a white linen trouser suit, worn as casually as if it had been jeans and a sweater. Instead of a shirt, she wore a pale grey T-shirt, the effect somehow teen rebel rather than garden party. James, after a smile in their direction, wandered over to the window. Iseult made her way straight to the girls – Laura noticed she didn't have much truck with Mrs O'Hagen's two-handed-clasp approach, just gave her a peck on the cheek, then moved firmly away.

'How's Amanda?' she said immediately. 'Don't worry, James told me everything. Or probably not everything.' She gave a quick smile. 'No one ever tells everything, don't you find? But enough.'

'We're not sure ...' Stella began.

'Not great, really,' said Laura. 'But at least it's done now. I'm sure she'll be fine. She just needs time to get over it. Definitely for the best.'

'Hmm,' said Iseult. 'Things that seem done often aren't. But we'll see.'

Just then, Amanda entered the room. She had showered and changed into a shimmery pale grey dress with pink panels, which Laura knew was Chanel because she had been with Amanda when Amanda had bought it, for an eye-popping sum that didn't cause her a second's hesitation. Her hair was loose around her shoulders, thick and golden, like a velvet snood, but her face was still wan and her shoulders slumped. She looks terrible, Laura thought. Worse than yesterday. Perhaps it was the hangover – a decent night's sleep might show her that life without Huw had good things too.

'Sorry I'm late,' Amanda said to her mother, then drew her to one side and began a low conversation. From the disapproving tightening of Mrs O'Hagen's mouth, and the way in which she said, 'Really, Amanda!' crossly, Laura assumed Amanda was filling her in on what had happened, and the reason for Huw's no-show. She wondered which version Amanda was giving her.

'What did you tell her?' Laura asked, when Amanda was able to extract herself and join them. Mrs O'Hagen had left the room, presumably to tell Ivana to change the table setting, her back set rigid with annoyance.

'That we had a big row, and broke up.' Amanda shrugged. 'What else am I going to say? I can't tell her the truth. I wouldn't be able to get the words out. Can you imagine?' She shuddered. 'So now she thinks I'm capricious and stupid. Luckily, I don't care what she thinks,' she finished. Then, smoothly: 'Iseult! You look amazing. How do you manage to be the youngest-looking person I know?'

'I haven't been out all night,' Iseult responded, laughing and hugging her.

Laura moved off to join Nessa and Stella's father, who were amiably laughing over the paintings on the wall. 'Other people's ancestors,' said Nessa, as Laura arrived. 'Someone else's dead Uncle Whatever. I never could see the point.'

'Lunch!' Mrs O'Hagen announced then, in tinkling tones, and they all moved through into the small dining room, where an oval table laid with a thick snowy cloth had been set in the bay window overlooking the formal back gardens, with purple hills in a distance made farther away by the clarity of the day. In the centre there was a round bowl of perfect deep pink roses, drooping just enough to take the sharp edge off their glory.

Laura, who had a headache and was longing for somewhere quiet and dark, winced slightly at the many brittle reflections of sunlight off silver and crystal. She was seated between Sinead and a man who introduced himself as 'Peter Morrison – friend of Mick,' gave her a bone-crushing handshake, then ignored her, much to Laura's relief.

Even the food seemed spiteful, she thought, as plates of thin, sharp asparagus spears alongside cold slices of scallop and shrimp terrine were served. Conversation was at first general – Mrs O'Hagen demanded to know what they all thought of the latest political scandal, something to do with police intelligence and who had known what and when, which Laura had been following only vaguely – then broke into smaller groups because only Stella's parents seemed to have any interest. Laura turned to Sinead and began asking about the night before – had she stayed much longer? Had anything interesting happened? Amanda was deep in conversation with Malcolm, who was still looking at her when Huw came into the room. Laura caught the dazed look of hope that floated across Amanda's face when she caught sight of him. Iseult is right: the things that seem done aren't, Laura thought.

'So sorry I'm late.' Huw came forward with all the confidence of his breeding and upbringing. Mrs O'Hagen rose instantly to greet him. Laura noticed that he did the two-handed shake as well, so that he and Mrs O'Hagen looked ready to play ring-a-roses for a minute as they clasped each other. 'I'm glad you didn't wait, Marie,' he said, kissing her cheek, then including them all in his smile and charming gesture of deprecation, with special emphasis of eyebrow-arch towards Iseult. Laura had noticed that he was the only one of Amanda's friends who willingly called Mrs O'Hagen by her first name. Not that Mrs O'Hagen had ever pressed them to.

'Huw,' she said now, calmly, although normally she reacted very badly to any disruption of her social plans, 'so pleased you could join us after all.' She threw a speculative look at Amanda.

She always became more English-sounding when she spoke to Huw, as if her early experience of smoothing out her own accent had left her unusually permeable to others. 'I'll have Ivana bring another chair.'

'Marvellous,' Huw said, as though he was doing her a favour. 'So kind. I wonder if I might have a word with Amanda first?' Laura looked at Amanda, who stared at Huw. Then she looked at Stella, opposite, who had her eyes fixed on Amanda and was silently mouthing, 'No, don't,' and shaking her head. Beside Stella, James seemed to be holding his breath. Laura willed him to do something, anything – turn the table over, smash a glass, make his own declaration of love. Anything that might change the course of what was happening in front of them. But he did nothing. Just sat. That's what he does, she realised. Nothing.

Amanda got up, as though in a trance, and walked over to Huw, who took her hand, at which she twitched but didn't snatch it away, then left the room with him. Would Mrs O'Hagen say something about 'young love'? Laura wondered. She didn't, just resumed her conversation. They ate chicken breast stuffed with goat's cheese and sundried tomatoes, served with a couscous salad, and chatted as well as they could, but with the two empty chairs and acute curiosity crippling most of them, conversation was stilted.

Amanda burst back into the room, holding Huw by one hand, waving the other aloft. She was now glowing with excitement, lit from within by a dancing flame.

'We're getting married,' she burst out, showing off a huge ring, diamonds and sapphires set in a star shape, antique, beautiful, and reaching almost to her knuckle. Beside her, Huw was smirking, like a painted marionette, with his smooth, even features and careful expression.

There was a pause.

Then: 'What lovely news!' Mrs O'Hagen rose smoothly after a steady look at Amanda, holding her arms out so that Amanda and Huw might dutifully kiss her. 'We must have champagne. How unexpected, but delightful.'

'He just asked me now but he had the ring with him because he knew he was going to. It's not a family ring but he says he'll give me that one later,' Amanda babbled, details dashing forth, like tiny waves breaking against a sea wall. Her father had risen, was shaking Huw's hand, and Huw was saying something insincere about how he should have asked him first but really he couldn't wait.

'Did he go down on one knee?' Alice asked, with a silly giggle.

'Luckily not,' Amanda responded. 'He was there to catch me. I nearly fainted.'

There was plenty of excited chatter and exclaiming but, looking around, Laura could see that half the table at least did not share in the general merriment. Stella and James's faces were almost identical masks of misery. Nessa looked worried, and Iseult seemed torn between upset for her son and apprehension for Amanda. Laura glanced at the couple again, and found that Huw was now staring at her, triumph on those neat features. He arched a dark eyebrow and smiled. Amanda, on the other hand, seemed to be avoiding her. She smiled at Laura once, almost shyly, then deliberately made herself very busy accepting the congratulations of others, fussing about champagne with her mother, holding Huw's hand, so that she didn't have to speak to either of her friends.

There was a general toast – 'To Amanda! To Huw!' said Mrs O'Hagen.

'To happiness,' added Nessa, which earned her a spiky look from Amanda's mother.

Any celebration of Stella and Laura's finals seemed forgotten now in favour of the more exciting news, but Laura didn't mind. She felt breathless, as if she hadn't recovered yet from the shock. To have gone from consoling Amanda and feeling secretly relieved, to toasting her and feeling secretly alarmed in the space of twenty minutes was a faster spin than she could assimilate. She kept trying to catch Stella's eye, see what was going on in her mind, but Stella, too, was keeping her gaze averted, staring at the table.

The party broke up soon after dessert. Malcolm had 'some people to meet', Alice said she'd take a lift from him ('She won't get anywhere with *that*,' Mrs O'Hagen said sniffily, after she'd left), Iseult said she must get back to the garden – it was the last day she could put in the lavender if she wanted it to take hold – and James said he would go with her. Stella's parents wanted to leave too, to Laura's relief. Nessa looked tired, white and drained, and Laura realised suddenly how little she had spoken, how drawn her face was. A sudden stab of fear made her frantic to get home, get away from these people and the terrible things they did, which required so much of other people's energy to make right.

'We'll come too, okay, Stella?' she said.

'Yes, fine,' Stella agreed immediately.

'Just come upstairs with me for a minute,' Amanda said. 'I have little presents for you.'

Once they were in her bedroom, Stella started to say something in a low voice about 'last night', but Amanda cut her off: 'I'm sorry our news hijacked your day.'

Laura moved to sit on the window seat, her favourite place.

From there she could hear wood pigeons cooing to each other as the afternoon sun slanted towards the house. 'Never mind our day,' she said. 'Are you really happy?'

'Really. Really, really.'

'Did you know?' Stella demanded.

'God, no. I had no idea. I wondered would he just go back to London. I thought it was possible I'd never see him again. That I'd have to make new plans. For everything. I wondered how I would do that.'

Laura had often suspected that part of the appeal for Amanda was the way Huw so constantly set the pace. Being with him meant she had very little deciding to do for herself: his more definite personality overrode the faint apathy that lay within hers.

'It is possible to change plans,' Laura said now. 'You could still do something else with your life. You could go back to college, finish your degree next year.'

Amanda just looked at her. 'But I don't have to. It's all right now.'

'It's not all right. How can you say yes to him,' Stella cut in, 'after what happened yesterday?'

'Can it really be only yesterday?' said Laura, dreamily. Could the world really change, and change again, so quickly?

'He explained it to me, and said he was sorry, and I can forgive him.' Amanda looked as if she dearly wished the conversation would end there.

'What possible explanation could he have? Did Dell somehow slip, and fall, and land with her mouth around his dick by accident?' Stella was vicious now.

'He explained it to me,' Amanda said again. When it became obvious that Stella and Laura were simply waiting to hear more, she continued reluctantly, 'He says the high is much more intense accompanied by a blow job. That you get a more amazing come-up. He says he wouldn't ask me to do that, but Dell was fine with it.'

'Good God, Amanda!' Stella looked as if she wanted to shake her.

'So it wasn't about sex, really, it was about drugs?' said Laura.

'Yes.'

'You know that doesn't make it any better?' Laura said, after a moment.

'Yes, it does. To me, anyway. And I don't want to talk about it any more. Look what I got for you.' She had bought identical gold necklaces, delicate chains hung with tiny gold leaves. She added, 'I hope you're going to be my bridesmaids?'

Neither Stella nor Laura felt able to respond to the question, or to the hope it carried.

○3

Mrs O'Hagen showed them to the door, chatting easily with Stella's mother, already rehearsing plans for the wedding. Safely outside, Laura leaned in to Stella and said, 'She knows this isn't right. She might not know what happened yesterday, but she must know he's not good for Amanda. Yet she's not saying anything.'

'Oh yes she is,' said Stella, bitterly. 'She's saying she's delighted. Didn't you see her? Lording it over everyone. She all but punched the air in triumph! This is exactly what she's dreamed of. She doesn't care that the details are so, so wrong. The picture is the right one.'

'Then maybe we should tell her about yesterday.'

'We can't. Especially not now. They're engaged. It's the last thing we can do.'

'But she needs to know,' Laura insisted. 'She's fooled by him.'

'She doesn't care,' said Stella. 'Amanda is the tribute she pays to her ambition. And, like all tributes, Amanda gets swallowed. Burned. Drowned. Dismembered. God, and I felt bad about leaving her behind last night! Mrs O'Hagen abandons her every single day of her life.'

'Well, I don't believe she's that bad,' said Laura, after a moment in which she weighed up the wisdom of siding with their own personal Wicked Witch of the West. 'I think she'd care, if she knew. And I think we should tell her.' But Stella wouldn't, and Laura couldn't, unless Stella did it with her. Fear of scenes, storms, with Amanda, with Stella, maybe even with Mrs O'Hagen, who, she knew, wouldn't like being confronted with something so poisonous to her plans, stopped her. So she said nothing, stuffed it down with all the other things she was scared to say.

Chapter Fourteen

New York

'STELLA?' SEAN APPEARED. 'A MOMENT?' HE CAME
into her office, shut the door behind him and leaned with his
back against it. 'How's the Sarah Travers thing coming?'

'It isn't. Still isn't. I haven't cracked it yet, but I will.'

'Right. Well, I've got your missing piece of the jigsaw.'

'Oh, yeah?'

'Look, she was fucking Carter. And he's prepared to say so.'

There was a pause. Not a very nice one. Stella let the new
information seep into what she knew already. It certainly
joined all the dots. Like ink, it swirled into all the fractured
parts and drew them together. 'You knew.'

'Sure I knew. But Carter didn't want it getting out if it

could be stopped. He wanted to see how they could handle this without but I just spoke to him. He can see now it isn't possible to just make it go away.' Sean snapped out the words as if he was slamming lids.

Stella understood that his aggression was more circumstantial than personal: he didn't like this kind of conversation – it was too revelatory – but that didn't make it any more bearable. She felt her own anger rising to meet his. 'So what happened?' she asked.

'What do you mean, what happened?'

'Well, why now? What went wrong with them? Why didn't he just end it?'

'They got caught. She got careless and stupid and they got caught. People began to talk, and he was walking right into a whole lot of fucking trouble. His wife is the type who knows how to make a fucking lot of fucking trouble.'

'So Sarah had to go?'

'And she wouldn't. Not quietly. She threatened him.'

'So he put this piece of bullshit together.' Stella didn't bother trying to hide how furious the conversation made her.

'That's the game.' He shrugged. 'That's how it goes.'

'For everyone, or just for Sarah Travers and Carter?' She stared at him.

'For everyone.' He sounded irritated. 'You know that. The person who has most to lose has to win.'

'I see. I understand perfectly. I suppose that's why you put me on the case. I must say, I did wonder.'

'No, Stella, that's not it. We put you on the case because we figured if anyone could make it go away, it was you. If you couldn't, no one could. No big deal. I'm just giving you what you need now to tie it up.'

But that wasn't all he was giving her. There was a warning, too – of course there was. She understood now why Barrington Fraser had attended their recent meetings. He was there as a fat, gloomy chaperone. Sean was shaken. Carter's near-miss, if it remained that and didn't blow into a full-fledged disaster, had spooked him. He was covering his tracks, strengthening his alibis, and delivering a clear message to her to stay in line. Unless she understood and acquiesced, she was now a threat.

So she smiled sweetly, choking on rage and betrayal, and said, 'I understand. And I'm so glad to be able to get this cleared up before I leave. Feels neater. I'll dictate a letter to you and Barrington before I go that should do the trick.'

He narrowed his eyes, stared at her, weighing in his decisive and fast-moving brain the possible implications of her answer.

She stared back, still smiling. 'It's okay, Sean, really. I get it,' she said softly.

So he smiled back, said, 'You're smart, Stella. A pistol. You'll make it. See you later, kid,' and left.

Stella waited until the door had snapped shut, then looked for something sharp to stab herself with. She wanted to feel an actual physical pain that would match the howl building inside her. A wound that she could worry and tease into sharper agony each time she needed to heighten the interior outrage that she knew would never leave her. It wasn't enough to carry the mark of her stupidity inside herself. She wanted to be able to touch it, see it, reopen it when necessary. So she found a safety pin, small but sharp enough to do the job, and jabbed it hard into her upper arm in one angry movement, then a second time, for emphasis. There wasn't much blood. Presumably you had to try harder for that, but the pain she craved as a reprimand was there.

She had never done that before, and wondered briefly if she was going to become one of those women who cut themselves repeatedly, out of stress, misery, isolation, carving out a story of rejection on their thighs and stomachs. Then she understood that never before had she walked into such a smithy of humiliation and waited to be cast as a fool. And that her rage against herself was justified.

C8

On the plane that evening, she touched the sore place often, forcing herself to remember the pain, drilling the lesson into herself so that it became part of her. As she tried to sleep, knees drawn up to her stomach, she made a confused sort of a vow: 'Stop being such a fucking idiot.' By which she meant Sean, her job, most of her existence in Manhattan, and the shallow, stupid direction her life had taken.

The revelation, and the pain that had followed it, had affected her like a shot of adrenalin, so that she looked back on the years of her life just passed with sudden wide-awake horror. For the way she had taken a few rags – the big salary, the affair with Sean, nights out in cocktail bars – and drawn them round herself, like a cloak, affecting to admire the richness of the fabric as it caught the light, when in fact it was threadbare and thin. Humiliation rose, like heartburn, in her, searing her throat until she choked it down again. How could she have been so stupid? She had let go of all the things she had sworn to believe in. Dumped the person she had chosen to be, and allowed life to remake her in such a pathetic mode.

She felt then how urgently she needed Laura and Amanda. Needed them beside her to tell her who she used to be. To list the qualities she knew she'd once had so that she could try to find them and tick them off one by one. Laura and Amanda would help her cut through this mess. 'The person who has most to lose has to win.' She remembered Sean's words and shivered under the thin airline blanket. Stripped of his presence, no longer playing out the film of their affair in her head, she could see it for what it was, and what she was within it. At best reckless. At worst – what? A cheat? A slut? A fool?

She searched to understand the point at which she had allowed all this to happen, the moment when she had subconsciously agreed to settle for so very little, and finally landed on the night before Amanda's wedding.

Chapter Fifteen

London

LONDON WAS BRUSQUE AND GREY, JUST AS
Stella remembered it. Her plane landed early and the cab took
her, in a haze of travel weariness and early-morning drizzle, to
the guesthouse where Laura would join her before lunch. The
bedroom was pretty and chintzy, deliberately English in a way
that only catalogues and a certain type of B&B could manage.
She lay down on one of the single beds, unwilling to go to sleep
but unable to face being anywhere else.

Her last proper trip to London, longer than an eye-blink,
had been six months before the wedding, a trip to buy clothes
for Amanda, who had flown in from Paris to meet them, and a
chance for Huw's parents to show their prospective daughter-
in-law to their acquaintances.

'Paris is amazing,' Amanda had exclaimed, jumping up from the kitchen table to hug them. Stella and Laura, just arrived, were still trying to get used to the house, hired by Mrs O'Hagen for the week – 'So much easier than a hotel,' Mrs O'Hagen had said. 'No having to say hello and thank you to people when you don't feel like it.'

Stella had been privately amazed that she would ever feel the need to say anything to anyone when she didn't want to. But perhaps, she thought, grim suburban habits died harder than you'd think.

The house was a four-storey monster on Montpelier Square, round the corner from Harrods. Everything was oatmeal-coloured, with touches of pale blue and primrose. The kitchen where they sat, with its skylights, pale wooden floor and charming duck-egg blue cupboards, was by far the nicest room in the house. Everywhere else, the furnishings were so soft and thick that Stella later imagined shutting her bedroom door and screaming at the top of her voice, confident that no one downstairs would hear her. Even the walls had fabric on them, rather than just paint or wallpaper, and the innumerable lamps, mirrors, immense vases and ornamental fireplace tools made her think how confusing a game of Cluedo would be, with so many potential murder weapons.

Amanda, naturally, had barely glanced around her. 'Sit down,' she ordered. 'Let me tell you everything.' She was wearing a long, bedraggled coat, made of something black and white and furry.

'Monkey fur?' asked Laura, gesturing at it.

Amanda glanced down, laughed. 'Astrakhan. Huw bought it for me in the *marché des puces* – the flea market. It's a 1960s' original.'

'Yes, probably Jane Birkin wore it,' Stella said, 'and no one's cleaned it since. Smells of Serge Gainsbourg. Not in a good way.' Amanda looked exhausted, haggard, with dark circles under her eyes and dirty hair. Maybe it was a Paris thing, a more dishevelled vibe. Beside her Laura, in a pink shirt and jeans, looked preppy and incredibly young. 'So, go on, tell us.'

'Oh it's amazing!' Amanda began. 'No one ever goes to bed. The whole city is full of tiny bars that are open through the night, full of the most wonderfully sordid stories. Tourists talk about people-watching on the Champs-Élysées or somewhere stupid, but the real Paris is to be found in those cheap bars — drunken arguments between elderly couples, or watching the *patron* give out to the North African kids who sit all night and buy hardly any beer. They fight like we chat — loudly, with no inhibitions. It's so wonderful!'

She was laughing, animated, brimming with excitement.

'Paris life suits you,' Laura said.

Stella wondered if she meant it. Was it possible she hadn't noticed the dirty roots and blotchy skin? Or was she just being conciliatory?

'*Life* suits me,' Amanda answered. 'You know, actually living life, being in life? Not just sitting around, waiting to grow up and be gone, always being part of someone else's plans. Now I do what I want.'

'And what's that? Tell us. Make us sick with envy,' Laura said.

'Nothing, really. The usual things. But it *could* be anything. That's the thrill of it.'

The week passed in a daze of getting changed and going to different places. Lunches, receptions, dinners, parties. The only meal they ate in the house was breakfast, which was laid out every morning by the Filipina housekeeper who came with the house. Stella and Laura's room perpetually looked as if the contents of a theatre wardrobe department had been turned upside down in it, with dresses, scarves, shoes, jackets and make-up scattered across every surface. They had declined the attentions of the maid, feeling she probably had enough to do ministering to the whirlwind costume changes of Amanda and Mrs O'Hagen, who shopped during every free second, coming home with carrier bags spilling pretty tissue paper and the designer clothes deemed necessary for the many celebrations of what was to come, only for those same bags to lie untouched, as they decided that something different was required.

Mrs O'Hagen was in her element, directing operations tirelessly. Stella and Laura would get up and make their way to the kitchen, fuzzy after yet another late night, silently grabbing coffee, croissants and some of the fresh fruit laid delightfully in glass bowls, and already they would hear her on the phone, giving orders, discussing arrangements. She had tried to get Amanda to join in.

'White or gold roses for Huw's mother?'

'Whichever. White?' Amanda said, shrugging.

'And while we're on flowers' – the *we* was either hopeful or deliberately dense, Stella thought – 'hydrangeas and roses, or peonies and sweet peas for the church?' They were all having their nails done in the smaller oatmeal sitting room by a friend of the Filipina housekeeper, who did massage and manicures.

'I don't mind, whatever you think.' Amanda was clearly trying to be polite, thought Stella. Couldn't give a damn was more like it.

'Well, the hydrangeas and roses will be more old-pink, sort of vintage. The peonies and sweet peas would be fresher, younger.' Mrs O'Hagen, naturally, pursued her course.

'Honestly, I don't mind. You decide.'

'Perhaps the hydrangeas and roses, then. They'll last longer. And the vintage feel will suit your dress. Not that the *dress* is vintage,' she emphasised to Laura and Stella, who knew very well what the dress was, having had to sit through interminable fittings at Vivienne Westwood, discussing every aspect of its fit and cut. 'But I do wish you would pay more attention, Amanda. This is *your* big day, you know, not mine.'

'Really?' Amanda had muttered.

Mrs O'Hagen had shot her a sharp look, but said nothing. She'd tried again: 'Do you want a band and a DJ, or just a band?'

'Both. Or neither, whatever.'

'Well, you have to have something,' Mrs O'Hagen said crossly. 'You have to have music. I have a string quartet for the church, but later, at the party, people will expect to dance. If you won't decide, I'll just get both. But I don't understand why you insist on pretending this has nothing to do with you. It's *your* wedding – the greatest day of your life.'

No wonder Amanda was stoned all the time, thought Stella, watching her tilt back her head in her chair, eyes closed, arm limply held in front of her to have tangerine polish expertly applied to her nails, disregarding the torn, ragged skin around them. And she *was* stoned all the time. She moved uncomplainingly through the various parties, lunches, dinners, coffees and dress appointments, changing as required, chatting politely, allowing herself to be introduced, congratulated and questioned, with resignation if not enthusiasm. She smiled, responded, but there wasn't much light or spark to her, Stella had noticed. She and Huw would slip away together late at night, once the formal requirements for the evening were over, reappearing only many hours later. In those moments Stella would see something of the old Amanda, something like excitement in her eyes as she threw a smile or a wink across at them as she left.

It was getting more difficult to get her up in the mornings, and longer again to magic her into the beauty she needed to be. Mrs O'Hagen was talking about sending her for 'a week or ten days to Barbados before the wedding. To relax.'

'Where do you go?' Laura asked her, as they sat over a late breakfast at the large, scrubbed-pine kitchen table. Stella was in jeans and a faded grey T-shirt, Amanda in an old-fashioned thick silk peignoir, the colour and texture of butter, which fell around her in thick folds. Sunlight came in above and behind them, picking out the corners and edges of things. The windows were open and the sounds of London traffic droned sleepily in the background. They had an unaccustomed free morning, and had decided to spend it doing as little as possible. Coffee percolated cheerfully on the hob, and the room smelt of it. Mrs O'Hagen had gone to meet Alice, who had 'popped over to London', ostensibly for some shopping, 'But really she wants to worm her way into what *we*'re doing,' Mrs O'Hagen had said, with grim satisfaction, tightly tying the belt of her Burberry trench coat.

'Sometimes to Huw's friends' places,' Amanda answered. 'Not the friends who come to all the parties. These are different friends. Sometimes we go to his house, but his parents are using it a lot at the moment, so that isn't really such a good idea. Last night we checked into a hotel, just a small place quite close to here, for a bit of privacy. Then we checked out again at six this morning and he dropped me back here and I got into bed, and then you two came and woke me up.' She laughed.

'Why a hotel? What did you do?' Laura was curious.

'Talked, listened to music, just hung out. Huw ordered room service for the fun, but it wasn't very good and we didn't eat it.'

'Drugs?'

'Some.' Amanda tucked a strand of hair behind her ear and bent her head. 'Although, really, you two are obsessed. We decided the desk clerk must think we were having an affair, or a sudden one-night stand, because we checked in so late and without luggage. We played up to that.' She giggled. 'It was fun.'

It was the first time the three of them had been alone together for any length of time since they'd arrived in London. Actually, Stella realised, it was the first time they had been properly alone since the lunch party that had become an engagement party. They had been out together at bars and clubs but never alone. She and Laura had agreed the night before that they felt like royal handmaids.

'There to admire and serve, but not get too close,' as Laura had put it. And it wasn't just Mrs O'Hagen who was keeping them subtly but firmly at arm's length. Amanda was allowing her to, seeming to want to avoid the usual intimacy between them, and Stella, who had always felt confident that she understood Amanda, knew what she was feeling, saw that now she didn't know, hadn't known since the night of the post-finals party.

'How is Huw enjoying it all?' she asked, hoping to open the door to some kind of confidence.

'Same as me. Putting up with it. Longing for it to be over and just the two of us.'

'Do you like Huw's parents?' Laura asked.

'I suppose so,' Amanda said slowly. 'I don't think they're going to feature much in our lives. Huw doesn't see them very often. But they seem nice.' She said it cautiously.

Having met them once, Stella thought that no one could have called Huw's mother 'nice'. She was more like a praying mantis than anything else. Shimmering, thin, always on alert, her large, faintly protruding eyes constantly flickering. As for his father, for all the laughter and show of geniality, 'nice' wasn't the word for him either.

'So, what are you two wearing tonight?' Amanda seemed eager to change the subject.

'My blue linen again. It'll just have to do,' said Stella.

'An old Diane von Furstenberg wrap dress of Nessa's, an amazing collection of greens, in an almost camouflage pattern, with broad collars,' said Laura.

'Perfect! But I'd love it if you'd let me buy you some clothes.' Amanda said.

'We know, but we'd rather not. The bridesmaids' dresses are quite enough.' Stella had answered for both of them.

'They're so gorgeous – just wait till you see them,' Amanda said happily. 'You two will totally upstage me!'

☙

The party had been 'for our city friends', as Huw's mother had said grandly. Imagine having categories, thought Stella. How many did they have? And how many in each category? The party was in the wedding-cake house, the Edsbergs' London house, where Huw and Amanda would live.

'Daddy wanted to buy us a house, but Huw prefers living there. He says it's where he feels most grounded, because he spent so many holidays there when he was at school and university,' Amanda had explained.

'The rich,' Laura had said later, 'really are different.' She sounded awed, as Stella would have been if she had, for one moment, allowed herself to believe that any of this was real. Actually real, instead of the fantastical trappings of someone else's life, which ceased to be the moment she stopped observing it. That was the only way she could cope with the vast gulf between them, a gulf that seemed wider every day, with Amanda an increasingly distant figure on the opposite shore, separated by the luxury and indolence of her existence, and her growing apathy in the face of it. Sometimes Stella wondered if she would like to be that rich, and how it might feel to be an object of inevitable deference and envy. She felt pretty certain that, curiosity aside, she wouldn't much like it. But Laura, she suspected, might. There was a look on her face at times, a secret wondering, as she watched the stacking up of excess around Amanda, which betrayed to Stella that she yearned, at least a little bit, for the kind of certainty brought by material things. It had surprised her, because she had thought Laura would be able to see how laboured it all was, this business of being rich, and for a moment she was disappointed that Laura couldn't, then decided it was a harmless failing. Like window-shopping, she thought, or admiring pictures of film stars.

Huw had been strange at that party, Stella remembered. It was a glittering set-up, full of international jet-set types. Beautiful older women with streaked blonde hair, year-round tans and long lean figures, wearing mostly shades of caramel and coffee in silk or fine linen. The men, equally graceful, in impeccably pressed trousers, discussed money and skiing in large, loud groups while waiters in black tie flitted between them with trays of champagne and cocktails.

The parents' generation had been so busy flirting with and impressing one another that, after an initial round of introductions and polite interest, she and Laura were largely left alone. Even Amanda and Huw were off the podium. This was not a young people's party. It was more like an O'Hagen party, Stella decided. Mr and Mrs O'Hagen looked at ease and perfectly at home, having been to many of the same resorts, stayed in many of the same hotels, as those around them. Cries of 'Never Sandy Lane in *March*' mingled with 'But then you must have met the O'Briens – you know, Tom O'Brien. Owns the golf course there ...'

So this was where Mrs O'Hagen belonged, thought Stella, watching from a doorway as she threw her head back in laughter at something the man nearest her had said, then reached for another glass of champagne. This world of plenty and ostentation, where she seemed welcome and recognised. How dull she must find Dublin. Stella jumped as Huw leaned on the wall beside her.

'Rich man, poor man, beggarman, thief,' he said, laughing.

'I don't see any beggars,' said Stella stiffly. She wasn't prepared to cease hostilities.

'You know, now that Amanda and I are getting married, you and I will have to find a way to live together in peace, for her sake.'

'No, we won't. We just have to avoid each other,' Stella had retorted.

'But I don't want to stay out of your way, Stella,' he had said, in a sneering parody of seduction. 'And I don't think you really want to stay out of mine.'

'Oh yes I do,' said Stella, adding, in exasperation, 'Must you always play the smooth-talking pantomime villain? Don't you have anything else in your repertoire?'

He looked momentarily surprised, then amused. He caught her arm as she tried to push past. 'You don't think Amanda and I are good for each other, do you?'

'I certainly don't think you're good for her.'

'I wonder if you might be right ...' he had said then, thoughtfully, eyes fixed on hers. 'We are rather ... extreme together.' He looked exhilarated, and scared. 'It isn't always clever to meet fire with fire, but pretty hard to resist.' He raised an eyebrow, drawing down the usual mocking distance behind which he hid.

Caught in his light green gaze, his hand warm on her bare arm, Stella had been horrified to find herself starting to blush, to feel a squirm of excitement in the pit of her stomach. She had a sudden urge to push him back against the wall and kiss him on that insolent mouth, drag him into the nearest bedroom and fall writhing onto the bed, letting him push up her dress and fuck her while the party surged around them. Huw for James, she thought obscurely, then remembered that both of them belonged to Amanda. She shook off Huw's hand, trying to settle the fire that had suffused her face, and walked away.

God, life just gets more and more complicated. She thought back to the St Assumpta days where, for all the cliques and shallow parades of prestige, there were at least clear goals in sight, as well as weekends and evenings off. Now nothing was clear, and no one was ever off. They seemed to be at the centre of a cat's cradle of impossibly interwoven strands, each doubling back on itself and ending God knows where.

'I'm so glad you and Huw are getting on a bit better,' Amanda said later, looking like a Greek goddess in a short silk dress of palest blue, and a pair of shiny black Chanel heels with thick gold chains around the ankle. 'He told me you had a good chat and that you understand each other better now.' She smiled, relieved, clearly still hopeful that all the elements of her life would come together.

'Bastard!' Stella raged to Laura that night as they got ready for bed. 'He knows perfectly well we did not have a good chat. He's just trying to make trouble.'

'Yes.' To Stella's surprise, Laura agreed readily, shaking out her pillow and settling herself. 'He's getting ready to cut her off from us, and wants to make sure it looks like our fault when it happens.'

'Really?' That he had a serious plan hadn't occurred to Stella. She sat up in bed. 'How do you know?'

'It's obvious. It's what men like him do,' Laura had responded, sounding, Stella thought, more than usually like Nessa.

'Well, he's not doing it here,' Stella said firmly. Then she added wistfully, 'It's all so interesting, the psychology of everything. I just wish Amanda could be here and chat about it too. She'd love this stuff. If it wasn't about her.'

೮ঽ

Now, as she tried to rest her mind but not fall into the blackout of jetlag, Stella thought about that week and how, for all the partying, shopping and lunching, it had been a kind of pause in Amanda's life, the animal crouching before it sprang.

Chapter Sixteen

London

LAURA'S MEMORIES OF THAT LAST TRIP TO London would always be overlaid by the shock of what she had discovered on her return to Dublin. Nessa had finally been ready to tell her the truth. 'It's cancer and it can't be cured,' she had said, almost cheerfully, once she had given Laura a cup of peppermint tea sweetened with honey and quizzed her about her doings during the week.

It was a wet evening, cold for the time of year, and Nessa had drawn the curtains early and lit the lamps. Light bounced off shiny surfaces – a beaten copper bowl, the silver back of an old mirror – and glowed warm against the orange velvet shawl that draped the couch. For Laura, who had persuaded herself that there couldn't be anything seriously wrong with Nessa, it was as if the world around her had rushed over the edge of a cliff while she stood still in the slipstream, feeling it pass.

'It can't be!' was all she managed.

'Of course it can,' Nessa had responded briskly. 'It often is, and so it is in my case. It's the liver, and there's nothing to be done except try to enjoy what time I have left.'

'But you've always been so healthy, so careful about what you eat, and you don't bottle up your feelings, you express them, and meditate ...' Laura was babbling now, the reasons why it *couldn't* be true tumbling out of her. She knew that if she allowed herself to accept what Nessa had said, she would have to begin to deal with the consequences.

'Cancer is the most capricious thing there is,' Nessa told her. 'It's like a giant eeny-meeny-miny-mo, with death as the mo. I mind for you much more than for myself.'

But as the months passed, Laura could see that she didn't, that the prospect of leaving her own life was clearly horrific to her mother. She avoided all conversations about 'afterwards', even those related to what Laura would do. 'You're old enough to look after yourself,' she had said, 'and that is what you will have to do. You will have the house, and you will not have to pay a mortgage on it because there isn't one. Other than that, I have nothing to leave you, and that is as it should be. Anything I have is intrinsically mine and will come with me.'

'Where? Come with you where?' Laura had asked. She wanted to know what Nessa thought now about an afterlife she had always claimed not to believe in.

'Wherever I go. Even if that is nowhere very much.' And Laura had seen suddenly that she was terrified at the impossibility of picturing it. Nessa, with her vivid visual imagination and love of beautiful things, couldn't soothe her own passing with an image of what would be. Laura was terrified then too, for her mother and for herself, so she stopped asking questions and began to do as Nessa did, dealing with each day as it came.

The wedding had been a relief because there was so much to do. Once Mrs O'Hagen had accepted that Amanda would not be at her side for the organising, or even available by phone in Paris much, she had turned to Stella and Laura, and because Stella ostensibly had a job with Amnesty, even though it was unpaid, and Laura was still 'looking', it was mostly she who accompanied Mrs O'Hagen on the many trips to try, taste and sample various strands that were going to make a most spectacular event. Would fillet steak be a good idea for the three hundred guests? The only way to find out was to try it, but try it as the guests would eat it, as part of a five-course meal beginning with champagne and watercress soup. They sat through an entire celebratory meal, just the two of them, after which Mrs O'Hagen decided that perhaps roast beef would be better. During those often tortuous sessions, Laura found herself puzzled by Mrs O'Hagen. Amanda had always encouraged her to regard the woman as half-monster, half-comedy witch, but when neither Amanda nor Stella was around, she could be very human too.

'How is your mother?' she asked one day, as they were checking the longevity of the flowers for Amanda's bouquet – 'We don't want them to wilt halfway through the ceremony.' The 'checking' mainly consisted of wandering around Belleville with a couple of bouquets to see which lasted best.

'She's not too good,' Laura confessed. She would never have volunteered the information, but saw no reason to dissemble when asked.

'I thought not. Amanda has told me a little. Nessa's face, when last I saw her, told me more. Who is she seeing?'

'Dr Stone.'

'Good. At least he's the best.'

Laura was relieved to hear it. Others had assured her of the same thing, but Mrs O'Hagen could be counted on to know. 'But is she public or private?'

'Public.'

'Not so good. Private would be better.' Typical of Mrs O'Hagen, Laura thought, that even in the middle of being kind, she couldn't resist rubbing your nose in it a little. 'I'll put in a word, so that Stone knows Nessa is a friend of ours. Mick knows him quite well from the club, and Malcolm knows him better again. Of course he'll do his very best anyway, even if she is public, but there's no harm in him – and the hospital – knowing that Nessa is not alone and friendless.' Typical, too, of Mrs O'Hagen to presume that anyone not ostentatiously known to them might be dismissed as 'alone and friendless', regardless of how many friends they actually had. 'How is she taking treatment?'

'Badly. She doesn't want to do it at all, says it makes her feel far worse than the actual illness. She wants to try her own remedies – lots of turmeric and wheatgrass juice. The only reason she does the chemo is for my sake. Which makes me feel terrible,' Laura confessed.

'Waste of time,' Mrs O'Hagen said brusquely. 'Guilt, like misery and shame, is a luxury we cannot afford. None of us. Your mother needs practical help. I'll do what I can. But wallowing in sorrow is for her, you know, not for you. Your time for that will come.' She was right, of course, and it had come, Laura thought now. In the meantime Mrs O'Hagen had been as good as her word, regularly sending deliveries of fruit and vegetables from Sinnott's, Nessa's favourite shop, and the one she said she could afford only for special occasions. With the fruit and veg – always beautiful, seasonal and varied – would come perhaps a tiny tin of caviar, or some smoked wild duck, of which Nessa ate sparingly but with approval. Once, when Mrs O'Hagen had wanted to 'borrow' Laura for an entire day, and Nessa was feeling particularly bad, she had sent Ivana, who had cooked borscht for her.

'The most perfect borscht imaginable,' Nessa had said, in some excitement to Laura later. 'Clear but strong, with the deepest ruby red colour. Most restorative.'

Laura and Mrs O'Hagen never mentioned Amanda by more than name – and then only in terms of colours she might like, the flowers she preferred. Never the deeper, emotional significance of the wedding. Once, Laura tried to steer the conversation into softer waters. They had been testing dessert wines, and the deliciousness of the Muscat de Beaumes-de-Venise inspired her to attempt intimacy.

'Do you think they will be happy together?' she had ventured.

'Who?' Mrs O'Hagen had wondered.

Her ridiculous answer should have warned Laura, but she ploughed on: 'Amanda and Huw.'

'If they're not, it won't be my fault. People are responsible for their own happiness,' Mrs O'Hagen said coolly. 'I can give her the perfect wedding. It isn't in my gift to give her the perfect marriage.'

'But do you think they're suited to each other? Do you think they should get married?' As she said it, she felt foolish, like a gushing schoolgirl dizzy with dreams of love.

'This thing about being "suited",' Mrs O'Hagen sighed, 'what does it mean? When I got married, there wasn't any talk of being suited. You got married and you made the best of it. And do you really think I could stop her if I tried?'

That, Laura realised, wasn't an answer.

⁊

Mrs O'Hagen's kindness to Nessa offered proof of what Laura had always believed – that no one could be the monster Amanda painted. It also highlighted, to Laura's immense confusion, the scant presence that Amanda was within her and Nessa's lives. At first she had expected that Amanda, when faced with Nessa's illness, would need nearly as much minding as Nessa, that she would be constantly underfoot, looking for reassurance and hope. Instead, she seemed to freeze at the news, delivered by Laura over brunch during one of Amanda's weekends home before the wedding.

'Nessa got her results back. Bad news.'

'How bad?' Stella said immediately.

'The worst.'

Stella rushed in with cries of 'No!' and 'Oh, my God!' and 'I'm so sorry', but Amanda just took Laura's hand and clasped it hard. Her face went red, then white, then took on a shuttered look, like a doll's. She didn't say anything. And neither, after that, did she do much, beyond a couple of almost cursory visits. At first, her reticence baffled Laura, then it hurt.

'It's as if she doesn't care,' she eventually said to Stella.

'That's impossible – you know it is. If Amanda loves anyone, she loves Nessa. It's something else – it must be. Do you remember when you first told her Nessa was sick, and she said she thought it was her fault?'

Laura had forgotten that outburst. 'Yes. And you thought she was being a drama queen. Making everything about *her*.'

'I did, but now I'm not so sure. She might really feel she's in some way to blame.'

'But that's ridiculous!'

'Utterly. But that doesn't mean she doesn't feel it. I think there's some kind of arrested development with Amanda. She always thinks everything's about her, but I've begun to think that it's a sign of her being still a child, stuck in the phase where everything *is* about her, rather than sheer selfishness. And think how terrifying that must be.'

'I suppose so. Every ache, every pain, every storm, every flood. Your fault.'

'Horrible.'

'And ridiculous.'

'Yes. But mostly horrible.'

Because Stella had largely persuaded her, Laura tried not to allow the crossness she felt with Amanda rise too close to the surface. But she decided that if Nessa asked about Amanda, about why she never called, then she, Laura, would have a word with Amanda. But Nessa never did. She was always interested in news of her, asked after her, with her usual warmth, but she never mentioned Amanda's lack of attention or asked to see her. When Laura asked if she was sorry not to see more of Amanda, Nessa simply said, 'No. She's not well enough to deal with other people's illness.'

Not that Laura or Stella saw much of Amanda either after that week in London. Her trips home from Paris were seldom, because filming was 'intense', and when she was home, it was always with Huw, and Laura felt even more uncomfortable with him than she had previously. 'He watches us now too,' she said one day to Stella, after an awkward lunch, 'just like he always watches Amanda.'

'Maybe he's afraid we'll run off with her.'

'Or that she'll ask us to rescue her.'

Huw and Amanda were far less social than they had been. They had given up the flat in town, and usually stayed in a hotel, ordering everything they wanted – food, drink, films, friends, drugs – from friends or room service, drawing the curtains and maintaining a kind of depressed, intense party scene like the colours on a paint palette that have all run together, losing their individual glory and becoming murky, until the regular Sunday lunches with Amanda's parents forced them out into the light. Sometimes they made arrangements to meet in a pub or club, but usually they didn't show up, occasionally texting, often not. On those occasions, Laura and Stella might call to the hotel late, after their night out, but they never stayed long. The room was always too gloomy and stuffy, and Huw, lounging in a chair or across an unmade bed, too obvious.

Even when Amanda did make it out, it seemed as if a thin layer of ash had settled across the burnished gold. The faint hint of danger that had always clung to her, the sense that exciting things were not far off, had sharpened into something coarser. 'Amanda's a disaster,' people said cheerfully, as she passed out yet again or tripped over a table. She smashed glasses, sometimes on purpose, failed to show up, refused to leave, ended many nights propped up by friends, being escorted out of nightclubs. Groups of which she had been the centre became used to having her on their fringes, physically present, but often silent. Where once she had been subtly teasing, she became outright argumentative, picking fights she couldn't win and often couldn't remember, slurring insults that were unworthy of her usually delicate mind. One such, in which Byron de Sade, by then shouldered out of actual friendship but still hovering on the edge, seemed to Laura to goad Amanda. It ended when Amanda chucked a glass of vodka and cranberry at him, missed, and stumbled over a barstool. De Sade had walked out, saying, 'Amanda O'Hagen is a joke.' Once said, it became a possibility.

Soon there were even clubs and pubs which once would have rolled out the red carpet and confetti, where Amanda was no longer welcome.

'She's not comin' in like that,' the bouncer at Trap said to Stella one evening when they arrived at the doors, all buoyant from an early round of cocktails, except Amanda, who seemed to be at the bitter end of her own personal night. He took Laura's arm, led her to one side, and delivered an almost fatherly lecture, leaning close in to her, jabbing his forefinger at the ground for emphasis. He smelt of tuna and vanilla – a sickly combination. 'I can't be seen to be lettin' her in here. It's not doin' her any favours, and it's not doin' us any either. Until she learns to take it a little bit easier, she's not gettin' in. Youse are grand, but Amanda's lost the run of herself.'

The funny thing, Laura thought now, was how little they had really understood what was happening. Stella was so blinded by her dislike of Huw that the deterioration of Amanda's life suited her because it matched her image of Huw: that he was a corrosive influence. But it wasn't that simple, as Laura had seen: Amanda was undoubtedly a victim, but she was an active, even eager one. Once or twice Laura even fumbled towards the notion that Huw, too, might be in the grip of something beyond him. It didn't make her dislike him any less, but it did make her wonder. A certain look that crossed his face, an occasional hint of weariness when Amanda fell into a heavy sleep in the corner of a nightclub or picked an unnecessary row. Those weren't impressions she could talk over with Stella: that he might be a victim, too, she would never admit. So Laura kept them to herself, unsure even if what she thought she'd seen was anything more than a false flicker. But that feeling prepared a place for something new between her and Stella: disagreement over Amanda and what might be happening to her.

'We need to tell someone,' Laura said one day. She and Stella were alone together, walking briskly through the park 'because it beats running'.

'Tell them what?'

Laura waited for a moment – of course Stella knew exactly what she meant.

Then Stella added: 'We don't really know what. How can we tell?'

'Well, we'll have to figure out enough to say something.'

'I don't agree. We don't do that. We're friends, not minders. We can't tell on her. And, anyway, who would we tell – her mother? How is that a good thing?'

'Mrs O'Hagen has no idea how bad things are. If she did, she'd do something. That's what she's like. She does things, gets things done.'

'Her *doing* is part of the problem as far as I can see.'

'Maybe. But we can't just let this go on. Things are bad, I can feel they are. And getting worse. There's no joy in what Amanda does any more. She gets wrecked and just looks miserable. Next day, she's even worse. This isn't right.'

'She'll be fine, Laura.' Stella's voice, always loud and full of conviction, was like a fist banging on a table. 'She just needs to, I don't know, grow up a bit, stop taking everything out on herself. Find something to do that isn't always with Huw. Really, she's okay. *Huw*'s the problem, and there's no point telling Mrs O'Hagen anything about him. She knows about him, and she likes what she knows.'

And Laura, because she wanted to believe the best, didn't want to be on any side that didn't have Stella on it, and had no idea what to do with the worry that nagged at her, pretended she believed what Stella had said. Except that afterwards there was a small nugget of shame at her own lack of courage. And anger that Stella, who should have listened, had used the greater force of her personality to smother Laura's fears.

❧

A month before the wedding, Amanda came home for good. By then it felt like half of Dublin was in a state of wild excitement at the prospect of a party that had become legendary in the foretelling. That half did not include Amanda, who looked tired and even more apathetic than usual. Mrs O'Hagen had revived her plan of a week in Barbados, but Amanda refused to go.

'You're mad,' Stella said. 'Why on earth not?'

'Huw doesn't want to. We're better off staying here and just getting through the next few weeks as best we can. Then we'll go to Thailand for the honeymoon, where Huw has friends. He's looking forward to that.'

They were at Stella's because her parents were in Kerry for the weekend, and Amanda 'couldn't face' any of their usual brunch spots. The table was laid with white china coffee cups and a plate of pastries in the shadow of a bowl of drooping tulips. Amanda was wearing a skinny black polo neck and dark blue jeans tucked into black Hermès boots, knee-high and shiny enough to have been made from coal. She was shivering slightly, though she insisted she wasn't cold and her long fingers, with the ragged nails, plucked at her sleeves nervously.

'Jesus, Amanda,' said Stella, 'it's your wedding! You sound like you're contemplating a corporate team-building away-day or something.'

Amanda laughed. 'Actually, it's a bit like that. Team Mummy! Which reminds me,' she said to Laura, 'I see you're a bit of a cheerleader these days.'

'She's been kind. To Nessa,' Laura said stiffly.

'Anyone would be kind to Nessa.' Amanda seemed far less discomfited by the mention of Nessa than Laura had expected. 'Don't be fooled. She never does anything without a reason, and that reason is never pure kindness.'

'You know,' said Stella hopefully, 'your lack of interest in the wedding may actually be a lack of interest in being married.'

'No go, Dr Freud,' said Amanda, laughing a little. 'I do want to be married, to Huw. Amanda Edsberg has such a nice ring to it. I just don't have any interest in the kind of wedding my mother wants. She keeps telling me I'll get the wedding I always dreamed of, but I never dreamed of any wedding. And if I had, it wouldn't have been like this. If she knew anything at all about me, she would know that.'

'But are you sure you and Huw both want the same things?' Stella persisted.

'Neither of us really wants anything, except each other,' said Amanda dully.

'Oh for God's sake!' Stella was enraged now. 'I suppose you've never read the bit in the Bible about burying talents? The absolutely criminal waste of squandering what you've been given?'

'No.' Amanda was indifferent.

There was a tense pause, into which the kitchen appliances poured various soothing sounds, low hums and hypnotic ticks. Upstairs a window was rattling in the wind. Laura longed to follow the sound out of the kitchen.

'When I look at you, I see that there really is such a thing as too much,' Stella said quietly.

'Too much, not enough.' Amanda shrugged. 'It seems to amount to the same.'

Chapter Seventeen

London

HUNGRY, BUT UNWILLING TO LEAVE THE guesthouse in case Laura arrived, wishing it were a hotel and she could order room service, Stella lay down and tried to read but was far too jittery to concentrate. The prospect of lunch with Mrs O'Hagen chilled her, not only for her own sake but for Amanda's too. It felt like a conspiracy, a ganging-up, when she and Laura should have been finding Amanda themselves, taking care of her alone, without telling any parents.

Partly, she knew, that was what still bothered her during her few interactions with Mrs O'Hagen — the fact that she made Stella feel like a child, was herself so much more in command, more profoundly connected to the grown-up world of influence and convinced of her position within it than Stella could ever be. She might lack imagination, sympathy, humour, but she always gave the impression of being exactly where she wanted to be.

When Stella stopped looking at her life in the belief that it was a success, stopped insisting to herself that she was happy, she felt she was able to see, clearly, the very moment she had realised that they were in far beyond their good-natured, willing capabilities. The very moment when the present distress had entered her future.

Across the years she saw herself and Laura arriving, so full of merriment, at Amanda's house for the wedding, 'with enough luggage for a week's holiday' . . .

☙

They were over a year out of college by then, and saw less of each other than they once had. 'The pressures of work,' Stella had joked, even though neither of them was earning any money. They were busy, Laura because the paper gave her regular bits of work now, even talked about having her on the staff, and Stella with Amnesty, although her time there was nearly up. They saw Amanda hardly at all. She was home, but mysteriously occupied, without much account to give of her days when they did meet up. The days before the wedding, Stella thought, would give the three of them a chance to be together again.

They had their dresses for the family dinner that night, bridesmaids' dresses for the next day, something to change into after the ceremony if they wanted, and something relaxed for the day after, the champagne breakfast.

'Don't bother about make-up. I'll have people here to do

that all the days,' Amanda had said, but even so, with shoes and pyjamas and just-in-case jackets and scarves, necklaces, earrings, bangles, they each carried a large suitcase into the house, which was filled with the sound of hasty footsteps and the sight of purposeful people striding in all directions.

'It's like the staging of a major opera,' said Amanda, leading them through the chaos. 'Outside is the same. There's really nowhere to go that we won't be forced to witness the erecting of Marie O'Hagen's Principal Production.'

'God, you're spoiled, Amanda,' laughed Stella.

'Jolly lucky I am. Otherwise, I'd have turned out just like them and actually be into all this stuff.'

'Hmm, okay. Fair enough. Three cheers for spoiling.'

They snuck upstairs to Amanda's room and hid out for the afternoon. Ivana sent up lunch, and every once in a while Amanda was called down to 'give an opinion' on something, but largely they were left alone.

'Where's Huw?' they asked, when she had come back from expressing views on the placement of the top table – 'Anything as long as I don't have to sit beside the priest or Mummy' was her verdict when she filled them in.

'He's with his parents. They arrived yesterday. They're all staying at the Huntington Hotel, just past Ashglen, where we're having dinner tonight. They'll be there for the next five nights, and Huw and I will stay in the penthouse there on the night of the wedding. If we ever actually leave.'

'Isn't the bride supposed to make a noisy and early exit?'

'Only in the days when the groom was so mad to shag her that he couldn't wait one second longer. He dragged her off early while all his friends whooped encouragement at him.'

'Which of his friends are coming?'

'Mostly ones you met in London, and a guy called Jake, who's great fun. You didn't meet him. Huw's parents don't much like him, so he gets invited only to the really big things.' With three hundred guests, the wedding was definitely a 'big thing'.

'God, how will you bear it?' Laura asked. 'All those people staring at you and wanting to talk to you. I'd hate it.'

'I guess Amanda's used to that,' said Stella.

'I guess I am,' said Amanda, 'and I won't be paying the slightest bit of attention. It's my wedding and I'm not going to talk to a single person I don't want to. Just because I've invited people does not mean I want to talk to them. I hope they understand that. Your main job is to keep people away from me. Seriously!'

Stella had visions of herself and Laura with crossed pikes, barring access to supplicants who came and begged for a few words. 'No admittance,' they cried sternly in her imagination. 'She may have *invited* you, but she doesn't wish to *speak* to you.'

'So, who's coming tonight?' Laura asked.

'Well, my parents, and Alice, and Huw's parents, and an uncle of his who lives in Spain and is apparently a bit of a rogue, and you guys and me and Huw, and James and his parents.'

'Why James?' Stella hadn't expected that.

'Well, he introduced us, so he's part of all this. And his parents know Huw's parents well, so we thought it would be more fun,' Amanda said blithely.

God, she really has no *clue*, thought Stella. Must James be given a ringside seat? Forced to form part of the inner circle at an event that might well break his heart? She just hoped she wouldn't be sitting next to him.

The Huntington Hotel had opened recently, owned by a

developer friend of Mr O'Hagen's. He called it a hotel, but had intended it as a private drinking club for his cronies. Except that it had opened almost in tandem with the financial crash that had forced so many of those cronies underground. The friend was giving a generous deal to the Edsbergs, who cared deeply about such things, and in return would be attending the wedding.

The gardens were still beautiful, with giant ancient chestnuts and an avenue of lime trees up to the house, which had been transformed from the rather shabby old spot it had once been into something so glittering and new that, despite the preservation order that had kept the structure intact, it might as well have been razed and rebuilt. The poor old stone had been so savagely sandblasted and polished that it twinkled, hard and desperate, like some ageing tart, thought Stella, staring in wonder at the quantities of glass and steel that had been added in new wings at either side. Inside, thick purple on walls, carpets and furnishings sounded an aggressively regal note. 'Like the King of the Travellers' palace,' whispered Laura, as they stared around at the huge paintings, all done by the same hand, cartoonish parodies of classic hunting scenes that were clever and grotesque, and up at the many large animal heads – bison, rams, deer – mounted on the walls, their great horns dipped in shiny gold paint, or possibly liquid gold, which gave them an unexpectedly smug air.

'Poor things,' said Iseult, beside them. 'I'm just surprised not to see Massy's head up there too.'

'Who's Massy?' asked Laura.

'The previous owner,' said Iseult.

'Nonsense,' said Mrs O'Hagen, joining them with a glass of pink champagne in hand. 'They got a very good price for the place. And it's much improved. Conor Mac showed Mick and me over it before they started work. Falling to pieces, rot in every corner, dry, wet, rising – everything.'

'Beautiful old place,' Iseult said firmly. Mrs O'Hagen moved sharply away.

James appeared, with a gin and tonic, Stella noticed enviously.

'Where did you get that?' she asked. 'I thought we all had to drink this stuff.' She gestured with the hand holding her pink champagne.

'I knew it would be that, so I stopped at the bar on my way through. Part of it used to be the gun room, before they did such a savage job here.'

'You don't like it either?'

'Not much to like. It's just another example of the new world biting huge chunks out of the world I grew up in, one that lasted for a very long time but seems to be disappearing rather rapidly now, as if it wanted to put itself out of its own misery.'

'What side is Huw on?' Stella asked curiously. 'He belongs to your world, but he doesn't seem to mind.'

'Huw is a survivor. He minds, I should think, but he's going to be on the winning team all the same. Like cockroaches and corporate avarice, he'd survive a nuclear war.'

'Well, I'm on your side,' Stella declared. 'A new world with hotels like this, cockroaches, big corporations and Huw isn't one I want to be part of.'

'Good for you.' He smiled. 'You always were good at picking sides and sticking to them. Loyalty. A very nice trait.'

If only you knew, thought Stella, giving in for one second to the fantasy that was ever awaiting her, of being in his arms, held so tightly that barely a breath of wind could have passed between their two bodies. 'How's the research going?' she asked quickly, to distract herself from an image that threatened to drag her under.

'Good. I've nearly finished my thesis. London is wonderful. You should come and visit.' He smiled.

'Mmm. Maybe one day. Amanda's moving there soon,' she said, then felt furious with herself for mentioning Amanda.

'Yes,' James said. Then, 'Funny, I don't think Amanda is a survivor like Huw.'

'I don't either,' said Stella. They both looked at Amanda, who was half-sitting on the back of a chair, swinging one leg and talking to Huw's parents. She was wearing a pleated, tunic-style dress in soft olive green with a wide belt and strappy sandals. On her arm, just above the bend of her elbow, she had a large cuff of beaten gold and leather. Her long legs were bare and brown, but so thin her knees looked misshapen and knobbly. Stella knew that brides often lost weight before the big day, but Amanda, despite having no part in the stress of organisation, seemed to have lost an awful lot.

'Her mother, on the other hand ...' he muttered, as Mrs O'Hagen tinkled her glass sharply, and said, 'Shall we go through to dinner?' into the ensuing silence.

'She sounds like the Queen,' Stella muttered. James stifled a laugh.

Dinner was in a private dining room in one of the new wings, overlooking the formal gardens at the back of the house. Making their way to it, Iseult caught up with them and pushed open a door. 'This used to be a little sitting room,' she said sadly, staring into a room oppressively furnished as a library, with shelves of heavy maroon-and-gold-bound books, a ridiculously large and solid desk, with the hotel's headed stationery laid out on it, and a forbidding dark green chesterfield. 'It was so beautifully arranged. There used to be an old daybed, Regency rosewood, just under the window.'

'What are we doing here again?' Stella asked.

'Celebrating,' James said, taking her firmly by the arm. 'That's enough, Mum. We're not here to lament.'

'Time enough for that later,' Iseult said darkly.

Does everyone know this is a disaster? Stella wondered.

At dinner she was seated next to Huw's father. Tall, ruddy, with evasive blue eyes, he quizzed her politely, but with an edge of mockery. 'So what do you do?' he asked, twinkling coldly down at her. Like a star that died a long time ago, but the light can still be seen, she thought. 'You do *do* something, don't you? All the young ladies now seem so frightfully high-powered and hard-working.' He said it as if it were a complaint.

'Well, I'm a legal intern at Amnesty International.'

'*Amnesty*! Well, aren't you *wonderful*?' he said, laughing.

James was opposite, beside Laura, and the play of candlelight across his features was almost too much for Stella, making him seem more familiar, more intimate than in the bright lights of the reception room. Huw and then Amanda were beyond Laura, with Amanda's father on the other side. Mrs O'Hagen sat between Huw's father and an uncle Stella hadn't met.

The food was silly. Towers of things on discs of other things, carrots pared into thin whiplash strips and potatoes peeled into thumb-sized chunks. Nothing tasted of what it should have or looked at all like itself. Waiters appeared and disappeared, with wine bottles, water bottles, side orders, so that conversation was desultory and fragmented. Amanda, thought Stella, watching her, had hidden even more of herself than usual. She and Huw seemed to be holding hands under the table a lot, Amanda clinging tightly to him, pushing food around her plate with her fork.

As a result of the waiters topping up their glasses after every sip, on the unfair principle of pouring more in than had been taken out, they all got drunk rather quickly, except Mrs O'Hagen, who seemed to be keeping a firm eye on her watch. By the time they got to dessert, a depressing deconstruction of a summer pudding, using brioche – 'Quite unnecessary, the sweetness should come from the berries, not the bread,' Iseult hissed to Stella – and a selection of tasteless fruit, the table was loud, if not exactly merry.

Once the wine glasses had been replaced with champagne flutes, the speeches started. Mr O'Hagen showed again that he could, when the occasion demanded it, be quite gracious, praising his daughter for her beauty and her sweetness of temper, the way she had never caused them a moment's trouble. Which was a lie, Stella knew, and, anyway, surely children are supposed to be trouble, she thought, watching Amanda, who smiled up at her father. Beneath the make-up, the expertly blow-dried hair and sparkling diamonds at ears and throat, she looked tired, harried. Next, Mr O'Hagen said how much he was looking forward to welcoming Huw to the family, and what a good opinion he had formed of his intelligence.

'And that's enough for now, or I'll have nothing left to say tomorrow,' Mr O'Hagen concluded, sitting down to loud applause.

'Will you be making a speech tomorrow?' Alice asked Amanda.

'No,' she said, looking a bit startled. 'I'll leave that to other people.'

'Quite right,' Huw's father said loudly. 'No need for you to say a thing. Bride rarely does.' He looked affronted at the idea.

'But perhaps you'd like to say something now?' Alice asked.

'Do!' several people called.

'Speech!' shouted the disreputable uncle, banging his spoon on the table.

'Speech!' Alice repeated, head on one side in what she must have thought was a charming attitude. Amanda, looking faintly hunted, got up.

'Well, it's lovely of you all to come, and I hope tomorrow is as wonderful for you as it will be for me.' Here she paused and smiled at Huw. Everyone clapped. The uncle banged his spoon again. 'And I'd like to thank my father for the dinner, and the wedding, and to say that I love him very much.' Huge cheers now. Amanda smiled, and moved to sit down.

'And your mother,' Alice called. 'You haven't thanked her yet.' A faintly uneasy silence fell, perhaps a chance dwindling in noise, perhaps not, Stella thought. Amanda got to her feet again, her face wearing the shuttered, painted-doll look that Stella knew so well.

'And of course my mother,' she said woodenly, 'whom I love exactly as I should.' This time the silence was much shorter, but sharper. Broken speedily, expertly, by Huw's mother and Mrs O'Hagen, who began to talk about the arrangements with practised ease. The moment was glossed over but not before it shot out a small but vicious dart.

'"Mend your speech a little, Lest you may mar your fortunes,"' Iseult muttered.

'What?' Stella said.

'Lear to Cordelia.'

'Oh. Right.'

Stella soon excused herself, heading outside through the nearest door for some air. Stepping away from the pool of light that lay before the windows into the shadow of the stone walls, she leaned back. The night was quiet and dark, with a heady smell of jasmine from somewhere. Stella was admiring the different shades of black before her that varied from charcoal to ink – once you began to look for it, there was always a darker spot, a murkier place to draw the eye. She had found the vanishing point of the inverted landscape in front of her, where the enormous branches of an old yew tree formed a deep V with the sky, and focused all her attention on it, when suddenly James appeared beside her.

'That was a toxic little scene, wasn't it?' he said.

'Utterly. Do you think Alice knew what she was doing?'

'God, no. I doubt she understands why she gets up in the morning. But she didn't need to: she brought the house down anyway.'

'Fools rush in … But Amanda could have faked it, just for once, and said something nice.'

'She never does, though, does she?'

'God, I'm sick of talking about Amanda all the time,' Stella said. 'Sometimes I think it's all we do, any of us. Amanda, Amanda, Amanda.'

'Okay, let's talk about you.'

'I didn't mean that,' Stella said uncomfortably, wriggling a little against the cold stone wall. 'I just meant in general.' The bank of heat created by his nearness was so dense, she felt she could have leaned against it.

'Well, I meant it. What about you, Stella? What will you do when this is all over? You're not going to stay in Dublin, working for Amnesty, are you?'

'I couldn't even if I wanted to. My time's up there. My dad wants me to do the New York bar exams. I might. I'm not sure what else to do. I feel like I'm in some sort of limbo, a state of suspended animation.'

'I think we all do. It's as if we had to see this through. Then maybe we'll be able to get on with things. Our own things.'

'You mean the wedding? Amanda?' said Stella, surprised that he was prepared to put into words what he must be feeling.

'Enough about Amanda,' he said, leaning in to kiss her. For a moment Stella was too startled to respond, but the delightful smell of him up close, the remembered feel of his arms, the touch of his lips soon shook her out of her surprise, and she kissed him back passionately, recalling with a start what she tried so hard to squash down – the memory of how much she loved him. But no sooner had she thought it than time lurched into motion again, and all the things she knew to be true, and didn't wish to consider, came to her in a rush. She stepped back, ducking away as he tried to step back with her.

'I'm not a consolation prize, you know.'

James looked shocked. 'I never said that.'

'No, but you thought it.'

'I didn't. Stella, I swear, I never, never did.' He reached a hand out for her, but she sidestepped, turned on her heel and went back inside, already trying to put a lid on the black feeling inside her. I will go to New York, she thought fiercely. Nothing could be too far away from here. I just have to get through tomorrow, and the next day, and then I'll make my plans and go.

⌇

And she had, she thought now, as she waited for Laura. She had made her plans, thrown herself into them, believed in them, and they had turned out to be no more real than any of the rest of it. Why must the ground keep shifting under her? she wondered. She decided that this time, with Laura and Amanda, she would anchor it once and for all.

Chapter Eighteen

London

WHEN LAURA ARRIVED AT THE GUESTHOUSE,
Stella was asleep, but she woke with a smile when Laura shook
her shoulder.

'Sorry. I didn't mean to.' She sat up and stretched. 'Lucky
you woke me, or I'd be awake all night. You look good,' she
said, with a smile.

'You look good too.' Laura hugged her. 'Thin, but fit. Still
running?'

'Always. It's my little piece of sanity in a very insane world
over there.'

'Is it still that bad?'

'It's full on. But I love it. Actually,' she added, 'that's

something I need to talk to you about. But later. What about you, anyway? How's work?'

'It's tricky,' Laura confessed. 'I'll tell you later.' The silence between them then was awkward. So many things not said, or said wrongly. So many laters.

'I'm glad we're here.' Stella broke the pause. 'Together. I know that if we can help Amanda now, we can change so much of what has happened. We went wrong somewhere, but we can make it right. I know we can.'

'I hope so,' Laura said. 'There's a lot to make right.' She wondered how much she could actually tell Stella. The story of her deception seemed more stupid every time she considered it. Her chest tightened at the thought of what lay waiting for her, growing more enormous in its impossible foolishness at every moment. By now she could hardly see around it to the plan she'd thought she would be able to follow through. Petrie had already rung her twice since she'd touched down in London. She hadn't answered, but the 'missed calls' icon on her phone, a reproachful little red receiver, was bothering her hugely.

'Okay, so what now?' Stella mercifully interrupted her thoughts with a request for action.

'Well, in a while we go and meet Mrs O'Hagen.'

'Oh, God.' Stella groaned. 'I'm not sure I'm ready for this. I feel fifteen again. And not in a good way. I think she's going to shout at me, as if I've done something wrong.'

'I know what you mean. Me too. But we haven't. We never really did, now that I think about it.'

'No, I guess not. Amanda did, and we just sort of tagged along.'

'Do you ever wonder what our lives would have been like without her?'

'Yes, actually.'

'Less exciting, I suppose. But maybe that would have been a good thing. Or maybe not,' Laura said, thinking of the many madcap, hilarious nights they had spent, the parties, talks, confessions, games and confidences. The way everything they had done with Amanda for so many years, certainly until after the graduation party, had been drenched in light, illuminated by her glorious looks and that faint aura of excitement that clung to her. 'We had some amazing times. Remember when that guy we met in Trap begged us to come to the South of France for a few days on his yacht? And he was going to fly us out on a private jet in the morning?'

'Yes, and we were going to go. Except you fell asleep on the sofa behind the piano, and Amanda decided what she really wanted was an early house and then breakfast at the truck-stop café on the quays.'

'So we snuck off without telling him.' They were both laughing. 'And when we finally got to bed in my house, then woke up later on, Amanda was furious that we hadn't gone. She kept saying, "We could be soaking up the rays *right now*," and trying to blame us for being "faint of heart".'

'Remember the Week of Leaves?' A guy Amanda had met one night in Trap had walked her home to Laura's house later, kicking through the autumn leaves as they went. The next morning, a black bag full of dry red and yellow leaves had been left on Laura's doorstep, with a note saying, 'We'll always have yesterday,' and a phone number. Amanda had ignored it, and the next day another bag of leaves was left, and another, one every night for a week, until finally Laura had left a note outside, saying, 'Amanda doesn't live here. Please stop leaving leaves,' and Nessa had made a bonfire in the back garden with the bagfuls. 'Literally burnt offerings,' she had said, with a laugh, watching them smoulder.

'God, yes!'

That time had led to another, and another. Do-you-remembers full of the adventures and scrapes of all the years together. Because that was easier than talking about the now of their lives. And maybe, thought Laura, with enough of an overture, enough blowing on the embers of their friendship, they might even be able to move into it. She was trying to muffle the panic at what she was about to do with these recollections, like tying rags around a horse's hoofs, she thought suddenly, but instead they banded together in a thick mass to reproach her. 'There were a lot of parties,' she said.

'When I look back, it feels like nothing but,' Stella agreed. 'We must have done other things, normal things, but it just seems like party after party, strung together like shiny beads.'

'And hardly any parties since.'

'No. Certainly not for me. Not since the wedding.' Then, 'That marriage was a disaster for Amanda, wasn't it?'

'Total. It wasn't even the beginning of the end. It was much faster than that.'

'Did you know it at the time?'

'Oh, yes. It was pretty obvious, no?'

'I suppose so. I didn't really know it. I prophesied disaster. But not this kind of disaster.'

'We don't know what kind of disaster it is yet,' Laura reminded her.

'No, that's true, but I presumed it wouldn't last. That he would break her heart and she would leave. I wondered how much it would all cost Mr O'Hagen. But I didn't see this.'

'I never wore my bridesmaid's dress again. Did you?'

'No. Even though Amanda chose them carefully so that we could.'

It had been the only thing Amanda had put any energy into, insisting that the bridesmaids' dresses be chic and understated.

'I want you to get loads of wear out of them,' Laura remembered her saying. 'I want them to be so timeless and perfectly cut that every time you're stuck for a dress, for a black-tie party, a lunch, meeting your fiancé's parents for the first time, these are the dresses that will come out and save the day. Later you can wear them to christenings and communions, and everyone will say, "What a stunning dress," and you'll say, "Oh, this old thing ..."' She had stuck to her guns, even when Mrs O'Hagen tried to steer them into something floaty and pale pink, which would have suited Amanda's Vera Wang better.

And the dresses had been lovely. Navy silk, with some kind of treatment to the fabric that made it slightly stiffer and heavier than normal, and gave a faint texture to the surface. Wide, puffed sleeves, a high collar, a broad waist and a bell-shaped skirt ending just above the knee. 'Not at all bridesmaid-y,' they had agreed, when they saw them, 'much more couture.'

'It's bad enough that my dress will be worn once and then ignored, folded into acid-free tissue paper. I'm not having yours go the same way.'

They were having tea, the three of them, in Amanda's house, after a morning of facials and massage, the week before the wedding, 'Because we all need to work on being radiant,' Amanda said mock-sternly. 'My mother is counting on us. It's part of your duties.' There didn't seem to be very many duties. Amanda had lain low since the return from Paris, then refused a hen party – 'I only like you two. The rest of my so-called friends can go to hell, frankly,' had been her response.

291

Huw had gone out for the afternoon, having said, 'Well, I'll leave you to it, I suppose,' rather reluctantly, as he lingered in the hall, picking things up and putting them down with an aimlessness that told Laura he had nowhere really to go. Amanda seemed brighter that day, without the dull heaviness that seemed so frequently to settle on her of late, as they sat around a highly polished coffee table covered with plates of tiny sandwiches and dainty cakes, delicate china cups and saucers and a large silver teapot, 'just ready to give us three wishes', Laura had said.

'The end is in sight,' Amanda said cheerfully, after Huw had finally left. 'Soon I'll be married and will never have to put up with this rubbish again. I may give up having facials and massages and things altogether. I can't bear people pawing at me. I've had enough of it. It makes my skin hurt.'

'But you used to enjoy all this stuff. Being on shoots, the centre of attention, everyone fussing over the way you look,' said Stella.

'I might have pretended to, but I'm not sure I ever really did. Acting is much better. You matter more. In a horrible way, the model is the least important person on a shoot. Sure, you get the most attention, but you're also the most replaceable. The photographer is the key. He has a vision, and the stylist helps him to deliver it. She is far more his muse than the model, really. Everyone follows him around, finding out what he wants and doing it. The model just sits there. Or stands there. You have people fidgeting with you and fussing over you and complimenting you but, really, it's quite humiliating because you know that if you fell down dead on the spot, they would simply step over you, ring the agency and get "the next Amanda O'Hagen" sent over. Never let your daughters be models,' she concluded. 'I don't think it's good for anyone's self-esteem to be so much scrutinised and so little respected.'

'But it wasn't bad for your self-esteem?'

'You're kidding? It was a disaster. And there wasn't a whole lot to work with from the start.' Amanda poured another cup of tea, took a small bite of a small sandwich and discarded the rest.

'But you always seem so ...' Laura struggled to find the word.

'You're confusing self-possession with self-esteem. Most people do,' Amanda explained kindly. 'And I do have lots of self-possession. Do you know how I acquired it?' She laughed, but only a little, and her mouth turned more down than up at the corners. 'My mother taught me. But not in the way she thought. No matter what she said to me, or how badly I hurt myself as a child, I learned not to show a thing. Any expression that crossed my face was a way in for her. She would begin to ask me questions, try to find out what I was thinking, what I liked, whom I liked, and she would go on and on and on until all I could hear was her voice in my head, banging on, telling me what to do, how to behave, how to walk, talk, look, dress. I would hear her judgement on the people I met, a second little voice behind my own causing me to doubt my impressions of them. Because her judgements were always nasty: "I don't think so, do you?" I'd hear her say, about some perfectly decent, normal person who just didn't happen to be any of the things she thinks are important. And it would colour my view of that person. Despite myself, I would find that I despised them a little, and that made me despise myself more, that I could have her values even when I hated them and knew they were wrong. Or "much more like it" would pop into my mind about some idiot who had nothing going for them except that maybe they were rich, or their dad was in the same club as my dad, or scribbled the same kind of numbers on the backs of envelopes. When that happened, I despised myself even more. So I had to start blocking her, and bit by bit I learned to do it. To keep her out entirely. But, unfortunately, it seemed to keep everyone else out too.'

Amanda sounded strained. 'I got very good at creating a no man's land between me and her. I did it because I had to. It was only afterwards that I realised the holding back impressed and intimidated other people. But by then it was too hard to dismantle it. And, besides, I still needed it. You two are the only ones who've ever really got past it.'

'What about Huw?'

'Oh, Huw's on the inside. Always has been. He didn't need to get past anything.'

'But your mother does love you, Amanda.' Laura tried valiantly to be positive, and fair to her secret regard for Mrs O'Hagen, but she knew it came out hesitant, more a question than a statement.

'I'm really not sure she does,' said Amanda. 'And if she does, she hides it well enough that it makes no odds.' She paused. It was a bleak silence. 'I always felt like a project to her. Something half-finished that had to be improved upon. The problem is,' she added sadly, 'you end up feeling like a project to yourself as well.' She stretched showily, set down her cup and said, 'That's quite enough tea. I'm going to roll a joint. Want some?'

'Not really,' said Laura. 'Too early.'

'Same,' said Stella.

'Okay, drink, then. Cocktail?'

'Oh okay, twist our arms. Mojito?'

They drank several cocktails, watching the afternoon slowly settle into lateness, past the mauves and purples of twilight, and on into the first twinklings of artificial light, the cars passing on the road beyond showing headlights suddenly huge, bleeding into the soft dusk around them. They talked about Nessa and the terrible toll of her treatment, and how angry she was beneath the show of resignation, of Stella's enthusiasm for law, 'real law, that changes people's lives', and Laura's steady progress at the newspaper – 'They ask me for something nearly every week now,' she said, with great pride.

'And everything you write for them is fresh and original, and they're damn lucky to have you,' Amanda responded stoutly.

They raised their glasses. 'To us!' they cried. 'To Nessa!'

'To you, Amanda.'

'To St Assumpta's and Dargle's,' said Amanda.

'That's going too far,' laughed Laura.

'No. It's thanks to those stupid places that I met you two. And if I hadn't, well, I don't know what I would be.'

'Don't speak too soon,' said Stella. 'None of us is out of the woods yet.' There was a pause, during which it seemed to Laura they all contemplated their private understanding of the truth of that.

Then, 'If it wasn't us here, I suppose it might be Sally and Nadine instead. And wouldn't that be nice?' Laura said, laughing.

'Oh, God – Sally! And *Nadine*! Can you imagine?' shuddered Amanda.

☙

Of Dell, there was no mention. She had vanished so completely that Laura had found herself concerned. All anyone could tell her when she asked was that Dell had gone home 'to chill out for a bit'. Her parents lived several hours from Dublin, but Dell had never been known to spend much time with them.

And then one day there was news. 'They found Dell in a pool of blood,' Christian said, with peculiar satisfaction, one night in the pub a couple of months after their exams.

'What do you mean? Whose blood?' Laura had asked.

'Her own, of course. She tried to kill herself. Tried properly, too, from what I've heard. Not one of those stupid nicks across the arm, a proper deep cut, all the way up both veins.' Christian was grimly approving. 'Her parents found her just in time.'

'Good God! That's hideous. Why?'

'I gather it's no fun crossing Amanda O'Hagen,' said Christian, doing the irritating tap on the side of his nose.

'This has nothing to do with Amanda,' Laura said.

'From what I heard, the ladder was pulled up pretty firmly, with Dell left at the bottom,' said Christian. 'No more parties, no more nights out, no more phone calls. No more friends. Just a lot of tumbleweed blowing past.'

'If it's true, it's because what she did was disgusting, not because Amanda had anything to do with isolating her. She'll be horrified by this, you'll see.'

But Amanda wasn't horrified. She took the news, when Laura told her, quite calmly, and when prompted by Laura to say or do something to show her shock, she resisted.

'Isn't it *terrible*?' Laura encouraged.

But Amanda just shrugged a little. 'I'm not going to pretend to be upset about something that happened to Dell.'

'It's not something that *happened*. She tried to kill herself.'

'Well, I don't care. And there's no point looking all shocked at me like that. I hate Dell, for what she did to me and Huw, and if she tried to kill herself, so what? I'd be a hypocrite to fake feeling bad for her.'

Laura was upset. 'A hypocrite? You'd at least be *human* to feel bad that someone, anyone, you know should be so miserable that they chose death. Is it really all just about you and Huw?'

'She's chosen Huw over everything,' Laura had said to Stella. 'Everything and everyone.'

The news about Dell bothered Laura deeply, both for what it said about the desperate state of mind of someone who was once a friend, albeit it a tough and bitchy one, and for Amanda's cool indifference. Driven by her incomprehension and disquiet, she wrote an article – 'Suicide Isn't a Cry for Help: It's a Cry of Rage'. 'You cannot hurt the world,' she began, 'so you hurt yourself, the only bit of the world you can reach, and cut, or hang, or drown, or poison.' It was, she felt, the first decent piece of writing she had done in a long time. The hopeless months of trying to get published, of sending in suggestions and article ideas to editors, only to have her efforts ignored, had taken their toll: every time she sat down to write, she carried the leaden burden of all those unpublished, rejected articles. That made her stiff, pompous in her writing, like a dull nineteenth-century essayist, rather than a modern young woman who might be expected to offer access, immediacy, youth culture to make up for her lack of experience. But the suicide article had something, she felt, something real and personal, so she sent it to the *Sunday Herald* and, to her astonishment, not only did they print it the following week but she got a phone call from the news editor to ask her if she had any more articles of that standard. 'Something fresh, showing the disaffection of your generation?'

Laura said she had.

But the article wasn't enough to subdue the nasty feeling that had grown up in her. It didn't come close. She knew that she wanted to see Dell, and was surprised to find that Stella did, too. She began by broaching the matter awkwardly: 'I know you'll think it's a stupid idea, but I want to know how Dell is.'

'So do I,' Stella had answered promptly. 'I've been thinking about it. We should go down, try to see her. She may not want to see us, though.'

'Should we ring first?'

'I guess so. A surprise is a form of aggression, as David Mamet says. We can't just turn up.'

'Text her. Say we're on our way, or passing through, or something, so she doesn't try to head us off.' Then, 'Why do you want to go?'

'I feel bad. I don't think Dell was meant to be involved in all this. I think she got caught, like in fly-paper, and the more she tried to twist away, the worse she got stuck. Whatever Amanda says, Dell is a victim of this, not some kind of evil mastermind.'

Stella didn't mention James or the way she had seen Dell differently once she'd considered that Dell might have loved him. It didn't make her like Dell, but it did make her think about her, and wonder if, beyond that sharp exterior, there might be something different.

Dell didn't say no. She said okay and that was enough. They borrowed Stella's mother's car, on a day Nessa was to be in hospital, and set off in grey and gusty weather, with sheets of rain blowing sideways across the windows. Stella drove fast and competently, and the directions Dell had texted were good. A little under two hours after they'd set off, they arrived at a bungalow on the outskirts of a small midlands town, painted a grimy eau-de-Nil.

'Not what I expected,' said Stella, as Laura was still trying to work out which part of the haughty Dell could possibly have come from this nondescript house.

'No,' she answered. 'I expected something more ...'

'Gothic,' supplied Stella.

'Yes.' Laura laughed. 'Turrets, at least. A portcullis.'

'A lurching man saying, "Walk this way."'

'And acres for Dell to stride around, bullying serfs and looking down her nose at decent folk.' They stared again at the pebbledash eau-de-Nil, the aluminium doorframe. 'The house looks like it landed on someone,' Laura said.

'I know what you mean. As if it fell from the sky. Kind of guilty.'

Dell answered the door. Her usually shiny pixie-ish crop was dull and coarse, sticking away from her head in dry tufts. Her face was puffy, although, under the baggy navy tracksuit, with 'American Apparel' written across the chest, the rest of her seemed stiff and gaunt. She held her arms defensively across her chest, and the frayed, grey edges of bandages that came down in criss-cross loops around her thumbs were visible under the navy. The smell of a cooked breakfast drifted past her, and a small dog, a Jack Russell cross, barked shrilly at her feet. They said hi awkwardly, trying not to stare at the grubby bandages, or make it too obvious how shocked they were to see her, usually so polished and self-possessed, looking so very ragged.

'Come on in.' She led the way down the hall. A door opened as they passed, letting out a blast from a television, and a woman stepped out to meet them.

'You must be Deirdre's friends,' she said comfortably, holding out two hands, which they obligingly clasped. 'You're good to come.' Her accent held a faint lilt, from somewhere north of the border. She was wearing a print dress with a purple cardigan over it, buttoned tight across her chest, and the smell that wrapped around her suggested she might have been the creator of the cooked breakfast. Feet planted far apart, she was round and strong, and altogether like the countrywomen Stella knew from holidays with her parents. But what was she to Dell? Or should that be Deirdre?

'This is my mother,' Dell said stiffly, still holding her arms protectively across her chest, her body at an oblique angle to the woman in front of her. Laura could not see the faintest resemblance between the two.

'Nice to meet you.' The woman already had hold of Stella and Laura's hands. Hers were warm and rough. 'I'll get ye tea. Go on in the sitting room, Deirdre – the fire's on.'

The fire was a three-bar electric one, glowing orange and creating a steady bank of dry heat immediately in front of it. The rest of the room was chilly, with a subdued smell of damp. Outside, the wind still blew strongly and flung handfuls of hard raindrops at the windows. Dell sat in one corner of the violently patterned sofa, knees drawn up close to her, so Stella took the other corner and Laura sat in the middle. Knowing that Dell's mother would shortly arrive with teapot and – if Stella was any judge of anything – a plate of cake and biscuits, there didn't seem much point in starting a serious conversation.

'Thanks for the directions. They were very good,' she began.

'Who's Deirdre?' Laura blurted out at the same time, so that Stella's remark got lost.

'I am. That's what I was christened after I was adopted. Only my parents call me Deirdre, and if you two start doing it, I'll kill you.'

'So you're adopted?' said Stella, thinking how much that explained.

'Yes. And spare me the psychoanalysis, please. I'm well capable of that myself.'

'Dell's much nicer,' Laura hastened to say. 'More original. More you,' she finished, a bit awkwardly. 'Was it a nickname?'

'Not really. I changed my name when I went to college. I didn't think Deirdre would have the kind of time I was hoping for.'

'So you invented yourself?' said Laura.

'Not really. This is who I am.' She shrugged, still cradling her elbows. 'But I always knew I'd fit better in Dublin than I do here. Deirdre was the name my parents gave me, and it belonged here, with the person they think I am. I put it back on when I come home. But in college I needed something that suited me better, and Dell was it.'

'Right,' said Laura.

'Complicated,' said Stella.

'If you think so,' she said coldly. 'It seems perfectly simple to me.'

She wouldn't meet their eyes, kept her focus on the floor in front of the sofa, the bit her feet would have been on if she hadn't tucked them up close to her. Tea arrived, carried in on a large plastic tray with an orange and brown pattern and a squishy beanbag type thing attached to the bottom, so that it settled solidly when Dell's mother placed it on a hard red leather pouffe. Broad mugs, a plate with chocolate digestives and slices of porter cake – 'My own,' Dell's mother said – and a thick teapot.

'I'll leave ye to it,' she said. 'Ye know where I am if ye need me, Deirdre.' She shut the door behind her.

Dell made no move to serve them and so, tea being exactly what both girls felt they badly needed, Stella poured full mugs, with milk, and put thick wedges of porter cake on plates. Dell accepted a mug, but shook her head at the cake and biscuits.

'You're not eating much,' Laura said conversationally.

Dell shrugged. 'Not hungry much.'

'So how have you been?' Stella tried.

'You know what happened. That's why you're here, isn't it? How do you think I've been?'

'Okay, not great.' Stella was trying to be placatory, wondering why they had come all this way to sit on a worn sofa, in a cold room filled with trying smells, and this hostile girl watching them from large, wary eyes.

'We're sorry, Dell. We were sorry when we heard what you did, and we wanted to see you,' said Laura, in a rush.

'Well, that's kind of you, I suppose. No one else has tried to see me. Or ring me.' There was a wobble in Dell's voice that made Laura want to put an arm around her, but she didn't quite dare.

'Did you have to go to hospital?'

'Yes. They stitched me up and kept me in for a night, and now I have to go and see one of their shrinks every week. As if I have anything to say to him.' Dell rolled her eyes.

'Does it still hurt?'

'A bit. Stitches come out in a couple of days. They say I'll have scars, but I don't really care about that. At least it means I can just follow the dotted lines if I ever decide to do it again.' Scornful laughter.

'Dell, don't. Please don't say that.' Laura did put out a hand this time, but Dell didn't take it.

'Well, I probably won't. But only because I don't want to

302

give Amanda the satisfaction of knowing how much she's got to me.'

'Amanda didn't mean any of this to happen,' Stella said.

'But you're not going to lie and tell me she's sorry for me?' Dell challenged. There was a pause. 'I thought not.'

'Look, you cheated with her boyfriend. What's she supposed to do?' Stella said.

'You must wonder why I did that. I wonder too.' Dell paused, and Laura's curiosity got the better of her.

'Well, I did wonder. I still do. Why would you do such a thing?'

'There's something about Huw,' Dell began slowly, 'something that just makes you want to be as bad as you can. Go as low as it's possible for you to go. Sink into your own depravity, knowing that he'll meet you there. It's a personal defilement that he somehow encourages, just by being. You must have noticed?' She said it mainly to Stella.

'I sort of see what you mean,' Stella said.

'I don't,' said Laura. 'I don't get it.'

'He kind of eggs you on, and you know that he's delighted with each new bit of badness, so you sort of keep going, daring yourself. It's like a dog rolling around in fox shit. You know the way they go into a weird kind of ecstasy, even though it's just shit? I don't like Amanda, but I don't hate her as much as you might think. And I certainly don't fancy Huw. Please don't think it's that. If I'm honest, he creeps me out. I suppose that was part of it – not fancying him but doing it anyway, forcing myself.' Another pause. Then, 'You must have got the shock of your lives, walking in like that.'

She sounded far more like the old Dell then, a bit teasing and mocking.

'Well, it was quite startling,' Stella agreed, with a smile.

'Not even dark outside. Not to be expected at all,' said Laura. And suddenly they were laughing, all three of them, Stella and Laura ignoring the disloyalty, allowing themselves to see the funny side of a situation that, until then, had had only a bad side.

Dell's mother poked her head round the door. 'That does me good,' she said, with an approving, unsubtle twinkle. 'Hasn't been too much of that lately.'

'So what will you do now?' Stella asked, when Dell's mother had withdrawn her head.

'Stay here for a bit. I have the last chapters of my master's to finish. I've been given an extension, because of this.' She held her arms out in front of her a little, the farthest they had been from her body since the girls arrived. 'I sort of let on that it was the pressure of work and study that had got to me.'

'That was smart,' said Laura.

'Well, I have my pride. I didn't want the rest of the world knowing that I'm in the doghouse because I did something Amanda O'Hagen didn't like. Quite enough people knew that already.'

'But will you come back to Dublin when you're done?'

'Not sure. I'm thinking of London, actually.'

'Where James is?' That was Laura, blurting out her first response.

Dell said slowly, 'Probably not. Not that James isn't the best of the lot, by far. As you know.' She gave Stella a sly glance as she said that. 'But, really, I think I'm done with the whole gang. Time to move on, get out. You can get stuck, you know. The opportunity for escape doesn't present itself endlessly. You have to seize it when it comes. Amanda may have been a total bitch, but I'm not sure she hasn't done me a favour. It can be hard to push yourself, but when you're pushed ...' she shrugged '... if you have any sense, you think about taking it.'

So everyone was drifting off, thought Laura. Like pieces from a shipwreck, breaking away, becoming caught up in other currents. She imagined Dell as a piece of smooth wood, disappearing over the horizon in the pull of a different force. James was already gone. Others – Sinead, Christian, even Byron de Sade – were all feeling the tug. Would it soon just be herself, Amanda and Huw left behind, clinging to each other? 'We should go,' she said.

Dell didn't attempt to dissuade them. 'My dad will be home soon,' she said. 'He works for the county council. As an electrician.'

'You know, you do it very well,' said Laura, as they set down mugs and gathered their things.

'Do what?'

'Your thing. Yourself. You're completely convincing as a snooty bitch.'

'Good.' Dell laughed. 'I hoped I was. Maybe my real parents are posh. Maybe my birth mother was the runaway daughter of a duke.'

'Who couldn't tell her father that she was secretly married to the son of a rival kingdom.' Laura entered straight into the fantasy. 'And then she died in childbirth and her husband killed himself, and an old nursemaid brought the baby here.' She stopped, suddenly aware of her tactlessness, but Dell ignored it, and for once didn't tear down the whimsy with her sharp sarcasm.

'Did you ever try to find out?' Stella, more pragmatic, asked.

'No. My parents would have been very hurt. They've always been kind and loving to me. I didn't want to do that to them.' It was a very un-Dell thing to say.

Dell's mother tried to make them stay 'for somethin' to eat. Somethin' proper. John'll be home in a minute and there'll be dinner put on,' but they insisted they couldn't. 'Well, but ye'll come again?' she asked. They promised they would.

Dell walked them to the car. The rain had eased and a thin strip of pale blue had appeared on the horizon, ready to offer up a brief glimpse of the sun as it set.

'We'll see you soon,' the girls promised. 'We'll come down again.'

'Or I'll come up before I go off anywhere,' said Dell.

'Great! See you then.' But it felt like goodbye.

'Nothing is ever what it looks like, is it?' Laura asked, as they drove back to Dublin.

'Or maybe we just see wrong,' Stella answered.

Chapter Nineteen

London

'I KNEW THE NIGHT BEFORE THE WEDDING,' Stella said, watching the past play across Laura's face as she thought back. 'I knew how awful it was going to be, but I couldn't think of a way out. By then, it seemed too late. God, what a mess.' And more of a mess than Laura knew, she thought.

❧

After the pre-wedding dinner and the devastation of James's kiss, the three girls had gone back to Amanda's and got ready for bed quietly. There had seemed too much to say and no place to start, so they had confined themselves to the plainest of chat.

'Wasn't the food awful?'

'Huw's uncle seems a bit rowdy, doesn't he?'

'Thank goodness the wedding's not till three tomorrow. I'm so tired.'

In the end, Amanda decided to spend the night in the spare room. 'Because I'm so keyed up, I might not sleep, and I don't want to keep you two awake. You need your beauty sleep.'

'Far more than you do.' Laura had laughed.

'Nonsense.' Amanda wrinkled her nose at them, then said, 'Goodnight. I've asked Ivana to bring breakfast up to us at nine. I still don't dare go downstairs.' She left, clutching the ragged copy of *Cold Comfort Farm* that Nessa had given her years before.

'Are you awake?' Laura had whispered a bit later. 'Isn't it weird being here without Amanda? It's like the night after James's twenty-first, when she stayed and we came home and were terrified that Mrs O'Hagen would come in and catch us.'

But Stella hadn't said anything, had pretended to be asleep, even though she was wide awake and crying very quietly. The house was silent, the bangings and hammerings and sounds of scurrying feet finally stilled, making space for memories of all the other nights they had spent in that room, the three of them, with all their dreams, hopes and determination, their boundless sense of life's possibilities, and the joyful certainty that, whatever they were, they would be kind. Stella didn't feel that any more. She felt she had come up against a brick wall of ill will, probably not personal, that life had built against the three of them. Amanda was disintegrating before their eyes, disappearing in strips and shreds, while her own life had lost its magic. Nessa was dying: Laura rarely spoke of it, but her face, in repose, showed a deeply etched misery that stood out against her features, like a mask. She presumed that James's life must be hard too, but found she didn't want to dwell on the what-might-be of his circumstances.

She couldn't sleep. The vividness of the memories and regrets was too intense. She seemed to see a hundred points where their paths had forked, and all three of them had recklessly taken the wrong route, leading farther and deeper into the bog in which they seemed mired. She wondered if they had all done something wrong that had angered an ancient, vindictive deity. If so, was there any kind of atonement they could make? A ritual or sacrifice? She wondered what she had to give, if sacrifice was required. Her slimness was definitely her best feature. The way she never had to watch what she ate. Maybe she could give that up. What would getting fat do to her character? And would it be worth it to get herself past whatever clutching mud currently held her?

What could the others give? With Amanda, it was obvious. The first thing any vengeful deity would require was the tribute of her beauty. Maybe that had been the problem all along. Perhaps she had angered a mean goddess, like Diana or Hera, and they were all suffering the consequences.

Stella decided to get up and see if Amanda was indeed having a sleepless night and, if so, tell her about the theory and see if she was prepared to give up her good looks to get them all out of their morass. How attached was Amanda really to the looks she always affected to ignore? Stella wondered if they could creep downstairs and grab a bottle of something. She felt like a drink. A hot whiskey would be nice, she thought. Settling.

The door to the spare room on Amanda's floor was ajar, with a dim light escaping through it. The room was usually used for unimportant single guests because it had no en suite, and the bed, although double, wasn't a king-size. Anyone important, socially or professionally, would be given the suite on the floor below, which had, as well as a bathroom, access to a small sitting room that looked onto the chestnut trees at the front.

Stella tapped lightly on the door, already planning what she would say to Amanda. There was no answer. She tapped again, a little louder. Still no answer. About to return to her own bed – she didn't dare creep down and look for booze on her own – she changed her mind and pushed open the door in case Amanda had earphones in and simply hadn't heard.

The door opened wide to the room. The window opposite, curtains undrawn, was a flat black reflection in which she could see her own form broken into several square panes. There was a dry, medicinal odour she couldn't identify but that she knew she had smelt before. To the right of the door was the bed and, beside it, a small ornate table and lighted lamp. Amanda was sitting half-upright, back against the padded headboard, half inside the pool of light, half in deeper shadow. Her head lolled on her shoulder and her hair was tumbled across her face. The thick yellow silk dressing gown she wore was pulled over one side of her body. The other arm lay bare outside it, resting heavily in her lap. Her bare legs were stretched in front of her, pitifully thin. Her feet, in comparison with the stick-thin legs, seemed huge and raw, lying just outside the pool of light. The perspective and chiaroscuro effect made Stella think at first of one of the Renaissance crucifixion paintings. Christ, as painted by Caravaggio, with the heavy yellow silk adding a touch of Raphael.

The familiarity of those images was comforting, distancing, so she allowed herself to look a little closer at the scene in front of her. Amanda was breathing, Stella could see the slow rise and fall of her stomach, but she made no sound and hadn't stirred at Stella's entrance. In her lap were an empty syringe and a flesh-coloured length of clear rubber. The bare arm that lay beside it, as though thrown there, had a foul patch of angry red just above the elbow, where the delicate skin was pitted and marked with scratches and holes clustered close together, black against the vivid red. One or two were so deep that Stella expected to see something slimy crawl out of them. It was, she realised, the place where Amanda had been wearing the heavy gold and leather arm cuff earlier that evening. With the cuff on, she had looked like an exotic slave girl or a beautiful cyborg. Without it, exposing the mess she had made of herself, she looked, Stella suddenly thought, like a living sacrifice. She thought of poor Prometheus, chained to a rock, having his liver torn out and eaten by an eagle, only for it to grow back, so that the sacrifice could be made again and again. Amanda, tearing herself up so slowly, seemed to Stella just as tragic.

It didn't occur to her to call anyone. Not even Laura. She moved the syringe, handling it gingerly, to the bedside table, placing it in the pretty octagonal box – mother-of-pearl inlay – that seemed to contain the rest of the drug paraphernalia, then the flesh-coloured bit of rubber. She took a fleecy rug from the end of the bed and laid it gently over Amanda, then turned off the light. She didn't mind Amanda knowing she had been into the room, if her friend thought to consider the implications of the altered scene, but neither did she want to draw attention to her intervention. She considered taking the rest of the drugs and flushing them, but decided there was little point. Amanda would just get more – and, anyway, the timing was all wrong. Maybe after the wedding there would be a moment of intimacy between them that would allow Stella to say some of what she felt: that this ugliness wasn't necessary. That there must be another way to cope with whatever life had done or become, a way that didn't require such annihilation.

Stella left the room, closing the door behind her, just in case, and made her way back to bed. She was briefly surprised at her own calmness, but saw she must have known, somewhere, for a long time, what had been happening.

Suddenly she remembered a conversation between Amanda and her mother, in which Amanda had refused the shellac nails her mother had been so insistent on.

'Your nails are a mess,' Mrs O'Hagen had said bluntly. 'You'll have to get a set applied.' Amanda's fingers were bitten and bloody, the skin torn around the cuticles where she had been worrying at them and down to the knuckles in some cases.

'I know they're hideous, but I'm not getting fakes.'

'You are not, surely, going to hold out that hand for Huw to put a ring on.'

'I am. He's seen them already. He'd be more astonished by the sudden appearance of a full set of witchy talons.'

'They don't have to be witchy. They could be perfectly natural-looking, and cover up those bitten monstrosities.'

'Nevertheless, I'm not getting them. These monstrosities will have to do.'

Now Stella reckoned Amanda must already have been scratching that poisoned spot, and figured that a set of falsies made from hard resin might do terrible damage to the worn, fragile skin.

Lucky the wedding dress has long sleeves, Stella thought, even if they are only lace, understanding now why Amanda had insisted on them. 'More elegant,' she had said at the time, to her mother's approval. 'I don't want to look like a Disney princess. Grace Kelly, not Katie Price.' They had all concurred heartily, commending the subtlety of the slender-cut ivory dress with handmade lace sleeves and a high lace neckline. Well, at least it would contain the hateful rawness of that arm, and cover the pitiful thinness of Amanda's limbs.

Back in bed, Stella decided not to tell Laura. She was afraid of making it seem even uglier than it had been. There wasn't a way of describing the troubling fact that, despite the material squalor of the set-up, Amanda – the central essence of her – had been peaceful, in repose rather than chemically absent.

ଔ

The morning brought rain and chaos. Breakfast appeared at nine, a tray brought up by Ivana with porridge, bacon, toast and grapefruit juice.

'Already house is jumping,' she said grimly, setting it down. 'Today, every time is going to be impossible.' The rain was unexpected – had been guaranteed to hold off until the next night – and even though the wedding was not planned with anything so foolish as sunshine in mind, some tables had been set on the lawn the night before, on what had seemed a reasonable gamble. They would now have to be taken in, dried, and set up elsewhere. From their windows, Stella and Laura could see men crossing the lawn hurriedly, not always using the wooden walkways laid down for the purpose.

'If she see that, he is dead,' said Ivana, with satisfaction, watching a man in blue overalls dragging a table backwards across the wet grass. 'I bring coffee later,' she said. 'After you eat.'

Laura complained of being hung-over. 'Today, of all days!

I hate sneaky waiters who keep pouring wine into your glass. I planned on having only two glasses, and I thought I'd had only two, and then I discovered I was drunk, without even noticing.' She picked up a spoon and drizzled honey over her porridge, straight fair hair sliding across her face. 'I see we're getting the hearty breakfast. I wonder if that means no lunch.'

Stella yawned. She felt . . . not hung-over but dull. The night seemed more nightmare than reality and she did for a moment wonder if she had dreamed the whole macabre scene. Except that she didn't usually have dreams like that, with such detail. Anyway, she never felt any doubt afterwards, always knew they were just dreams. That scene, she knew, had been reality. Her calmness of the night before now struck her as surreal complacency. How could she not have told anyone, raised the alarm and brought Mr and Mrs O'Hagen running? Their daughter had been lying in a drug-induced slump, possibly an overdose, with a needle all but hanging from her savagely pockmarked arm, and all she, Stella, had done was drape a blanket over her. In a fit of panic, she jumped from the bed and ran to the door.

'I'm just going to wake Amanda,' she called to Laura. 'Her big day and everything.' She ran to the spare room, terrified of what she might find. Heart thumping, she banged hard on the door, then opened it without waiting. The window was wide open, despite the rain, and the room smelt fresh and wet. Amanda was sitting on the bed, with the yellow silk dressing gown pulled tight around her, feet in slippers on the floor. She yawned and stretched her arms high over her head as Stella barged in.

'You're excited,' Amanda said, with a smile. 'I guess it's everyone's big day.' She stretched again, pushing her golden hair off her face and over her shoulders. 'Lucky the hairdresser's coming.' She laughed. 'I must have slept on it funny.' Her hair was matted at the back where she had lain against the headboard. All night, Stella wondered, or had she come to at some point and made herself more comfortable? She didn't know what to say. Should she mention her midnight visit? How? Would Amanda think she was judging? Being censorious? A memory of the mangled arm came to her, and she shuddered at the thought of touching the pitted surface, seeing it up close in daylight. She wondered if it was actually rotting, or if it only looked as if it was.

'Breakfast's ready,' she finally mumbled. 'Bacon and porridge. It'll get cold.'

'Coming.' Amanda stood up. There was no sign of the mother-of-pearl box on the bedside table. Amanda must have been up long enough to hide it.

'Did you sleep well?' she managed.

'Perfectly, in the end,' Amanda said. Something in Stella's voice or face must have chimed with her because, after a pause, she said, 'Thank you for the blanket. It was you, wasn't it?'

'Yes,' Stella said, unable to say more. Was it better or worse that Amanda knew she knew? But Amanda seemed perfectly easy with it.

'It was kind of you.'

∞

Thinking back now to that night, she was still astonished at her response to what she had found, unable to work out if her inaction was the result of sang-froid, fear, or just the self-obsession of youth that believes everything is an adventure and nothing bad can happen.

'Let's have a drink before we go and meet Mrs O'Hagen,' she said, wondering how to tell Laura about that night, and explain why she had kept silent for so long. 'We're going to need it. I bought a bottle of vodka in Duty Free. We can get ice sent up.'

'I don't drink any more,' Laura said.

'What? Since when? Why?' Stella was astonished that something so significant should not have been mentioned in the email dispatches between them. Although, now she came to think about it, those dispatches had become gradually briefer, more mundane, as if they were both too tired, or confused, to lay bare the big things that were happening to them. But soon it would be okay, she thought. Now that they were here together, and with Amanda somewhere close, they could stop pretending to be grown-up, separate and making successes of their lives. They could go back to the muddle of being together, without clear distinction, and perhaps later try again to emerge into separate, grown-up identities.

'I don't see the point,' Laura was saying. 'It's just a big lie. You get drunk, everything seems suddenly great, but it isn't. You come home, laughing and feeling like a supermodel, and it's all fake.' She shrugged. 'Life isn't wonderful. It's the same as ever. You're just letting yourself be fooled. So until life is actually wonderful, and I can enjoy it sober, I'm not going to let myself pretend.'

'But surely the point of being drunk is that you have those few hours of feeling like things are great.' Stella was bewildered. 'You know they aren't really, but you get a chance to stop having it shoved in your face, just for a little bit.'

'Nope. If it's not real, I won't do it.' Laura was adamant.

When had she got so controlled? Stella wondered.

Chapter Twenty

London

TURNING DOWN THE DRINK HAD BEEN HARD. Laura had fought to resist the old urge, the urge learned in childhood, to slide in with Stella's wishes and lay aside her own troublesome desire to be someone more definite. But she had done it, despite Stella's irritation, and she was glad she had. So tell her now, the voice in her head said. Or, rather, the sudden increased banging of her heart told her that she was about to say it. Because she couldn't keep pretending that nothing had changed, that she was there for the same reasons as Stella. That they were in harmony.

'I'm going to write about this,' she blurted out.

'About what?' Stella said.

'This. Amanda. Everything.'

'Write it where?' Stella asked, rather stupidly, Laura thought.

'For the paper.'

'You can't!' It was a gasp. 'Laura, you can't.'

'Yes, I can,' Laura snapped. 'She owes me.' The more she had thought about it in the last few days, the more she had believed it, so now it was easy to say, loudly and with conviction. Once said, she believed it all the more.

'Does the paper know you're here?' Stella asked.

'Yes.'

'You've already promised them, haven't you?' said Stella slowly.

'Yes.' Laura was a little shame-faced, then rallied. 'I need this, Stella. I'm going to get fired otherwise, and Amanda has always had everything and never valued it, and we have always protected her, taken fire for her and put her first, and now I have to get something back from that.'

'That's not fair,' said Stella. 'Everything we've done for Amanda, we've done because we wanted to, not because she asked.'

'Well, maybe,' said Laura tightly, 'but now I want to do this. Have to do this.'

'It's just a job,' said Stella. 'It's not worth so much.'

'Yes, it is!' Laura shouted. 'It is. It's stupid to say it isn't, and choose friendship and honour over it when friendship and honour haven't given us much, not with Amanda anyway. Not recently. It's just babyish to pretend they mean more than getting paid and having a career and making something of your life. I'm sick of living like I do, Stella. Of being at the bottom of the heap at work and not knowing what the point of my life is. Of having no money and no idea what I'll be doing in a year.

It's all very well for you, with your *hotshot* career in New York,' she said, with bitter emphasis. 'I don't have that kind of career, or any kind much, really, but I can do with this story. It's the only thing I have of any value and I'm going to use it and build on it. And it's my story too, anyway.'

'It's not yours to tell, though,' Stella said.

There was a strained silence.

'If not mine, whose?' asked Laura.

'No one's. Or all of ours,' said Stella. 'At least ask Amanda first.'

'Okay, I'll ask. But I don't promise to do as I'm told. Not any more.' The silence between them felt as if it weighed a hundred tons, as if it would eventually pull the entire room down into it.

'Laura, I know it's been horrible for you in the last couple of years.' Stella tried to breach the silence. 'Since Nessa. It's been horrible for all of us. I miss her, too, so much. And things have been crap in my life.' She paused, seemed to be gathering force to speak again, but Laura wouldn't let her.

'I know you think we all suffered that together,' she said, 'but we didn't. Only I did. You could always go home for a while. That was my home. Nessa was my home, and she's gone. And after she went, I saw how little she was able to leave. Nothing concrete. Nothing for me.'

'But that wasn't Nessa's way—' Stella began.

'Don't tell me what her way was,' Laura yelled. 'I don't care if it wasn't her way. It should have been. She should have tried harder. Fought harder. And not assumed I'd be okay just because she wanted me to be.' Her voice broke on the last words but she refused to give in to the tears that waited.

'Okay, I'm sorry,' said Stella, after a pause. 'Of course

we didn't suffer it together. Not really. But I did love Nessa. Still love her. And miss her.' But Laura wouldn't let herself be reached, thawed, by the appeal in Stella's words. She held firm to her sense of purpose, bitter as she knew it to be. 'And I think it's partly because of that that I let myself get into a really stupid situation at work,' Stella went on. This time, Laura let her continue. And she told it all. The affair with Sean, the adrenalin of long hours and being good at what she did, which allowed her to forget how little of anything else there was. The cutthroat nastiness of all her professional engagements, the guarded disappointment of her private ones. The way a gap had grown between her parents and her because they were proud but baffled by what had become of their avenging-angel daughter. Because they could see that, beyond the big salary, she had so little. And because she couldn't tell them, admit to them, just how little.

And Laura, offered the opportunity to be kind, comforting, chose instead to be cruel and dense. 'I can't believe you would sleep with another woman's husband,' she said, once Stella had finished. 'After everything you've said about female solidarity and never letting yourself be someone's fool.'

She turned away, bent over her case so she wouldn't see the shock on Stella's face, or show Stella the shock on hers. She wished she hadn't come. Why had she come? The story, Petrie, Amanda – suddenly none of it seemed worth the effort and she wished she had let it all lie. The friendship with Stella, which had so far fallen away that this could happen between them; Amanda and the many problems to which she had her own solutions, hopeless as those were: why was she there, thinking she could salvage something from their days together? Why was she bothering with any of it? Really, the wedding had been the end for all of them, except that they couldn't see it at the time, had still seen only their own belief in a bright future.

ം

They had breakfasted together, in Amanda's room, from a tray Ivana had brought up. Around them, the house was pulsing with purpose. Amanda had looked tired but surprisingly relaxed for a bride. Stella had seemed the uptight one.

'It's like being in a tree house on a windy day,' Amanda said, after she'd had a bowl of porridge and three pieces of toast with bacon. 'I can hear all the bangings and shakings going on below us, but we're safe up here out of it all.'

'For now,' said Laura, laughing, 'but the storm's a-coming.'

'Big storm,' Amanda agreed, laughing too. She glanced at Stella and gave her a tiny ghost of a wink that Laura didn't understand.

'Lucky the SWAT team are on their way,' Stella said. 'I think we could all use a little help today.'

'Two hairdressers, two make-up artists. You think it'll be enough?' Amanda asked.

'Just about,' said Stella.

'What are we supposed to do until it's time to dress?' asked Laura.

'Stay out of my mother's way,' Amanda answered promptly. 'I think I'll go back to bed for an hour.'

'I'm going downstairs,' Laura said. 'I can't sit up here all day. I don't mind helping, and, anyway, Nessa will arrive soon.'

Nessa had been given a room in the house, and Mrs O'Hagen had arranged for her to be collected from town early so she would have a chance to rest before the ceremony. It was, Laura had reflected, the kind of practical help she had become used to from Mrs O'Hagen. Efficient, thoughtful, and invariably the best possible thing.

The day passed faster than she'd expected, and the house emptied steadily as tasks were completed, and those responsible left. The rain cleared, leaving a thin mist that muffled sound, like straw in a busy street. The flowers were finished first – huge banks of spectral-pink hydrangeas and glossy roses – and the florists set off for the church to give their work there a last look. The setting-up men thinned out steadily until they were all gone. The marquee – gorgeously draped in swathes of white, with real chandeliers and real trees, through the branches of which were twined ropes of fairy lights – stood stately and aloof in the centre of the immaculate lawn. The wooden walkways had been dressed up with rustic handrails through which were twisted garlands of wild flowers. Three smaller marquees, 'Gazebos, really,' Laura had said, sniggering at the silliness of the word, had been set up with drinks tables and a few chairs for the elderly and infirm.

'We'll know where to avoid so,' Amanda had muttered bitchily, when Mrs O'Hagen explained the reasoning over an early and very light lunch in the white drawing room. It was the first time they had seen her all day, and Laura marvelled that she could look and seem so cool, the calm centre of a feeding frenzy all around her. Of course, she reflected, Amanda was cool and calm too, but she wasn't involving herself much with the organisation.

Hair was already done, although make-up not yet, so they could eat without taking undue care. Stella and Laura had matching chignons, smooth and classical with a faint sixties beehive look. Amanda's was twisted into an elaborate but wistful series of curls, soft at the front, flowing into a mass of golden waves and plaits at the back. She looked like Aphrodite ceremonially coiffed, Laura thought.

Mrs O'Hagen had opted for a far more severe look: hair swept off her face and back into a thick knot, exposing the angularity of her cheekbones and slight under-bite, which gave her thrust-forward face a constantly challenging look.

Perhaps because of the hairstyles, or the importance of the day, the conversation was stilted. Amanda said almost nothing, just yawned loudly every once in a while. Laura tried to engage Mrs O'Hagen about various guests and plans, but found her unusually reluctant to communicate, while Stella was surprisingly silent.

'I wonder is this the last time we'll sit here together, like this?' she said suddenly.

'Of course it isn't!' Amanda insisted.

'Of course it is,' Mrs O'Hagen contradicted. 'After today, Amanda, you will be a married woman. You will have your own house, different cares and worries. Things will not be the same.'

'You sound as if I'm going to turn into some sort of little *hausfrau*,' Amanda said lightly. 'Warming my husband's slippers by the stove and baking bread. I don't intend to change my life, you know. And Huw doesn't want me to. We'll carry on exactly as we have been. We've promised each other that.'

'Nonsense,' said Mrs O'Hagen firmly. 'Life does not carry on as before, no matter what you think now. You'll have a house to run, for a start. And Huw has plenty of position to keep up.'

'We don't want people coming and visiting,' said Amanda. 'We won't be running little salons where we invite important people to meet each other and maybe find ways in which they can work together so that the crumbs of their approval fall on us for bringing them together.' Her voice dripped with sarcasm. 'We just want to be left alone.'

There was an uncomfortable silence. Stella and Laura stared at their plates, conscious that Amanda had half-turned in her chair and was staring sullenly out the window. She yawned again.

'Must you always be the victim of your own life, Amanda? Never the heroine?' Mrs O'Hagen asked, looking directly at her daughter.

Amanda stopped mid-yawn, and flashed back, 'I thought you were heroine enough for both of us.'

Mrs O'Hagen seemed ready to say something swift and bitter, but instead said coolly, 'That's enough of that. If everyone has finished, it's time for make-up. You know ... I don't expect thanks for all I've done for you – that would be to consider you an adult, Amanda, something you very clearly are not, but I do not expect rudeness.' She rose from her place. 'After today, I suppose it will no longer be my role to try to guide you, but let me tell you one thing. Life does not stay the same. It cannot be made to. And you had better get used to that idea.' She swept from the room.

The girls stayed silent a moment longer.

'You can't really mean you want life to stay the way it is now,' Laura said, thinking how desperate she was for her own life to shunt forward, change in almost any way.

'Well, I do,' Amanda insisted. 'I don't see what's so great about "moving on" and "personal growth" and all that rubbish. Things are fine now. I want them to stay this way. I can't think of any way my life could change that would make it better.'

'What about being cast in a really big film?' Laura asked eagerly. 'Surely that would be a good thing.'

'Not really. I'd have to be away from Huw for long periods, and no one ever leaves you alone on a film set. Even when you don't have anything to do in a scene, they're always looking for you, for costume or make-up or to run lines or whatever. Always intrusions, always hassle. Everyone's in a panic because there's never enough budget, and always more time needed than expected, so there's all this suppressed hysteria and hurry.'

'What will you do for money if you aren't making films?' Stella asked.

'We'll order everything from Harrods on the charge account,' Amanda said wickedly. 'Even loo paper and toothpaste. The newspaper, too. Anything that Harrods doesn't have, we just won't be able to get.'

They laughed, and Laura wondered what it must feel like never to have to take care of yourself or worry about how to manage, how to pay bills and still have something left over. The thought made her dizzy. 'I'm going to see how Nessa's doing,' she said.

'Yes, time to get on,' Amanda agreed. 'Nearly there now.'

The church was visible from Amanda's bedroom window, its stone steeple rising through a gap in the trees beyond the field where the horses had been. Surrounded by a small graveyard softened with moss and weed, it was pretty and far too small for the number of guests, but Amanda had insisted.

'We may not have spent much time there, but at least it's familiar,' she had said. 'I'm not driving miles to some horrible mausoleum I've no connection with. I've always thought that when I die I'd like to be buried there, so I could see the light from my own bedroom window at night. But, in the meantime,

I want to get married there.' And so a Silver Cloud Rolls-Royce was booked to take her the mile or so by road to the church.

Fully dressed, Amanda was breathtaking. Aphrodite indeed, subtly arrayed to the most heartbreaking effect. The dress was exquisite, and discreet enough not to swallow her whole. Instead, it was the perfect frame. The lace added contour and substance to her too-slender arms and shoulders, while the elegant length and sheen of the fabric gave her added height, pooling softly on the floor behind her in a kind of demi-train. Her make-up was no more than a clever enhancement of her natural features, so that she was entirely herself.

'You look amazing,' Laura said simply, when she appeared before them at last.

Amanda twirled around. 'I *feel* amazing.' She laughed. 'I can't believe I'm actually going to marry Huw today, and be with him for ever. I hope the same thing for you two,' she added seriously, 'that each of you will marry the man you love, and who loves you.' Laura smiled, careful not to look at Stella. 'Although,' Amanda continued, 'I think I'd spare you the whole circus. Run away and do it in a register office!'

'Or we could hire your mother as event planner and do nothing,' said Laura. She meant it mostly as a joke, but somehow it came out sounding censorious.

There was a pause.

'You'd better go down,' Amanda said. 'It's nearly time to start.' They kissed her, then the three of them clung together, feeling the weight of the moment's emotion far more than Laura had expected.

'It's not goodbye,' Amanda said eventually, although her voice wobbled. No, they agreed, not goodbye.

'See you in church,' Stella said, trying to laugh.

'It's like sending off a maiden of Athens as tribute to the Minotaur,' said Laura sadly, as they made their way downstairs to the waiting cars.

'Huw is definitely half-beast, and ready to devour her.'

'Maybe marriage will settle him,' Laura said doubtfully. 'They say it does settle men.'

'Doubt it. The only settling will be what Mr O'Hagen coughs up as a wedding present.'

Amanda kept no one waiting, arriving at the church barely moments after Stella and Laura, and sweeping up the nave on her father's arm, fast and with purpose, to the gentle strains of Schubert's 'Ave Maria', the hymn that spoke of a young world in solemn worship. Despite the packed church and audible, even theatrical, gasps of admiration as guests caught their first sight of her, she looked neither left nor right, just kept her eyes fixed on Huw. Beneath the delicate misty ambiguities of her Irish lace veil, there was no doubting at all the set of her shoulders or her determination.

Neither did she hang around outside the church afterwards, to the despair of the photographer, who was counting on her to become the gemstone of his portfolio, and had lined up a hundred artistically irresistible shots featuring old stone walls and Amanda's golden beauty. Within minutes of accepting the stream of good wishes that flowed steadily their way, Laura could see that she and Huw were twitching with impatience and irritation. Amanda's smile was fixed, glassy, while Huw, who looked impeccably handsome in his morning suit, his compact frame enhanced by its formality, was sneering behind the polite laugh with which he greeted the well-wishers, his sly eyes casting about him in a way that barely masked his boredom. Amanda had dropped her glorious bouquet against the wall of the church and pushed her veil impatiently back on her head, disrupting the careful gathering of plaits and curls.

'The bride wore a tissue of lies,' Stella whispered gloomily to Laura.

'No, she didn't,' Laura retorted. 'She is clothed entirely in sincerity. And she's the only person here who is.'

'Apart from us.'

'Apart from us. We ache sincerity!'

For all the undoubted magnificence of marquee and gazebos, the carefully calculated generosity of the dinner and the lavish speeches, the reception was noticeably flat. Amanda and Huw remained aloof, staying close by each other's sides and watching, rather than participating. So strong was the feeling of exclusion they carried with them that the guests gave them a wide berth.

'They look like they're talking about us all,' Iseult said to Stella, Laura and Nessa, watching Amanda and Huw with their heads close together, whispering and giggling.

'Yes, and not necessarily nice things,' said Stella.

The only real entertainment had been provided by a previously unknown friend of Huw's who had accosted Stella as she passed with glasses of champagne for some of the elderly and infirm.

'Jake. Friend of the groom,' he said, winking at her. 'Nice to meet you. I 'ope to see a lot more of you later.' He winked again, the other eye. The effect, coming so soon after the first wink, was to make him look like a clockwork toy – an owl, maybe, with those large eyes. She half-expected him to make a whirring, clicking noise up close. He had a hearty Cockney manner that struck Stella as fake, even as she was wondering how Huw could have such a friend, so unlike the polished contemporaries from school and university, and that Amanda could possibly have thought she would like this grinning, impertinent fellow.

'What a ridiculous person that Jake is,' she said later to Laura. 'Like an extra out of *Oliver!* or *Withnail and I*.'

'I agree. Total caricature. He's already tried to sell me some purple hearts. What does he think this is? A festival?'

ꣷ

Amanda and Huw left early, and hastily.

'I thought you weren't going to do the dashing-off-early thing?' Stella asked. 'That you were going to stay to the bitter end?'

'I thought so too,' Amanda answered. 'Except it feels as if it isn't so much the end that's bitter as the whole thing. I'm sick of it. Huw too. We just want to get out. And,' she added, 'I'm not doing all that ridiculous bouquet-throwing and being cheered off by well-wishers. In fact, maybe you could tell my mother I've gone.' She gave Stella and Laura a hopeful look.

'No chance,' said Stella promptly.

'No chance,' Laura echoed.

'Okay, fine, but don't think I'm going to make a thing of this, because I'm not. And I'm counting on you two to get me clean out and away.' She looked giddy and unfocused, Laura thought, belatedly stuffing a few final things into a battered Louis Vuitton bag. 'I don't want people queuing up to say goodbye. I've done enough of that today.' That wasn't true, Laura reflected. She had barely spoken to a single guest.

'Exit Amanda,' said Stella, watching as she and Huw got into the car that was to take them to the hotel.

'Pursued by a bear,' Laura added.

ೞ

The next morning, Amanda had refused to turn up for the champagne breakfast, sending her mother, Stella and Laura a text, saying she and Huw were tired and going to stay put in their honeymoon suite. After that, she had refused to answer the phone when Mrs O'Hagen tried to ring her. Instead, Mrs O'Hagen had called Laura and Stella into her bedroom, where she was having a cup of tea. They stood awkwardly beside the bed, because there was no question of sitting cosily on it. For all the opulence of the room — thick creamy carpets, heavy curtains, the inevitable fat cushions — her bedside table, Laura was fascinated to see, had exactly the same sort of faintly disgusting clutter as anyone else's: crumpled tissues, a nail file, a half-full tube of ointment for the Treatment of Fungal Nail Infections.

'Did you know about this?' she had demanded, gesturing towards the phone that lay face-up on the table beside her. 'That Amanda and Huw won't be coming back for the breakfast?'

'Only now,' Laura said, flushing red.

Mrs O'Hagen looked at them both, head to one side. 'I always thought you two would be a good influence on Amanda,' she said. 'You especially, Laura. I was pleased with the friendship. Even though neither of you is precisely brilliant.' She paused, to let the sting sink in. 'But now I wonder if you weren't always just too compliant. Perhaps Amanda needed someone of stronger character.'

'That isn't fair,' Laura burst out. 'We aren't her keepers. We're friends, not *influences*. It doesn't work like that.' Her voice carried a faint whine, and shook at her own audacity.

'No. Perhaps not.'

'And as for brilliant, we're not a hand of cards, you know,' Stella said, surprisingly steady.

'Cards?'

'Yes – ace, king, queen, whatever. You know. Separate, complementary, carefully chosen. We're friends with Amanda because we like her. Love her.'

Mrs O'Hagen seemed faintly surprised. 'Of course you do,' she said. 'As do I, you know. And let's hope that's enough. But don't say you never wanted anything from Amanda. You know she has a loyal nature, and that where she goes, you may go too. Don't tell me that means nothing to you.' Stella stayed silent but Laura felt her quiver.

Mrs O'Hagen stood up, her breakfast mostly untouched. 'Well, I'm not going to cancel now, so we'll just have to entertain without Huw and Amanda. You two will be staying.' It was an order, not a question, but they nodded anyway.

∞

Laura, unfolding her fleecy pyjamas from her case and putting them carefully under the pillow of the bed nearest the window, was thinking. If I can just talk to Amanda, she'll say it's okay, and then Stella won't mind. She put on a pair of spiky black-patent heels and stood up. 'We'd better hurry. We'll be late for Mrs O'Hagen.'

Chapter Twenty-One

London

AFTER EVERYTHING YOU'VE SAID ABOUT FEMALE solidarity and never letting yourself be someone's fool . . .

The cruelty of Laura's words had been deliberate, Stella knew. Not the product of awkwardness or ignorance, but carefully chosen to hurt. And that had been the end of the conversation. The end, too, of Stella's certainty that all the three needed was to be together again, for a path to be traced and begun anew. With that, the happy forward momentum of her life came to a halt because, she realised, it was built on simple optimism. The undemanding belief that tomorrow would be better than today. No matter how bad things had been, there had seemed always the chance of good things happening just around the corner. That belief had sustained her through the worst of everything, and without it she felt very little interest in her life.

They got ready for lunch with Mrs O'Hagen in silence, moving politely, angrily, around each other in the bathroom and between the two beds. The cosy chintz of the room seemed to mock their estrangement, looking on in plump, floral disapproval at the distance between them. Stella felt an exhaustion so profound, it was as if her mind and limbs were moving through treacle. Jetlag, she told herself. She splashed vodka into a tooth mug and drank it, not bothering to ring for ice. Laura ignored her, putting on make-up and dressing far more carefully than Stella had ever seen her. Instead of the casual, boho look she had more or less inherited from Nessa, she was now businesslike, snappy. And nasty, thought Stella, missing the soft colours and layers she was used to.

Worst of all, she thought, she would have to face Mrs O'Hagen alone and without allies. The idea made her uncomfortable. She was no match for Amanda's mother. Stella remembered the grudging admiration she had felt the morning after the wedding when, confronted with Amanda's careless disruption of her plans, Mrs O'Hagen had refused to bow down. Once the guests had gathered – and most of the wedding party seemed to have been invited – she had made a short speech, sleek and shrewd as an old cat, explaining that the bride and groom, while so grateful to everyone for sharing their day, were tired and wouldn't be attending. The guests, clutching champagne flutes and lining up for a buffet brunch that included wild smoked salmon, blinis and exotic fruit salads, looked, Stella thought, pretty indifferent to the fact that Amanda and Huw had failed to appear.

'They aren't really here for Amanda, are they?' she said to Iseult and Laura.

'Lord, no. Free bubbly and a chance to tell their friends they were invited,' said Iseult.

'I see Huw's parents aren't here either,' said Laura. 'Maybe they're at the hotel with him and Amanda.'

'I don't suppose so,' said Iseult. 'Not the kind of thing they go in for. I imagine they feel they've done enough and are getting ready to leave for home.'

'They aren't a very close family, are they?'

'God, no. I doubt they see each other at all, if it can be avoided. You know, if I had expected ... well, any of this, I wouldn't have let James bring Huw within a hundred miles of here.' There was a pause. 'James once asked me to have a word with Amanda, in the beginning, before the engagement, but I wouldn't. I felt I shouldn't interfere. I'm rather sorry now that I didn't.'

Stella thought about that – James asking his mother to intervene and save the girl he loved. Save her, or save her for him? She presumed the latter.

The string quartet were playing Bach's *Art of Fugue*, distinctly melancholy for the supposedly celebratory nature of the morning, but entirely in keeping with Stella's mood. The guests were greedy and merry, jostling each other at the buffet table, refilling glasses recklessly, keen to cram in all they could of the lavish hospitality around them. She could see James on the other side of the lawn, talking to Malcolm. Stella and he had avoided each other the day before, yet she had felt acutely conscious of where he was at all times, her body seeming to catch a vibration off his so that she was angled towards him, even when he was on the other side of the room. Each time she looked up, her eyes slid across to his so that their glances snagged and tangled. She longed to tell him about Amanda, what she had seen, laugh with him at stupid Jake, ask him why she felt so dreary, and if he felt the same. But she did none of those things, only made polite small talk when they were obliged to be close together and resisted the urge to fold herself into him. At that moment, she realised that staying in touch would be much harder than allowing themselves to drift apart. The future lined itself up before her, and contained very little of the bright hilarity of the past.

℘

The happy couple had left for Thailand two days after the wedding, Stella recalled, so it was almost a month before they saw Amanda again. By which time she had gone from party girl to full-fledged drug addict. Stella still found herself astonished at how the old Amanda had vanished on that honeymoon, replaced by a sullen, solipsistic changeling.

Amanda had been scruffy and spotty at the reunion lunch, ludicrously pale for someone who had spent nearly a month on one of the most beautiful beaches in the world. She was wearing a wide-sleeved cotton top and grey maxi skirt, and looked like a backpacker, Stella remembered thinking, as if she'd been sleeping rough – she knew, though, they had been staying at an obscenely luxurious resort. And she smelt ... New-Age-y was the only way she found to describe it. Patchouli incense, spices, dirty hair.

'What was it *like*?' Laura was asking. Amanda had flown in that morning, would be leaving for London the next day. Her lips were dry and chapped, so that she kept picking at them with bitten fingers. The effect of all that torn skin, Stella thought, was tragic. Her hair was dry too, the ends rough and frizzy, her skin blotchy under the make-up. Looking at her, Stella itched for one of those magazine makeover sessions, a day of exfoliating, moisturising, self-indulgent pampering, so that Amanda could hide what she had become for a little longer. And if she couldn't hide it, Stella realised, they couldn't ignore it. They would have to do something. And what that might be left Stella reeling. Where to begin? Detox? Psychoanalysis? Huw-aversion therapy? A good night's sleep?

'It was okay. Nice, I guess.' Still wearing sunglasses, Amanda pushed bits of pineapple and mango with chopped mint around her plate, having asked for 'just a fruit salad' instead of a main course. 'The water is beautiful but it's really too hot to sit out. Huw went fishing and scuba diving a bit with a local guy, and some friends of his came from Bangkok for a few days.' She scratched at her arm through the cotton top, then speared a piece of mango with her fork. She didn't eat it. 'Look, we got tattoos.' She pulled up her top a few inches, leaning back from the table. Just above her hip bone, which protruded sharp against the pale skin of her concave stomach, a tiger was etched in blue-black ink, prowling down towards her groin. 'Tigers are for protection. Huw got the same one, in the same place.'

To Stella, it looked like nothing so much as the crystal panther on the black marble plinth in Mrs O'Hagen's white sitting room. Imagine going all the way to Thailand to get a two-dimensional replica of an ornament they had all scoffed at. Nevertheless, she made admiring noises, then said, 'You always swore you'd never get a tattoo. That they were tacky. What changed your mind?'

'It just seemed different over there. Everyone has them. And when you're on the beach, wearing hardly anything most of the time, they can look pretty good. I wonder do they travel, though?' she added thoughtfully. 'Maybe it was a mistake. Maybe they're like shells — away from the beach they just look sad and dusty.' She seemed suddenly deflated, so Laura rushed to change the subject.

'You didn't do much sunbathing?'

'We mostly weren't up in time. We went out a lot at night.'

'Where? Clubs? Bars?'

'Both. There's every imaginable type of nightlife there, from the smartest Euro-trashy clubs to squalid little dives.' Amanda perked up a bit while delivering this description, animated by the idea of badness in a way that beauty couldn't get to her. 'No matter what you do, no one ever bats an eyelid. It's like everyone expects Westerners to be walking cesspits of debauchery, and none of it bothers them. They just say, "Yes," and "No," so politely, no matter what's going on around them, and whatever you ask for, they can do it, from a dog fight to probably a murder.' She sounded as if she was boasting.

'Which friends of Huw's? Have we met them?' Stella wanted to know.

'No. One of them lives there — he's married to a Thai girl and they have a fancy little hotel in one of the other resorts. She's some kind of Thai Mafia, I think. She never said very much, but I saw her giving out to him one night when he was drunk and falling around rather. She looked scary and he was pretty terrified. I didn't blame him. The others were friends from university and London, who seem to have been drifting around the world for a while now. They were in India and Vietnam before Thailand.'

'Trust fund dropouts?'

'I suppose so.' She began to tell them tales of various parties and nights out. To Stella, it sounded grubby, full of chaos and excess, typical of the entitled young let loose in hot countries with cheap booze. Huw seemed to have behaved like a thug and a bully in too many of them, once apparently rounding on a German tourist with a broken bottle. Nights when fights broke out and deals were done, against a backdrop of cheap party music and cocktails in coconuts with paper umbrellas, populated by a shifting population of tourists. It all sounded very downmarket, Stella decided, entirely in keeping with the tattoo but quite different from anything she would have expected of Amanda.

'Tell me what's been going on here,' Amanda said at last, having run out of momentum.

'Not a whole lot,' they had to admit, which pleased her.

'Is life duller when I'm not around?'

'You know it is.'

'But dull isn't always bad,' Stella muttered darkly. Since the wedding she had chosen dull, studying hard for the New York bar exams, to her father's delight, and refusing so many invitations that they had almost dried up. Dull, she had decided, was the way forward. Forward and out.

But Amanda didn't hear her, or pretended not to. 'I must go. I'll see you later. I have to meet Huw.' She reached for her bag, a soft brown leather Mulberry satchel, impeccable in its simplicity. The wide sleeves of her cotton top fell back as she slung it over her shoulder, revealing track marks, like spiders' threads, crawling down her inner arm.

'She never took off her sunglasses,' Laura said, into the long silence that followed her departure.

'Or dropped her guard,' Stella answered.

CB

After that, they had seen less of Amanda. She had moved to London and the four-storey wedding-cake house, where her career prospects were better. Stella had been glad. Uncertain how to deal with the situation, she held back. She wasn't, she dimly knew, ready to give herself over to Amanda any more, so she squashed down the faint feeling that, if anything was to be done, she and Laura would have to do it. That no one else knew what they knew, or cared as they did.

Laura made no protest, seemed ready to let Amanda go, for it to be her and Stella again.

Amanda seemed ambiguous, dancing back and forth between neglecting and requesting. Once in London, she and Huw were swallowed into his crowd – models, filmmakers, the young and reckless – and often they did not hear from her for long stretches. Then, suddenly, there would be a barrage of calls. Could they come for a weekend? There was a great show at the National Gallery they'd love. A few days in the country? She and Huw had taken a house and it was far too big for them. A week in Ibiza because a friend had a yacht? Stella always said no, because Huw would be there, and because she could feel the edge of desperation in Amanda's voice and didn't know what to do about it. Gradually she and Laura drifted into a way of mocking her, which helped to distance their confusion. Stella was shamed by her failure to act because it went against everything she believed herself to be. Not knowing what to do, but that she should do something, made her defensive and sometimes cruel.

'You'd probably get stoned just from breathing the air they exhale,' she joked to Laura, after one such invitation for a few days near Nice.

'I'd say the combined urine would be enough to contaminate the entire water supply of the South of France,' Laura quipped back.

'I wonder does Amanda still show herself in a bikini?'

'She must need a burqa to cover the damage by now.' Thus they had coped with being forgotten but still needed. The pain of the one played off against the guilt of the other. Both were busy with their future, trying to make something out of what seemed the inadequate hands they had been dealt: 'A degree, a few qualifications, Grade Five in piano,' Stella had remarked one day. 'What are we supposed to conjure up out of that?'

When they did snatch a few hours together, for lunch or a drink, they spoke of their plans and hopes, the minor triumphs – Stella passing the bar exams, Laura being invited to sit in on editorial meetings at the *Sunday Herald* – of their new lives. When they did mention Amanda, it was with a careful sneer for her party-girl lifestyle and habits, safe in the vast distance between her life and theirs. And, anyway, neither of them felt there was anything unexpected in the story that had evolved. Amanda was living almost exactly the kind of life they had imagined for her and it didn't occur to them that the childish fantasy of glamour and danger they had dreamed up should not have been so faithfully copied.

After Stella had moved to New York, she heard from Amanda more often. She would ring, usually late at night when she knew Stella would be at home, and talk until Stella said, 'Amanda, I have to go, I have work in the morning.' Then Amanda would say how sorry she was, that she hadn't meant to keep her up, but always with a sudden coldness, as if Stella were criticising and she couldn't bear it.

Sometimes she rambled, speech softly slurred, pursuing stories that she seemed to think Stella was already familiar with.

'You know that guy? The one who said he'd put me in a film he's making based on *Don Quixote*?' she would begin, out of nowhere, the faint echo of nearly three and a half thousand miles between them, and Stella would try to explain that she had never heard of him until that second. But Amanda rarely listened enough to backtrack, simply carried the story forward from the place where, in her mind, she had broken it off. Often, the stories seemed to be of betrayal, double-dealing, let-downs and lies. People who promised her jobs that never materialised, who offered contracts that were then withdrawn, who spoke of exciting roles that went to other beautiful girls. Amanda was ever the victim in the stories, duped and dismayed.

'What does Huw say about all this?' Stella asked cautiously one night, after a particularly long tirade involving the offer of a starring role in a government-backed public service campaign aimed at teenagers, which had then been snatched from under Amanda's nose when she had failed to turn up at the agreed location. 'But they changed the location,' Amanda kept saying, bewildered. 'They changed it and they didn't tell me. They said they had, but they hadn't.'

In response to the question about Huw she said, a bit sadly, Stella thought, 'Oh, he doesn't get involved. He's probably right not to.' She didn't sound convinced. 'He says it's my career, that I need to manage it better and I should be more reliable.'

It was the first time Stella had ever heard the slightest suggestion of discord between them. She wanted to put her two hands into the faint dim gap she had discerned in that moment, and pull them far apart. But she held back. Life in a legal firm had taught her patience, even when the cause was righteous. 'Why don't you have an agent?' she had asked instead, practical and business-like, tapping her foot against the edge of the sofa, aware that the clock in the cupboard-like kitchen must be edging past one a.m. 'That's the way most people do it.'

'Oh, I couldn't bear it.' Amanda sounded horrified. 'Another Mummy. Can you imagine? Telling me what to do and how to be and who to be nice to … I'm never doing that again.' There was a pause. 'I suppose you have to go?' she said then, wistfully.

'I sort of do. It's late.'

Stella found the conversations unsatisfactory, one-sided and obscure. Amanda never really asked after her so Stella never really told her anything. Neither, though, did she get any real sense of Amanda in those phone calls. She was just a slightly defeated voice, droning on in a way that Stella secretly thought was spoiled, not the beautiful, vital girl she had known. Maybe you had to see Amanda to get her, she thought.

And then one night, two years into the marriage, Amanda rang, breathless and excited, words falling over each other.

'Guess what?' She left no time for guessing. 'I'm pregnant!'

'Oh, Jesus.' Stella hadn't known what to say. 'How amazing. God. I mean, you're pleased, right?'

'I'm so happy!' Amanda had gushed. 'Everything will be different now, you'll see. I'd much rather be a mother than a muse or a model. We weren't planning this, but I think it must be Providence intervening. I know this is going to change everything.' She was doing it again, Stella thought, painting herself a nice new scenario. A new backdrop. Like Paris. Like being married. But maybe she was right this time. After all, a baby was real life, really grown-up. No more play-acting.

'That's wonderful,' she had answered. 'You'll be the first of all our friends to have a baby! What does your mother say?'

'I haven't told her yet.'

'Right.'

'I need to limit the amount of time she has to try and take over. I'm thinking of getting Huw to tell her once I go into labour,' she joked. 'Or maybe when the baby is eighteen.'

They hadn't spoken much during the pregnancy, and Stella had been delighted at Amanda's new-found sense of purpose, her energy.

'I'm so damn good you wouldn't recognise me!' she had laughed during one conversation, early on. 'I'm drinking endless green juices, made with spinach and things – so much that Huw reckons I'll give birth to a goblin. A cute little baby goblin. Wouldn't that be adorable?' Stella had said it would be, had laughed, and felt persuaded by the courage of Amanda's conviction. Everything *would* be all right now. Things *would* be different.

It was Laura who told Stella the baby had been born, ringing early one morning, nearly three weeks before Stella had expected such a call, to say, 'Amanda had her baby. It's a girl! She just rang.'

For a brief, cross moment Stella wondered why Amanda hadn't rung her, then squashed the flash of jealousy. 'How wonderful! Trust Amanda to catch us off guard. Are you going over?'

'Of course. You?'

'Of course.'

And she had paid a fleeting visit that weekend. Feeling far too nervous to ask for any time off from Davies Darn and Slate soon after starting, she had arrived on the red-eye on a Saturday morning, flown back on the Sunday afternoon, guiltily aware that an entire weekend without going into the office 'just for an hour or so' would not go unnoticed. Not mentioned, but noted.

'I'll be too fast to even get jetlag,' she had said, when Laura had worried about how tired she would be. But that hadn't been true. She had felt profoundly exhausted for many days afterwards. Although that, she knew, might have been the depression that set in on seeing Amanda with her baby.

'She's not Flora,' Amanda had said, tears running wearily down her cheeks. 'She can't be. Not now.' Stella hadn't understood the reference, until Laura, standing behind her, out of the line of Amanda's tears, explained it to her in a hiss.

'That book she used to read, one of Nessa's, *Cold Comfort Farm*? You remember she always said she'd call her daughter after Flora Poste.'

'I'll call her Dora. For nearly being Flora,' Amanda had continued rather wildly. Her skin was muddy, her teeth discoloured and translucent. No evidence of the healthy juicing, Stella had thought, looking at her in quiet shock. The private room in the Portland Hospital was filled with lavish bouquets, so fleshy and dense they appeared to be sucking up the oxygen Amanda needed, leaving her breathless and struggling.

She and Laura had stayed as long as they could bear to, chatting as best they could, mostly talking around the topic in front of them, too vast to touch. They talked about what Amanda would do when she left hospital – 'Go away for a few weeks, I suppose,' she had said listlessly.

'With the baby?' Laura asked. 'Or just you and Huw?'

'With the baby, of course. At least, I think so.' Amanda looked suddenly panicked. 'If I can. I mean, what do you think?'

'I'd say wait a bit, then all go somewhere nice together,' Stella had said soothingly.

They had even tried the old 'Black or White' game they had played together since St Assumpta's days.

'Nurse or doctor?' Laura had blurted out, into a longish pause.

'Doctor,' Stella answered automatically.

'Of course,' Laura had said, laughing. 'Okay, doctor or surgeon?'

'Hmm, doctor, I think,' said Stella.

'Smart move. Amanda, queen or princess?'

'Princess, definitely,' Amanda said. But it hadn't really taken off, had died out after a brief, rather forced flurry, and they were back to trying to find something to chat about that wasn't the one thing they all knew they needed to talk about.

Huw arrived, with a carrier bag from Harrods.

'Still with the charge account, I see,' Laura said.

'We should go,' Stella said. 'Leave you to it.' Leave them to what? she wondered. Huw looked tired and slightly sick, a yellowish tinge to his skin. The circles under his eyes were real, not the dash of debauched glamour he used to wear. He looked like a man who had started a game, only to find that now it wouldn't let him go.

'Stay for some lunch,' he said, rather desperately, Stella thought. 'I got *foie gras*. And crackers. That cheese you like, Amanda.' Amanda made a face. She didn't look as if she liked any kind of food very much. 'And fruit cake. Someone said it was good for new mothers.'

'Someone who was taking the piss out of you, I suspect,' said Stella, aware that he was struggling – with what she didn't know. Fatherhood? Husbandhood? Life? The impossibility of buying food for someone who didn't want to eat? – but not ready to see any side of him that she wasn't already familiar with hating. 'Congratulations, I guess,' she said instead, making no move to kiss him.

'Yes. I guess,' he agreed.

Amanda pressed them: 'Do stay! We've hardly talked about anything. I have so many questions for you both, about how everything is, how you are. Please?' Her voice cracked a little, more desperate than ever.

'Don't leave on my account,' Huw had said. 'I'll go to the café.' So they had stayed, but it hadn't done any good.

Amanda's refusal to allow them to do the one thing they could think of to help her – tell someone, a 'grown-up', as Stella still thought of them, someone who would be effective and determined, who would know what to do and how to do it – was absolute. Because the person who most clearly needed to be told was Mrs O'Hagen – even Stella had at last been able to see that – and Amanda made them swear not to.

'It'll only make things worse,' she had begged. 'I can do this by myself. I can, I promise. I'll go away somewhere and do it properly this time. I really will. Telling my mother will make everything worse, and then I won't be able to do it. Now that I've seen Dora, held her, I understand so much more. I have the reason I need.' It was, Stella knew, the old optimism, the old belief that new circumstances would deliver her a new self, so many times misplaced.

Instead, she found Huw before she left. He was drinking tea in the café on the ground floor, with a newspaper in front of him.

'Things had better be different now,' she had said, conscious of the nearness of her flight time, unwilling to enter in a protracted and subtle dance.

'They will,' he had responded. 'I'll make sure of it.'

And where Stella had been unable to trust Amanda's shaky optimism, she was forced to trust Huw's bald assertion.

☙

At first after Stella got back to New York, they had spoken often, difficult conversations in which Amanda had cried and promised, and Stella had soothed and encouraged. But after a few weeks Amanda had abruptly retreated from any willingness to admit to need, had seemed stronger, ready to be let loose in her own life and determined to draw down the veil of 'fine' across herself and her child. 'How's Dora doing?' Stella had asked one day.

'Very well,' Amanda had said, with a chilling lack of elaboration. In the silence that followed, Stella realised that she must no longer ask that question. That was what Amanda was like. She didn't admit, didn't ask for help. The clues she let fall were ambiguous, easy to misread or ignore for anyone minded to do so. The honesty of a simple appeal – help me – was alien to her. Which meant that, for Stella and Laura, their interventions were always short-lived: a swoop in, then out, let all believe that need had been served.

After the closing down of conversation about Dora, the energy it took to stay in touch, to remain close and connected when there was so much unsaid, was more than Stella had to spare, more than any of them had, she suspected, so they had allowed the ready excuse of distance to cloud their friendship.

'Can't chat now, just wanted to say that …'

'I'll talk to you properly later, just a quick call to see how you are …'

'No time, just tell me quickly. Everything okay?'

Even that had dwindled after a while to texts and emails: 'How u doing? Skype at wknd?' But the weekends came and went and somehow they never did Skype, or talk.

But Stella had believed those things were only temporary, to be resolved by one long and honest conversation, one laugh that went on long enough to reach the bits they'd put out of sight. Perhaps a weekend together in New York would do it. Or London. Or back in Dublin. Time together, where they could get past all the awkward barriers and dig up the things that held them together.

Instead she had this: Laura, bitter, furious, who wouldn't talk to her, planning on doing what they both knew was rotten. And Amanda, who had made everything so wrong, suddenly the only one who could make it right. Why, she wondered, had she come? What did she think could be salvaged from all this mess? Perhaps if she hadn't left Amanda on the night of the graduation party, she'd be able to leave her now. But she had, so she couldn't. She needed to find her and put everything back into some kind of shape they could all live with.

Chapter Twenty-Two

London

THE RESTAURANT MRS O'HAGEN HAD CHOSEN for lunch was almost entirely pale grey – carpet, walls, thick curtains, even the artwork: large canvases with shades of grey splashed with more vivid hues. Enormous Regency-style chandeliers hung from the high ceilings, and the pale grey menus had little silvery tassels. It wasn't what you would call trendy, Stella decided, but was clearly so expensive and discreet that it didn't matter. The maître d' glided across the carpet, murmured something at Laura, who sounded as if she was shouting in comparison when she replied, 'We're joining someone. Marie O'Hagen.' He inclined his head respectfully, then glided away, swift but supple as he negotiated tables.

Smart women were lunching in pairs or threes, sometimes interspersed by attractive couples who managed to look illicit even while in full view, and as if they were part of an ad for some exquisite piece of jewellery – an anniversary piece, Stella thought, not engagement. There were no young people, except the perfectly trained waiters, who were uniformly young, male and handsome. A steady hum of conversation on all sides, a soothing wall of sound, from which the odd word escaped every now and then, like a dolphin breaking the waves: 'Impossible ...' they caught, as they passed one table, 'Exactly ...' from another, and 'Sherry Francis says ...' escaped intriguingly from a third.

They followed their guide to a round corner table, perfectly placed in a shallow alcove with a view of the entire room, enough space around it that it was entirely private, but without being cut off. Sitting at it, martini in hand, back ramrod straight, was Mrs O'Hagen, wearing a beautiful grey suit with an orange Hermès scarf twisted carefully around her neck, the exact colour of a hibiscus flower. She's like one of the paintings, Stella thought, wondering if she had done it on purpose.

'Girls.' She stood up carefully, held out her hands and caught one each of theirs, as was her wont. Her fingers were thin, slightly bony, with huge flashing rings. The rest of her was thin too, much thinner than before, and her face more deeply lined. She had let her hair fade slightly, a few threads of grey woven artfully through the pale blonde. She looked elegant, efficient and steely, as always. A force to be reckoned with, never discounted, never underestimated. Stella leaned in to kiss her, without thinking, and felt Mrs O'Hagen draw back slightly. She had always avoided too much physical contact, and now Stella felt the woman's hard fingers pressing onto the back of her hand, pushing her down into her chair. 'Do sit,' she said. They sat. 'Drink?'

'Yes, please,' Stella said.

'Martini?'

'Please.' Was more alcohol a good idea after such a long flight and very little sleep? Stella decided she might need it.

'I'll have a sparkling water,' Laura said primly.

They talked about New York, the things Mrs O'Hagen had done on her last trip there, whether Stella knew any of the places she liked to frequent. Stella knew them, but had never set foot in most of them. They were Sean-type places, expensive and watchful. Places, she saw now, she had never dared go into in case he was there. In case Tory was there.

Then Mrs O'Hagen switched, asking Laura about her work, listening closely to her answers, nodding approvingly. It was obvious, from the level of detail, that Laura talked to her far more often than Stella had known. The conversation was a speedy resumption of something close to hand, rather than a resetting of the basics.

'Mick and I know John Mangan, who of course is on the board,' Mrs O'Hagen said thoughtfully, at one point. 'It might be an idea for you to meet him at our house. A Saturday lunch, perhaps. With some other people.'

'I'd like that,' Laura said coolly, when Stella thought she should have been sniggering at the vile worldliness of it.

'How's Dora?' she blurted out eventually, unable to take any more of the light dance of mutual approval that Mrs O'Hagen and Laura were conducting.

'She's fine. The nanny came over with her. She seems happy.'

'Does she ask for Amanda?'

'Not much. She's quite like Amanda, you know. Very self-contained. She doesn't need much.'

'Until she decides she needs so much that there simply isn't enough of anything to fill the need,' Stella blurted out.

Mrs O'Hagen considered her with an eyebrow faintly raised. 'Is that what you think this is? Some desperate, driving need of Amanda's that can't be filled?'

'Of course.' Stella was surprised. 'What else could it be?'

'This is just a mistake,' said Mrs O'Hagen, carefully. 'A mess that Amanda has got herself into and we must get her out of. It happens. People drink too much, pick up bad habits that get them into terrible trouble. It's unfortunate, unpleasant, nothing more than that.'

Neither Stella nor, she thought, even Laura knew what to say. The gap between the story they knew and the one Mrs O'Hagen had just told them was too vast. And the distance between the two friends was too great for a concerted approach.

'Even the best families have this sort of problem,' Mrs O'Hagen went on. Another pause. Their starters arrived – oysters, because Mrs O'Hagen had said that was what the restaurant was famous for.

'What do Huw's parents say?' Stella asked at last, squeezing lemon into the pearly shell, mainly because someone needed to say something, and there seemed no obvious place to start.

'Well, I spoke with Margot. She says they don't interfere with how the boys want to run their lives. That it's a matter for themselves. I asked if she had seen anything in the papers, and she said they didn't read them.'

'Too vulgar, probably, to actually know what's going on.' Stella was withering, but Mrs O'Hagen didn't rise to it.

'Perhaps, but she might be right, you know. This may all be

a lot of silly nonsense. You know very well what those gossip columns are like. They make most of the stuff up.'

'So why are we here?'

'Because neither Amanda nor Huw has been in touch for several weeks, not since they sent Dora over, and I want to know what's going on.'

'What do the police say?'

'Not much until now. But there have been signs of disturbance recently. The neighbours have complained, a known drug dealer has been seen going in and out, and no one has answered the door when they've called to investigate.'

'Jake,' said Stella. 'The dealer was probably Jake.'

'You know him?'

'We've met him.'

'Where?'

'At the wedding.'

'So, one of Huw's friends.' She said it as if that actually made things better, and Stella could see her rearranging the pieces again in her mind, reducing the space in which any admission need be made of how squalid and ugly the whole thing was. A friend of Huw's. A party that had got out of hand, perhaps, or at worst a temporary excess of self-indulgence on Amanda's part. Nothing that a new haircut, a holiday in Barbados, a word in the right ear couldn't put right.

Stella couldn't hold back any longer. 'You know that Amanda went into rehab after Dora was born? Because Dora was born addicted to heroin? That she spent the first days of her life being given morphine, so as to gradually withdraw her from it? You didn't come to the hospital, so you didn't see her.'

'Stella, you can't!' Laura gasped, but Stella ignored her, kept her eyes fixed on Mrs O'Hagen.

'Amanda didn't want me to. She said to wait until Dora was older and more fun, and see her then.' Mrs O'Hagen spoke only after a lengthy pause, and so quietly that Stella and Laura had to lean in to hear her. 'I knew she had gone away for a rest. Why do you think I've been paying for a nanny all this time? I knew Amanda wasn't coping very well, but people often don't with the first baby. It's a shock, especially to someone like Amanda. I understood that. But she didn't want help from me. She asked me not to come. I respected that.'

'Of course she didn't want you to come. One look at Dora and you would have known she wasn't right. And if you didn't, the social workers would have told you.'

'Social workers?' Mrs O'Hagen nearly vomited on the word.

'They didn't let her take Dora home for weeks. Amanda told me. Even after she came out of rehab, she had to attend clinics weekly, and allow them to visit unannounced at any time. And Huw had to make a huge parade of his family's venerability and their support, which in fact was non-existent. His parents came once and said how "rather sweet" the baby was, and didn't want to hold her because she cried so much, and then they left. That was one of the things that weakened Amanda's resolve to keep trying. She said it made her realise how little she could do to protect Dora from all the hurt and pain, and how she couldn't bear her own inability to shield her.' Stella stopped, drew breath, and found herself shaking.

Laura reached across to Mrs O'Hagen, took her hand and squeezed it. Mrs O'Hagen, Stella noticed, let her. Even squeezed back.

'That's enough of that,' Mrs O'Hagen said. 'My daughter is not some kind of filthy addict. That is not what this is.'

'You didn't see her,' Stella said.

'Stella, stop it,' said Laura shakily.

'Who? Dora? Amanda?' Mrs O'Hagen said, ignoring Laura.

'Both of them. It's the saddest thing I've ever seen. The baby cried and cried, a desolate little howl, with stiff limbs and a desperate need, which only the ugliest thing in the world could relieve. And they actually gave it to her, because there was nothing else they could do. Amanda cried too, with shame and guilt and horror, and I cried because I couldn't see any way to help them, except the thing that would destroy Amanda altogether: tell you, and have someone take the baby away. I thought she would have a chance if she kept her and had something to come out to after rehab. I believed Dora would be the reason she needed. I reckoned that if she had something else to live for it could show her a better way. Laura, you were there too. You also cried. How could you not? So we all cried, as if that would get the misery out of us and make an end to it. Except that wasn't the end obviously.'

'No, and neither is this,' Mrs O'Hagen said urgently, as if she needed to believe, needed the security of her own unflinching moral compass, the one that always pointed forwards and onwards. 'This will not be the end.'

After a pause, Mrs O'Hagen continued, 'My upbringing wasn't a particularly good one.' She waved away Laura's knee-jerk protest. 'I don't mean that horrible estate I grew up on. I mean the way my mother was with me. How little she told or taught me. How little she involved herself in my life. We grew up like weeds, like cabbages, without care. I never wanted that for my daughter. But maybe I've made as many mistakes, just different ones. I never expected all *this*.' She waved her arm, including in its sweep the restaurant, their table, the remains of their excellent lunch, her handbag, the chic jacket that hung on the back of her chair. It was a silent, eloquent summing up. 'But even without it, I would have been fine. I've always had spirit for the fight. Amanda lacks that. And perhaps that is my fault. Maybe giving too much is as bad as giving not enough.' They all sat silent, contemplating the truth of this.

'So what is wrong with Amanda?' Laura asked slowly, and Stella marvelled at how far they had come that such a question was now possible.

'I'm not sure,' Mrs O'Hagen responded. 'Something, I suppose.' It was a tremendous admission. 'Everyone said how good she was when she was a child, but I suppose I found her to be not so much good as unresisting. When something went against her, she could be as stubborn and cross as anyone, but mostly she let things happen around and to her without much protest.'

'And she's always been like that since we've known her,' Laura said.

'Except when she thinks you want something from her. That has a very bad effect on her,' Stella added.

'That's true,' Laura conceded.

Stella wondered if Laura was taking mental notes. Would this dissection of Amanda's character appear somewhere in the article, served up for readers to speculate over? The thought made her feel ill. 'But why is she like that?' she asked. 'Why does she want to disappear out of her own life? Because that's what it feels like with her. As if she's retreating into the background of her life, and the more you try to pull her out, the more she retreats. Sometimes you can coax her by seeming not to care whether she comes or not, but as soon as she sees you do care, she slides away again.'

'It is, of course, part of her allure,' Mrs O'Hagen said. 'I noticed that quite quickly. Not always with children her own age, that could be difficult, but with older children and adults. That way Amanda has of keeping herself aloof has always been a big part of her appeal.'

'It sounds like it's a big part of her problems too,' Stella said bluntly. 'Didn't you ever wonder why she was so evasive?'

'There was a teacher when Amanda was about ten,' Mrs O'Hagen began slowly. 'She once asked me if I had any "concerns" about Amanda's emotional development. She wanted me to refer her for what she called an assessment. I refused, of course.'

'Why?' asked Stella, after an appalled silence.

'I don't believe in all that stuff,' Mrs O'Hagen said firmly. 'I don't believe in giving labels to people and allowing them to think they can shirk responsibility because of something that a psychologist says they are. And I certainly didn't want anyone to look at Amanda and think there was something wrong with her. I did it to protect her, to protect the future I knew she could have. And because I presumed she would grow out of whatever it was that teacher saw in her.'

Stella recalled that she had always felt Amanda was locked in behind something, that life came to her at a distance, then thought about the ways in which some clever person might have helped her, when she was still a child, to overcome that distance. She started to cry. To her astonishment it was Mrs O'Hagen, not Laura, who reached a hand across and gripped hers, hard.

'Perhaps I was wrong,' she said. 'But I did it for the best. Now, I suggest that we go and find Amanda, and get her into some kind of centre or hospital. There's still time for a second chance, a way to do it right. For Amanda and Dora.'

Chapter Twenty-Three

London

INSPECTOR DAVIES WAS WAITING, THE TWO stripes on his epaulettes proclaiming a solid confidence in all matters that fell within his judgement. With him were two constables, standing discreetly back. The October air was chill and thin, with a gleeful jeer to the wind that spoke of winter. Late-afternoon sun lay across the bottom steps and iron railings, and the black door looked carefully bland. Beside it, two evergreen box hedges, of the type rich people always had outside their front doors, Stella thought, were starting to brown around the edges.

Mrs O'Hagen knocked and rang a couple of times. They could hear the bell pealing into thick silence. The people who passed on the street seemed to do so hurriedly, half-turned away. No steps, no shift in atmosphere behind that door to suggest the presence of anything other than furniture and dust.

After a decent interval, Inspector Davies said, 'I think we can proceed from here, madam.' He took out a key that looked like a microchip, opened the door and, when it caught on the chain bolted from the inside, beckoned the two policemen forward. Together they put their shoulders to the door and, on the third go, knocked it smartly open.

The hall was cold and dark, and their feet echoed on the polished black-and-white marble as they crossed it. No sound came from anywhere, except the noise of traffic and London life through the open front door, which Inspector Davies now firmly closed.

'We'll check these rooms, madam, if you would like to stay here,' he said. So the three of them stood in a tense knot in the centre of the hall, underneath the grand staircase curving into the upper reaches above their heads, while the three men opened doors around them, disappearing then emerging. There was no one, as Stella knew there would not be. She could feel the emptiness clearly. Past a policeman's shoulder, she saw into one of the front rooms: dust covers draped across the bigger items of furniture. Perhaps they actually had gone away. Taken off to Thailand without telling anyone.

When the police were satisfied, they suggested going upstairs. On the first floor were the reception rooms where the engagement party had been held, so long ago now. They, too, were quiet and fallow, subdued, even, except that the small Turner wasn't in its usual spot over the fireplace. Instead, there was a pastoral scene in oil in a heavy gilt frame. Was that a sign? Stella wondered.

'The painting's gone,' she whispered to Laura. 'The Turner she liked so much.'

'Maybe Huw's parents took it back. They could hardly have intended to give it to Huw and Amanda. Too valuable.'

'Maybe. Amanda loved that painting, though.'

Once the police had given the all-clear for that floor, they moved upstairs again, the police with measured tread, Stella, Laura and Mrs O'Hagen keeping pace.

On the floor above, the bedrooms were equally silent and echoing, with no signs of habitation in any of them. The beds were made up, duvets lying creaseless across high, firm mattresses. One room, clearly Dora's, had a brown rocking horse with flowing mane and tail, and a beautiful doll's house that seemed no more painted and empty than the one they stood in. In another room there was a dressing table with two silver-backed brushes, clearly for show as much as the antique perfume bottle beside them. Nowhere was there a newspaper, a toothbrush, a paperback left open, anything at all to suggest occupancy.

They carried on upwards. Mrs O'Hagen was breathing heavily by now, although with anticipation or exertion Stella couldn't be sure. Laura, just behind her, was humming nervously, taking it all in. Rounding a curve in the staircase, Stella became conscious of a sickly smell, like the time she and her parents had gone away and there had been a power cut: everything in the freezer had spoiled. She could tell the police had smelt it too, because they both speeded up and slowed down: they moved faster, but they became more deliberate and purposeful.

Reaching the upper landing was like crossing London, she thought. Moving from plush Knightsbridge to some squat in

Kilburn. The wooden floor was bare and scuffed. Clearly a long rug had covered the centre of it at one time, because there was a faint mark to show where it had lain, but it was now bare, except for scrape-marks and balls of dust lying in corners, like the nests of mice. The doors along the corridor were open, but little light was coming through them. Peering into the first room, Stella saw a mattress stuffed into the window frame, blocking it almost entirely. The smell was much worse now, and her heart beat faster. Her breath shortened, as the full force of where she was, what she was there to do, hit her. After the last days of thinking about Amanda, recalling the run of their story from the beginning, she realised now how much she wanted to see her, to see her being okay. She wanted to hug her, mind her, say that she didn't understand how in the last years they had drifted so far apart, that she still loved her and that everything would be all right. But what everything? she thought. There must, by now, be much in Amanda's life that couldn't be okay. Well, they would just have to make it better, like they had always tried to do.

She and Laura kept pace with each other, but Stella didn't know whether she was looking with Laura or watching her look. In every room clothes and blankets lay in heaps; furniture appeared to have been kicked around. Could the police have been here already? Or drug dealers to whom Huw and Amanda owed money? The place might have been torn through by some reckless, hungry thing searching wildly, turning over everything in its path, or perhaps it had been abandoned in a hurry. The progress seemed chaotic, the debris left behind worryingly flimsy. Everything seemed used up, discarded, although she could see that, technically, the furniture was as good up there as that in the rest of the house.

Nausea at the smell was growing. At the smell and the surroundings. Although the police conferred in low voices, Stella, Laura and Mrs O'Hagen were silent, stunned by the possibility that Amanda was living in this. Where was she hiding? Stella imagined her in rags, crouched behind one of the violent heaps of viciously discarded household items, afraid to come out. She wanted to call to her, reassure her, shout loudly to dispel the thick webs of silence that lay across everything, but she didn't dare. She was afraid of what else she might wake in the place.

None of what she saw made sense to her. Huw was a creep and a blackguard — her own private word for him — but surely this wasn't his place either. What were any of them doing there? She, Laura, Mrs O'Hagen, turning over the foul debris of someone else's catastrophe. How had it happened? All the silly, reckless, vulgar things they had done as children — the posturing and drinking, the drugs, cheating, flirting and teasing, the endless parties. How could those things, those foolish games, have led to this?

Stella kept walking, because she felt that if they could only check every room, establish that all were empty, they could get out of there, find a company with mops and send them in to repair the mess before Amanda and Huw came home to it.

'Someone must have broken in,' she whispered to Laura. 'They might still be living here. Lucky the police are with us.'

Laura nodded, but didn't say anything.

They were the first into the room at the very end of the corridor, the largest room, and the most savagely abandoned. It was lighter than the others — instead of a mattress, the windows had blankets over them, held up with masking tape, through which the last rays of sun were gently diffused. What they saw reminded Stella of the images of bombed refugee camps she sometimes caught on the news, places where the business of living had been ousted by something more basic.

The sofa was torn apart, frame exposed, stuffing ripped into as though a giant dog had worried it in a frenzy. The huge, gilt-framed mirror above the translucent pinkish marble of the fireplace had been crudely painted over in thick black, by hand it seemed. Was that to spare someone seeing their own reflection, or prevent spies looking in? she wondered, seeing anger and fear in the thick sweep of the brush strokes. Books, DVDs, magazines, ashtrays, shoes and clothes lay in a jumble. Stella spotted a pair of Christian Louboutins, their distinctive red soles standing out, like a gash, in the mud-coloured heap. There were dirty syringes, empty biro holders and burnt beer cans mixed with old foil takeaway trays. The floorboards were scuffed and worn, the rugs kicked around into wrinkled heaps.

Bowls of cat food lay everywhere, rotten and covered with flies. This was the source of the smell, Stella thought, looking around for a cat, for any sign of life. Maybe not the only source, she decided, seeing a syringe full of something brown at her feet. Specks of dust danced in the soft light drifting in through the blankets, showing Stella clearly that this wasn't something haphazard, the product of burglary. This was by design. She put her sleeve over her nose, wanting to open a window but afraid the police wouldn't like it.

Nearby, Laura scribbled something on a scrap of paper, then stuffed it into her coat pocket.

'Don't do that,' Stella said sharply. 'Don't take notes.'

Laura didn't answer her. She turned away and kicked softly at a heap of stinking things, clothes and blankets, knotted together by the fury with which someone had at one time searched through them. Stella thought she could almost hear echoes of that search, vibrations from a disrupted past still blundering against the streaked walls.

It was impossible to associate this room with Amanda, her swinging curtain of golden hair, her strong, lean arm as she threw a tennis ball into the air, and her bright, ready wit. Yet it was consistent with the disgusting sore on Amanda's arm, seen once but never forgotten. With the birth of Dora and the misery of that hospital visit. This, Stella thought, looking around, was what it all actually meant. This was where all the stuff about living on the edge and the beauty of the dark side ended up. The silly fantasies of teenage girls flirting with an idea of excitement and danger culled from books. She took her sleeve away from her nose, the better to breathe in a reality so putrid, she knew she would never forget or misinterpret it again.

Now she understood Huw's face at Amanda's hospital bed a little better.

She glanced over at Mrs O'Hagen and could see that she, too, had found her nose pressed up against the kind of realisation she couldn't avoid. No talk of 'mistakes' or 'bad habits' now. She, too, was silenced by the necessity of imagining Amanda in this scene, sprawled on the savagely ripped-up sofa, or casting through the evil debris on the floor to find . . . what? A syringe? A screwed-up piece of tinfoil?

Mrs O'Hagen, who always had 'people' everywhere, people who could get her the best table, an early look at a collection, an Hermès bag when there was a waiting list, access to information and influence, people who knew things, owned things, found things all in her service, didn't, for once, suggest that any of them be deployed here. Not to clean or cover up. Not even for the comfort of deploying them.

'She's not happy unless she has plates spinning all around her,' Amanda used to say of her mother. No plates were spinning now. Instead they lay, smashed, at her feet.

Inspector Davies joined them and had his own slow and steady look around the room. Then he said, 'There is no one on the premises and no reason to remain here. We will be returning to the station.' No one said anything in response, just followed him back out to the corridor.

It was only then that they saw the cat. A large marmalade with thick glossy fur and stately demeanour, it jumped from a shadowy window ledge with a heavy thump and stalked slowly across the hall towards the stairs, tail twitching. A dog, Stella thought inconsequentially, would have cared.

And then she wanted to vomit. There was nowhere to go, no sink or toilet that she could recall seeing, so she vomited into the closest corner. Laura and Mrs O'Hagen stood and watched her silently, made no move to help.

By the time they reached the street and the mercifully fresh, sharp air, evening proper had fallen. Stella's clothes smelt of vomit and she felt her hair carried the sickly stench of the upper floor. Perhaps her skin did too, she thought, feeling a fresh wave of nausea rise within. Her legs shook and her mind would gather only the most immediate pieces of information. The cold of the evening, the fact that it was now almost dark. Laura beside her, teeth chattering.

Mrs O'Hagen was fumbling with her bag at the side of the street, one foot nearly off the kerb. She looked at them, older by years than they had ever seen her, all the lines of fatigue, worry and disappointment etched clearly into her face. She seemed to teeter on the brink of something, then her eyes snapped shut, the light in them fading quickly. 'I need a taxi,' she said.

Stella watched her in a daze, but Laura ran forward. 'Let me call you one. I'll take you back to your hotel.' Then, to Stella, 'I'll see you later, back at the guesthouse?' It was very much a question. It hadn't occurred to either of them that they wouldn't find Amanda, would have to spend the evening there, alone together.

'I don't think so,' said Stella slowly. 'I think I might stay somewhere else. I'll come and get my things tomorrow.' She knew she couldn't bear an evening spent listening to the tap-tap of Laura's laptop, as she spelled out the whole sorry story, laid it bare for the world to read in their morning paper, to be sent online around the world over and over, so that anyone who had ever known Amanda, seen her in a film or an ad campaign, heard her name or uttered it with envy, would know what she had become. 'Please don't do it, Laura,' she said again.

'I have to.' Laura's face was shut tight, and she half-turned away to hail a taxi.

'What about her?' Stella gestured towards Mrs O'Hagen. 'What on earth do you think she'll make of it?'

'Oh, I think she'll understand.'

And Stella had a horrible feeling she might be right. 'Okay,' she said. 'Well, I'll see you later.'

'Here, let me help you,' she heard Laura saying to Mrs O'Hagen, as she ushered her into the taxi. 'I think a cup of tea. Maybe a brandy …'

What is she? Daughter-in-waiting? Stella thought angrily, revolted by Laura's parade of virtuous concern.

As Mrs O'Hagen and Laura drove off, Stella looked up at the

house again, pressing her fingers into the still-painful pin mark on her arm. She thought she could see the glowing orange eyes of the cat staring out at her from an upper window. She wondered if Amanda was there after all, hidden in some secret corner they hadn't discovered. Had she been watching them the entire time?

Chapter Twenty-Four

London

SHE HAD NOWHERE TO GO. SHE HAD KNOWN that before she'd told Laura that she wouldn't come back to the guesthouse. She didn't really know anyone in London and didn't know what part of London she was in. She knew the firm had an apartment somewhere, possibly somewhere close, but she also knew she wouldn't ask for it. So she walked, through the cold streets, hands deep in her pockets, following a system of traffic-light colours – first a red light, then a green, then an amber, then a red and so on – until she had no idea where she was, knew she could be just a couple of streets away from the Knightsbridge house or halfway across the city. The people who passed her did so in a rush. It wasn't an evening for lingering. Everyone, she thought, had a plan, even if it was to do no more than getting home. She pictured them all, in cosy houses or flats, beside warm fires, telling the news of their day to someone who cared to listen.

Gradually, though, she became aware that under the veil of the rushing and purpose, there was another layer, of people like her, without aim or direction, who walked slower or didn't walk at all. Whose commitment was only to the next five minutes and the next cup of tea. They were the sedimentary layer of the streets, where the things that drifted or hurtled were trapped and came to rest. Was this where Amanda was? A skinny hand holding a ragged cup?

She thought again about what Mrs O'Hagen had said at lunch. Would knowing what was 'wrong' really have made a difference to Amanda? Stella couldn't imagine her any other way. What would a more focused, determined sort of Amanda have been like? Not as lovable as the Amanda she actually knew, she decided. And anyway, she thought, Laura was mistaken. This wasn't about what was 'wrong' with Amanda, it was about what had gone wrong among the three of them.

She tried to think more about Amanda then, but mostly she thought about herself. She seemed to have lost everything, and in such a short time. Sean, Laura, Amanda. Perhaps her job – certainly her enjoyment of it. She had lost her belief in the invisible structure, the network of silken threads that had held her up. They had been removed, one by one, leaving her unsupported. She had even abandoned herself, she thought. Her famous certainty and sense of right had abruptly deserted her.

'What's the quickest way between two points?' Amanda used to joke.

'Stella!' was always the answer.

'Stella-for-certainty', Laura had called her, ever since they were about eleven. Now, she couldn't even decide between green tea and a cappuccino, as she stood in line at Pret A Manger, hands red and raw with cold, hair a frizzy halo around her head, sprung by steady drizzle from the neat bob she schooled it into back to the childish mop of curls. She had walked for nearly an hour, she saw, checking her watch. Sean's watch. She fought the urge to remove it and throw it into a bin because she disapproved of such reckless gestures. 'Pantomime rage,' she called them, always insisting that anger was a useful emotion, something to be turned to a good end – revenge, creative achievement, self-improvement – not squandered on show-off play-acting.

'Harness it,' she would say to Laura, only half-joking, when she fumed about being humiliated by a teacher, ignored by Mrs O'Hagen, overlooked by all, except those who knew her well and loved her. 'Use it. Show them what you're capable of and make them sorry they shrugged you off. Use the anger as rocket fuel, to take you somewhere you want to go.' Laura had usually looked sullen and mutinous at the idea.

What a slow burn, Stella thought then. That Laura should have squashed down so much, for so long, only now allowing the rage that was clearly within her to blunder to the surface. What, she wondered, must the last year have been like for her, for this to happen? She had always believed that Laura would process the hurt and anger she refused to express in writing, creating. Well, in a way she had, she thought, imagining Laura even now slowly gathering the story, using all her skill to tell it well. She could see the Amanda who would emerge from that tale, and the cartoonish resemblance she would bear to the real Amanda, their Amanda, who was subtle and fluid enough to have been all the things Stella knew of her, but who seemed to have lost her ability to slip from one role to another and become trapped in the least lovely of these.

Stella sat outside, on a wet bench, unable to cope with the damp bustle inside, sipping her tea – a sudden nausea had turned her off cappuccino – indifferent to the continuing drizzle.

She didn't have much money on her, and wondered, with momentary panic, how to get more. Would her cards work here? And why didn't she know? The high-intensity cocoon of her working life had left her unused to the practicalities of daily existence. All that dry-cleaning being collected and lunch delivered to her office, and now she didn't know how to get herself out of the mess she was in.

She fought another urge, stronger than the desire to hurl away Sean's watch, to ring her PA and set in train the efficient mechanisms of Davies Darn and Slate. She knew perfectly well that, if she did so, within the hour she would be booked into a smart hotel or the company's flat, probably with a wad of cash to keep her going and clear instructions on how to leave London, the time of her plane, the name of the driver sent to collect her.

Or would she? With a sudden jolt of paranoia, she wondered if Sean – worse still, Barrington Fraser – would give a silent headshake of refusal to the suggestion of rescue. Perhaps she was no longer one of the employees to be looked after. Not everyone was. You had to earn it. She had earned it, but did that carry over? Maybe not.

She could ring her parents. Hadn't they said, 'There is nothing you can't tell us', 'Whatever happens in your life, at any time, we are there to care for you'? A kind of mantra of devotion, part of the chant of their domestic existence, ever since she was old enough to leave the house by herself. And, of course, she knew that she could, but knew, too, the fatal flaw in the mantra: when there was anything she really needed help with, she was too proud to ask.

'Why do they always say that?' she had asked, one evening, after she, Amanda and Laura had left her house to go into town. They had been, she reckoned now, about sixteen at the time.

'Because they mean it,' Amanda had said, swinging her bag in the air with the sheer excitement that struck them all on such nights, when they left the cosy certainties of home for an evening out.

'Yes, but why must they always say it? Once is enough. Nessa never says it, and neither does your mother,' she had pointed out.

'That's because Nessa doesn't want me to think like that. She wants me to sort out my own problems. Be resourceful. She doesn't say it because she knows I'm only too likely to call her,' said Laura.

'And my mother doesn't say it because she knows damn well I won't,' Amanda said. 'No matter what happens. You're lucky.'

'I guess,' Stella had said. 'Except that it's kind of a paradox. Anything bad enough for me to need to tell them is going to be far too bad to actually tell them, and anything that isn't too bad, I can sort out for myself anyway. So it's nice. But useless.'

'Oh, well, better nice and useless than just useless,' Amanda had said, finally swinging her bag so high that a shower of make-up, wallet, coins and phone had scattered in a high arc down to the pavement.

Now cars whooshed by, their soft lights bleeding into the fuzzy wet air, leaving bright streaks behind them. Stella thought she could sit there the entire night, go and collect her things in the morning and simply leave, almost as if she had never been there. But she had come to find Amanda, and if she could achieve that, she believed that something of their joint past could be salvaged. Enough, anyway, to take them forward a turn or two. She was hungry, cold, tired. Lonely. So she rang the one number she had, the one person she could call.

'James?' When he answered, Stella started to cry, the warmth of his voice acting like sunlight on ice.

'Stella? Stella, what is it?'

She cried so hard she couldn't get any more words out, only managed to choke out the necessary information when he nearly shouted her name, panic in his voice. 'It's okay,' she sobbed. 'It's okay. I'm somewhere in London. I came to see Amanda with Laura but we can't find her and now I don't have anywhere to stay. Please tell me you're here. Please say you're not in Ireland.'

'I'm here, Stella. I'm in London. Where are you? I'll come and get you.' She described where she was sitting – 'There's a tube sign, for Green Park, and a Pret A Manger behind me and a big park on my left.' Then she sat some more, her tears making her feel colder than ever, so that by the time James arrived, jumped out of a taxi and ran to her, she was shivering so much that it seemed entirely natural to stand and step into his arms, into the heat of his embrace, and stay there.

'Let's go,' he said at last, into her hair, because his arms were still tight around her. 'We'll go to my flat and we'll work out what to do there.'

In the taxi she tried to pull away, sit in her own corner and put distance between them, but he wouldn't let her, kept his arm tight around her.

'The hunt is properly on,' he said. 'My mother rang me.

Half of London seems to be looking for Amanda now, and Huw, including the police. They don't like what they saw in the house.'

'No one could like it,' Stella said, sitting up but staying close. 'James, you can't imagine. It was so disgusting.' She tried to tell him, aware that her words were like stepping stones across a swamp, conveying only isolated glimpses of a horror that could have overcome them all. How to convey the smell? How to express the story that sickly odour told? The glimpses it gave of the life Amanda had been leading?

Describing it to him was like putting together a thousand-piece jigsaw, each piece a new kind of squalor. As she talked, she remembered more than had sunk in at the time, such as the many fine strands of blonde hair that had lain on surfaces, dusty and dry, too many not to be remarkable, like a nest torn asunder and the poor little scraps scattered.

'When's the last time you saw her?' she asked at last, wondering how much James already knew.

'Shortly after the baby was born. I called round to see them with a present for Dora, and some books that Iseult wanted me to give Amanda. They didn't look very happy then. The baby cried and neither of them knew what to do with her, so they gave her back to the nanny. Huw looked anxious and rather worn, I thought, although he was easier with Dora than Amanda was. She seemed defensive, as if she thought I would accuse her – say she should have been doing better.'

James's flat was on the second floor of a red-brick house with deep bay windows and a row of dustbins in the small paved front garden. 'It's London,' he said, with a smile, when he saw Stella staring at the bins, and the tufted weeds that grew along the inner garden wall. 'We can't all live in Knightsbridge.'

Inside, though, the flat was nice, with dark wooden floors, uneven but highly polished, and a few faded rugs, of the type Drumcranig must have millions of, Stella thought. Persian or Afghan, in glorious colours, but worn and frayed at the edges. There was a bedroom and study besides the living room, and everywhere there was evidence of James's life, the existence he had, by himself, away from all of them. His books and papers, clothes, the pictures on the wall that he had chosen, the sofa angled towards the television as he liked it, so that Stella wanted to hug armfuls of the jumpers she saw half-spilling out of a wardrobe in the study, or curl up in his bed with his covers pulled tight around her. Just by looking, she knew he had managed it, made the break he needed and got quite away.

'You're happy here, aren't you?' she asked.

He looked surprised, but said, 'Yes. Very, actually. I wasn't at first. I felt as if I had left too suddenly, but I needed to go. You know how Dublin can be. A small city, too few people playing too many roles in your life. It's stifling. But I'm sorry I didn't help more,' he said seriously. 'I can see now that I could have, and that you all needed it more than I knew. I thought getting out of Amanda's way was the best thing I could do, but I see that it wasn't. So what about you? Happy?'

'Not very. Actually.' She tried to smile, but it came out wrong, so she muttered, 'Tell you later,' wondering which bits, if any, she would tell, and ducked her head, pretending she was studying the titles of the books on his shelves.

They talked about Amanda then: of all the things they could have done, interventions they could have tried, desperate courses of action they could have taken. 'After the first overdose,' they agreed, had been the moment. But what exactly they could have done, how they could have played their intervention, they still didn't know.

Until at last Stella said, 'We couldn't have, you know. And we did try, in our way. We were too young, and the adults were too strong and they didn't help us. They let Amanda go because they wanted her to be something for them. So they didn't see what was actually happening, only what they believed *could* happen.' That, finally, was what she blamed Mrs O'Hagen for. For being stronger than them all, more ruthless. For not listening or seeing. She wasn't the monster Amanda had painted her — her kindness to Nessa, to Laura, to Amanda herself in a funny way, proved that — but maybe she was a different kind of monster: selfish, with small ambitions that demanded large sacrifices of those around her.

James made them spaghetti with tomato sauce and opened a bottle of wine, which Stella drank, too fast at first, slowing down as warmth returned, and with it a sense that, after all, things might be all right. It felt studenty and fun to be sitting there with James, on the sofa, arms touching at times, part of nothing more than the jostle for space to wield a fork, but easy, comforting, all the same. They joked, teased each other, making up for the seriousness of the Amanda conversation with good-natured silliness that, to Stella, was precious.

'So how's New York?' he asked. 'Everything you dreamed of?'

'Sort of,' she said slowly, finding her way through it as she spoke. 'The lifestyle is like I imagined it — furious, lots of take-out and taxis, runs around Central Park, flea markets in Brooklyn at the weekends, cupcakes. You know the sort of thing. I mean, Manhattan really is exactly like they show it in films. But working life is different.'

'How so?'

'Well, I don't do anything useful or important. I just process documents all day, often all night, reading about the dirty tricks big companies try to play on one another, the ways they find to renege on deals made, and I give recommendations and I'm never even really sure what happens in the end. The senior partners are always pleased and say I've done great, but the stuff all drags on for years, so even if I find a way out, a loophole for our clients, nothing ever seems to happen. The litigation just enters a different phase.'

'Sounds dreadful.'

'It is dreadful, really. And you know what? I'm not going to do it any more.' As she said it, she knew, with rising excitement, that it was true. Of course she wasn't. You couldn't see things clearly without taking action. That was what the pin in her arm had done: punctured the absurdity of it, the way she had let it inflate her from the inside. 'I'm done. My time there is up.'

'So what will you do?'

'I'll do things I always said I would. Cases with actual people in them, people who have been wronged by their employers or by the government, and who can't speak for themselves because they don't know all the tricky ways the law uses to keep them out. But I know the ways, and I'll cut through them and out into the air where the shitty things that powerful people have done can't be hidden or disguised. In fact, I'll do the exact opposite of what I'm doing now.'

'You could do all that here, in London,' he said, gazing thoughtfully at her.

'I could,' she said slowly, staring straight back. There was a silence, a look between them that dragged out, long and viscous.

'I'd like that,' James said at last, with a smile.

Her phone rang. Laura. 'I'd better take it,' she said, wishing Laura had chosen a better moment for the apology she must be about to offer.

'Stella, can you talk? I need to check a few things with you.' And, with an audacity Stella would never have credited, she proceeded to do just that. Despite herself, her shock at the enormity of what Laura was doing, the code she was breaking, Stella found herself admiring the cool precision of Laura's questions – When had Amanda started doing drugs, did she think? Was it the year they'd left school? Might it have been a thing among models, or was it her college friends? How was it possible that she had hidden it for so long? That, Stella saw, was the crux of it: how had Amanda for so long played such a double game? And there Mrs O'Hagen held the answer. Amanda's habit of obedience to her mother meant that she shirked the grosser reality of what she was doing for the longest time. She had her facials, her full body massages, her hair appointments. She got up and went to shoots, castings, launches and parties, because Mrs O'Hagen expected her to. Until Huw had taken over as the driving force behind her, the cracks hadn't shown. Amanda hadn't looked or behaved like a junkie, because her mother simply wouldn't have allowed it. Only when she'd put her hand into Huw's on her wedding day, and walked away from her mother's control, had she started to slip under.

Amanda Edsberg. It certainly did have a ring to it. A very hollow ring.

So did that make Mrs O'Hagen the cause or the correction? They would never know.

'I have to go, Laura. But before you do this, you need to think about one thing. You said that Amanda owed you because we were always there, picking her up and breaking her fall. Well, we weren't, and I think that has a lot to do with it. The night of the party, in Trap, when we left her. That was wrong. You know it was.'

'You left her, Stella,' said Laura, furious. 'You insisted, not me.'

'Well, if you knew it was wrong, you should have stuck up for yourself and not been so wet!' Stella snapped, horribly aware that Laura was right. She hung up, conscious that James was watching her.

She explained Laura to him as much as she could, hampered still by loyalty and an unwillingness to put into words what Laura was doing. So she didn't say 'betrayal' or 'abandonment', even though they were the words that screamed in her head. She used lawyerly phrases instead, careful, allowing of ambiguity. Laura, she said, was 'exploring the possibility of writing a story about Amanda'.

'And what about the night at Trap, when you said you left her?'

'It was the night of the graduation party.' Stella blushed a little, remembering the earlier part of that night, James's mouth hot on hers, the misery when he pulled away. 'Amanda was wasted, remember? She didn't want to come with us and we should have made her but we didn't. I didn't. I was annoyed with her,' she avoided looking at him, 'so I didn't. Normally I would have.'

'But why was that so bad?' James looked honestly confused.

'I don't know. I don't even know if it *was* bad, but it always felt like it was, as if I betrayed her, and I never dared ask her what happened, if anything happened. And the next day she got engaged to Huw, and then everything just moved faster and faster, and further and further out, and then this.'

'You once gave out to me because you said that all we talked about was Amanda,' James said then.

'I did,' Stella agreed, remembering that night, all the nights, so well.

'Well, just so you know, I'd much rather carry on talking about you,' James said. 'About us?'

Stella smiled at him. By now she was warm, so fuzzy with wine and giddy with possibility that she had almost forgotten why she had come. 'We can talk about us,' she said, 'if you like. Although I don't really know where to begin.'

And she didn't. How far back do you go? she wondered. *I've loved you since the first time I saw you*, perhaps. Even when you knew the other person couldn't say *me too*! Couldn't lie, no matter how much they might want to. And then she knew it didn't matter. Now mattered, that moment. The future mattered. The past? It would have to find some kind of arrangement with itself.

His phone rang. 'My mother,' he said, checking the screen. 'Might be news.'

It was news.

'Huw's turned up,' he said. 'He arrived at his parents' house about an hour ago. Margot just rang Iseult.'

'With Amanda?'

'No. Apparently he left her, about two weeks ago. Walked out. Said he couldn't take it any longer.'

'Left her? Just like that? Without telling any of us? Without making sure there was someone to be there for her?' Stella's voice was rising to a shriek. 'What kind of an arsehole is he? And where has he been all this time?'

'Iseult said Margot wasn't too sure, but said he looked "very tired and thin", so presumably on a binge of his own.'

'Jesus, James, we have to find her now! If Huw's gone, God knows what she'll do. Or has done already,' she added, after a faint pause, during which her mind leaped to provide terrifying images. She saw Amanda wandering, disoriented, alone through the streets Stella had so recently come in from. Abandoned by Huw, heartbroken and with Dora already safely at her mother's, there was nothing Amanda might not do. 'Did he have any idea where she might be?'

'Apparently he seemed surprised that she wasn't still in the house in Knightsbridge, but said there was a chance she might be at Jake's.'

'Jake's?'

'Yes, you know, that guy from the wedding.'

'Why on earth would Amanda go to him?'

'Maybe she didn't have anybody else.'

They both stayed silent a moment, contemplating the hollow sound of that possibility.

'And she didn't ring you. Or me. Not any of us,' Stella said, in a small voice. 'James, I don't like this.'

'No,' James agreed. Then, 'Let's go to Jake's. He lives in Neasden, Iseult said. Even if she's not there, he might know something.'

Chapter Twenty-Five

London

YOU SHOULD HAVE STUCK UP FOR YOURSELF AND
not been so wet ...

Stella's words rang hard in her ears, accusing in the silence of her room. Was Stella right? Laura wondered. Probably, but not necessarily about that particular night. There had been many times when she had tried, but feebly, to make someone do something about Amanda, had tried to persuade Stella to do something, but she had never persevered, never succeeded. That night, though, was that a failure of hers? She thought back, trying for as much detail as she could recall after all the years, but all she could really remember was Stella, how rattled she had been. She remembered the look on her face as she had said, 'She'll be fine. You heard her, she wants to stay', and how she had seemed as if she might vomit, had actually vomited later, although that wasn't surprising, given all they had done and taken.

Of Amanda, she had a far hazier recollection. How had she seemed? Wasted. And beyond wasted? Fine, the same as ever.

Deciding that Stella was just looking for accusations to throw, she put the night out of her mind, because whatever Stella said about needing to set the past right, for Laura it was the now that mattered, the future, what happened to them all when the weekend was over and London left behind. She deliberately hadn't asked where Stella was or what she was doing. She couldn't. She knew that if she gave in to the need to know that Stella was okay, had found somewhere to stay, someone to be with, she wouldn't be able to continue her course. Nothing about what she was doing fitted with the Laura who had been best friends with Stella, and so, because she couldn't see a way to reconcile the two, she had to turn away from one to do any kind of justice to the other.

The piece was nearly finished, and it was the best thing she'd written, she knew that. Not just because of the access, the wealth of detail she had. She had kept faith with herself in the telling of it. With all of them. Hadn't squandered the opportunity on anything obvious. The story was gripping, subtle, careful. She could see it in *Paris Match*, even *Vanity Fair*. This was the piece that would make her. Already she was thinking of follow-ups: the story of where Amanda had been, once they actually found her, the what-next of her life, a whole separate piece on Mr and Mrs O'Hagen. That drew her up short. Even bent double by such a blow, Mrs O'Hagen was still a force, not to be confronted without care.

She had accompanied her back to her hotel, sat with her while tea was ordered, suggesting a bowl of soup to go with it, then recommended a bath, all while Mrs O'Hagen had said very little, just sat, twisting the large, glittering rings on her fingers.

Finally, with visible effort, Mrs O'Hagen said, 'I must ring Mick. Make some calls.' She'd sounded vague, distant, but Laura could see she was trying hard to shrug back to her usual self, the Mrs O'Hagen who did, who managed, who set so many balls in motion that only she could possibly keep them in the air.

'I have to go,' Laura had said, 'but I'll call you later. Will you ring if there's any news? If I hear anything, I'll ring you.'

And Laura had left her there, gone back to the guesthouse and begun to piece together the story as she knew it must be told, beginning in the moment and moving backwards then forwards again, across their common landscape in the effort to describe what had been.

She steered clear of fault, as Petrie had warned, and barely mentioned Huw. This was a story about Amanda, herself and Stella. As she retold it, she saw how each of them, not just Amanda, had struggled with becoming. Was it the same for everyone, she wondered, or had the sticky grip of the cocoon clung more tightly to them, making their movements leaden, exhausting them so fast that they could move only in short bursts? She saw them as insects – Amanda a pale, gangling daddy long-legs, Stella a sturdy, shining ant, herself an uncertain, blundering moth. Mrs O'Hagen was a spider, obviously. Nessa? Perhaps a ladybird, all humble vulnerable bravado. The exercise amused her, kept her mind off the aftermath of what she was doing. Gave her courage for what she knew must come next.

Finished, she reached for her phone. There were four more missed calls from Petrie, calls that she had ignored, alarmed at her own daring. Now, though, she was ready.

'Petrie, it's Laura. I've finished the piece. It's written.' And then, driven by the images that still played in her head, the laughing days of youth and conviction, she made another call.

Chapter Twenty-Six

London

NEASDEN WAS YET ANOTHER LONDON, STELLA
thought, as the taxi motored through squat streets with sandy-
coloured brick houses into which too many people seemed
crammed, judging by the numbers of bicycles and bins outside
each one. Everywhere windows were lit, sometimes covered
by a thin sheet, hung badly, so that whatever happened behind
them seemed a shadow play projected onto a backlit canvas,
black outlines approaching and retreating. Others, hung
with exotic shawls in orange and purple, tasselled edges and
sequined bursts, made her think of elephants and circuses.
In general, though, the houses were quiet, unassuming,
the inhabitants hunkered down for the night in preparation

for another day at jobs where effort far outweighed any outcome.

Jake had the basement of a flat-fronted, two-storey house, built more to provide an address than comfort or security, Stella thought. The windows on the upper floor were boarded with sheets of plywood onto which someone had spray-painted 'WMB' in fat, sagging letters. Stella wondered what it stood for.

Jake opened the door promptly, beaming as if he had been expecting them. Yet again Stella was struck by how like a clockwork toy he was, bowing forward and rocking backwards on his heels as they launched into an explanation – 'Looking for Amanda … Huw thought you might know … Came over from New York to see her …'

His large eyes opened and shut with an almost audible click. 'Come in, come in,' he said jovially. 'You're in the right place. She's here all right. Been here a while now. Best place for her.' He smiled approvingly. 'Bit of peace and quiet is what she needed.'

Peace and quiet, thought Stella. As if she'd had a busy day at work, or a hectic time at the shops. Relief surged below the surface with an intensity that surprised her. Only in the letting go of it did she understand just how much she had feared not finding Amanda here. Not finding Amanda at all.

Jake was leading them down a cramped hall, over-full of boxes, bikes, bags, with a smell of damp. At the end, a door into the sitting room: low-ceilinged with a grimy brown carpet and sagging sofa covered with ancient tweed. A large, framed poster from the film *Scarface* hung crookedly on one wall, surrounded by takeaway menus thrust through nails so that the effect was like a crown of thorns.

'Welcome to the 1970s,' she whispered to James.

'It's not much,' Jake said happily, 'not what you'd call smart, but we do all right here.'

'It's very nice,' said James politely. Then, looking round the rather bare and empty room, 'Is Amanda actually here?'

'She is. In the bedroom. She hasn't been up long, only a couple of days. Still finding her feet.'

What is he talking about? thought Stella. Amanda wasn't a newborn calf. She imagined her tottering on impossibly thin legs, woozy with disuse, collapsing after one heroic effort. 'Can I see her?' she asked.

'You can.' He nodded at a door set almost at right angles to the one they had come through. 'An awful mess she was in when she arrived. Better now, though – much better.' As Stella reached to open the door, she heard him saying companionably to James, 'Cup of tea, mate?'

And James responding, 'Lovely, thanks.'

How strangely ruthless men are, she thought, how good at keeping drama where it belongs – on the margins, in the small print.

The bedroom was dark and smelt oddly of root vegetables. Turnips and earth, Stella thought, like an old-fashioned greengrocer's. In the gloom she made out a bed, and in the bed a shape.

'Amanda?' She shook the nearest bit of the shape very gently. 'Amanda, it's me.' Nothing. Through the door she could see Jake bearing a large mug and a carton of milk. 'Amanda?' She shook again, a little harder.

At last the shape stirred and a hand emerged from the heap of covers, fingers outstretched. Stella took it in hers.

'I hoped you'd come,' Amanda said very quietly. Then,

after a while in which the two simply held hands, she said, 'Wait, I'll sit up. It takes me a minute.' Slowly, she rearranged herself with some groaning and leaned against the greasy headboard. 'You can turn on a light, if you like. There's one by the bed.'

The light, an old desk lamp with a bare bright bulb, showed Stella an Amanda unrecognisable from the thousands of photographs of the glowing, golden girl the world knew. On the wall above her head, incongruous as the soft glow of a lamp in the jungle, was the Turner.

'I look like an extra in *Planet of the Apes*, don't I?'

'A bit,' Stella answered honestly, scanning a face drawn sharp down to a pointed chin, muddy skin stretched too thin over jutting cheek- and jawbones, the nose large and coarse in comparison, then adding, with a rush of the protective feeling that Amanda had always inspired in her, 'But I'm sure you won't stay looking like that. You just need a bit of time, and some decent food.'

'Is James here too?'

'He is.'

'Good. I need a bath. Can you help me? I can't exactly ask Jake. Although I nearly did. It's so horrible being constantly reminded of your mistakes by the squalor of actually sitting in them.'

Stella ran a bath, allowing a cracked piece of Imperial Leather soap – the only toiletry the sparse, chilly room contained, except for shaving foam – to dissolve in the hot water. Thank God there was hot water. She had had visions of herself boiling kettles and saucepans. The bath was small and made of scratched pink plastic. Getting Amanda into it was a question of stopping and starting several times from the bed. Jake hadn't been exaggerating when he'd said she was still finding her feet. She was wearing a black T-shirt with 'Hard Rock Café' printed on it in faded letters and a pair of old grey tracksuit bottoms. She leaned heavily on Stella, and up close, the smell of earth and turnips mingled with something sweetish that made Stella force herself not to turn her head away. The intimacy of the smell – which seemed to confide just how long it had been since Amanda had last been clean, eaten properly, had a refreshing night's sleep – was overwhelming, told her things Amanda would probably never say.

She was indeed filthy. Hair matted and smelling of grease, snarled into a bird's nest at the back so bad that Stella suspected she would have to cut it out. She wasn't sure if the dull, dun colour was dirt, or if Amanda's golden tresses had actually changed and aged. Once out of the T-shirt and tracksuit, her ribs could easily be counted, pelvic bones brittle and protruding, the stupid tiger tattoo now wrinkled so that it no longer prowled but limped, an angry rash where her knees seemed to have knocked against each other. Scabs and sores stuck up from her shrunken flesh, knobbly and gnarled. Like Braille, Stella thought, imagining that if she were to run her fingertips lightly over them, they would tell the story of Amanda's self-mutilation.

'It must be like volunteering at a leper colony,' Amanda said lightly, although Stella could tell by the way she sat, shrinking even from herself, how hot was the shame she felt.

'It's not so bad. More like a heroin-chic photoshoot.'

Amanda shuddered. 'With added real disgustingness ...' Her hands were the worst, the skin around the nails torn and bitten raw.

'They hurt like hell,' she said, seeing Stella look. 'The days

I was withdrawing, I chewed on them. I couldn't stop even when they bled, and it made me vomit.'

'Why here?' Stella asked, sluicing water up and over Amanda's shoulders, gently rubbing at the bony, goose-pimpled flesh.

'Couldn't think of anywhere else. At first, after Huw left, I stayed in the house, because I thought he'd come back. But that became unbearable. It was so silent and lonely and I kept thinking I heard Dora, even though I knew she wasn't there. The only person who came anywhere near me was Jake, so eventually he put me in a taxi and brought me here, although I had to pay. He's kind in his own way. And he'd seen me all along, so I wouldn't have to put up with the shock I'd cause anyone else. I looked even worse then,' she said, with a wry smile. 'So I came here, and when Jake suggested it might be time to quit, I knew he was right, that there wasn't any other way. He got me enough Valium and clonidine and stuff that I was able to get through the worst days. And nights.'

'Why did Huw leave? Shouldn't he have stayed with you?'

'No.' Amanda sounded resolute. 'I see now he was right to go. It was too crazy. And he was angry about Dora. He didn't want me to send her to Belleville. I think that was the last straw. I know you don't much like him,' she said, with characteristic understatement, Stella thought, 'but he really loves Dora. He changed after she came, much quicker than I did,' she finished sadly.

'There's still time to change,' Stella said, wondering if it could possibly be true.

'Of course there is,' Amanda agreed. 'That's why I'm here now, doing this. Everything is going to change.' She said it not in the way she used to talk about how wonderful things would be once she moved to Paris, or once she and Huw were married – as if constructing glorious fairy castles in a distance she could barely see – but with a quiet conviction that made Stella want to cry for its fragility.

So completely stripped of her beauty was she that Stella now couldn't find the Amanda she had always known. The glowing creature. Was this really what they had all come tearing over to a squalid corner of London for? Looking at her, she realised that whatever they had all thought was in Amanda wasn't there. There was, after all, no great secret beneath the fascination of her beauty, her poise, her mystery. Just the small collection of things that Amanda actually was: her sense of humour, of decency, the desire to have a good time that had infected everyone around her, the need to escape notice that had nearly killed her. She couldn't take them away with her – Stella was at last honest enough to admit that that had been part of it, the feeling that Amanda might lift them up and out, just as she had done when they were schoolgirls back in St Assumpta's. Behind the vast promise of her looks, she was simply who she was. Empty, maybe even rather shallow.

But she was also their friend. If she was full of anything, it was the years they had spent together. And, after all, she had never claimed to be what she wasn't, had even tried to tell them, only they hadn't wanted to listen. They had read into her something that spoke more clearly of their own dreams and hopes than of anything that was actually there. Photographers saw a muse, her mother had seen glory, Stella and Laura escape, their friends from college excitement. What a lot of reading, she thought. Poor Amanda. No wonder she was always on the run.

'I'm going to have to wash your hair with soap,' she said. 'There isn't any shampoo.'

'Not surprised,' said Amanda. 'Jake isn't exactly a devoted consumer. He's like one of those survivalists. He says he doesn't want to be dependent on The Man, and that when society finally breaks down, which he reckons is about four years away, we'll all have to get along with barter.'

'His *Scarface* poster should get him some good trades,' Stella said, gently pouring water over Amanda's hair. She was shocked to see how much of it seemed to be coming out in her hands as she rubbed the soap and water through, but said nothing. She was surprised at how fast they seemed ready to slip back into their way of being together – the jokes and one-liners that still came more easily than the unvarnished contents of their hearts. Before they could entirely disappear into the old, teasing ways, and because she knew she had to say something of what had brought her there, Stella blurted out, 'You could have told me. You know I would have tried to do something,' hoping as she said it that it was true, that if Amanda had ever asked for help, she would have known how to give it.

'I did mostly believe that,' Amanda said quietly. 'And I wanted to see you so much, but I didn't know how to call, what to say. Before Dora, I didn't think I needed to. I was perfectly happy, although it probably wasn't the kind of happiness you would have admired,' her mouth twisted in a wry smile, 'and after Dora, I just couldn't. There weren't words.'

The doorbell sounded, a thin, nervous squeal. 'I'll get rid of them,' Jake called hospitably from the sitting room. 'Not really the moment, is it?'

He came back accompanied by Laura, who stood in the doorway of the bathroom for a moment, taking in the tableau in front of her. Then, finally, in the silence that had gathered round the three of them, she came and knelt by the side of the bath, reached into the water for the bar of Imperial Leather and began gently soaping one of Amanda's ravaged arms, drawing the bar carefully around the whorls and scabs.

'How did you know?' Stella asked, into the silence.

'News travels,' she said. 'Half of London is looking for you, Amanda, and a fair amount of Dublin too.' She said nothing else, just continued her gentle manoeuvrings of the soap. She said nothing about the scars and scabs, the protruding ribs and dull bruises. There was no need. Amanda closed her eyes, lay almost as though dead.

'I'm sorry I left you,' Stella blurted out at last.

'Huh?' Amanda opened her eyes.

'The night of the graduation party. I shouldn't have let you stay, but I was angry about James.'

'James?' Amanda sounded vague.

'You made a play for him that night, when you knew I wanted him.' The words sounded hollow, pathetic, to her own ears, and when she looked at Laura, Laura wouldn't look back.

'I never knew you wanted him until you turned up here with him, Stella,' Amanda said, with a resignation that had a ring of truth. 'Truly. You think you wear your heart where anyone can see it, but you don't. You keep it so much out of sight that I have to guess at what you might be thinking, or wait until you tell me. Like now. And anyway,' she went on, with more spirit, 'if you wanted him, you should have just taken him. I wouldn't have tried to stop you. I don't even really know what you're talking about.'

'You kissed him.'

'I kissed everyone that night, Stella. Anyone who wanted me. Do you know what I felt like? One of those tiny birds the French eat. First they blind them, and in their pain the poor little things eat and eat and eat until they're so stuffed they die. It's not even because they think the food will dim the pain, they eat because it's the only thing they know to do. That's what I felt like. I stuffed everything that night. Drink, drugs, boys. I didn't think anything would stop the pain, but I knew that eventually I'd consume so much that I would just shut down. And I did. And when I came to, I found myself in bed with Christian and Byron, and then I discovered that there were more types of humiliation than even I knew, and that you had left me to it.' So she had known. All these years, she had known and never said.

'So you were right,' Laura said slowly, 'to keep going on about that night. You were right.'

'I'm sorry.' The words nearly choked Stella. 'I always wondered if you knew. Or even if anything had happened to you. I'm so sorry.'

'I don't blame you,' said Amanda. 'Really I don't. Think of all the times you didn't leave me when you could have.'

'No, I'm sorry.' Stella was crying.

'It wasn't your fault,' Amanda said. 'I do know that I can't keep blaming other people, not even my mother, for the things I do. But it didn't help, that's for sure. Just one more thing I couldn't look at. After a while there were so many of them that the only way was to be stoned all the time.' She sank gingerly back into the water that had turned a pale brown round her. 'Anyway,' she went on, 'you're here now, with James and Laura. We're all here again.'

Stella made an indistinct noise that might have been agreement.

'Whatever happened to those guys?' she then asked. 'Byron and Christian?

'I saw Byron recently, although he looks much less like a romantic poet now, far more like plain old Tim,' Laura said. 'Apparently he wasn't able to get himself any kind of a job, so his dad got him one. In an abattoir. When I saw him he had a streak of blood on his cheek. I told him it was there and offered to spit on a tissue and wipe it for him, and he was mortified. He said he'd had no word of Christian for a couple of years, that he had dropped out of his postgrad and kind of disappeared.'

'Into thin air I hope,' Amanda said robustly.

In the sitting room, Amanda settled onto the tweed sofa, wearing cleaner versions of the tracksuit and T-shirt combo – this one from London Zoo with a picture of a cartoon penguin on it – and holding a mug of tea. Stella searched James's face for clues as to his feelings for Amanda, knowing that she no longer cared. Or, at least, not that she didn't care but that she could finally, perhaps, separate youthful infatuation from something more grown-up. And indeed, she saw shock, self-reproach, love made gentle by pity, but not love of the old, awed kind.

Jake bustled happily around, seeming delighted at the company, offering bowls of soup. 'Oxtail,' he said. 'It's what I've been giving Amanda.'

'Tinned,' Amanda hissed to Stella. 'I'd say dating back to the First World War. It's all he has in the kitchen. But surprisingly good.'

'Well aged,' Stella hissed back. 'Good vintage.'

'So,' Amanda said, with a grimace. 'What hope of keeping this quiet?'

'No hope at all when Laura's piece is published,' Stella said. The brief truce of the bathroom was behind her and she felt again the outrage of Laura's betrayal. Laura, sitting on an armchair opposite the sofa, gave her an angry stare. Her arms were folded, hands tucked defensively into armpits, her face dividing into patches of angry red and translucent white that came and went, replacing each other with a rapidity that told Stella she was very agitated.

'What piece?' Amanda and James said together. Even Jake turned from laying a fire made of twisted newspaper and sticks in the tiny grate.

'She's written a piece for the *Sunday Herald*. It'll probably be run all over the world. About you, and what's been happening,' Stella continued, still bitter.

'Oh,' Amanda said, then fell silent. Then, 'Here we go again,' she said wearily, shifting awkwardly on the sofa, as if any possibility of getting comfortable was remote.

Not surprising, thought Stella, remembering the sharp bones protruding, vicious reminders, beneath the tracksuit bottoms.

'What do you mean?' said Laura.

'Everybody always wants something,' said Amanda. 'Everybody. My mother, obviously. Even my dad, although he never said it and I never knew exactly what he wanted, but I knew it was something. Sally and Nadine when we were at school, wanting me to take them to parties and introduce them to people. All those photographers and stylists and fashion editors and directors. Everybody pushing and pushing me to be something so they could *coat-tail*.' She brought out the deliberately vulgar word with vehemence. 'Even you two,' she finished sadly.

'We didn't!' Laura shouted.

The anger in the room made the air thin and sharp. Much of it, Stella realised, was coming from Laura, who normally folded any such feelings deep inside herself but had now obviously decided to do things differently. Amanda, who usually absented herself from situations she didn't like, who didn't look as if she had the strength to sit up straight, was coiled like a sinuous reptile. They were, Stella saw, two scared, desperate creatures fighting each other.

'We did,' Stella said suddenly. 'We did. Laura, you know we did. But not in the horrid way you mean, Amanda. The thing is, no one who knew you then could have helped believing you were going to do something amazing, and we just wanted to go with you. Because we love you.' She felt James move to stand behind her. Jake was back in the kitchen, clattering things.

'You know why I wanted to be friends with you?' Amanda switched the conversation. Stella, who had long wondered, shrugged. 'You always seemed to be having fun. Even though no one bothered much about you, or even liked you much, you had each other and you were always laughing and giggling. It looked nice.' She sounded wistful. 'I wanted that. I'd never had it. Sometimes, seeing the two of you just being silly and funny and teasing each other made me feel lonely.'

'So that's why? I did always wonder a bit,' she said. Laura, she could see, was still holding herself aloof.

'Yes. And it was like that. But ...'

'But?'

'Well, it wasn't the answer either.'

'The answer to what?' asked Laura, abruptly. Then, without allowing Amanda to continue, carried on, accusations falling from her mouth like curses. 'All I ever wanted from you was that you would, just once, admit that you had more than other people – more of everything – and be grateful for that instead of always chucking it away as if it was nothing. How do you think that made the rest of us feel? Those of us who had so damn little and were hanging onto that tiny bit with both hands and, even so, watching it disappear away from us.' Her voice broke. 'And as for your mania of not wanting people to want things from you, well, that's what being human is, Amanda. That's what being a friend is. It's wanting things and giving them and getting them. It's not some kind of creepy, vulgar way of trying to use people, it's just normal life. But you're pathological about it. We give you plenty. Why shouldn't we get something back? Why should we be made to feel so bad, as if we're trying to steal your soul or something, every time we want a tiny thing from you? For God's sake! It's so childish, and stupid, and annoying!' She was ranting now, words coming out in a great rush.

Stella, who had tried to halt her, stopped. Laura was sort of right, she decided.

When the torrent of angry words dried up, the room fell silent again. Sneaking a look at James, Stella saw that he was staring carefully at a ripped corner of carpet, avoiding all possibility of eye contact.

'Okay,' said Amanda, at last. 'Fine. Show me the piece. Let me read it. Maybe you have a point ...' She sounded uncertain.

Laura, after a pause, settled the laptop on Amanda's knees, then stepped back. 'I haven't sent it yet,' she muttered. 'I waited ...'

Amanda read quietly, scrolling through the pages slowly. The rest sat in silence while Jake made yet more tea. Stella didn't know what to say to Laura. The leap of relief that had greeted the news that she hadn't sent the piece was restrained by the knowledge that she yet might, the admission that she had a point about Amanda undermined by the persistent feeling of disloyalty. Beside Stella, James reached for her hand, took it in his warmer one and squeezed. She squeezed back, wondering if she would ever let it go, and why she hadn't taken hold of it before.

'It's very good,' Amanda said at last. 'Send it. It's okay.'

'Really?' Laura said. 'You mean that?'

'I do. You have a right to tell it. And there's been enough lying and covering up.'

'What about Dora, when she's old enough to read it?' Stella asked, wanting Amanda to understand that, once it went, none of them could ever call it back.

'When the time comes, she needs to know the truth,' Amanda said. 'That's the only way I have any hope of being able to do this.'

'And what about your mother?' Stella asked.

'She of all people needs to read it. Needs to read it as it was, and is. The things that actually happened, rather than the things she thinks happened just because they're what she wanted to happen.'

'Well, I'm not going to send it,' Laura said then.

They all stared at her.

'What?' Stella was first to the question.

'I'm not going to send it. I just needed you to tell me I could. To admit I had a right to.' Laura looked uncomfortable, but determined. 'I rang Petrie and told her I wouldn't be sending anything. She was furious, of course. Then I rang my dad. Or my not-dad, the painter.' She had always struggled to find a word that defined their relationship. 'He once offered to help me, if I decided to write books. Apparently it was him who paid my school fees all those years ago, but Nessa didn't want me to know.' She knew she was blurting out more than she needed, but couldn't stop. 'He said that he thought I had more a novelist's eye than a reporter's, and that my sentences went on too long, except that finally they did something interesting and I should work on that instead of trying to be crisp and curt.' Her words tumbled out, almost breathless. 'So I rang him, after I rang Petrie, and he said he'd like to help. That he was my dad for nine years, and he'd like to go back to being that, regardless of blood lines.' She was smiling now, broad and steady.

'Laura, that's amazing!' Stella's delight was immediate, profound.

'It's perfect,' Amanda agreed. 'You'll be a brilliant novelist, I'm sure of it.'

Laura went over, hugged her. 'I'm so glad you're here, not in that horrible other house.'

'Oh, God,' said Amanda, with a shudder, 'you didn't go there, did you?'

'We did.'

'I'm not sure I can ever go back to it. No matter what happened to that top floor, even if it was gutted completely and rebuilt, I could never forget what it had been.'

'It was like falling through a rabbit hole,' Laura agreed. 'One minute you're in the interiors of *Gracious Living* or something, and the next it's Harlem in the 1950s.'

'I suppose I'll have to get Dundee though,' Amanda said. 'Jake was going to, but couldn't find him.'

'Dundee?'

'The cat. Huw bought him for Dora but she's frightened of him. Not surprised, he's not exactly cuddly. But I guess I can't just leave him. Maybe Huw would take him.' She was starting to work herself up, worry and fidget. Stella saw her hands going to her mouth, watched her start to gnaw at her thumb. She reached over, gently pulling the hand away and down, leaving her own hand over it.

'And what about Huw?' she asked quietly.

'I don't know,' Amanda said. 'I really don't. I can't see him now, and I know he won't see me. But maybe, later, because of Dora …' she trailed off. 'This isn't his fault. He didn't do this. I did it. But he didn't help, or at least not for a long time, and when he did try, it was far too late. Funny, I always thought he was exactly right for me, but I suppose he was exactly wrong.'

'About as wrong as hydrogen and nitrogen,' said Stella with an attempt at a smile.

'And maybe now that you know that, he won't have the same hold over you,' Laura said hopefully.

'Maybe,' said Amanda.

And for all that Amanda would never be the same, none of them really would; for all that the scars she bore would remain as shadows in all their lives long after her skin had thrown off their imprint; for all that there would always be things between them that couldn't be talked about, except at an angle and carefully distanced, Stella knew then that they would be okay. They would find their way back to friendship and it would be both stronger and more tentative than before. No longer so unreflecting, but more precious even for that.

'What about your mother?' she asked. 'We'd better tell her you're here. She was pretty shocked back in that house.'

'I never imagined feeling sorry for my mother,' Amanda said, 'but I do. It can't have been anything except horrible for her. Yes, I suppose we had better tell her.'

'Actually, she's on her way,' Laura said. 'Margot told her where you are.' She looked up, met Stella's eye, saw James's hand curled around hers, the way he leaned his body protectively over her, and smiled a tiny, shy smile. Stella smiled back.

'Well, I suppose I have to face her sometime,' Amanda said.

'You will stay though, won't you?' She sounded suddenly desperate.

'Yes, we'll stay,' Laura and Stella said together. And in that moment Stella saw them, she believed, in a future where they were together, the three of them with Dora too, happy and with purpose. It wasn't the kind of vision they used to share with each other, giddy, after late nights or lines of coke, glittering, excitable descriptions of doing and glory, full of swirling dresses and bursts of gay laughter. This was a smaller thing altogether, neater, more modest. But if it dazzled a little less, it also, she realised, convinced a little more. The shapes were softer, kinder. Maybe because she now knew where, and how, to look.

'We'll always stay,' she said.

Acknowledgements

I've been writing non-fiction for years, and like many journalists, I always wanted to try my hand at fiction. There was of course the 'novel in the drawer' – commissioned by a publishing company which then went bust – but even at the time, I knew that novel wasn't good enough to be published, but was essential practice. Writing a semi-memoir, *How to (Really) be a Mother*, returned me to my childhood. *The Privileged* isn't autobiographical – any resemblances to real persons, living or dead, etc. – but I couldn't have written it if I hadn't remembered exactly what it's like to be an adolescent and a student.

My agent, Jonathan Williams, a man as kind as he is discerning, read the first half of the first draft of *The Privileged* and told me it was worth finishing. My sister Bridget, as exacting as she is discerning, read two further drafts and managed to be both critical and encouraging, not easy when your standards are as high as hers. I asked my friend Domini Kemp to read an early manuscript, because she and I share similar taste in novels, and she said, 'It's really good and the sex scenes aren't at all creepy', which seemed like high praise.

When the novel went out into the wide world, looking for supporters, it was my good fortune that it came before Ciara Doorley at Hachette Ireland, whose immediate enthusiasm was wonderful, and whose later comments were excellent. At every point, from editorial to design, the team at Hachette have shown the kind of wisdom and flexibility that you really hope for from the publisher of your first novel. Particular thanks to Hazel Orme for a very fine edit, Joanna Smyth and Breda Purdue.

The Privileged had a charmed gestation, but, a few months before publication, I was diagnosed out of the blue with mouth cancer. The type I contracted is very treatable and tends not to recur but I wouldn't wish the treatment on the worst character in this book. You can't not be changed by cancer. I feel lucky that I managed to write, and have accepted for publication, my first novel before my diagnosis. Although it takes a dark turn, *The Privileged*, for me anyway, retains a prelapsarian innocence, which feels right because it mostly deals with the wonderful stupid courage and bravado of adolescence.

I also feel lucky in the remarkable proofs of friendship, support and kindness from all around me during my worst days. The practical support and resounding cheers from my friends, neighbours, people I barely know and some who I don't know at all, got me through some very dark days.

I could not have survived my treatment, nor written this book, without my husband, David. To acknowledge his 'unfailing support' feels like bathos. Our household is fed by his wit as surely as by the electricity grid.